THE GREEN GODDESS

Mystery of the Green Woman

Edward Spencer Dyas

Arise of Athena

Copyright © 2015 by the author of this book Edward Dyas.

The author retains sole copyright to this book.
All rights reserved.

ISBN: 1508677344
ISBN 13: 9781508677345

A tall and lovely woman, instinct with beauty in every part, and with a ...grace that I have never seen anything like before.

> H. Rider Haggard. 'She'

She is more beautiful than the sun, and excels every constellation of the stars. Compared with the light she is found to be superior.
I loved her and sought her...

Apocrypha. 'The Wisdom of Solomon'

ACKNOWLEDGEMENTS

Are due:

To Darius and Helen of Radmanesh Publishing for their cover design and advice.

To the literary agent who had confidence in my book.

To Alexandra Bazhenova of Cambridge University for her enthusiasm and encouragement.

PROLOGUE

The aging knight, silent, with eyes unflinching, gazed at the king. Standing without weapons, head uncovered he felt alone before the might of the French monarch.

Each side of the knight a single line of armed men stood at ease but there was clear evidence of discomfort as they shuffled their mailed feet and coughed. All of them knew the famed soldier standing before them as well as the evil monarch before whom he was being accused.

To the right and left of King Philip le Bel stood six Cardinals of the church.

'You are not a Templar?'

'No Sire.'

'Then to what order do you belong?'

'We have no name.'

'But you associate with Templars.'

'Yes Sire and with all *good* men.' The accused knight emphasised coldly the word good.

'We are told you worship a goddess and not the living Christ.' The king glared at the prisoner. 'Is this true?'

'No your Majesty.'

'They tell me you worship a relic. Is that true?'

'No Sire'

'What is the truth then?' The king asked vehemently, 'Tell me *if* you wish to save your life.'

'We are soldiers of the living God but we revere the Goddess who turns all life green again, who gives life to all. You and these men of the church can pray as much as you wish but without her guidance you will achieve nothing,' the knight answered, his sunburned, bearded face, showing no emotion or condescension.

'Sacrilege!' Shouted a cardinal and leaving his place beside the king struck the knight across the face.

'Cease.' The king ordered angrily, 'Or you will join him. Is this what we are to expect from our church? Whether true or false Chevalier Gules is correct in this one thing at least you have not, any of you church men, achieved anything for me. Step back or I swear you will join him.'

The Cardinal abashed hung his head, returning to his place.

The Green Goddess

King Philip had already determined the fate of the knight that no matter what the knight said, he had to die with the whole of the mystical order he represented and all who collaborated with the hated Templars. They were too powerful these soldiers of God or Goddess, whatever the truth was, and dangerous. He was hostile towards their order because of their growing international power, their arrogant independence and fabulous wealth. They could hold all the world to ransom if they wished for they were owed so much by the God elected monarchs of Europe. He the king of France was in debt to them for more than his country could afford. They had to be destroyed. If he could do it before any of the other grumbling monarchs, too afraid of the church to act, were aware of it then their incredible wealth would be his.

The king leaned forward intently.

'What is the origin of your great wealth?'

'You yourself deposit and borrow from us. Many gifts flow to our order for our knightly services to the kings of Europe and the Holy Pope himself.' The knight answered unbowed by the cardinal's assault.

'How is it that a knightly order could become so wealthy?' The king asked turning to the cardinals and bishops beside him.

'The devil himself, your majesty.' A cardinal answered for them all. 'Did not Satan offer the world and all its treasures to the Living Christ if he would but obey him?'

'Our wealth comes not from a devil but the Goddess proclaimed in the Holy Scriptures. It is she who teaches virtue and wisdom and understanding of all things. She brings to those who love her all they need.'

'Where in the scriptures does it say this?' A cardinal asked cynically.

The beleaguered knight whose time had been divided between warfare and ecclesiastical study replied.

'You are a leader of the Holy Church and do not know? In "The Wisdom of Solomon," it says, "All good things came with her. She brought me untold riches."

'Is this so?' The king asked turning to his cardinals, somewhat taken aback by the knight's answer.

Whispering among themselves before giving their reply a cardinal answered. 'The passage refers to our blessed Mother your Majesty.'

'So your so called goddess is the Virgin?' Philip asked.

Without answering the King's question the knight replied,

'She is the one who was with God from the beginning, without which he could do nothing. She gave design to all things. She is holy and wise above all and cannot be harmed or destroyed, she is kind and a friend of all who are pure of heart. Like the wind penetrating all things, she is the spirit of God's power.'

'Blasphemy,' screeched a cardinal.

King Philip waving his hand, to calm the frenetic cardinals, said with genuine interest at the idea of wealth and power, 'So! I am intrigued by this relic some claim you possess. What is it?'

'A relic nothing more. We speak to it as you yourself speak to images in the Cathedral of Chartres.'

Bending towards the king, one of the cardinals whispered to Philip. The king nodded in assent.

'Tell us more of your beliefs so that we may condemn you the more easily,' the cardinal who had spoken with the King said sarcastically.

'We believe the only way to escape punishment and death is through piety, by fighting to preserve virtue and by the intercessions of our goddess.'

'Chevalier Sir Gules du Bois knowing of your services to the crown it is without pleasure I am sending you to the torturers for your sacrilege and refusing to divulge the names of your companions or to tell us the truth,' the king said.

'The truth sire stands forever and even lies cannot alter it.' The proud knight replied as the guards tried to take him away. Shaking them loose he spoke fearlessly. 'I will die with a clear conscience but you Sire will not. When you yourself were fleeing the Paris rioters you sort refuge with us, the very men you are massacring at this moment. On your orders, yes sire your orders, two Popes were murdered. What will you say on the day of your judgment?'

'Go, before I execute you on the spot.' The king replied reddening sullenly, angrily.

After months of interrogation and refusal to reveal the location of the relic or name of any of his companions in the order Chevalier Gules du Bois died, physically broken by his torturers.

On the day of his death with the connivance of guards and French Comtes attached to the kings court the knight's companions stole the corpse, wrapping his body carefully in a white shroud, as was their custom, and by night hiding it in a chancel of a remote church.

When the knights came to honour and remove the body the following day, for secret burial, the corpse was no longer there. The white shroud Sir Gules had been wrapped in was found speckled with dried blood from his wounds and strange dark images stained the cloth as though it had been singed by fire. This blood stained winding sheet was sent secretly to Besancon Cathedral in the French province of Doubs as a memorial to the piety and courage of Sir Gules.

After being moved from cathedral to church, to fortress and back again, exhibited in numerous processions and hung from castle walls, the shroud of Chevalier Gules du Bois ended its days in the Cathedral of Turin.

CHAPTER ONE

Lady Eleanor Allan was sitting at a small easel that rested on her desk. She was painting in water colours wild flowers she had collected on the Allan Estate that evening. It was already pitch dark outside. Lord Henry, her husband, was on his way from London where he worked as director of several international companies and this time also fulfilling an obligation to sit in the House of Lords. Lady Eleanor waited eagerly for his return. He had promised he would be home before midnight.

They had been in love from the moment they first met at Beauchamp Palace. On these occasions when he was away she felt restless thinking of him constantly. Opening a writing table drawer she took out a free verse letter he had given her years before and read it through several times. It was a poem he had sent once when absent in Europe.

Around eleven she heard a vehicle rasping along the gravel but stopping some distance away. That seemed strange because he usually drove right up to the entrance. She dismissed the question hanging at the back of her mind and hurriedly, exuberantly happy to see him, ran down the blue carpeted stairs in her satin robe folding around her like a second skin to welcome him home.

Before reaching the long hall below the marble stairs Lady Eleanor heard her housekeeper remonstrating angrily at the entrance door.

A despairing cry for help broke the silence of the house and stopped Lady Eleanor where she stood on the lower level of the stairs. Panic and a dark premonition took hold of her. She turned to run back up the flight of stairs but it was too late. Three masked men burst through the inner door and one sprang up the steps to take her forcefully, violently.

Using a stair for leverage Lady Allan thrust at her assailant with a desperate lunge. The man toppled backwards, heavily, down the flight of stairs unable to grip the wide, marble banisters.

Eleanor continuing her flight up the stairs away from her attackers ran with a desperate speed that fear and adrenalin gave her. Tearing along the

The Green Goddess

upstairs gallery she reached its end and turned abruptly right before any of her attackers had reached the top of the stairs.

Opening an oak door she rushed inside the room and locked it.

She was in the bedroom of her three year old daughter Sophia. The small girl looked at her in surprise her large violet eyes staring at her mother knowing something was dreadfully wrong.

'Mommy,' Sophia cried clinging to her mother's gown.

Opening a door that led to another stair Eleanor lifted her daughter in her arms and closed the door silently behind them her hands nervously shaking as she locked it.

As quietly as her racing heart allowed she moved slowly down another corridor and a narrow flight of stairs until reaching what appeared to be an oak wall. Listening with her ear against the wood she strained to hear noises beyond. Satisfied, she thrust heavily against the oak panelling. A swivel bookcase opened onto Henley Hall Library. Pushing the bookcase back into its recess she stood her small daughter beside her and placed a finger to her lips gesturing silence. Going to another bookcase Lady Eleanor pulled at a shelf that swung free to reveal a steel safe set into the wall. Fumbling, forgetting and trying again with trembling fingers the sequence combination the safe door swung loose to reveal an oblong, tooled silver casket with a lid that sparkled even in the unlit cavity of the safe with gemstones.

The casket measured some twelve by eighteen inches and Eleanor knew she couldn't carry both it and her daughter.

Kneeling beside Sophia she whispered, 'Follow me my darling and run fast, very fast. Do you understand?'

Sophia nodding, whispered, 'Yes Mommy.'

Eleanor kissed her daughter desperation flushing her cheeks as she hugged her tightly.

Sophia nodded again at her mother, assuring her, somehow realising the danger they were in.

Pausing to listen at the door, Lady Eleanor could hear men's voices further up the stairs. Carefully opening the library door taking Sophia's hand she held the silver casket under her other arm and they moved rapidly silently down the hall to the far side.

Her heart pounding, her hands trembling, Eleanor stopped beside a large door and felt for her keys, 'Please, God,' she breathed a silent prayer.

Bolts clunked open as she turned the key. Rushing inside with Sophia she locked the great door behind them.

The room they were in was constructed almost entirely of onyx.

Near the centre of the room a gigantic green marble statue of a woman rested on a white stone pedestal.

Lady Eleanor went to the statue and kneeled down. Sophia knelt beside her mother mimicking her movement.

Several years previously Eleanor had rested against the statue's pedestal and to her surprise, and delight, discovered a panel of the plinth slid open to disclose a three feet deep receptacle inside. It was empty and feeling sure she was the only person living who knew of its existence kept it as her own secret telling no one. From then on she had used it to store intimate love letters from her husband.

She pressed forcefully against a side of the pedestal. It swung open and she slid the silver casket inside behind bundles of letters and documents and once more pressing against the block closed the panel.

Taking Sophia's hand she led her daughter behind the statue furthest from the entrance door.

'Darling be a brave girl for mummy and stay here. Please stay here, until I or Daddy call you. Can you do that dearest?'

The child smiled and nodded, 'Yes. Is it a game?'

'In a way, yes my dearest but the most important we have ever played. You must stay here and be silent. Will you do that darling please?'

The child looked at her mother and kneeled behind the green marble statue.

Holding her daughter in her arms, tearfully kissing her, Lady Eleanor went back to the door, opened it and locked it behind her leaving her daughter inside.

Moving down the hall towards the entrance she threw the keys to the marble room behind a display cabinet.

Hearing footsteps behind her she raced away once more. Close behind now flinging himself at her one of the men knocked her from her feet. Falling heavily forward in the full momentum of flight Lady Eleanor struck brutally the corner of a mahogany hall table. She felt and heard her left ribs break and cave inwards. Unable to breath she felt blood choking her throat. She tried calling her husband's name but the words were silent and drowned.

The three men, removing their hoods, stood gazing down at the beautiful broken woman on the floor in front of them. Blood oozed in red foam from her mouth spreading over the carpet at their feet and her eyes remained open in frozen astonishment. The leader of the men, without looking at his companions, stood in silence his head bowed.

'To kill the housekeeper is one thing but to kill Lady Allan another. I should never have bought you imbeciles with me.'

'We haven't found what we came for,' the man who had lunged at Lady Allan replied.

Ignoring him the leader said, 'The most beautiful woman in England. You bloody fool. She couldn't have got far. Now we have no chance of finding it.' The speaker squatted beside Lady Eleanor listening for her breath, touching her jugular a genuine remorse clouding his face. 'Forgive me,' he spoke to her lifeless corpse. Raising himself to his feet he turned to the men and said 'Valuable it may be but no fortune is worth a life in prison. Let's get out of here.'

Avoiding the blood beginning to soak and stain the hall carpet the men stepped over the dead housekeeper lying at the entrance of Henley and fled to their vehicle. Without turning on the car lights they drove away into the night.

Lord Henry reached home a little after midnight and peeped his car horn loudly. Running up entrance steps, a bouquet of flowers in his hand he realised at once something was wrong. Eleanor didn't open the door to meet him the way she usually did. Unable to open the door he rang the bell impatiently. Fumbling to find his key he unlocked the heavy oak door.

Consternation rooted him to the spot. Maria, their housekeeper was lying on the floor near the entrance. The sight of her lifeless body filled him with a cold, apprehensive fear. Dropping his case and flowers where he stood he rushed into the house.

'Eleanor, Eleanor,' he called as he ran into the hall. When he found her he closed her eyes and kneeling in her blood cradled his wife in his arms and wept uncontrollably.

CHAPTER TWO

Since boyhood Alex had been adventurous to the point of foolhardiness. His father had given him Victorian stories of exploration, adventure novels of the early West, India and Africa and dropped them onto his bed, magazines filled with tales of daring exploration and he had read them over and over. In silent hours, unable to sleep, he had imagined fighting Indians, shooting animals in Africa, travelling with Stanley, exploring Australia with Stuart, hunting tigers with Jim Corbett, crossing unknown lands.

After university he realised almost everywhere had been explored and the only way to live that kind of life would be as a travel writer.

Finishing his education he set off to tour Europe.

One late evening on a train journey through Switzerland, during the bleakest of January's, he had met an American travel writer.

'Would you like to share my whisky?' The writer asked, 'Keep the damn cold out.'

'Why not? That's a welcome offer.'

'I only have these plastic, railway cups if that's Ok?'

The writer who was employed by a Missouri newspaper combine told him some travel stories to pass away the time. Alex listened fascinated.

Outside their carriage a blizzard was turning the mountains white with piling snow drifts and threatening to block the Simplon Pass.

It was at this moment Alex knew for certain that this had to be his life, travelling, writing, recording his perceptions of the world.

He began with articles for travel magazines, then books, followed by assignments and his skill as a professional photographer enhanced his popularity.

After particularly long contracts he needed time to recuperate, time in which to prepare the essence of his journals and catalogue hundreds of photographs and materials he had meticulously collected.

This time after months of privations, and a relentless bout of fever, he was physically fragile, but something more, a cloud had settled over him. For the first time he was aware of an emptiness, a lack of direction. He began to question if this was what he truly wanted to do with his life. A haunted feeling settled on his thoughts. Sleep came broken by dreams of shadowy figures he couldn't understand.

To escape this mood he boarded a ship home. It was easy to find a berth on a merchant vessel. The journey might add colour to his travellers' tales. Once he had journeyed from South America on one of the last oak built, square rigger, sailing ships that still carried timber to the ports north of San Francisco. That experience had given life to one of his books. Maybe this trip would prove as profitable.

The vast, mysterious life of the boundless ocean healed his spirit as nothing else could have. One grey morning he rose to take the air of the sea and walk the decks before breakfast. Completely alone that morning he leaned on a deck rail and gazed across the expanse of the great ocean. It seemed a living soul breathing and sighing as the waves clashed against the ship beating their relentless eternal rhythm. This morning none were strong enough to spray their salt foam heads into the wind over the deck side.

A distant horizon evaporated in mist and above it a watery sun had begun stretching an inviting cosmic yawn. He breathed deeply the exhilarating sea air that woke his sleepy senses.

There were no other paying passengers aboard the merchant vessel. His cabin was spacious with everything necessary and he dined with the ship's captain. They struck up a good friendship and before long he was able to share rollicking tales with the Danish crew.

The sky was clearing dramatically. A sparkling sun broke over the waves. He stared across the wide unruffled ocean, at ease, at peace with himself and life in general.

A sudden greeting disturbed him.

'Looking fair this morning but we expect some wind this afternoon.'

The captain joining him to lean across the deck rail was sunburned, in his fifties, above medium height, broad shouldered and cultured.

'Not a storm I hope.'

'Not at all. The sea won't have a bone in her teeth, if that's what you mean, and we needn't batten down the hatches at least not today.'

The captain smiled and looked wistfully out across the sea.

'The ocean is forever changing like a beautiful woman, magnificent, unpredictable, turbulent and dangerous. You can fall in love with her just the same and at your peril. She will take all you have

The Green Goddess

if you let her and give you the happiest moments of your life. Wouldn't you say?'

'What was it Kipling called her, "The old grey widow maker." Like you I love the sea. A longing for our primordial home I suppose.'

'Yes, perhaps. The blind miles of the sea. We really have no idea what happens out there. You lead a lonely life I believe from what you tell me. I understand that, sailing the world as I do, but still I have a wife on land that I can go to at the voyage end.'

'This time when I reach England I've decided I'll find a place of my own somewhere away from London and from city hassle.' Alex answered thoughtfully.

Staring out to sea, lost in some memory, the captain seemed not to have heard him, then turning to Alex said, 'You know there's a place I can recommend. It's a small village, unaltered for centuries *and* there's a railway line still working. A lovely, beautiful place of green hills and valleys, not too far from the Welsh Border mountains. You can walk there undisturbed for days. I stayed once and have never forgotten it. I remember a strange story I heard about it. There's a large hill overlooking a valley, once an iron age fortress, that is said to be the residing place of a pagan goddess.'

'I think you mean, *was* once the residing place of a goddess.' Alex bluntly interrupted, though not intentionally impolite.

'No, I mean, *is* the residing place of a pagan goddess. The locals refer to her as 'The Green Goddess.' There are stories of men who fall in love with her and disappear forever.'

'A delight of England, ghosts, goblins and fairies.'

'I'm an old sea dog and superstitious. In any case I commend the place to you. It has all the things you are looking for away from it all. Come up to the bridge and I'll show it you on a map if you like and give you an address of a good hotel'

On their way to the bridge the captain said, 'I also recall the place from an incident I heard took place there some years ago. The hotel proprietor told me a countess or baroness, or something like that, the wife of a local lord was murdered nearby and the case never solved. Apparently the culprits were looking for some kind of relic owned by the poor woman's family. The murder was reported in all the papers but the husband refused to discuss the object with anyone, even the police.'

Back in London, Alex impetuously decided to follow through on the Captain's recommendation. Close friends in Kensington had stored his car in their garage.

The Green Goddess

'How long this time Alex? What a life you lead.' His friend Joyce whom he had known since university days leaned over the open door of his car, deliberately flirting.

'Oh a long time, a short time, I'm not sure.' He laughed at her. 'I'm looking for a place I can finally call home.'

She leaned into the window and kissed him. 'I've told you my home is your home. Come back soon and don't forget we're always here if you need us we really care about you Alex.' As an afterthought she shouted after him, as he drove away, 'And eat properly.'

From London he drove for three hours before reaching the rolling hills and green valleys of the borders where he booked into the ivy covered hotel the captain had mentioned. He was tired and as Joyce had noticed a little emaciated from months of travelling. He slumped on the bed and fell fast asleep.

The next day found him among russet hills, emerald valleys and half- timbered villages. No modernisations, housing estates, no motorways or widening of country lanes. It was Hardy's image of England undisturbed.

At breakfast one sunny morning he asked the hotel manager, 'Where's the nearest Estate Agent?'

'Walmley Village, that's about 5 miles from here. There's nothing local.'

'Any properties for sale in this area?'

'Not many I'm sure. Most families have been here for generations and the majority of cottages are tied to the Henley Estate.'

That day driving down hedge grown country lanes he came across Barrington Hall, a seventeenth century country house laying back among the trees so well hidden he almost missed it. Stopping the car he grabbed his camera and walked up the dirt drive. He was enamoured of its isolated neglected beauty.

Autumn leaves blew in a silent golden breath over its neglected stone terraces. Mirrored light, reflecting the clouds and trees in its tall and stately windows gave it an air of loneliness and secrecy. The house appeared deserted. Certainly no cars had disturbed the grass strewn driveway for ages.

After a walk around its wild gardens he realised it had been vacant for a considerable time. A neglected orchard tumbled with ripe fruit and the once carefully landscaped garden still perfumed the air with forgotten flora. Wild white byrony had grown between flagstones of the terraces and were heavy with their deadly scarlet berries. A Neptune fountain above an enormous bowl, and a pool, beyond the weedy terrace stood sadly in a mantle of green and orange algae.

About to leave he noticed a window at the rear had been left open. Looking round to be sure he was alone he climbed onto the sill and jumped inside.

The interior was filled with period furniture covered carefully with protective dust sheets and all was well maintained, no signs of damp or flaky paint or broken windows. He browsed the spacious rooms admiring the charm of the place and began to climb the stairs. Then an unexpected noise of running feet startled him. He turned on the stairs to catch a glimpse of a man bolting from one of the ground floor rooms and this was followed by the noise of a door being flung open on its hinges and slammed shut.

Bounding down the stairs Alex gazed from the windows to the drive of the house just in time to see a man running into the lane.

Shocked by the disturbance Alex left immediately.

Gazing back at the hall from the pillared entrance gate he looked for a 'For Sale' notice but found none.

Inexplicably during the following week whenever he made enquiries about the abandoned house his question was received coldly with raised, suspicious, non-committal eyebrows.

'We don't have any information about it.' A girl in the Walmley Estate Agency told him.

He knew she was lying.

In Henley village library the assistant stared at him guardedly.

'Our local history collection doesn't have anything on it, I'm afraid.' She was polite but didn't want to help.

Why such reticence about this magnificent country house?

A search at the county planning office gave the name of the owner of Barrington as Lord Henry Allan of Henley Hall.

Later efforts to contact Lord Alan were frustrated. It was impossible to gain an audience with him or anyone else at Henley Hall.

After writing several letters, and a half dozen attempts at phoning, his efforts were eventually rewarded. An interview was arranged after Lord Henry heard Alex was the writer of travel books of which it fortuitously turned out he was an enthusiast.

They met at Henley Hall.

The eighteenth century Hall dominated the landscape between tranquil green hills its entrance hidden from view down a lane quiet as a forgotten coach road. It was a stately affair set in fifteen hundred acres of woodland, pastures and gardens.

Alex drove down the well maintained winding access drive and parked near the entrance. There seemed little life in the place yet as he walked up the terrace steps to its huge double entrance door it was opened before he could ring the bell.

'So you are the famous traveller I've read so much about. Well I must say you look every bit the man I imagined. Please come in Mr Roedale.'

Lord Henry led him through a wide hall.

'I am delighted to welcome you to our village and my home.'

'Thank you.'

'Our valley as you probably know by now is one of the loveliest parts of England.'

They entered a grand living room.

'Perhaps it will surprise you but I have most of your books, missing only one I believe.'

Sixty or so in a grey suit and yellow tie Lord Allan spoke in short staccato bursts of energy. He led Alex on to another smaller room.

'My reading room, it's more cosy in here. What would you like to drink, beer, wine, tea, whisky perhaps or port.?'

'Coffee's fine, too early in the day to drink anything stronger.'

'Yes indeed, well said, wish everyone here thought so.' Lord Allan smiled. Going to the door he called loudly.

'Kevin, old boy, bring us a pot of coffee and those cream biscuits you keep sneaking off with.'

The panelled room was lined with bookcases along two walls. A red and blue carpet displayed a coat of arms. Victorian chairs had been set along its edge and in the centre of the room a bottle of wine and two glasses rested on a French inlaid table.

'Kevin's my butler, been with me twenty years. He takes advantage because he is, well, part of our family I suppose. Lovely Irish rogue, a great tippler all at my expense I must say'

Lord Allan's eyes flashed in humour.

'When I heard your name I thought it a mistake not here of all places. I have most of your books, you know, in this very room.'

'I can sign them if you wish.'

'That would be a great pleasure for me. Please sit down. I asked my son Shenley to get your phone number when I heard you were in the village and he said you are interested in Barrington Hall?'

'I wondered why no one lives there at the moment.'

Lord Allan frowned briefly unsure how to answer.

'Barrington's history is rather chequered and unusual if that is what you are enquiring about?' He raised an eyebrow in anticipation.

'I just noticed that it's empty. I know nothing about its history. I need a place to live that's all and it's obviously been vacant for some time I'd say. I suppose it seems a little too much to ask but would you consider selling it? Failing that perhaps renting it?'

Before Lord Henry could answer they were disturbed by a loud knock on the study door and the butler entered.

Thin, athletic in spite of his years, with a brown weathered face of lines, that reminded Alex of wallpaper, a disarming insolence shone from the man's eyes. Alex's experience told him something was incongruous about the man. He was no ordinary butler, too physically fit, and his eyes too alert and observant.

'Your coffee Lord Henry', the butler said in a pronounced Cork accent.

'Kevin! This is Alex Roedale, the author I mentioned.'

'Welcome. Is that all sir.' Kevin was already moving to the door, and closed it gently behind him.

'Been at the whisky again I can always tell, the flush on his face, the don't give a monkey's attitude.' Lord Henry laughed. 'Lovely chap for all that, reliable and protective. You wouldn't believe it to look at him but when the occasion merits he is meticulous down to every detail, has a phenomenal memory, never forgets a face or a name or an overheard conversation, and a formidable fighter.'

Alex believed it.

Lord Allan broke off thoughtfully.

' I *would* like to get rid of Barrington Hall.'

Alex held his breath.

'It's a big drain on my income while it's empty. It needs someone to look after it and take pride in it, someone like yourself perhaps would be perfect for all of us, and return some status to the place. My guess is you are the man and I might add respectfully, have enough money to keep it in the manner to which it is accustomed.' Lord Allan laughed disarmingly. 'You know, once upon a time royal heirs dissipated there with their mistresses and wives, or someone else's. I'll be sad to see it go, but, to be honest, at the same time glad to get it off my hands. I did try to sell it years back but with all the rumours of its bad history and strange happenings.' Lord Henry looked quickly towards Alex, 'Did you know about those?'

'No, but I don't pay much heed to rumours or superstitions in any case.'

'Yes just superstition, that's all,' Lord Allan re-marked thoughtfully changing the topic perhaps too quickly, Alex noted.

'I'm willing to rent it to you or let you have it on a ninety nine year renewable lease to you and your heirs.'

'A kind offer and I will think about it.'

Alex was prudently unwilling to show enthusiasm.

The Green Goddess

'Of course. Let me in any case show you around the place. If you decide you would like to buy it we can come to an agreement and everything will be drawn up by my estate solicitors, without any small print,' Lord Henry laughed. 'You can have the house as it is, furnishings, everything and the books in the library, if you wish. I would be delighted to have you there.'

'When I first saw it someone had broken in. It was clear I had disturbed them.'

Alex explained what had happened.

'It's something I've been afraid of.' Lord Henry cast him a furtive, surprised glance. 'Before I show it to you I will make sure nothing has been stolen or damaged.'

Barrington needed little doing to its interior and on inspection Alex decided to buy. Months of solicitors wrangling, unnecessary delays and visits to his bank followed until it was finally settled and he became the owner of Barrington Hall.

A neutral, grey washed sky belied his mood on the day he moved in.

Two men in a red Porsche watched from the lane leading to the hall.

'So I wonder who the devil he is.' The driver of Porsche asked.

'Must know the Allans.' The passenger companion said casually.

'We need to know more about him. See what the villagers are saying. Can you do that? The bloody thing we are looking for might well be in that house.'

'Ok Ralph I'll do my best. Maybe he's a friend of Sophia.' The passenger cast a sly sideways glance at the driver.

A flash of angry jealousy clouded and narrowed Ralph's eyes. 'Find out whatever it is.'

CHAPTER THREE

Sometimes it seemed all the sorrows of life condensed and fell on his secluded valley to say in spite, 'You live in such an Eden that it's necessary to remind you of the world outside.'

Rain was drawing curtains across the fields and squalls tearing across the landscape. Not a friendly star lit the gloom. Alex stared from his study window towards the rain engulfed hills and the clouds rolling angrily across the sky. Thunder savaged the night with such a violent reverberating sound the ground shook. Lightning furiously broke across the hills like a gigantic cosmic strobe as the land withdrew into itself like a frightened animal.

Alex watched the wild turbulence among the trees.

On a path crossing his land he caught a glimpse of Will Perrin, an old man, struggling against a squall of rain, as he followed the public right of way across the fields.

Pausing at a gate Will sheltered beneath one of the great oaks that bestrewed Barrington. Wind was tugging his clothes angrily. Wiping rain from his cheeks and beard Will took deep breaths to fortify his frail body from the new onslaught of wind and deluge.

Slate grey clouds rushed across the troubled skies and terrified him. The wind howled like warriors racing towards a Valhalla doom.

Opening his window the storm almost took the pane from Alex's grasp.

'Will, Will, come in here, please,' he shouted. The noise of the storm drowned his words in the wind.

On a fine day this was one of the most beautiful parts of England. Alex had chosen the Hall because of its mystery and lovely views. Gentle hills of sandstone undulated in voluptuous curves like a sultry woman in repose. On clear days, that did often happen, in spite of this storm, he could scan the Black Mountains far to the southwest and much nearer, Houseman's "Blue remembered Hills".

Majestic elevations of sandstone were covered in forests of pine and beech, oak and chestnut. Some of the most beautiful stately homes in England graced the meadows and woods of its countryside. Fallow deer roamed the estates, elusive crossbills were abundant and sometimes the mournful cries of the exotic ring ouzel pierced the air.

The rolling incomparably fertile countryside and plains of Gloucestershire were clear to see.

Misty, timeless, villages hidden in hollows and valleys were skirted by wide and peaceful rivers. Ancient forests and groves engulfed the landscape in a history out of time.

Lightning shook the old oak above Will causing its boughs to tremble momentarily. For a few seconds the tree was lit by a phosphorescent green glow in a remarkable emerald display.

Looking around him fearfully Will stared up in horror at the tree as though he had seen something ghastly there. He coughed then spat into the hedgerow and hid his face in his hands.

Feeling ashamed of his safe shelter while the old man struggled against the awful night Alex unlatched the window to shout again to come inside but before he could do it Will sprung into action.

Unsteadily, his rickety limbs trembling, Will broke into a disconnected trot that took him out of vision. Behind him lightning created an ominous silhouette of Druids Hill and for a moment the ancient mound dominated the landscape like an angry Titan.

The morning, after the storm, came with a tired peace and clouds of steel grey.

Several days passed before he met Will Perrin walking the lane near Barrington Hall.

'Hello,' Alex greeted.

'Nice day Mr Roedale, after that awful storm.'

'Yes, absolutely. My paddocks are still soaked and the old barn. I need to fix the roof if you know anyone.'

'I'll send someone, Mr Roedale, good at his job.'

'You know something has been bothering me for days now.'

'I hope I have'n done anythin' wrong I certainly wouldn' mean to.'

Alex laughed disarmingly.

'No, of course not, nothing like that. It's just the other night, you remember, during the storm.'

'I got a real soaking that night on my way home.'

'Well, I saw you from my windows, on the footpath, and noticed you beneath the oak tree opposite. I called you to come in but you didn't hear me. You should have knocked my door.'

Will's face paled noticeably at the mention of the tree. 'Aye,' he answered almost inaudibly.

'You seemed to be very afraid I noticed. Tell me what frightened you?'

The Green Goddess

'Just the lightnin.'

'What was it you saw in the tree?' Alex asked coming directly to the point.

Will remained silent until Alex coaxed, 'Tell me Will, I would like to understand. I thought I saw a green glow emanate from the tree. Did you see it?'

Will had been a sergeant in the war and knew men well. He liked Alex. He noticed the set of his mouth, the quiet loneliness, the direct, pained look in his eyes, the fearless independence.

Will turned away without answering then thinking better of it turned back and said, 'If I were you I'd leave that place Mr Roedale.' A grim determination set the old man's face like rock.

'Why do you say that?' Alex asked in surprise.

'That light, I knew when I saw it, was none other than the Green Woman herself.

'Ah! the local legend.'

'I don't think you understan' Mr Roedale the Green Woman is a living thing. I saw the green light in the tree just as you did and I heard her laugh. I know it means trouble.' Will shook his head. 'Take my advice sir an' leave. I heard that storm was just over our village nowhere else and then she appears again.'

'What on earth is the Green Woman?'

'She's a creature that guards a treasure hidden in the hills and in doing it takes men's souls and sometimes their bodies. She lives up there as eternal as God himself.'

'What treasure are you talking about Will?' Alex was intrigued by this new slant to the folk tales.

'My grandfather saw it once when he fell into a cave an' he was never the same after. Many strange things beneath that hill.'

'Well why do you think I should leave?'

'The house you live in has a bad history. Terrible things happened there.' Will shook his head.

'What bad things?'

'Men disappeared from there and some say taken by the Green Ooman.'

Will turned and walked away without saying goodbye lost in thought.

Alex smiled, another way of adding interest to the otherwise sheer boredom of living in a remote village.

Walking on Alex came to a bend in the lane and ahead of him he could see the tree clad hill Will had been talking about.

Druids Hill, one and half miles from Barrington, was an enormous prehistoric hill fortress, the second largest in Britain a local archaeologist had told him. Almost entirely covered by oak and an extensive grove of evergreen yews it was enveloped in mystery, probably because no one had ever conducted an archaeological survey of the site. For many people it had become a hallowed spot not so known as Glastonbury or Stonehenge but nevertheless sacred. Some superstitious villagers he was told avoided the hill so strenuously they walked miles round it rather than use public footpaths that ran over it. A Ministry backed contractor once attempted to tunnel beneath the hill to build a motorway. The villages threw themselves together in such determined stance that the ministry rerouted the planned road further west.

Alex himself began to think of it as mysterious. He had never seen birds sheltering in its trees nor seen rabbit, hare or squirrel dart across its green paths yet in April its trees burst into fragrant blossom and the hill was covered in an exquisite, gently shaking sea of English bluebells.

Perhaps from a considerable variety of mushrooms and fungi, rare plant species, a mix of beech, alder, oak, yew and buckthorn, the air close to it took on such an intoxicating quality in the Spring it left people light headed. Villagers adamantly maintained that in the springtime it exuded an aphrodisiac on the wind. Alex grinned at the thought.

The moment he had seen Druids Hill he had been reminded of mythical Celtic tales.

It was not the tallest prominence overlooking the valleys but it had a charismatic presence in the surrounding countryside. You couldn't ignore it and little wonder generations of villagers had built up a repertoire of phantastic tales about it.

CHAPTER FOUR

It took months before he knew the district or its eccentric villagers. His few neighbours, farmers and businessmen, were scattered over miles.

The nearest pub was an old coaching Inn, The Red Bull at Henley village. Before long he had a quiet corner in the lounge. Eight or nine regulars dropped by every evening and one night soon after his arrival they turned to look at him with more than usual interest.

'Something will happen to him, it always has to everybody who ever was there. What do you think Judith?' A heavy bellied farmer asked the barmaid.

Judith tossing her dyed blonde hair paused long enough to blow her cigarette smoke in the air away from the men.

'I hope nothing happens to him.' She turned from the speaker to eye Alex. 'He's the nicest man we've seen here in a long time *and* the best looking.' Judith spoke a little louder hoping Alex overheard her. 'So polite and kindly with it.'

'Aye Yo'm right there, you know the t'other day he saw me cutting the Allan hawthorn hedges an he stopped his car, pulled out a six pack and gave me a beer.' A hedge cutter, piped in.

'What's Ralph Morville doin' here tonight?' Judith asked. Staring, meanly across the room.

'Nothing good to be sure. He usually drinks at the Talbot.'

Ralph Morville was sitting alone at a corner table drinking whisky and observing Alex with interest.

'I don't like him being in here.' Judith remarked.

'He's a bad seed like all his family,' a bearded man standing at the far end of the bar joined in.

'I don't like the way he keeps lookin' at Alex either,' Judith answered.

For a moment all the men at the bar fell silent.

'Miss Sophie Allan will like him.' Judith added.

'Alex?' The hedge cutter asked.

'Who else?'

The three friends clinked glasses and laughed.

Judith agreed thoughtfully with her eyes and turned away. Suddenly all she wanted was a quiet smoke.

The glances in his direction from the bar and the watchful gaze of Ralph Morville hadn't escaped Alex. He finished his pint and left.

Alex' neighbours, just as old Will had done, hinted without being specific, at a notorious history connected with Barrington Hall. Old ladies shuddered at the mention of it but said nothing except to make quiet warning assertions as though afraid to even speak of the place.

On a wet day of drizzle that forbade anything better to do, Alex visited the county library, a Frank Lloyd Wright affair, set in acres of parkland and surrounded by woods and pasture.

There wasn't much about Barrington Hall in the archives.

A female librarian, red haired, slim, beautiful, wearing glasses and the perfect stereotype of hidden passion beneath a studious face came to help.

'You won't find much about Barrington Hall, I'm afraid, not in the library. It's mostly at Henley Hall. They have an extensive archive there of manorial records that they refuse the County Archivist access to or even copy. We would like to retain them for safe keeping but they refuse.'

'Why?'

'Who knows? Ridiculous really, unless they have something to hide. You'd need to speak to someone there a secretary or estate manager probably. Would you like their phone number?'

'I have it thank you.'

In the library catalogue he discovered a detailed account of Druids Hill and some articles about local folklore and superstitions. In one there was a fanciful history of the stone age fortress that said the name Druids Hill reached back into an undiscoverable past. First extant records in early Saxon documents referred to it by that name from a Celtic derivative and described a colony of Druidic priests who had lived there long before in its fortified settlement. It was they who had planted the sacred yew and oak trees he could see from his windows at Barrington.

At one time, it continued, a formidable tribe of Celts had inhabited the region. They or someone long before them had built the Stone Age settlement that crowned the Hill. At the time the moated fort, seven and one quarter acres in extent, was set amid difficult marshlands that gave no easy access. A broad ditch of this great defensive moat still surrounded the Hill and from its edge, protective ditches and banks and a strenuous escarpment rose steeply to the summit.

The article suggested it had been a revered Druidic temple.

Then in the eleventh century a military order of monks arrived from Palestine, where they had been defending Jerusalem, and built a temple on a hill crest adjacent to Druids Hill. The article maintained *that* much was fact but a local legend added they had used a maze of limestone caves beneath the Stone Age fortress to hide their considerable, and fabulous treasures.

In addition to these snippets of historic detail the writer mentioned superstitions that were not so easily proved. These stories gleaned from records five hundred years old and more told of apparitions, of men being lost and never seen again, of ghosts of Roman soldiers, witches and a supreme eternal goddess who lived among the yew trees and beneath the stone age fortress.

Alex photocopied the article and returned to Barrington.

From his bedroom the first thing Alex saw was the mysterious hill. Early morning it was a pleasurable scene with the sun shining across its mantle of green luxuriance. On wet days, when the wind was bending the greenwood trees, it took on the aspect of a wild strength and enduring stability. After a while every tree became engraved on his memory.

A farmer, at the library looking through land deeds, told him Barrington Hall was inhabited by the ghost of a man who had lived there and disappeared without trace. Alex had laughed at the story.

Checking two references about Barrington in a volume of Victoria County History Alex came across the following.

'Lord Hungerford, an eighteenth century owner of Barrington was said to have wandered over Druids Hill one August day and was never seen again. His ghost it is said is heard weeping among the Stone Age yews trees on the anniversary of his disappearance.'

"Two other owners, the brothers who had given the house its name, were said to have been enamoured of a beautiful goddess who lived on Druids Hill. They supposedly fought a duel over her but only one body was ever found. Local superstition states that Sir Thomas Barrington disappeared into a mystic realm with a green goddess. Circumstances however suggest he fled, after the duel, and sailed overseas but in any case Sir Thomas was never heard of again anywhere in the kingdom."

Alex photocopied the articles and left.

CHAPTER FIVE

In the leafless wintry rime garlanding the fields Henley Hall stood proudly isolated in the landscape. In the distance Alex could see, in a meadow below the great house, a thoroughbred striking the frozen earth with impatient hooves and snorting, the sound carrying on the icy air, but apart from that there was silence and no signs of life whatever.

A public footpath led beside fields of corn across a sunken drovers road towards Henley Hall and past the village church. Too early yet for Lord Allan's invitation to the Hall he decided on a whim to visit the church hoping its history would throw light on the Barrington family.

Opening the withered oak door Alex entered the gloom of a dimly lit nave. Inside near the entrance, on a narrow table, he found a small booklet mentioning the memorials of Hungerfords, Barringtons and Allans locked in their cold sarcophagi towards the altar. He browsed the booklet quickly. An acquaintance with some of these would give a talking point at the Allan's home later that morning.

Looking up the nave of the church he didn't see her immediately his eyes adjusting to the gloom and dim pale winter light shining through the stained glass windows. When his eyes became more accustomed to the interior, a movement near the altar startled him.

A woman rose to her feet, tall, slender with long hair fastened off her shoulders. Facing the communion table she made a barely perceptible curtsy before turning away to walk down the nave towards the exit. Her strawberry blonde hair caught rays of sunlight from the side windows. She wore white, mud spattered riding breeches. As she walked towards him she moved willowy as a cypress and as undulating as a wave of the sea.

She would have passed without a word had he not spoken first.

'I've disturbed you, I'm sorry,' he said quickly in an attempt to prevent her leaving.

Pausing beside him she flashed smiling, violet coloured eyes.

The Green Goddess

'I had finished anyway. Is this your first time here?'

He had never seen anyone so beautiful. Eyes framed by long lashes stared at him, kindly and expectantly.

'It is. I'm new to the area.'

'I thought so. I've never seen you before and I know everyone in the village.'

'It is a lovely old church and quite unusual.'

She smiled holding out her hand. 'My name's Sophia. I have some time would you like me to show you the church? It is a unique parish church.'

Without waiting for assent she turned to a stained glass window and pointed upwards.

'This is fourteenth century glass. The saints depicted are Peter and Paul. Below, there, you see is the coats of arms of the Barringtons and Allans.' She smiled, quickly and secretly to herself he thought, as she turned away.

'Over here is the tomb of a Knight Templar.' She led him to a stone coffin beside the church wall beyond the pews.

Barely visible a sword cross of a medieval knight adorned the weathered, crumbled, stone lid.

'I find this more interesting than the Elizabethan tombs on the south side. We know nothing about the knight. He may not strictly have been a Templar but one of an order of knights who had a small church on a hill nearby.'

Sophia, glanced at Alex shyly, 'When I was a girl I used to look at him and dream of lands far away that he must have fought and jousted in. I imagined him wielding his sword against impossible numbers and always the victor. His coffin was found covered in grass near the churchyard and long forgotten. There was no name inscribed just the coffin and his Templar Cross.'

She was, he guessed, in her mid- twenties and with such violet blue eyes and rounded cheek bones she looked far more European than British. Her arm gestures and graceful movement suggested ballet training. Everything about her, every strand of hair, every eyelash, her long fingers, the way she jutted her jaw when she smiled, the wave like cadence of her voice, enchanted him.

'Over here is a Barrington tomb.'

Alex listened carefully. This had been the owner of Barrington Hall.

'He wasn't a nice man, had a reputation for immorality.' She smiled, watching closely to gauge Alex's reaction before turning away. 'Before a church was here this place was a pagan religious site. The old baptismal font, over there,' she walked towards the church porch. 'With these funny dragons is from the Welsh Marches,twelfth century we believe.'

Sophia enlivened with enthusiasm said, 'I want to show you now one of our real treasures, I mean *a real treasure* of English architecture. You know many English churches boast of green men, but up there,' she raised her arm lifting her breasts tightly against her dress. 'Is something original, a Green Woman.'

Sophia lowered her arm and watched closely Alex's reaction.

The carving she pointed to was of a woman floating from the bole of a web like tree that spread its branches protectively over her. The figure was carved delicately, exquisitely. A medieval super-model Alex smiled. Praxiteles would have been proud of it with its large eyes, long neck, perfect breasts. Unlike the solitary facial images of green men the sculptor had carved a full nude figure that left nothing unseen and in her green vibrancy she seemed almost alive.

Sophia was watching him closely.

'Local myth claims men fall in love with her.' She eyes flashed humorously. 'People claim to see her in their dreams.'

'Strange object in a church. A fertility goddess?' Alex asked.

'Perhaps but we don't know. Like most mythical creatures in Norman churches she is of pagan origin and my own view is she doesn't represent fertility or spring, but whatever her symbolism her fascination lies in being uniquely local, and green of course.'

'Why do you believe local?'

'You probably haven't heard the story but I believe she's the Green Woman of Druids Hill. Anyway that's what I think.'

Sophia looked at him as though debating whether to tell him more but changed her mind.

'Well I will leave you to look around.'

'Before you go can you tell me the quickest way to Henley Hall?' Alex asked not wanting her to leave.

Her beautiful eyes squinted, momentarily and inquisitively, in fleeting distrust.

'It isn't open to the public I'm afraid.'

Walking to the door the conversation over she turned, feeling guilty, and said,

'Follow the path at the front of the church. Where the path forks go left and you'll be there. The best view is from the gardens. No one will mind if you walk around or take photos.'

Now he'd found her he wasn't going to let her go from his life so easily.

Following her to the door to open it he asked. 'I'm new to the village, would you have time to show me around sometime. You know the area well. Perhaps, let me take you to dinner. I've no friends here yet.'

The Green Goddess

Slightly embarrassed, she gazed down at her riding boots, feeling for the first time self-conscious and vulnerable, her jaw jutting, she smiled.

'Alright, dinner, I'll be free on Wednesday evening.'

It was said determinedly as though she was struggling free from some long confinement that only an act of courage could free her.

'Where? I have no idea of the best place.'

'It doesn't have to be the best place. The Talbot, in Mawley, a village about five miles away. I can be there about eight.'

'I will be there.'

'See you there then.'

She smiled and was gone.

His invitation to Henley Hall that morning had arrived now that the papers had been signed for ownership of Barrington.

Lord Henry had rung to ask, 'Would late morning be welcome to you. My daughter loves to ride early mornings and my sons are always involved with something or other private but I would like you to meet them all.'

'Yes, of course. What time?'

'Good, well then, let's say eleven thirty would that be alright? I've invited a few country friends, I thought you'd like to meet and you should *certainly* meet them.'

A first fall of snow littered the fields. A muffled silence permeated the valley. Rooks flew in arcing flight over bare limbed trees wheeling to their roosts under an elevated soft focused grey sky that glowed with gold rimmed clouds. The distant hills were vaguely outlined beneath a motionless pale blue mist. He could smell snow on the wind. A shepherd's dog barked coldly across the hills and thin layers of ice filled the ditches and puddles along the country path.

The snow fall of the previous night, crisp and turning to ice, crunched like glass beneath his feet as he climbed the steps of Henley Hall, and a bitter wind was blowing a flurry of snow from the trees as he rang the bell.

CHAPTER SIX

The Irish butler Kevin welcomed Alex at the door. 'Ah! It's you sir. The master's waitin.' Kevin's face shone in a cheerful smile. 'I've read your books, you know, as well as Lord Henry. When you've finished sir then come round the back and have a drink with me.'

Alex trying hard not to smile hid his laughter and agreed, 'I will'.

You couldn't ignore the charm of this Irishman and Alex was convinced there was more to the man than being a butler. He had noticed it the first time they'd met.

'I'll return the favour, come to Barrington one evening and tell me about yourself.'

'Sure enough I will. The moment I set eyes on ye I knew there was a Celt in there just waiting to come out.'

'Well, don't tell my father then.' Alex quipped and they both laughed.

Across a great entrance hall he was led to a drawing room that exuded warmth and family content. Everything gleamed, cabinets waxed till they shone, a fireplace glowed with flames of burning logs, a Christmas tree waited to be removed now its lights had been extinguished for the season, wall lights combated the January gloom giving the place a cheerful brightness. Through tall windows he could see the heavily wooded hills. An enormous Persian carpet centred the floor and on it a magnificent inlaid coffee table.

Lord Henry standing with his back to the fireplace came over the moment the door opened.

Alex took in the guests at a glance.

'Punctual. I wish all my visitors were so precise. How has your morning been? My sons Shenley and Marston and daughter Sophia will be here shortly. Come in Alex I'd like to introduce you to our friends.'

Lord Henry introduced, 'This is Hugh Haversham Kingsley.'

A man of medium height, dark curly hair and humorously raised eyebrows came to shake his hand.

The Green Goddess

'Henry has been telling us about you. What an interesting life you lead.'

Before Alex could reply an immaculately preened twentyish woman with rapturously wide eyes came over.

'Are those things true about you? That you once killed a man in New Guinea and I think were almost killed yourself by an African elephant, that you crossed the Mongolian steppes on horseback?'

Alex lowered his head not sure how to reply.

'Not everything one reads is true,' he replied.

'Oh!'

Lord Henry noticing Alex's discomfort came to help by introducing the young woman.

'Meet the charming Alexandra Morley, later no doubt she will talk your head off, but please Alexandra not right now.'

'Come and meet Sir Gerard and Lady Victoria Blount.'

Gerard Blount stood to shake Alex's hand, 'Pleased to meet you.' Then looking at his wife, who was still seated but staring at Alex quizzically, analysing him from top to toe, he said, 'And this is Victoria.'

Suddenly, her curiosity satisfied, Victoria stood and held out her hand, took his gently and reaching up kissed his cheek.

'Welcome Alex. I have read some of your books and am delighted to meet you.'

Looking askance at her husband she said impishly, 'A real man at last Gerard.'

Lord Henry intervened. My family are a varied lot. Sophia is a professor, would you believe at her age, of Medieval Studies. Shenley's a gentleman of the old school, a true Victorian squire, works hard, manages the estate mostly and genuinely cares about the staff and farmers and knows all of their families. If he has a fault it's that perhaps he's too much an intellectual like Sophie. Marston now there is a black sheep if ever there was one. I wish you didn't have to meet him but you will have to sooner or later. He is beyond description. A word of caution don't be offended by him and answer him aggressively if he pushes you too hard. He always backs down. He tries it always without exception.'

A rowdy sound of laughter and voices were heard clamouring in the adjoining hall.

'Here they are.'

The door of the drawing room swung violently open as though a gust of wind had struck it petulantly. Two men stumbled in laughing boisterously. In appearance they were Cain and Abel.

The youngest, clean shaven, with bright blue eyes and auburn hair was dressed in moleskin trousers and woollen roll neck sweater.

The other man, the same height but more heavily built was tanned deeply. His dark brown eyes

The Green Goddess

scrutinised Alex cynically. There was a virile charisma about him that electrified the room. His clothes, worn and soiled by the farm he worked, made him look like a gypsy except for an expensive designer short coat that quickly removed the image of Romany vagrancy. Approaching Alex, without waiting for any introductions, he shook Alex's hand vigorously.

'I have heard much about you from father. I have to admit I never read any of your books.'

'Pleased to meet you.'

The younger brother came over to interrupt, 'At last an intelligent man I can converse with,'

'This is Marston.' Lord Allan introduced the older brother, 'And this is Shenley.'

Shenly's face revealed quiet, confident sophistication and a controlled keen mind.

Before Alex could reply the door was opened again. Everyone in the room turned toward it expectantly.

Alex's breath faltered. The woman at the door was the one that had enchanted him in Henley church. Gone were the riding breeches and tight fitting blouse. Sophia was dressed in a black three quarter length dress that played about her thighs freely revealing every curve and movement.

Halting in surprise at the sight of Alex, an embarrassment not missed by her brothers, a hint of colour flushed her cheek.

At his daughter's hesitation lord Henry walked Alex over to her.

'This is my daughter Sophia.'

Surprised at her blushes Lord Allan said, 'Meet Alex the new owner of Barrington'.

Swiftly regaining composure Sophia held out her hand raising her eyes unflinchingly to his.

'So nice to meet you at last,' Sophia said. 'Has father offered you anything to drink, perhaps a sherry? I think I need one.'

'Perhaps you would like something stronger?' Lord Henry asked Alex.

'Sherry's fine'.

'Looks like you've made an impression on our sister', Marston butted in mischievously.

Sophie turned to her brother riposting smartly, 'How would you know?

Their sibling rivalry sliced across the room like a hatchet.

Marston laughing moved alongside his sister and wrapped his arm gently round her and said to Alex, 'Feisty woman.'

Shaking his arm loose Sophie asked her other brother. 'What would you like Shen and you father?' She came to Alex first with a tray and a sherry glass filled to the brim before going over to the other guests.

'You should ask Kevin to do this,' Lord Henry coolly admonished.

Marston watched her with smiles creasing his face, while he poured out for himself a glass of mineral water, then asked Sophia, 'Has that bloody fool Ralph Morville been bothering you much lately? If so tell me and I will hang him off the nearest oak in Gibbet Wood.'

Sophia's eyes narrowed as she shot a quick warning at her brother. 'No he hasn't. Thanks for the offer.'

Lord Henry sighed and confiding to Alex said, 'They've been like this since childhood'.

'Nothing for me Sophie dear, too early,' Shenley refused.

Marston taking a seat near his father and Alex said, 'Sooner or later you will be told I have a wife and a mistress living, guess where, in the same house.' He laughed uproariously. Switching his attention to Sophie, he teased 'And that proves you wrong about not understanding women.'

Lord Allan's friends, listening intently, pretended not to overhear.

'That only proves my point. It shows you hate them in your heart. If you are going to be honest, for a change, tell everyone how you treat them.' Sophie glared at him.

Ignoring her Marston grunted, 'And that's why most of my family ostracise me. Never mind. Women like strong men Alex and, since they are herding animals, subconsciously recognise the need of a powerful stag.'

Instead of being shocked the guests were smiling. Everyone knew the affection and regard Sophia held for her devilish brother and they had heard these banters before.

'Settle down both of you we have a guest. I don't want heated skirmishes in here and certainly not in front of visitors. If you wish to play your childish games, and continue this behaviour, then leave the room.' Lord Henry warned, 'I'm ashamed of you.'

Lord Henry turned to gazed sadly through the windows at the blue grey mist lying over the distant fields. His children he thought would have been different had Eleanor lived. Suddenly all his energy left him. He sat down in silence.

Lady Alexandra, who had not been blind to Sophia's attraction to Alex came to join him with more questions. Touching his arm gently she asked, 'Tell me about the adventure with the elephant.'

She looked up into his eyes, knowing her lean, angular, aristocratic face, her perfume and wide confident smile assured her of attention.

Alex to himself acknowledged she was beautiful and graceful

The other guests overhearing drew closer to listen. Even Marston stopped his boastful talking to hear the story.

Alex hated these moments.

Taking Sophia's arm gently he turned to Lady Alexandra and said, 'Excuse me for a moment.'

Leading Sophia out of earshot he whispered, 'Get me out of here.'

'*After* the story.' Sophia smiled enjoying his discomfort.

Unable to escape Alex said, 'Well, it sounds adventurous and romantic to you I'm sure but in reality I can assure you it wasn't. A small Kenyan village of farmers, asked me to hunt a rogue elephant that had somehow gone on rampage and killed several people. It isn't an easy task stalking dangerous animals but I had a good black African with me who could follow any spoor to the ends of the earth. We expected it would be over in a few days. I don't like killing but I had to help the villagers they had become friends and always made me welcome whenever I was near their lands taking photos.'

By now all the guests had formed an attentive group around Alex.

'Rogue elephants are always male and we confirmed it by its urination pattern. He wasn't hard to follow because he had an injured foreleg that left a distinctive spoor. We tracked him for days. Wild animals know when they are being tracked. Using some natural instinct he quite plainly realised we were on his trail and to evade us sought the protection of a herd of elephants close by. We had to be more than usually alert.

Elephants are intelligent creatures and dangerously unpredictable, especially in the mating season.'

'Please excuse me all I have to make a phone call.' Gerard Blount apologised.

Victoria Blount looked at her husband disapproving and quizzical. After he had gone she said, 'Gone out for a fag I shouldn't wonder.'

Outside Gerard looked around to be sure no one was near enough to hear and rang a number on his mobile.

'Ralph? He's here at the moment. You asked about Sophia, I'm sure he doesn't know her at all. Now's the time for you to go over there and take a look around. Personally I don't think he knows anything about the object, or whatever it is, but as you say he may be working alone. Right! Of course I will keep you informed if I hear anything.'

Returning to the other guests Gerard stood silently among the group listening to the end of Alex's story.

'Behind us, and approaching at full gallop was the rogue. He suddenly stopped at about twenty metres, raised his great head and trunk, and let out a bellow that was terrifying in its anger and pride. It gave me the chance I needed so I raised my rifle and took aim. The bullet hit him square but seemed to have no effect.

The creature lowered its head and charged. Matabla the tracker and I had just one more chance to fire before we scattered in opposite directions in an attempt to confuse the animal. Unfortunately my foot caught the root of a tree and I fell. The animal was on me in a second and my rifle several feet away. I heard Matabla's gun go off just as the elephant raised up onto its haunches to crush me with its fore legs.'

Alex paused remembering the horror he had felt and the sight of the great creature above him.

'What happened?' Alexandra burst out.

'It collapsed lifeless both of its seven feet long tusks hit the ground on each side of me and sank into the soft earth propping the animal, on its bent knees, over me. Its head and trunk pressed against my chest.

Had it fallen any other way I would have been crushed to death. One tusk gouged out the side of my ribs as the animal fell. One of its eyes stared at me pitiably before it closed. A truly magnificent creature.'

'Show me the scar,' Alexandra begged impetuously.

'This isn't the place to show scars,' Lord Henry reproved coming to rescue Alex.

'No indeed,' Alex agreed laughing.

'Perhaps you could tell me more of these exploits another time soon?' Lady Alexandra said with a cool, sophisticated tilt of her head and direct flirting gaze.

Listening intently Sophia had been surprised to learn Alex was the writer her father had so often enthused about. A moment of destiny had brought him to her in the church.

'Alex would you like to see the house and our lovely gardens.' Sophie asked. She felt satisfaction at Alexandra's pouting when he agreed.

'Father?' Sophia looked to Lord Henry for permission.

Lord Allan nodded agreement fully aware that Alex wished to escape.

Sophia led him through to the main entrance hall and beyond that into an adjacent corridor. To the left she opened a tall double door and waited letting him pass in front of her.

They were in a great vestibule the splendour of which astonished him. Ahead of them a wide, double flight marble staircase was lit by a stupendous crystal chandelier. At the conjunction of the stairs were two crystal lamp stands that were inverted images of the chandelier above them.

The Green Goddess

Sophie was delighted at his wonder.

'The stairs were designed by a French architect. They're Carrara marble. I believe the chandelier lamps were from Italy, about the same time, the early eighteenth century. It was a fad among the wealthy in those days to use Italians. All the interiors were completed by Italians designers and architects.

Walking up the flight of stairs ahead of him she pointed out several marble sculptures recessed into the walls and the glorious ceiling painted and portraits of her Allan ancestors on the stairs.

It was Sophia's own beauty, delicate, svelte, feline, complimenting the great house that captivated him most as she led him through an interminable series of drawing rooms, Green Room, Red Room, Orange and Blue. In the last, walls of blue fabric matched the colour and texture of two enormous couches and seven chairs. A blue and red carpet was embossed with the Allan family coat of arms. The ceiling displayed scenes from Greek tragedies.

Sophie leaned on a wide window ledge to survey the gardens.

'Alex come here and see.'

Standing close to her, their bodies touching, he wondered if the way she pushed her hip against him was deliberate. The casual revealing dress, lean straight back and delicate shoulders stirred longings that made him draw his breath slowly and deeply.

Resting her head on folded hands Sophia stared over the snow filled landscape.

Impulsively Alex put his arm around her as he followed the line of her gaze.

A long avenue of matured trees formed a great arch with their winter branches. Coldly on a hill to the left he could see a mock classic folly and beyond that the rising point of an obelisk. In the distance the rising flank of Druids Hill dominated it all.

'Do you ride much?' Sophie asked, turning to him.

'I haven't a horse yet, not here, but yes I used to ride almost daily.

'You are a man of parts as my father told me. Come Alex, there's a lot more to see.' She took hold of his hand.

'This is the ballroom. In the old days George Fourth danced here and the Prince Regent and once Lord Byron. Wish I'd seen that. I like this room I used to practice ballet here, with a private tutor, in front of that tall mirror.'

Sophie walked towards the mirrored wall and broke into dance.

She was still wearing high heels and her graceful movement seduced him as she spun and pirouetted until her short dress became a sea of black

The Green Goddess

waves. Stopping she leaned forward, her hands on her knees, catching her breath and laughing like a teenager. He clapped his hands and laughed.

She led to more rooms and marble statues of angels and Greek heroes and a gallery of ancestral portraits.

'I want to show you a very special room.' She said.

Sophie led him to a room decorated in wall fabric the colour of her eyes. An onyx fireplace dominated one wall and on another a tapestry of an English country scene lit by a carved lamp. A stately four poster bed dominated a side of the chamber and close to it a door led down a dimly lit passage. Leading him down this they came to a door that was securely locked.

'Wait here a moment,' Sophia said and rushed back along the narrow passage.

Returning she thrust a heavy iron key into the lock and to Alex's surprise bolts disengaged from all sides of the door. Pushing hard she thrust open the heavy door and turning on the dim lighting revealed a marble walled room without windows. One side of this room was filled with what appeared to be antiquarian books but standing in the centre of the room was a magnificent nude sculpture of a woman carved from green marble.

The larger than life size figure, hands clasped across her navel appeared to be welcoming them into her domain. It was an image of female perfection. Her green eyes stared with such hypnotic intensity Alex imagined her alive. A strange refulgent glow, caused no doubt by a refraction of the light on the marble, increased this strange impression of animation.

Sophie gazed at the figure with an almost religious devotion.

'Do you recognise her?' Sophie asked.

'I don't think I have seen *anything* like this before, in all my life, nor anything so beautiful.'

'Doesn't the colour remind you?'

'I can't say it does.'

'She's the goddess from Henley Church.'

'Ah! Of course, but in comparison the difference between a garden gnome and a Canova. So much more exquisite, this is the work of a true master. Who created it?'

Alex walked over and touched the green marble.

'Don't touch Alex,' Sophie ordered in a mock urgency. 'You will fall in love with her.'

'This is a shrine to her isn't it?'

'Not really. Well, maybe, in a way I suppose, yes. All the books you can see over there are about mythology and goddesses. No one reads them except perhaps Shenley.'

'Where did this marvellous statue come from?'

'No one knows, certainly we don't. It used to stand in Barrington Hall where you live. The first

The Green Goddess

owner of Barrington brought it to the house but never recorded where or how he came by it. He was an amateur archaeologist. There's some conjecture it came from Druid's Hill.'

Standing beside the green statue Alex couldn't help comparing Sophia with it. The statue could have been modelled on her but Sophia was alive, flesh and blood, and this an artist's representation of what could be.

'What marble is it?' He asked, intrigued by the phosphorescent glow that shone like a halo around the statue.

'My grandfather once asked a geologist to examine it and was told by the man he'd never come across anything like it before. Last year Shenley had a Gemmologist take a small sample from the heel but the report was inconclusive. Of course it's marble but the source of it is what puzzles everyone. Nothing like it is recorded in the Gemmology Society records. The only suggestion he could give was it bore some resemblance to a rare artefact found at a Hittite site about three thousand BC.'

'What do you think?' Alex asked.

'Wherever Barrington got it from we have no idea. He was, like you, a great traveller so it could have come from anywhere. Lord Barrington, perhaps you heard, disappeared, mysteriously. The villagers say the Green Woman took him,' Sophie laughed. 'See what a haunted, mysterious place our house is.'

In the drawing room they found Marston had left ordered out by Lord Henry for some incivility to the guests. Shenley was waiting for their return and talking genially to his father and friends. The whole room paused in mid conversation to stare at Alex and Sophia as they entered.

Afternoon light was already fading from the windows and everyone was preparing to leave.

Alex looked at his watch.

'I'll have to leave too,' he said, addressing Lord Henry.

'Come over to my house if you can one evening.' Shenley requested, 'I'm in the phone book. It's Chiswick House, just down the road'.

'Sorry we haven't really had much time to talk,' Lord Allan apologised. 'Do come next week, if you can, we'll show you the estate and you can meet some of our staff. That way you'll feel a part of our home and the village.' Lord Henry held out his hand and shook Alex's warmly. 'Thanks so much for coming.'

'I'll see him out Papa,' Sophie offered.

At the door she gave him her hand and reminded, 'See you Wednesday.'

CHAPTER SEVEN

The Talbot, three miles past Walmley village was a black and white timbered Inn that had once been a squire's manor house. It lay so far back from the road Alex passed it in the dark but catching a glimmer of its lights through the trees doubled back. Driving through a narrow farm gate that led to a large car park it was deserted except for a few farm vehicles.

Frost hung in icy streamers from the silent, naked trees surrounding the Inn. A wintry smell of moulding farm fields hung on the night air and the stars shone brilliantly in a cloudless deep purple sky.

Inside was oak panelled and discreetly lit lamps retained a vestige of its seven hundred years of history.

A tall, powerfully built man met Alex at the bar to ask, 'What can I get you?'

'Any local ale?'

'Three and I'd recommend Hatton's. This time of year I put a poker in it from the fire if you like.'

Just what was needed on such a cold night. 'Is it usually this quiet?'

In a snug corner Alex noticed a dark suited man in his forties talking intimately to a pretty younger woman and in an adjoining room he could hear men brusquely shouting and laughing.

The barman, his face squared and hardened like a rugby player's, replied as he drew the pint, 'At this time, yes, but in an hour you'd be hard put to it to find a seat.'

A rush of cold air blew in as a man about Alex's age brusquely entered and stood brushing snow off his jacket.

Alex saw the barman give the man a fleeting but loathing glance. The visitor's blonde hair contrasted dramatically with his dark brown eyes and though handsome he had the arrogant sneering face of a bully.

Eyeing Alex quizzically, disdainfully, as though he were about to ask what he was doing there the man decided not to and ignored him.

'Brandy, Tom, please,' he called walking past the bar and taking a seat near the fire.

The Green Goddess

Alex left the bar and in an alcove found privacy away from the draught of the door and where he could see when Sophia came in.

Two more men entered, went to the bar, and then noticing the blonde haired man one went over and greeted.

'Ralph, can we get you anything?'

'Already ordered.'

'Should have ordered us one as well. Bloody cold night, I'll have a whisky I think.' The man left to join his companion before they both joined Ralph at his fireside table.

Alex noticed they were speaking secretly, quietly, in muffled voices. The blonde haired man named Ralph said something, nodded, and both men turned to stare towards Alex.

Alex looked at his watch, she was late. If it had been anyone else he would have finished his ale and walked out. He had looked forward, anticipated this evening with Sophia, but now was suddenly filled with a heavy foreboding. Through the window he could see more snow falling. It was a bad night and anything could have delayed her.

Tiny drifts of snow were rising on the window pane obliterating his view of the car park. Taking a notebook from his oilskin jacket to jot down ideas for an article he was writing he was prevented by the outside door opening and closing rapidly with a thud. Looking up he saw Sophia.

Sophia wearing a tightly tailored jacket, with turned up fur collar, beneath which she had tucked blue jeans over riding boots had already noticed him. She approached, smiling warmly. Her blonde hair tumbled from beneath a grey fur hat. She glowed with flushed sparkle of winter purity.

The three men who had been watching Alex stopped their conversation and turned to stare at her in unconcealed admiration as Alex stood to greet her.

'I'm so sorry. I was held up at the uni, then my car wouldn't start in the cold.'

'What can I get you?' Alex asked pulling out a chair for her.

Looking around, as she removed her coat and noticed the three men at the fireside table. Her smile narrowed in a rapid almost imperceptible look of alarm then just as quickly regained composure.

'I'd like a Bailey's please.'

Alex thought her more beautiful now than when he had first seen her. Aware of his attention she sat down a smile curling the corner of her mouth.

'Am I mistaken, but you seem uncomfortable at the sight of those men sitting to our left.' Alex said.

The Green Goddess

'No you aren't mistaken, that's Ralph Morville, owns Morville Hall, he's someone I know and don't like much.'

Their conversation was interrupted, by Morville himself who without being asked walked over and sat at their table.

'Nice seeing you again, especially here, Sophia,' Morville said making no attempt to greet Alex.

Sophia remaining silent looked angrily away towards the bar.

'How's your gentle brother, still searching the woods for his goddess?' Morville asked.

Sophia turned to Morville, coldly, venomously.

'Gentle? Yes in an old world sort of way but not the way you mean. You have a short memory Ralph.' Sophia said cuttingly. 'Don't you remember that thrashing he gave you in that boxing tournament at Trelgate ten years ago. Didn't he put you in hospital?'

Taken aback at her onslaught, Ralph moved uneasily in his seat.

'Then,' Sophia continued, 'There was that horse race over the Sheepwalks. They tell me he was 100 metres ahead of you, *and* all your cronies. I think the word Ralph is not gentle man but gentleman.'

Ralph fell into silence.

'Just in case you want to know this is Alex Rodale the new owner of Barrington.'

Morville stared angrily at Sophia then at Alex.

'Ah! So you're the new owner. I was wondering who you were. I knew it had been sold.' Ralph acknowledged, then addressing Sophia, sniggered, 'They tell me old Will saw the Green Woman again. Must have pleased your brother.'

'There have been stories of the Green Woman ever since people lived here, you know that. Your ancestor two hundred and fifty years ago found a wooden carving of it on Druids Hill.' Sophie corrected.

'All nonsense,' Morville retorted. 'What do you think Alex?'

'Don't know much about the story.'

The men at Morvilles table were watching, listening, laughing in close camaraderie waiting expectantly for Ralph's denouement of this village intruder. Like villagers everywhere they were territorially distrustful of any trespass in their tribal kingdom.

Alex had seen it in every village community in the world.

'I've known of too many unexplained phenomenon to be as certain as you.' Alex commented.

'Sophie, your brother will at least have one friend here.'

'One more than you then', Sophie rejoined acerbically.

Ralph's friends laughed with delight at Sophie's reply. A great favourite in the village they all knew about her witty, feisty repartee.

Ralph shot his drinking pals an angry over the shoulder glance.

'Do you ride?' Ralph asked.

Alex leaned forward resting his forearms on the table wondering where this conversation and evening were taking them.

Before he could answer Sophie joined in, 'Better than you. Alex has just completed an eight hundred mile ride across the Caucasian Steppes'. She glanced at Morville deliberately, provoking.

Subdued, Morville noticed he had lost the attention of his friends who were engrossed in their own private conversation and drinks.

'I should have asked do you hunt?' Morville recovered.

'Once I shot a bear at close range in Canada after some overzealous hunters disturbed its lair. I felt ashamed I'd had to do it. I killed a charging rhino once to save my horses and companions and last year, in the Russian Taiga, where I'd been five days without food I shot an elk' Alex's ire was beginning to display itself openly now.

Vanquished, struggling not to express vitriol, Ralph rose to leave. 'I'll ring you, sometime,' he said to Sophie.

Sophie dropping her gaze didn't look at him or answer.

After Ralph had gone she said quietly to Alex. 'I suppose you had to meet him one day or another but be careful Alex, he's dangerous.'

Ralph and his companions emptied their glasses and left casting cursory, unfriendly glances at Alex and Sophia as they passed.

The ancient inn began to fill with people as though all they had been waiting for was Ralph Morville to leave.

'Let's meet the local's,' Sophie suggested. She felt happier now Morville and his cronies had left.

'Our villagers are a classic country litter and this is the best place to find them.'

Sophia led Alex to a petrified oak door over which was written 'Gun Room'.

'It was once a bar of sporting gentlemen, in Squirearchy days, but now it's the local smoker's.'

A score or more men were talking loudly. Two aged dames were sitting silently alongside a white haired patriarch speaking to them quietly. A diaphanous, hazy, smoke cloud hung beneath the lights and the room smelled of beer and tobacco.

Recognising Sophia the men fell silent to look at her.

Sophia stared them down with a disarming smile as bright as the morning.

The Green Goddess

Two men at a crib table stood to offer their seats.

'Miss Sophie', one of them greeted bowing his head as he and his companion left their seats to be with the boozers at the bar.

At the table the only person who hadn't moved was Will Perrin who took off his old felt hat when Sophia joined him.

'What are you drinking Will,' Alex asked.

'I'll have a pint o' Bertram's thank you sir,'

Cold shouldered by three farm hands at the bar Alex pushed past and ordered drinks.

Taking up his beer Will raised his glass. 'Cheers Sophie, Mr Roedale'

Sophia in exuberant mood left her seat went to the bar and standing on the lower rung of a stool banged a pint glass on the table.

'Gentleman all, ladies, I want you to welcome Alex Roedale the new owner of Barrington.' Sophia swept her arm in Alex's direction.

Alex, embarrassed, nodded an acknowledgement as the room raised their glasses.

'Alex wants to buy you all a pint or whatever it is you are drinking.'

The men turned as one towards Alex and once more raised their glasses laughing boisterously.

Returning Sophia laughed, 'Hope you have enough money.'

'Will was telling me I ought to leave Barrington,' Alex said smiling at her.

'Why do you say that?' Sophie prompted, in controlled humour.

'She's movin' off the hill again, an' it'll only mean heartache for all caught up in it,' Will answered.

'Who is moving off the hill?' Alex asked perplexed.

'What was it you saw?' Sophie asked.

The bar fell silent as everyone tried to catch Will's words. Noticing it Will didn't answer and took a long drink from his glass.

Sophia resting her hand on Will's arm cajoled, 'Will'.

Staring at his pint glass Will said, 'I saw her in that great oak, her green eyes staring at me, burning into me, calling me to the grave. I was afraid and knew I daren't look at her wild beauty or I'd been gone like all o' them others. I ran away'.

'Where do you get such wild ideas?' Sophie admonished. 'In any case stories of her say she helps people and protects them.'

'True but she also takes em, an they're never seen again. Scoff if you like Miss Sophie but I know what I saw and my grandfaither fore me.'

The bar room overhearing the conversation was beginning to warm to the story. One of the older ladies joined in so that all could hear her.

The Green Goddess

'Once I was walkin' my dog on the slopes of Druids an I saw Roman soldiers racing down the bank, the sun shining on their helmets and shields. My old dog took fright, poor thing, and left me, the first time he'd ever done that. My old Bob, a good old boy, was home when I got there, shivering like a leaf.'

'You left your glasses at home you old bugger', one of the men called, and the room flooded with laughter.

'You wouldn't even know what a Roman soldier looked like,' someone shouted.

'You can laugh, but it don't alter anything,' the woman answered.

Recognising a man near the bar Sophia turned to him and asked. 'Do you have your fiddle?'

The man rose from his corner. 'Aye,' he said expectantly.

'Is John here with you?' Sophia called.

'Yes, here.'

'Give us a country song both of you and let's liven up this winters evening and show Alex what we are really like without this superstitious nonsense.'

Within minutes the room was filled with music, spirited laughter and the sound of happy voices.

It was almost midnight when Alex and Sophia left to a chorus of voices shouting, 'Good night both.'

Snow was mingling with sleety rain when they left the Inn and a bitter cold wind made them tug their coats tightly around them. Alex wrapped his arm around Sophia's to pull her close. Sophia's car wouldn't start, the battery indicator was shining red and it was too foul a night for Alex to check the car electrics for her.

'I'll take you home and we'll fix it tomorrow. Alex said.

On the way to Henley Alex asked, 'What did Ralph Morville mean about Shenley?'

'Shen, just like those folk in the Talbot, really does believe a Green Woman lives on Druids Hill. What's more he accepts *all* those superstitious folk-tales about her. He told me once he'd seen her himself. According to him, she was the most beautiful woman any one would ever see.' Sophie laughed, 'You'll have to ask him about it. He might be able to introduce you.'

'What do you think about it?'

'Shenley has a brilliant mind. He doesn't accept anyone's judgment but his own. He did see something I think because it changed him quite dramatically. If you are asking if I believe in a goddess of course I don't. You know in the stories she never appears to women. I think it has something to do with male phantasy. There *is* something strange about Druids Hill though and there are a lot of written accounts of a goddess on Druids Hill going back to Norman times. You can find sites all over Britain where pagan deities were once worshiped but this is the only one I know of where people actually believe such a deity still lives there. The answer lies perhaps in Jungian psychology a kind of folk archetype residing in the unconscious of the local people but who knows about these things. Another possibility a chemist suggested to me is that the soil on Druids possesses hallucinatory properties but then why are only men susceptible to it? You have to realise Alex this is a backwater. Not much has changed here for a thousand years. People have been brought up with this legend from childhood and especially Shenley with that statue at the Hall and the figure of her in the family church. It made a great impression on him as a child that's what I think. That's my theory anyway. Why not in any case ask him yourself? It would be a good way of getting to know him. He needs someone like you. He has girl friends who come and go all thin as bamboo and very, very attractive but he needs a male friend to share things with.'

Sophia turned to Alex as he stared at the road ahead but he could feel her violet eyes pleading with him and her feminine dependence touching his very soul.

'I'll ask him. I've come across things of this kind in primitive cultures and to find it here in England intrigues me.'

'Sometimes I worry about him. I think perhaps you'll be a good influence. He's become something of a recluse these days working at the Estate Office long hours then hiding himself away.'

Parking below Henley steps Alex got out first and opened the car door for her.

'I'd love to ask you in Alex but it's late. I hope you understand. I have early lectures tomorrow. I'll have to use Papa's car. I had a lovely evening.' She leaned forward and kissed his cheek. Perhaps you'll ring me?'

She held out her hand but instead of taking it he pulled her close, tightly to him by the lapels of her coat and kissed her. Parting from his embrace her face had flushed her purple eyes staring at him like a child. Leaving him she walked up the stone steps then changing her mind came back kissed his cheek and said, 'Ring me on friday night.'

Then she was gone leaving him staring at the dark expanse of Henley Hall in its wintry isolation as though she had never existed.

The fields of Henley lay under a blanket of white, silent as the falling snow, the wind moaning a dirge that resonated to his aching loneliness.

Ralph Morville had followed them from Walmley and had been watching them from a narrow lane on a rise above Henley. Lowering his binoculars he wondered if this would lead him closer to his goal.

'It's in that damn house somewhere,' he whispered to himself.

CHAPTER EIGHT

'Ah! It's you. Come in Mr Roedale,' Kevin the butler greeted, 'Miss Sophie said you'd be comin'. I'll take ye to the library. I believe that's where master Shenley is.'

Shenley stood up from behind his desk and books.

'Hello Alex. I've been looking forward to seeing you again.' Shenley held out his hand. 'Come over here.'

Shenley pulled back a chair for Alex, 'Take a look at this.'

The library was brightly lit by wall lights and a desk a lamp fitted with magnifying glass that shone rays onto a yellowing vellum manuscript.

'I thought you would like to see this. My sister said you're interested in Druids Hill. I'm not surprised Barrington Hall is historically connected with its stories I suppose you've heard about that.'

'I'm not sure.' Alex replied wondering what on earth Shenley was about to reveal. The manuscript they were looking at seemed indecipherable and in places too faint to read where it seemed to have been rolled and folded so many times in its long history. Some words he noticed had quite disappeared.

'Tell me what it's about.'

Shenley laughed at Alex's perplexity. 'Yes it looks impossible but with darling Sophie's help we've managed to translate most of it. We used oblique lighting on the lettering and managed to decipher it.'

Shenley straightened up and looked at Alex. 'It is such a great find. I found it while browsing some of our antiquarian books and saw it folded inside one of them.'

Shenley leaned over the illuminated parchment again tracing a finger above each word as he read;

'My master of late had become most strange in his behaviour. At times he refused the food we brought him and when I tried to raise him in the mornings he lay silent as death itself. Often

I asked the maid to have a doctor attend him. At night he rarely slept and I would hear him go outdoors into the fields and return at dawn. One evening I secretly followed him. He took paths that led to Druids Hill. Heaven forgive me I wish I had never been so foolish. In the dark grove of trees above the old fort, the Master stopped in front of a tree and gazed into the branches. I heard him calling in a foreign sounding tongue. Then what I saw made me want to flee in terror but I was unable to move as though some unseen power held me in its grasp. A green light filled the grove as bright as the sun so that I was near blinded and then out of it a woman walked from its glow. I had never seen a woman so beautiful. The woman approached my master and began to speak with him, though I don't recall seeing her lips move, and I heard an echo as sweet as valley springs or distant church bells. The phantasm took his hand then led him beyond the green light and out of my sight. Then it all died from the woods just as quickly as it arose. I never saw either of them again. In fear and trembling I ran away and stopping at the church I woke the vicar and told him what I'd seen. He was deeply troubled at the news of my master and the apparition and said he had expected it. He led me to the church and prayed over me at the altar of Christ.

Signed:
   William Harwood.
   Witness: Robert Thomson.
   March 25 1628.'

Shenley looked up elated his handsome face animated in the reflected gleam of the lamp.

'Until I found this everyone believed the Barrington brothers fought a duel and one of them had been buried secretly by the other but this manuscript is evidence from the Barrington butler. It's quite clear now to me this statement was withheld from the County Court Sessions. It must have appeared in those Puritanical times as the work of the devil and would have incurred the crime of witchcraft. It was most likely discarded as fanciful and worthless as well as dangerous in their deliberations over Barrington's disappearance. They would hardly have wanted to convict the other Barrington brother.

'Either that or the butler was in on the murder.' Alex suggested.

'Yes maybe but I don't think so you see there is something unusual about this date. The twenty fifth of March was the beginning of the New Year until about seventeen fifty.'

'What do you mean?'

'Well, it was the pagan traditional day when the Earth Mother appeared to renew Spring.'

'I suppose as a piece of history it is quite interesting but why is it so important?'

Shenley's passionate monologue ebbed away. He sat down drained of energy.

'I'm sorry I forgot you know hardly anything about it and here I am ranting away. I'm sure Sophie thinks I'm deranged. I've been trying a long time to unravel the centuries old legends of a Green Woman but besides that there's something else about it I am far more interested in. Some of the stories tell of caves beneath Druids Hill and a rare artefact, hidden by crusading knights, that bestows a mystical power to all who see it. Alex I want to find it.'

'Perhaps villagers just connected mystical beliefs with a Goddess of the seasons. We know in Shakespeare's time people believed in elves, fairies, ghosts and witches so it shouldn't come as any surprise really. We don't believe those things now. I think you should consider it a country folk tale.'

'A few years ago, I would have agreed with you, whole heartedly, but something happened to me to change all that. Tell me have you ever been on Druids Hill?'

'I feel a bit ashamed to say so but after months here I still haven't ventured there even though it's right on my doorstep. Most of the time I've spent browsing libraries, writing, seeing my publisher, arranging photos in some kind of order for another book and I've had little time for walking.'

'Come with me on Sunday why don't you? If that's convenient. If you wish we can ride up there and leave the horses to graze. It's all Henley land including the Hill and I'd like to show you the Stone Age fort and yew grove.'

'Without apparitions I hope.' Alex laughed. 'Well, if the weather's clement, then gladly. It's about time I saw more of the place.'

A noise in the passage cut short their conversation. The library door opened.

'Alex! I'm sorry, I wasn't quite ready.' Sophie entered her face flushed and cheerful. Noticing the aged manuscript she gave Shenley a disapproving glance then softening kissed her brother's cheek.

'This parchment needs better care'. She pouted an admonishment, switching off the spotlight,'No bright lights'.

'No of course.' Shenley put his arm around her waist. 'But sooner or later Alex will hear of these things.'

'Yes of course darling Shenley and I want you to tell him, you know that. We met your friend Ralph the other night at Walmley.'

'Some friend,' Shenley scowled, 'I suppose he was trying to get beneath your dress?'

'Not him please'

'Wonder what his new wife thinks about his phone calls to you, day and night.'

Sophie glanced guiltily at Alex trying to measure his thoughts.

'Oh! You didn't know Alex?' Shenley asked goadingly. 'He rings her constantly, even follows her in his Porsche. We've had a bad time with him. We told her to go to the police but she refused as always. You will know by now I'm sure she knows better than anyone else in everything, everything under the sun.'

'I'll handle it. In my own way,' Sophie responded acerbically annoyed by her brother's temerity.

Taking Alex's arm, she led him to the door anxious to leave.

'Can't blame him, you're the most beautiful woman I've seen, or any one has ever seen.' Shenley repented. 'What do you think Alex?' He asked playfully.

She was the kind of woman it was impossible to ignore the way she held her head when speaking and grace in every movement. Alex agreed but said nothing.

'You're a born troublemaker, Shen,' Sophia teased from the door.

'Good night Alex,' Shenley called as they left the room.

Sophie kissed Alex' cheek and whispered, 'Don't let these problems with Ralph trouble you.'

'I don't.'

CHAPTER NINE

Sunday morning, the bells of Henley church were ringing across the fields and country lanes when Alex and Sophia entered and took seats near the rear. Light shadows spasmodically flitted across the mediaeval windows.

A smell of flowers from the altar, centuries old wood, mould and decay of eight hundred year walls filled the interior. Sitting beside Sophia he felt happier more than he could remember when.

Throughout the service his attention was caught by a shimmering light from a stained glass window that shone a brilliant green hue, flashing and fading, with passing clouds and animating the seductive image of the Green Woman. Alex realised the glazier had skilfully, perhaps knowingly, designed

The Green Goddess

the window to always envelope the carving with this brilliance of green flame. He had no doubt that as the seasons progressed a viridescent light from the other windows would replace this one to illuminate the lovely figure. There was a mystery in this place, all his instincts told him, that strange pillar, the green sculpture, the way the church had been built as though to give her prominence.

In the shaft of light the Green Woman beckoned as though wanting to reveal some great secret only she was capable of telling.

After the service they stayed for morning coffee in the vestibule.

Owen Thomas, the vicar, came over. Clutching bony hands together he urged 'Do come again'.

Tall, angular, sombre beyond all description Alex thought him the epitome of the Grim Reaper. A tortured stare in his eye said he had met the devil somewhere. When he spoke it was in a nervous, high pitched tone. Owen definitely belonged here among the tombstones of this Allan family mausoleum Alex thought.

'I am told you've taken over Barrington', Owen burst out concern apparent in his raised eyebrows and inquisitive frown and direct troubled stare.

'Yes. A lovely place, I'm very happy there'.

Noticing the slight rebuff Owen re-joined enigmatically and awkwardly, 'Well, if you ever need me,

I've had some experiences of these things,' then he rushed off to fraternise with someone else.

'Are you alright?' Sophie asked, gliding next to Alex, a glint of humour creasing her beautiful eyes.

'Just met the angel of death.'

Sophia laughed. 'He's a really wonderful man. When mother died he was the strongest support to our family. 'Come!' She guided Alex to the Church porch. 'Meet Tamara, Owen's wife. She's his antithesis.'

Tamara Thomas was indeed the opposite of her husband. She smiled and shook everyone's hand as they left asking how they were and their families. Twenty years or more younger than her husband, slim and tall, she exuded confident beauty in a fawn trouser suit complimenting the russet brown hair tied back off her face and tumbling down her back.

'Pleased to see you Sophie', she greeted them, 'And you, eh, Mr Rodale I think? Glad to have you join us.'

Tamara smiled warmly, flirtingly, lowering her eyes like a coquette, when she spoke to him with a feigned excitement of arousal. Touching his arm she invited, 'Come to our party next Saturday night at the Vicarage'.

In the cool February morning Sophie grasped his hand.

The Green Goddess

On the church lawns, virginal white snowdrops drooped their heads like spotless saints, daffodils and crocuses had already risen in the shelter of the trees, a crow swooped a warning alarm from a solitary beech.

'Bye Lady Sophie,' called a thin red haired mid-thirties from the church steps.

'Bye Miriam' Sophie waved. 'Miriam lives close to you. You'll hear more of her I think. She gets that lovely pre- Raphaelite hair from an Irish grandfather. She's one of our more memorable personalities. If you need a house cleaner, she's the one to get.'

Over Sophia's shoulder Alex caught a glimpse, of the dark and haunting figure, of Owen Thomas watching them from the Church lych-gate.

Walking together to Henley Hall Sophie said inquisitively, 'You're pensive Alex.'

'The vicar I think.' He replied, but in his heart he was reflecting on the effigy of the Green Woman.

'For an intelligent, strong man you're surprisingly sensitive,' Sophia tried to drag more out of him, without response.

At Henley, opening his car door to leave, he took Sophia's hand impulsively, pressed it behind her, drew her close and kissed her.

When she broke away her violet eyes clung to him and pressing herself more closely, arousing him, she returned the embrace.

'I'm going over Druids with Shenley. Shall I see you afterwards?'

'So, he's taking you up there. I would *love* to visit you at Barrington, late evening, if you wish. I do hope you and Shen get along.'

'Why shouldn't we?'

'He's very strange these days. He wasn't always like it. If you'd known him eighteen months ago he was the opposite, a real party goer and sociable, I mean *very* sociable, nightclubs, the phone screaming with his girlfriends. I lost count of them all and so many I couldn't remember their names and I was always afraid I'd call them by someone else's name. They came as unexpected as an avalanche.'

'And now?' Alex asked.

'Now, he hardly ever goes out except to walk or ride over Druids. If not that, he's absorbed in his work on the estate. In some ways I suppose he's a better person, from a woman's point of view that is, contemplative, reads a great deal.'

'Broken heart? '

'Not him, but they were I think.' Sophia thought affectionately of her brother's quiet strength.

'So what is the problem?' Alex asked thinking Sophie's appraisal inconsistent.

'I suppose when I think of it he has always been something of a saint. He went through all those teenage things, the cerebral bored occupation of the idle and affluent. Then one day he rejected all of it. All he desired, he told me was to be perfect. Come twenty five all he'd wanted to do was party, experience hedonism to the full dissipating tide.' Sophie laughed at the cherished memories. 'If you knew him you would be as fond of him as I am. He's never dull. Shen is a real man. Like a Greek hero, at heart. He's fearless, always on the side of right, the underprivileged and neglected. He's been like that as far back as I can remember.'

'I don't understand why you fret then about my getting along with him'.

'He's very melancholic, these days, disillusioned with everything. He's stopped cavorting and spends too much time alone absorbed with that Green Goddess at the Hall. Daddy ought to get rid of it. I remind myself he's brilliantly intelligent, that it's just a phase, but I'm not so sure. I don't know what is happening to him. If he was one of my students I would say he needed medical help.'

Sophia drifted into reflective silence distress clouding her lovely face.

'It maybe he's going through a spiritual or personality crisis, or just trying to find himself. See if you can help Alex.'

Ralph Morville was waiting that morning for Miriam Round to return from Church.

'Miriam,' Morville shouted from his Ferrari.'

Miriam went over asking herself what he wanted this time.

'Is it true you'll be cleaning for that newcomer Roedale?'

'Miss Sophia mentioned it was an idea. Is there a problem? I can do yours and his without any difficulty if that's it.'

'No, I didn't mean that.' Morville said brusquely. 'I need to ask of you a favour.' He gave her an insincere smile.

'If I can help.' She had never liked his crafty, double face.

'I'm interested in Roedale's work. He's researching the village and its history. Is it possible you could let me know if you see anything on his desk relating to some lost relic?'

'I'm not sure what you mean. What kind of relic?'

'I'm not sure either, to be honest, anything about the middle ages, anything, an art object perhaps.' Ralph felt exasperated for not knowing. 'I tell you what, anything mediaeval you see him working on let me know, notes, photos, books that sort of thing.'

'Will he mind?'

'We won't tell him Miriam, will we? I'll pay you well.'

'Why do you need to know?' Miriam was suspicious of anything Ralph was involved in.

'I think it might have something to do with my family history,' Ralph lied.

'Well, I could do with the extra. If there's nothing to cause him or anyone trouble, I wouldn't want to be involved in anything like that, then yes of course. No harm done.'

Miriam watched him bowl off down the lane much too fast for the narrow road. She didn't like him, wouldn't trust him with anything, but she had to live. The money would come in useful. She'd find something to make it all worthwhile.

CHAPTER TEN

Alex drove to Henley stables, changed quickly into riding breeches, and pulled on boots and a waterproof. Shenley who had been waiting for him led two horses out of the stables by their bridles.

'This mare's seventeen and a half hands as you can see. I know quite well Barrington Hall hasn't a stable. I used to tell father it detracted from the place somewhat. If you haven't bought a horse yet father and I would like you to have this mare as a welcoming gift from us.'

Alex looked at the mare as Shenley spoke. She was a magnificent creature.

'You can leave her in our stables if you wish of course and the girls will groom her with the rest. We named her Gazalla because as soon as she was born she found her legs and began springing around like a deer. With such huge eyes the name seemed to suit her well. Gazalla is Arabic for gazelle so it stuck. Father said she would be the finest hunter in the stable and so she's turned out and an added bonus will be if you need an excuse to see Sophia you have one.' Shenley smiled brightly, 'We have our own farrier by the way and that's worth a shilling or two.'

Gracefully powerful the mare exhibited with quiet disposition nudging Shenley affectionately.

Alex liked her at first glance. She'd make a good endurance horse as well as hunter, he judged.

'Let me buy her, I would feel much happier doing that.'

'No father wouldn't agree. He's a fan of yours and would be deeply offended.'

'In that case then, gladly,' Alex said shaking Shenley's hand. 'Say thank you for me.'

Shenley had fitted the mare with a working, hunter saddle, a good all- rounder for the hilly terrain of Druids.

Tightening the girth straps they mounted, Shenley leading, over the well ridden bridle paths and open fields that crossed the extent of Henley lands.

The noon air was cool; several hares broke cover and at least a dozen pheasants. From a coppice, wild with thistle, a flock of goldfinches took to the air. Dark threatening clouds and a playful easterly wind brushed the trees. Already green buds were whispering of spring.

Henley Estate, much larger than Alex had realised, encompassed tied houses and farms, whole hamlets and a thriving mediaeval fishery After Shenley had given him a quick survey of it late afternoon was beginning to dim the skies as they began the ascent of Druids Hill.

'You are fortunate to inherit so much, hardly you couldn't expect more,' Alex said not without envy.

'It takes a lot of maintenance; it's a business like any other. Many county families have gone forever because they failed to see that. I don't consider myself fortunate Alex it really gives me little pleasure. It's hard work and it's easy to fall into enormous debt. You are right of course, I should be grateful. I am not oblivious of the less fortunate and if I succeed with the estate then the hundreds of people who depend on it will keep their livelihood and cottages. The wealth side of it doesn't give me pleasure at all apart from that. Once, I thought myself the luckiest man in all of England, the Hall, title, wealth, women, and there were a lot of those, and travel of course but suddenly out of the blue I saw the emptiness of life.'

The Green Goddess

'Lonely?' Alex suggested.

'No not lonely, just searching for something more.'

'Is there no consolation in women?' Alex said humorously.

'Yes, some, our imagination creates an image that is unobtainable. Even the sex act itself often leaves us despondent. There is always a great hunger that, no matter what we do, can never be assuaged. Our souls yearn for something but we never know what. Don't you think so Alex?'

Approaching Druids along a sandstone bridle path the horses swished their flanks as a florid jowled farm labourer came towards them carrying a fishing rod and basket slung across his shoulders.

'Afternoon Lawson, nice day, catch anything?' Shenley greeted, holding his horse steady.

'Some but not enough for all of a mornin'. Off to Druids I see, be careful there Master Shenley. I hear she's been active again an' last week somebody stuck a rams head in the yews.' Lawson shook his head in disbelief.

'I'll have it removed.'

'We don't want them new-agers up there especially if she's appearin' in the woods, somebody'll get hurt. It's a bad omen and my advice sir is you'd be better not goin'.' Lawson gave Shenley a vexed, reproving glance.

They waved goodbye and moved on.

'What does he mean new-agers up there?' Alex asked smiling at the thought.

'Often we have people who've read about Druids Hill in some magazine or other try to hold pagan rituals in the middle of the night. At the solstices they come up here in robes. Father tends to ignore them but we have to beware of fire. On the whole they're no trouble and sometimes they get more than they bargained for.' Shenley tilted his head back and laughed gustily.

'In what way?' Alex asked.

'There really is something in Druids Wood no matter what. It frightens the life out of some people. Local papers carry stories from time to time and you know I'm sure very few villagers are seen up here. Wisdom comes with experience don't you think?'

In the fields below sheep were grazing near a large tumulus rising from the steeply sloping landscape. In the distance Alex could see Barrington and Henley Hall to the east. A light wind rippled the grass on the fields below.

Noticing his direction of gaze Shenley said, 'Father won't allow archaeological digs anywhere on our estate. He's right of course. Practically the whole of Henley has burial remains in it, Celtic and Saxon. That mound you are looking at is no doubt a burial of some sort, iron age perhaps, some say Celtic. I found a manuscript in our library saying our statue of the Green Woman, the one Sophie showed you at the hall, was found buried inside that tumulus but the stone it's made from apparently doesn't come from this region so that's unlikely. The author conjectured it had been hidden by Druids when the Roman legions attacked. There were other remains found here and fortunately left undisturbed. I presume they are there still. An archaeologist found some three miles of burials scattered across the area. They were definitely stone age. Some of the hills around have been identified as pagan worship sites as well fortified places of refuge.'

'I'd say that's where all those stories come from.' Alex suggested.

The horses were sweating from the rigours of the climb. Steam rose off them like a mist around the two men.

Reaching a level of high ground Alex noticed it had been a first line of defence for the old fortification. A winter woodland of oak and yew, interspersed with other deciduous trees, birch, ash and beech, rose even more steeply ahead of them. Dismounting they left the horses grazing and proceeded to climb the rest of the steep escarpment on foot.

'As you see it's an extensive site, one of the largest in England,' Shenley pointed out.

At the top they paused for breath. The ground levelled into a plateau and along this they walked through a dense growth of trees until, without warning, the ground fell away sharply into an enormous man made ditch.

'A moat defence,' Shenley explained. 'The good news is we don't have to climb down the thing to get to the other side.' Shenley lead Alex across the brow of the hill and walking around the rampart they came to a sandstone bridge that led over the moat defence. From here the plateau continued, dense with trees, through a ten foot wide avenue of the most enormous, gnarled, grotesque yew trees.

There was no movement of air inside the grove, so sheltered was it from the outside world, only a dead calm set in motionless time.

'Miriam, that red haired neighbour whom you met at church, Sophie told me, was terrified when she came here. She said all the failures and weaknesses of her life came to overwhelm her. She wept for days after visiting this place. A team of horses wouldn't drag her up here again,' Shenley laughed. 'Father wouldn't let any of us come up here as children but of course we did.'

On the top of Druids Hill it was deathly quiet. The venerable avenue of yews ended abruptly in a small glade bulwarked by a circle of aged trees. In its centre was an astonishing sight. A yew of great girth had entwined an equally immense oak, clasping it tightly with tentacle branches.

It was one of the strangest and most extraordinary spectacles Alex had ever seen. Not in all his travels across the latitudes of the world had he come across anything like it.

'It looks as though the yew has suffocated the oak doesn't it. In fact however it has kept it alive.' Shenley pointed out. 'The oak at best would have died fourteen hundred years ago but that yew holds it up and somehow imbues it with life. Father asked an arborist to examine the age of the trees. The yew is estimated at three and a half thousand years old and the oak two thousand one hundred which under normal circumstances is quite impossible. Here's another mystery the oak is not native to this country but of a variety found in the Mediterranean. How it arrived here we have no idea.

'This was confirmed?'

'Indeed.'

'How incredible.' Was all Alex could mutter in surprise.

Shenley tilted his head back and looked up at the giant trees. 'This Alex is where the Green Goddess dwells.'

Alex shrugged, 'I can understand why people think so. That union of trees and their age could easily have given rise to the myth.'

Alex stared at the great yew still hanging with yellow blossom as Shenley, using a short fallen branch of oak, walked over to the yew and struck one of its limbs. A golden smoke of pollen rose from the yew like a cloud to envelope them in a golden shower. Then a most strange thing happened, the other branches of the yew began to move in resonation with the vibrating branch, like the strings of an ancient lyre.

The two men were encapsulated within a yellow translucent mist that obscured all but its golden illumination. When the air had cleared Shenley chuckled boyishly in delight. 'Let's go we've seen enough for one day.'

They retraced their steps through the grove. Evening light was fading from the sky and at the edge of the woods a breeze had begun to fidget the trees.

'There really is a Green Goddess, you know. I can tell you this because I've seen her,' Shenley said thoughtfully.

'I wouldn't tell anyone that if I were you.' Alex scowled.

The sadness of evening enveloped them drawing a chilled quiet over the meadows as they rode towards home.

Alex was relieved that the hill was behind them. All the time they had been in the grove an inexplicable sensation of being watched and the eerie silent exudation of the woodland made him ill at ease.

Lord Henry Allan stood gazing from the window of his Westminster suite. Below mingling among the traffic were the usual tourists though being Saturday the traffic was lighter. He thought of Shenley. His son was so like his mother, looks and personality. The memory of Eleanor and the tragic way she died made his heart miss a beat. Since that awful day he had desired no other woman nor wanted one. There had been many who had shown interest but always he had rebuffed their advances.

Instead his energies were expended on the goals of the order he belonged to. Political and financial clout and his influence with European aristocrats made him effective at this. He was a wedge that kept any door open the order wished to enter.

Through the centuries they had opposed dictators, kings and rulers, military regimes, removed oppressors, had helped to organise resistance during wars, relieved poverty in the world and all achieved by their secret subtle influence. They were hurt sometimes by those who resented their power but Eleanor had never harmed anyone. He thought of her with a groan and emotion that bordered on tears.

The order never recruited members, membership was inherited all of them traced their ancestry back to the original founders and even then membership was only offered if a candidate revealed consistently the qualities that were necessary for the continuance of the society. Rules and discipline were strict and very few were chosen. Without them the world would undoubtedly be a worse place to live in.

Shenley, without knowing it, had been a candidate for the order since a child. Marston would never have qualified and, because it was an all-male alliance, Sophia was excluded. Lord Allan thought of his daughter and smiled she would have made an excellent candidate. Soon the time would come to enlighten Shenley and make him ready for initiation that is if he wished to join them. You never knew with Shenley and it all rested on them finding their lost relic. Failing to do so? Then their thousand year old ceremony could never take place. Without its unique power, to prosper their way, all they tried to achieve would inevitably fail. That they truly believed.

CHAPTER ELEVEN

After the horses had been stabled Shenley asked Alex to stay.
'There are plenty of spare rooms here. No doubt Sophia would be happy if you did.'

'No. I have things to do.' Alex said not divulging that Sophia would spend the night at Barrington.

It was already dark when he drove from Henley but he noticed, parked on the exit road out of the estate, Ralph Morville sitting alone in a maroon Ferrari. He turned his head away, when Alex passed, but in the car headlights Alex recognised him. Why would Morville, be parked there he wondered and recalled Shenley saying Morville stalked Sophia. He dismissed the notion immediately and continued the short drive to Barrington.

Sophia reached Henley late. Looking at the clock in her car she knew Alex would be waiting for her to call him perhaps worrying whether she intended coming or not. Grinning she decided not to ring, she would she would keep him guessing. Turning her car into Henley drive she was forced to slam on her brakes. Morvilles Ferrari was partly blocking the estate entrance. Morville flinging open and slamming his car door ran to her and tried to tug open the passenger door of her car.

Sophia instinctively dropped the lock on all her doors and drew back in panic her seat belt held holding her like a vice. In the glow of the head lights she recognised Ralph. She beeped her horn loudly, repeatedly, as he tried forcibly to get in beside her. No one at Henley seemed to hear. Recovering from her initial shock Sophia released the door locks and angrily jumped from her car to confront Ralph.

'What do you think you are doing?'

'I just want to talk to you.'

'We don't have anything to talk about. If you don't leave I will ring the police and have you charged for harassment.'

Sophia stood her ground, facing him venomously. She could smell the alcohol on his breath. Quickly she turned to look at Henley and realised she could never outrun him that distance.

The Green Goddess

'You wouldn't want to do that Sophie everyone knows we've been friends since childhood.' Ralph moved closer placing his hands on her shoulders. 'And you know I have always been in love with you.'

'How can you say such a thing you have a wife or have you forgotten.'

'Marriage for money, Sophia.'

'You are despicable like all your family, immoral and without any decency. For centuries your family have been a curse to this valley and hated for it.'

'I hoped one day your family and mine would unite through us Sophia.'

'That's more like it, hoping you could get your hands on our estate, now you and your father have ruined your own.'

The thought of her in the arms of another man galled Ralph. He was behaving like an adolescent, knew it, but was unable to set himself free. Surely rejection was the cruellest pain of all. Since her school days he had loved her. At a Garden Party on the Henley Estate, they had played volleyball over a beech hedge, Sophia had run away, teasing him, laughing and screaming across the lawns. At twelve she was five years younger than he and precociously blossoming into a woman. Already her breasts were swelling and pushing hard against her cotton dress and already tall for her age her long legs attracted attention.

Roisterously he had chased her into a vacant marquee where they struggled over the ball and fell to the grass, exhausted, giggling and panting. At seventeen a newly found virility confused and aroused him. In a swift moment of recklessness he had kissed her.

At first she had been shocked, then excited, and finally smiled at him, got up and ran towards Henley Hall laughing. From that moment Ralph had been in love with her. Every year through her teens he had waited for her return from her Cheltenham college. Over the years they had socialised, as all their circle did, rode, and dined together, but she had always rebuffed his ardour.

'I want a career, freedom, not love, not marriage, not an affair.' She had always told him.

Disappointed, Ralph married and in the newness of it Sophia had fallen away for a time only to return more fervently to haunt his every lonely hour. He felt he could bear it no longer. He pulled Sophia to him holding her in his arms tightly, pushing her against the car, pressing his loins against her so that she couldn't escape.

She struggled to free herself then quite suddenly relaxed and as Ralph leaned forward to close his lips on hers she moved her head and, driving her teeth viciously into his neck, bit hard. She felt blood, warm and sticky on her lips and trickling down her chin. Ralph let go, grasping at his neck in pain. She stood back afraid trembling at what she had done.

'You vixen,' Ralph spat.

Fear giving the strength she needed she lifted her legs high in a sprint and raced towards the safety of Henley. Ralph recovering from his astonishment and filled with fury was not far behind and closing rapidly. Once drawing close he grabbed at her but she zagged out of his way throwing him loose as he paused to gain his breath in his drunken stupor. He was panting, in laughter, by the time she reached for the Henley doorbell. Clutching at her, his arms around her, he tugged at her dress attempting to lift it as he pulled her to him. He was determined now to take her whether she wanted it or not.

Sophia repeatedly rang at the door of the Hall and shouted for help as he put his hand between her thighs.

Lights came on in the great house and Ralph let go.

Opening the door hastily, taking the scene at a glance, Kevin thrust Ralph forcefully down the hard, unrelenting, stone steps of Henley. At that moment the lights of Shenley's car arced across the circular drive as he swerved to clear the gravel path and drive onto the lawns of Henley to avoid Ralph and Sophia's vehicles parked across the entrance gate. In the car headlights he could see the door of Henley open and the silhouette figure of Kevin and two other people shouting into the night. Putting his foot down at such speed he skidded on the gravel he raced towards the Hall.

Shenley got out in time to see Ralph picking himself up off the drive where he had fallen.

'Glad to see you master Shenley,' Kevin hollered, 'And nice timin,' if I may say so.'

'What's going on here?' Shenley spoke sternly to all of them.

'Morville here tried to assault ye sister.' Kevin shouted from the top of the steps.

Angrily Shenley struck Ralph with such wild ferocity Ralph dropped heavily backwards once more to the hard, gravelled driveway.

Shouting to Sophia and Kevin, Shenley ordered them both inside before turning his attention to Ralph who was slowly rising to his feet.

'If you ever come near my sister again or anywhere on this estate I will have you shot. Do you understand, in that thick useless head of yours? This is private property, now leave immediately.'

Shenley watched as Ralph, his pride wounded, slunk away down the drive.

Turning, at a safe distance away, Ralph called out, 'You'll regret every minute of this and all your family.'

Shenley stood in silence until he heard Morville's Ferrari purr into life. It wouldn't be the end of it. They both knew that.

At Barrington Alex was arranging his articles and lecture notes into catalogue order. His study was his haven of escape, a desk with green leather top, two spotlights at each side, two enormous tropical plants to add colour and life to the room and the tall windows that viewed out over a panorama of valley and fields. In the evening, when too tired to work or he had lost continuity, he would open the velvet curtains, as he did now, turn off the lights, and look out across meadows and woods and the night sky beyond.

Tonight a swollen, yellow, full moon shone directly into the study and onto his desk. Filling a glass with brandy he stood by the window watching the clouds, moon and freedom of the fields. He heard the alarm call of a pheasant from a nearby meadow and the sharp cry of a lonely woodcock where the meadows embraced the trees..

It was after ten. Sophie was either late or unable to come, he conjectured, perhaps she hadn't really intended coming after all. To ring would be a sign of weakness. Turning back to his work he saw lights approaching on the lane that ran past his home. The vehicle slowed at the entrance to Barrington and turned in through the gates towards the house.

Opening the door for her Sophie pushed passed Alex unceremoniously without a smile or word of greeting. She slumped disconsolately, wearily, in an easy chair, anger and anguish etching her beautiful face.

'What happened' Alex asked.

Without acknowledging him or answering Sophia stared ahead nervously fidgeting her fingers.

'Shall I get you a drink of some kind?' He put his arm around her shoulders.

'Yes.'

Returning she was crying silently. Handing her the glass, he waited for her to recover.

'What happened? Is it something I can help with?'

'When I left Henley Ralph drove his car across the entrance so I couldn't get passed. I opened my window and shouted at him to move. He jumped out of his car and tried to get into mine. I managed to reverse up the drive and kept beeping for help. No one came. I got out and he molested me so I ran up the steps to the door. Ralph chased me. He caught me at the door but I managed to ring the bell. Kevin came out, bless him, saw what was happening and thrust Ralph down the steps. Kevin might be middle aged but he's strong as a bull. He loves me dearly. Ralph came back towards us but just then Shen came up the drive. He shouted at Ralph and asked what was going on and why was he there. Ralph just stood laughing, drunk I think, looking at us, sneering in a supercilious way. Shenley saw red and hit him so hard I think he must have broken his jaw. I heard an awful crack.'

'Then what happened?'

'Ralph left and when everything had calmed down I came here.'

'Police?' Alex enquired.

'No. Shen would have been just as guilty as Ralph.'

Alex could feel a heat of anger rising in his chest, restricting his breathing and rousing male aggression. All his instincts told him to find Morville and punish him physically. He fought it back but his hand trembled.

Sophie wiped her eyes. 'Ralph's uncle is a judge and his cousin a magistrate. We've been through all this before. We never get anywhere. I thought that now he was married it would all stop. Ralph gives the local constables backhanders to patrol his farms and house at night, there's always a patrol car running up and down the lanes near his home even though nothing ever happens there unless he did it. If villagers walk anywhere near his residence they're stopped and questioned. Father spoke to the Commissioner about it nothing was done of course you know what British police are like.

'Yes, I do know, in every country blue mafia.'

Their first romantic night together had been doused into a wet ember by Morville. There was little Alex could do for the present but that would change. Giving her another martini he changed the subject. After a short while she placed her head on his chest pressing close to him. Her perfume reminded him of when he had first seen her. Kissing her forehead he said gently, 'Let me take you home now. I'll bring your car first thing in the morning.'

Curling his arm around Sophie's slender body his fingers could feel the fragile ripple of muscles tightening along her spine. She was warm, beneath her open coat, as she turned to face him and wrap her slender arms around his neck her nipples pressing hard against him.

'I want to stay.' Sophia insisted clinging closely. 'The thought of being there alone terrifies me.'

'But you'd be better at home after what happened to you.'

'I don't want to be alone.'

She moved away from him determinedly, energetically, a new found sparkle in her wide eyes. Taking off her coat and throwing it over a chair she poured drinks for them both and sitting beside him on the long sofa she snuggled into his shoulder.

'We should never let bad things destroy, or get the better, of us. Daddy taught me that after mother died. Never let evil inside the hearts of other people take away, not for one second, your personal goals and happiness. I'm not letting Ralph ruin our evening together. First promise me you won't cause trouble with Ralph.' She gazed into his eyes testing his honesty.

'Morville should be taught a lesson.' Alex said through clenched teeth.

'But not by you. Your reputation would be ruined here and I feel afraid for Shenley really. Ralph is dangerous, there's something evil about him, not just male testosterone.'

Sophie rose from the sofa. 'Can I use your phone?'

Alex could just make out Kevin's Irish rippling voice over the receiver.

Sophia re-joined him.

'They all know I am safe here until morning.'

Sophie fell asleep her head cushioned on his knees. Lifting her in his arms he carried her to a bedroom at the rear of Barrington where she would sleep undisturbed. Laying her on the covers he kissed her and sleepily she helped him remove her dress before sliding into oblivious peace.

Alex slept only fitfully. Dreams floated like reflections of another reality past his half consciousness. In one of these a beautiful green woman was locked in a prison like cell. He gazed in wonder at her overpowering beauty. As he watched her, through the steel bars of her cage he tried to photograph for all time, this mythical, incomparable creature, the sight of whom would steal the hearts of all who saw her. In anger at his audacity the green woman lifted a short handled axe and swinging it sharply through the bars struck his head. In the dream he fell lifeless to the ground, then men dressed in white robes came and kneeling beside his corpse one of them touched his head and life returned.

When morning filtered into his room he was woken by Sophia calling his name. She was naked beside the bed. Lifting the sheets she snuggled herself in beside him.

CHAPTER TWELVE

Dropping Sophia off at Henley Hall Alex was unable to shake his thoughts free of Ralph Morville. He tucked a sheepskin numnah, under the saddle of Gazalla and rode determinedly over the Allan estate. He rode until he reached a steep limestone ridge. Below in the valley he could see the Morville Estate, Ralph's impressive home. On the wind he could hear an angry, male voice, across the expanse of fields, shouting, without dignity or control, and a woman crying.

Fearing it was Sophia, the memory of the previous evening still fresh in his mind, he immediately realised it couldn't be. Alex pointed the mare in the direction of Morville and galloped down from the ridge, over a stone cluttered, purling brook, through open gorse to finally cross the sloping fenced woodland that bordered the Morville estates.

Before the mare reached the manor he heard once more the same growling, male voice and recognised it at once. He was close enough to see Ralph's car driven away, raising dust in a smoky cloud. It was too distant to prevent it's roaring exit even if he could have. Descending from the woodland he held the mare back until reaching a narrow path where he reined in. Ahead of him were the stone pillars of Morville, with a family crest bridging an arched gate.

Surrounded by open fields from which all protecting hedgerows had been removed, Morville Hall in part dated to the twelfth century. Three hundred yards away across the open fields, enigmatically, stood a Norman Church devoid of village. It rose from the farming landscape like a folly, without purpose except that of aggrandisement. It spoke unmistakeably of Morville's ancestors. Once that graceful, twelfth century church, remote in its ploughed fields, had been the spiritual home and centre of a thriving village community. The Lords of Morville considering the village and its inhabitants despoiled their view across the landscape towards green distant hills obliterated the village. They had their view and the church remained a mausoleum to generations of Lords of Morville.

The Green Goddess

Alex rode into a former coach and stable yard. The grey stone edifice of the hall beyond the stables spoke of hard times. Windows, doors and walls without exception breathed decay on the morning air as though the building itself cried out for redemption. Whatever the disturbance there that morning it was now quiet. Riding around looking for the woman he had heard crying, so wildly in her misery, he found no evidence of her anywhere.

Cantering back to the green fields of Henley Gazalla seemed to rejoice at heading home and needed no encouragement. Stabling the mare he climbed into his car to return to Barrington but was prevented by Shenley driving up beside him.

'Afternoon, Alex. Been riding?'

'Among other things' Alex replied abruptly, his anger still with him and wishing to get away.

'You're unhappy about something? Can I help?'

'No, it's a private thing.'

'Come into the house and let's have a brandy, Shenley persuaded.

Not wishing to offend Alex followed his friend into the Hall.

'I've some things I'm working on I'd like you to see. It will take your mind off whatever your thinking about I guarantee,' Shenley encouraged.

Lights were already on in the study illuminating paper and journals on an enormous desk. A phone rang somewhere in an adjoining room interrupting their conversation.

'Excuse me Alex.' Shenley apologised, 'Make yourself comfortable while I answer this.'

Going to the desk Alex noticed Shenley had left a scatter of working papers and a journal open. Casually thumbing through these, to see what his friend had been working on, an entry in the journal that had been underlined in red caught his attention.

It was such a lovely afternoon I decided to leave my office early to stroll across Druids. This month, being exceptionally warm a cloud of blossom adorns the woods and meadows. For the first time in years I heard a skylark trilling above Long Meadow, our welcome pheasant and elusive partridge were friskily active, hawks were out over the hedgerows, with their low secretive flight, searching out pigeons and a kestrel hovered, beautifully.

I noticed part of the fence broken at Tom Dovey's field. I will need to have it repaired now lambing's near.

The colours of nature, the sunshine, the smell of blossom and meadow, on the windless afternoon air, filled the hills and valleys with an indescribable peace. In the very depth of my soul a great tearing loneliness filled me, an incomprehensible sadness at this vista of Arcadian splendour.

Besides this I wanted to visit the sacred yew on Druids to hopefully uncover some of its mysteries. I'm sure there is a living presence in that tree and the ancient oak it embraces. There's something more than mere fable to these persistent stories about a spirit living on the Hill.

That was the content, more or less, of my thoughts as I climbed the track to Druids. The grove seemed to draw silence into itself with the force of a vortex, as it always does at this time of year.

No birds fly over Druids. I've observed that from a distance and indeed birds only skirt its borders, never entering or flying above it. The Hill is like some mountain monastery, a natural temple, as I am sure it used to be. Here also is the presence of a spiritual being. People have always felt it and a few individuals, if we can believe the stories, have met it.

Walking down the avenue leading to the centre of the grove, the yews seemed to close preventing my exit. I suppose I was imagining that the long avenue had somehow disappeared from view in the dappled afternoon light. The trees around the grove shone like a borealis in a brilliant lucid emerald that even the sky above mirrored back onto the path ahead of me.

When I reached the circled glade it was as silent as the heavens. The old yew in the centre stood like an ancient god of the forest, eternal, indestructible.

I'm not sure how long I sat there enjoying this peaceful place as I sat on a fallen trunk worn smooth by centuries of visitors. For minutes I just gazed at the tree, attempting to define its mysterious attraction, but getting nowhere with that I closed my eyes, shutting my mind from all distractions and just waited in meditative silence.

Through my eyelids I noticed the afternoon light changing. When I opened my eyes the whole temple arena was engulfed in yellow light, almost white in its blinding intensity, and emanating from the old yew. Had I fallen asleep? I asked myself. Was this a dream springing out of my imaginings or perhaps a hallucination?

Staring into the light, I trembled in astonishment because I saw I was not alone. A partly obscured figure stood immediately in front of the yew. Fear clutched me then. I rose from my seat ready to run from this awful sight but found I was unable to move, my legs and arms were bereft of all energy. I called out but though my lips moved no sound came to relieve the terror of that afternoon.

The phantasm walked towards me and to my utter surprise I saw it was a woman. Her graceful movements rippled like the rhythmic undulations of a sunlit sea. Her naked body was the colour of new born leaves vibrating translucent greenery.

I knew then it was the Green Woman of folk legend in all her incomparable perfection. I felt humbled and worthless in her presence. She was the epitome of all that was good and enduring in nature and the great, eternal universe, a vision of feminine grandeur only to be experienced and never fully known defying all description for she was beyond the power of words.

This amazing creature paused ten feet or more in front of me, her face filled with flirtatious humour, her green, wide, eyes staring deeply into mine. All fear left me as suddenly as it had arisen. I felt I had known her always.

Recovering from my surprise I gazed at her in rapture and would have fallen at her feet in worship had I been able to move. Tall, slender, more beautiful than idealised imagining this goddess in her nakedness overwhelmed my senses, filling me with a longing for life and love I had never dreamed of.

'You have been calling me.'

I heard her voice like a sound of distant water or breath of wind in the blossom of trees. I wasn't sure if I had heard the voice audibly or it had sounded in my heart.

'Who are you?' I asked,

'You have called to me and you are ready now.'

The creature smiled, her eyes gleaming like pale stars, as she tossed aside tumbling, autumn gold, hair that fell over her shoulders like shafts of light in a forest glade.

I can't describe the irresistible allure and enchantment of her. From that moment onwards I longed to be in her presence always. Nothing else in life mattered to me. How can I ever explain what happened to me, the effect she had on my heart, her beauty, the finely sculptured face, the graceful neck, fragile shoulders, perfectly formed breasts, the flawlessly curved waist and loins, long legs, ankles and delicate feet. Inwardly I trembled at the sight of her yet I felt no burning lust for her, only bewitchment.

She was watching me, her eyes flashing as the sun on a lake of dappling blue.

'I have known you always, since your life began and I have waited for you.' She spoke sonorously.

'Tell me who you are, please?'

My words came as though spoken by someone else.

'You will know in time and that knowledge will give you immortality.'

Her image faded from the sacred grove and with her the golden light that had filled the circle of yews trees.

I think I lost consciousness.

When I woke I was lying on the brown earth chilled to my extremities. A cool breeze rustled the trees, feathery fingers of horizontal light shone through the trees from the setting sun at the edge of the sky.

I rose from the ground, looking about me for physical evidence of the things I'd seen, but all was as it used to be, there was nothing to prove I had ever met the enchanting creature. The avenue that had been so obscured from me before was clearly visible now and I made my way home.

Have I really seen the Green Woman or did I merely fall asleep in the tranquil swaddle of the mysterious hill?

Alex closed Shenley's journal guiltily. He had glanced into someone's private life but still it was

The Green Goddess

an intriguing entry. So this is what Shenley meant when he said he had seen the Green Goddess.

His thoughts were abruptly interrupted by the study door swinging open. Sophia entered, her face flushed. Dropping her briefcase on the parquet she tumbled her arms onto his broad shoulders, trusting, and pleased as a child in his embrace.

'Oh, how nice to see you here,' she greeted, pressing herself against him, kissing him. 'Will you stay tonight?'

Shenley entered the study before Alex could answer.

'Ah! The love birds. Unfortunately Alex the things I intended showing you haven't arrived yet. Apparently there's a slight problem with the tradesmen's deliveries. Can we meet again soon?'

Alex nodded casually.

'I'll leave you two alone then.'

With half closed eyes Sophia glanced at Alex, raised her brows happily, picked up her briefcase, switched off the study lights and took Alex's arm.

Sophia's apartments were in a self-contained wing of the Hall. In the warmth of her bed the smell of her hair and neck subdued him like incense.

They didn't hear Shenley arrive, nor Kevin's undignified shuffle later that afternoon, nor the animated conversation between Shenley and his father. Eventually when they entered the drawing room they were startled at being met by Lord Allan and Shenley at the door.

'Alex we were just talking of you,' Lord Allan greeted kissing Sophia's cheek.

'I wondered where you both had got to,' Shenley remarked, devilishly

Sophia blushed and sailed passed them into the room.

CHAPTER THIRTEEN

'May Day celebrations on the weekend. It's great fun, believe me'. Sophia persuaded. 'It takes place on fields below Druids and goes on into the wee hours.'

'Enjoyable?'

'Most certainly.'

'Then why not? Of course,' Alex agreed.

The day was exceptionally warm. Below Druids hill stalls circled a field. A marquee served alcohol and beer flowed copiously. Crowds came from surrounding villages to meet each other. Many, young and old, wore wreaths of oak leaves for the men and spring flowers for the women. All smartly swaggered, laughing, enjoying sunshine and spring. A brightly coloured young woman came and thrust an oak wreath on Alex's head and one woven in all the colours of the spring fields on Sophia's.

'Oak for men because it represents power, virility and success,' Sophia laughed.

'And yours.'

'It is woven of twenty seven different flowers symbolising beauty and fertility.'

'Amen to that.'

'It's a unique festival, nothing quite like it anywhere in England it goes back to God knows when.' Sophia explained, 'Its pagan of course a celebration of life, newness and resurrection of spring.'

At the top of a Stone Age barrow three men and two girls in medieval costume were playing and singing English folk songs. A noisy group of revellers, with pint glasses in their hands, accompanied them in boisterously discordant choral breaks.

Further below Druids a group of archers, in Lincoln Green, were competing in a Long Bow, tournament.

'Let's go to the booze tent, shall we?' Sophia squeezed Alex hand.

They bustled through, Sophia doing her best not to be recognised. Sliding her sunglasses over her eyes she draped a baseball cap low over her forehead.

Barrels of ale, mead and country wine glowed enticingly on trestles each side of the marquee and the moment they entered Sophia was recognised.

The Green Goddess

A barman dressed as a troubadour addressed her.

'Ah! The fair Lady Sophia what a pleasure to see you. What can I get you both?'

'All this stuff is locally brewed so I warn you Alex it's very, very potent. One glass of plum brandy and you're anybody's.'

Wrapping his arm around her all he could think of was laying her beside him in the long grass.

By late afternoon the crowds were stretched out exhausted on the fields. A May Queen was chosen.

'Are you competing Miss Sophie?' A young man, in Elizabethan garb, with lascivious glint in his eye, smiled.

'Let the others take a chance,' Sophie shot back cheekily.

'Every fair from fair sometimes declines, but not you my lady.' The rakish Elizabethan said graciously.

Sophia laughing at this impudence stood up from the grass and kissed his cheek, 'Well said, you charming wag, find thee a wench and win renown.'

Alex his hands behind his head, eyes closed, lay on the grass smelling its summer freshness, feeling the solidity of the earth beneath and the warmth of the sun on his face, quietly smiled to himself as he listened to this quirky conversation. All so different from the tormented places he had returned from only nine months before.

After an hour of hurrahing and laughter a May Queen was chosen and accompanied to a brightly coloured tent by a group of youthful followers to loud witticisms and cheers from the young men.

The Queen was robed only in flowers that left nothing of her to imagination. Silence fell over the watching youths as she walked blushingly between them. Gathering round her the young men lifted her to a Victorian farm buggy, painted and covered with blossoms and fruit, drawn by a white horse similarly garlanded with the brilliant bold colours of spring.

A rose hued sunset sweeping across the horizon gave the signal to begin. The cart, accompanied by the crowds was supported on each side by young men as it trembled and rumbled its way around Druids Hill to the sound of marching musicians, a harness bell and jovial procession.

'By tradition the women never follow the carriage,' Sophie pointed out.

'Hardly fair.'

'Their moment comes later.'

After slow circumambulation of the hill fortress the carriage was halted at the start of the steep incline that led into the heart of Druids Hill. The May Queen, flushed and pretty, waited in silence as she shook out the folds of her floral dress.

Sophia led Alex back to the beer marquee, laughing as exuberantly as anyone else.

The Green Goddess

The wine was strong and Alex's head floundered in the heat. From the marquee door he could see the May Queen surrounded by young women freely drinking, excitedly, shyly glancing in the direction the young men and listening to their voices across the open space of the meadow. At last the youths came running back towards the May Queen. In their midst the most handsome of them, a wreath of tree blossom adorning his dark unruly hair, ran perspiring, shirtless, a garland of flowers trailing out behind him, to climb onto the decorated cart where the May Queen welcomed him like a hero into her arms.

Young men and women screaming and laughing after much chasing and compromise chose themselves a partner and were led by the May Queen and her chosen hero up the steep path to Druids Hill. This was the moment everyone had been waiting for and the fields and stalls were deserted for the parade. All that was left were empty stalls and canvas blown quietly in the wind.

'This festival is so old we have no idea when it began. There's a story that when the Israelites were taken captive to Babylon some of them escaped and joined the merchant ships of Phoenicia who traded with Cornwall. These Jewish families moved up the Severn Valley until they reached this place. They then tunnelled catacombs below Druids Hill and built a temple beneath it where they worshipped in secret. With them they brought a middle eastern form of worship a female goddess whom they revered just as much as their God of Israel.'

'Do you believe it?'

'If there is truth in it, she was Astarte. The Welsh language does have Semitic origins and ancient Hebrew is an offshoot of it. The legend says this festival began at that time.'

'Did anyone ever discover these catacombs?'

'Not to my knowledge.'

'I did read once somewhere that the Welsh were a lost tribe of Israel.' Alex spoke without sincerity.

'Who knows? The language has some distant similarities.'

Revellers, swarming like bees into the shaded depths of Druids grove reached the sacred yew and oak and fell into silence to gaze in expectant awe.

At the edge of the amphitheatre on a fallen log, hewn centuries before into a rustic seat, the May Queen and her companion sat closely together holding hands as their silent entourage walked in front of them placing dolls and gifts of flowers at their feet before beginning their May dance, in which all held hands, three times around the May lovers and the ancient trees and along the yew avenue to leave the pair alone in the silent glade.

'What next?' Alex asked breathlessly.

The Green Goddess

'Sometimes the girl has been known to become pregnant,' Sophie laughed.

At the end of the yew avenue the procession spilled into the meadows below. Alex held Sophia back at the brow of the incline and waited until all had gone and they were alone. Laying Sophia down beside him on the green sward he kissed her fiercely in his throbbing need for her.

Sunset was turning the sky into a plum coloured hue. The air was clear and a range of hills, thirty or more miles distant, could easily be seen their every contour pencilled against the fading evening light. The painted light reddened Sophie's cheeks and turned her hair to flame. Slipping his arm beneath her waist and holding her tightly he kissed her.

'It is true four of the May Queens, in the last twenty years, did conceive nine months after their May Day crowning. Too much of a coincidence wouldn't you say.' Sophie said mischievously smiling at him. She raised herself to her elbows her breasts curving out and upwards beneath the fragile thrust of her shoulders.

They sat there laughing, happier than either had been before.

Alex reclined on the grass, pretending to speak seriously but she would have none of it and keened over him as he lifted the billowy folds of her dress and pulled her on top.

At their moment of union something happened that later he couldn't understand or forget. Gazing into the violet blue of Sophia's eyes at the height of his desire the world changed around him. Place and time ceased to exist. He was lost somewhere in another dimension where all things were one and he himself the universe.

Sophia was sitting across his loins her breath escaping in soft broken sounds but when he looked into her face he almost thrust her away in horror for it was not Sophia but the Green Woman staring back at him her emerald eyes enveloping his soul to its very depth taking all strength from him. She was the glory and beauty of all worlds, of the heavens, of all created and exotic things. He had no strength to break away from her. Looking down at him, smiling, she was the most beautiful creature that ever lived. No sounds escaped her throat but somewhere, somehow she was speaking to him inside the lonely, dark abyss of his being.

'Don't be afraid.' She whispered in the silence touching his lips before fading away.

He must have been dreaming. He woke with his head in Sophia's lap. She was laughing at him, tickling his ears with grass.

'You slept like death itself.'

Alex gazed around, disoriented, and at Sophia half expecting to see the Green Woman.

The Green Goddess

'It must have been the wine,' he apologised.

Night had fallen and a fat yellow moon shone between flying clouds. Rising to his feet, stiffly, his head throbbing as he waited as Sophie straightened her dress.

The path from Druids to Henley Hall lay directly below them and in the darkness his arm wrapped around Sophia's waist they almost stumbled over someone's legs protruding from the shadows of a gigantic, old Maple tree. The enormous black, overhang of the branches were hiding a couple in an act of copulation. A sudden break in the cloud cover revealed their faces in the moonlight.

Alex choked back his gasp of surprise, the woman on the meadow grass was none other than Tamara Thomas, her eyes closed pretending she hadn't noticed them or was determined not to know, or see, who passed by. The man with her, young, casually dressed was definitely not her husband the tall and fragile vicar Owen Thomas.

Gripping Alex's hand Sophia led him hurriedly, silently down the steep slope of the hill and when too distant from the lovers to be heard, smiled at him and broke into laughter.

'It happens in these villages on May Day.'
'Owen knows?'
'Unlikely. Like all good people he is too trusting.'
Alex didn't reply.

Aware of his reserve and reluctance Sophia squeezed his arm. 'Tamara was born in the village and her beliefs don't exactly follow doctrines of the church. I would say rather they are pre Christian. You know she really vehemently believes in our Green Goddess. Besides all our village women try to find a lover on May Day."

'You also?'

'Jealous? 'Sophia laughed, 'I never had the opportunity. During holidays I was sent to my grandmother's or overseas to distant relatives but oh how I used to wish I could have been here on May Day.' Sophie raised her hands over her head in adulation. 'There isn't anywhere like this place in the whole of England.'

'Why here?'

'Tradition and the presence of the Green Woman.'

'Not a family oriented goddess I'd say.'

A wild flutter of pigeons rattled the trees above them, warning them someone was approaching. Simultaneously they turned at the muffled sound of voices and saw three men behind them in the darkness. Sophie, recognising them, fell silent a fleeting uneasiness creasing the corners of her delicate mouth.

'Well, if it isn't the magnificent Lady Allan herself,' A drunken voice called.

'Ignore them,' Sophie warned.

The Green Goddess

The three men, approaching rapidly spoke in lowered tones followed by drunken, laughter and began running along the grassy track to join them.

In moments Ralph Morville with two of his cronies came panting up beside them. Stumblingly, aggressive, the men separated Sophia from Alex. To his left one bully was sneering at Alex the other to his right grinning foolishly as Ralph taking Sophia by the arm led her yards ahead of them.

Alex felt fear but not for himself. Glaring at the two men beside him he judged how much of a threat they were, they were worse for drink and he guessed too far gone to offer serious resistance if he needed to go to Sophia's help. It was still a nasty predicament to be in. He had seen too many moments of confrontation end in sudden injury or death not to be aware of the danger they were in. Ralph was trying to kiss Sophia, his arm around her waist, as he drunkenly leaned his face over to reach her lips. For the moment at least she was managing, with defiant tenacity, to push him away.

'You have something, I want Sophia.' Ralph grunted.

'Whatever that is you're not getting it.' Sophia flared back at him

'You misunderstand me. You may not realise it but you are my key to the most valuable object in the world.'

Sophia didn't understand his drunken raving all she wanted to do was get herself and Alex away from there.

Trying to kiss her once more, Ralph breathed, 'I will have you both one day the treasure your family are hiding and you.' He was becoming frustrated and angry as she forcefully resisted his every move.

Sophia turned to glance at Alex, more anxious for his safety than her own, and in her eyes Alex caught her look of desperation. Gesturing with a nod to assure her he could see in the pale light of the night sky the shock on her childlike face.

One of Morville's bullies sniggered at his gesture to Sophia. It was the last straw and it broke Alex's control spurring him into action. Raising his right leg he furiously drove his foot downwards, with all his weight behind it, against the side of the thug's knee. Immediately letting go of Alex's arm the man fell forward groaning, and cursing his pain, grasping at the knee joint that had broken and skewed inwards.

Using surprise for his next attack Alex faced his other opponent. The man was staring in disbelief, frozen in restrained violence. Reaching forward and grasping the man's dark curly hair, with a rapid thrust forwards and down Alex struck the man's face hard against his lifted knee. There was a sound on the night air like a dry stick being snapped as the man fell to the grass shielding a broken nose.

Swivelling round Alex turned his full attention to Morville who at the commotion had forgotten all about Sophia. Staring nervously, alarmed, at his companions groans as they lay on the ground he then faced Alex. There was a palpable aura of fear in the way Morville stood with neck extended forwards.

Swiftly moving to Sophia's side Alex thrust Morville violently away from her half hoping as he did so that Ralph would begin a retaliation. Alex felt an almost uncontrollable desire to reduce Morville's arrogant, supercilious visage to a bloody mess.

Through clenched teeth Alex growled. 'If you ever try to manhandle Sophia again you will wish you had never seen the light of day. Attempted rape is a serious offence. I'm sure you know that.'

'I had no intention of raping Sophie.'

'This is what you say now. I think you are lucky I prevented it. Do you think these drunken fools you associate with would help you in any law court? I don't think so nor could your relatives protect you from Lord Allan or me. Go near Sophia ever again and I will make sure you pay for it dearly.'

'Threatening me? You don't know who you are dealing with.'

Sophie reached for Alex's arm pulling him away and curbing him.

Ralph had wilted, and paled noticeably, even in the darkness of the night.

Alex and Sophia turned and walked away leaving Ralph arguing with his cronies.

Over the following days whenever she thought of the incident Sophia recalled Ralph's innuendo about the treasure her family had hidden and wondered what he meant when he said she was the key to the most valuable object in the world.

CHAPTER FOURTEEN

Landing on the lawns of the Italian Castello the helicopter had flown directly from Rome. Touching down the helicopter door was flung open by a man of middle years in a crumpled well-worn suit. Stepping onto the grass, instinctively lowering his head to avoid the down draft from the helicopter blades he moved quickly, briefcase in hand, towards the entrance of the mansion.

A short, older man with youthful jet black hair and open neck shirt was already striding across the lawns to meet him.

Shaking hands, the older man greeted his visitor with a broad, self- important smile. 'Angelo, so pleased to see you,' he said taking the arm of his guest and leading him towards his villa.

Angelo looked at the older man weighing his personality. He had heard much of this corrupt, dangerous and affectedly charming politician who had moved from the ranks of banking businessman with Mafia laundering operations to be the light of Italian politics. The doll like face of the politician revolted him. He was unable to read its intention through the controlled poker faced impassivity.

'Licio, I am pleased also to meet you at last. Of course there was no chance of that before my new appointment.'

'I suppose it would be in order to tell you Angelo but it was I who recommended you to the Holy Father himself.'

By now they had reached the portico of the great house.

'It's the first time I heard of it,' Angelo answered in surprise.

'Our fathers in the banking world knew each other so it seemed to me you would be the most appropriate choice to head the Instituto per le Opere de Religione.'

'Thank you to be made the head of the Vatican Bank is something I never imagined could happen to me.'

Licio laughed. 'God is a God of surprises, Angelo.'

Both men laughed knowing full well that God had nothing to do with it.

Licio had once remarked and meant that he himself was more powerful than the Pope. A remark the Vatican warned him was most unwise. Licio had merely shrugged at the rebuke and reminded them that as head of a universal financial brotherhood the Vatican relied more on him than he on them.

Over drinks and sumptuous dinner at which neither ate much Licio suggested the Vatican financier stroll with him around the gardens and estate in the cool of the late evening sunshine.

'You can only see it from above but I designed it myself in flowers a rampaging red dragon the symbol, of our brotherhood.' Licio remarked showing Angelo a verdant flower garden.

'Do you think that was wise?'

'Only the brothers would ever know its meaning.'

Licio screwed up his face assuringly, then asked, 'What did the Vatican think of my offer?'

'His Holiness has agreed the relic, you mentioned to us, would complete the Vatican collection and be its most holy and prized possession. It would increase the faith of the Church, bring in phenomenal revenue of course and draw countless more people to the faith. More than anything it would establish gospel truth. I was advised to inform you however that His Holiness will have nothing whatever to do with arrangements to procure the object, such matters must only be left to you, nor will His Holiness be involved, or connected in any way, in how the object is to be recovered.'

Licio smiled to himself, thought for a moment, and asked. 'Did the Holy Father's advisers agree to the sum asked for this unusual item?'

'Indeed they said no value could be placed upon so sacred an object.'

'Then you agree.'

'I spoke with the Papal Cardinals and we all agreed no price is too high for such an object.' Angelo nodded.

'Three billion dollars in a Swiss account.'

'Agreed and it was also agreed that for your valuable services you would be rewarded in other ways.'

'In what ways?' Licio asked with concentrated attention.

'In furthering your political aspirations. We have great influence in these matters as you are aware. The Church Council agreed we need such men as yourself in our political arena. One point however, I am sure you will understand, is stressed by all the cardinals, there must be no question of violence.' Angelo glanced disdainfully at the placid, inscrutable face of the politician.

'You need not worry over details just as long as the object is discovered.' Licio smiled charmingly.

The Green Goddess

'We cannot agree to violence.' Angelo insisted.

'The Holy Father knows I am the Grand Master.'

'Nothing is hidden from us not even your own secret organisation.'

'Popes have persecuted, and tried to suppress, us in the past.' Licio pointed out, 'And failed.'

'Those days have long gone. Now the new word is cooperation with all who serve the purpose of God.'

Licio laughed, 'And their own.'

'Your Mafia friends and Zurich Gnomes have made you very cynical.'

'Less gullible,' Licio corrected.

'One question, why did you choose our Church? Other religions have as much claim to its possession, Orthodox, Coptic, *and* large museums.

'Or any numerous international investors,' Licio grinned.

'Then?'

'Simply put? Whoever will pay the highest price.'

CHAPTER FIFTEEN

The months passed. Spring, in a delightful enrobing of colour, tumbled blossom on an unusually torrid summer landscape. Martins flitted over Barrington, swooping in tumbling flight across the sultry valleys; pheasant and partridge thrashed their wings colourfully across luxuriant meadows, noisy squirrels fought among the trees and hawthorn covered the hedgerows of Henley with white.

For weeks it was oppressively humid, enervating and sultrily warm. Afternoons waited indolently for storms that never came as rivers fell to their lowest levels in a decade to leave fish gasping for air in the breathless heat.

The Green Goddess

From the windows of Barrington Alex saw each night the moon grow into a watery yellow pumpkin during peaceful evenings devoid of wind. By the end of July the luxuriant trees of spring were already dropping yellow leaves beside the lanes.

Alex spent more of his time with Sophia but one morning when he discovered a small private airfield, fourteen miles from Barrington, he hired a light aircraft and flew over the borderland. Fortified towers, manor houses, castles, steepled churches, Roman roads, sunken forgotten drover lanes and lost villages, a Saxon dyke, secluded private lakes and deserted farms fell away beneath in intoxicating beauty. Who could blame anyone for believing in a Green Goddess in a landscape such as this?

In August Alex was persuaded by his publisher to spend two months travelling on a literary circuit that never seemed to end, lectures to Americans, signing books in New York, Milan, Munich and Petersburg.

He missed Sophia and the beloved quiet comfort of Barrington more than he cared to admit. Long legged Slavic women, Teutonic models and immaculately preened Yankees rubbed their delicate shoulders and knees against his at endless dinners. It meant nothing without Sophia. If your heart is in someone else's heart fleeting intimacy is no compensation.

When he returned to Barrington the evening was well advanced, a nightjar called across the fields and his resident owl swooped across the trees to welcome him home.

Sophia was waiting with dinner and wine, her smile like sunshine on a wintry day. She clung to him in a lingering embrace held long enough for him to know she was deeply unhappy. Over dinner Sophia smiled, charmingly as ever, but humour had all but gone from her eyes. Every glance spoke of a singular sadness she was trying to hide from him.

She just didn't want to spoil his homecoming.

Finally unable to put up with the pretence any longer he asked, 'Tell me what is wrong. It isn't any good hiding it Sophia, you are making me feel uncomfortable.'

Drooping, as though at any moment she would collapse into tears she sipped her wine and told him, 'Shen is in hospital'.

Silenced momentarily Alex asked, 'How?'

'He and Kevin were physically assaulted.' Sophia's eyes narrowed in anger. 'It brought it all back to me after so many years.'

'Brought what back?'

Sophia's hand was shaking.

'My mother was killed by burglars along with our housekeeper when I was a child. I was only four. I remember nothing of it except being left alone, in the marble room with the Green Woman statue I showed you, by my mother. That was the last I saw of her. She locked me in there for safety before they killed her.'

Unable to hold back her grief any longer Sophia placed her hands over her eyes and wept through her fingers.

Alex was lost for words at the revelation. Sitting beside her he comforted her placing his arm around her slender shoulders.

'To be truthful I think I have suppressed it all these years, that's why I never told you about it, or anyone else,' Sophia sighed. 'Now this.'

'Tell me what happened to Shenley and Kevin?'

'Someone broke into the Hall and Shen and Kevin got in their way. I am not sure that was the motive because it seemed to me like unwarranted, deliberate violence.'

'Do you think Ralph is behind this?' It was the first thought to enter Alex mind.

'Definitely, that was my conclusion also but we can't prove it. Kevin was knocked unconscious without seeing them and Shen has been in a coma since the night it happened. Poor Shen the hospital say his ribs are broken, there are bruises all over him and his skull is fractured, a lung punctured and internal bleeding. Whoever did it meant to kill him I'm sure, his legs and arms as well as his body are covered with bruises.' Sophia stood in her agitation. "They beat him mercilessly Alex. The hospital said he's lucky to be alive.'

Alex paced the floor, a dozen questions racing through his thoughts. Perhaps it was his fault for threatening Ralph and his cronies that night on Druids Hill but Shenley and Ralph he knew already had a long and lasting feud, he had made it worse. Maybe they'd hoped to find him and Sophia at the Hall and not Shenley.

'Why do you think it was Ralph?' He asked.

'For the same reason you do. Shen and Kevin were at Henley, Daddy was out and about ten thirty someone rang the doorbell. Kevin thought it was me and opened it wide but found there wasn't anyone there. When he stepped outside to look around he was struck brutally on the side of the head. That's what we think happened. He must have been knocked unconscious. Kevin saw three men running away and he thought one of them was Ralph. He asserts it was definitely him but that's to be expected, I suppose, because he hates him.'

'Could they have been burglars?'

'Doesn't seem it to me, nothing was stolen but they *were* looking for something, father's library, and Shen's desk, were ransacked. They must have been after something specific, files or documents maybe. Every room was searched, they even tried to break into the room where the goddess statue is kept but it's centrally locked with bolts top and bottom, as well as sides, as you know. When they were disturbed by Kevin they left in a hurry but without taking anything.' Sophie spoke rapidly, nervously.

'Does your father know what they were after?'

Alex was curious. Why should robbers have been there if they hadn't stolen anything? After all Henley was full of valuable paintings, centuries old vases, glass and antiques.

'Maybe you are right they just wanted it to look like a robbery.' Sophia considered. 'They wanted to brutalise Shen that's for sure but whatever they really came for Daddy said he didn't know. To tell you the truth I believe he does know. He doesn't lie and his words were, 'I couldn't say.' With daddy that is a sure give away meaning he didn't want to tell me. I thought he looked afraid and, most unusual for him, very afraid not just for Shen but for me also. He was the first home and rang the police immediately but he never saw anything of the men. Shen can't help. He hasn't spoken since it happened.' Sophia sobbed quietly, unable to continue.

Ignoring her emotion Alex asked, 'Did Kevin see or hear a car at all?'

'No, he said they ran round the side of the Hall and into the trees. It was dark and of course he was hardly in a state to see much. When he went outside he found Shen and just then Dada arrived.'

'Why didn't you tell me?'

'I knew you'd just drop everything and fly home.'

'How terrible for you,' Alex comforted.

'The police believe Shen put up a fight, his knuckles are bruised so whoever did it will most likely have some noticeable injury. Shenley was a marvellous boxer in his student days, a university champion, but these men hit him with something very heavy, to crack his skull.'

Alex took hold of Sophia, gently pulling her to him calming her, stroking her hair.

'Sophia, listen to me, we'll find who did this.'

'Shen is badly injured Alex.'

'I don't know him well of course but if he has the fighter's spirit as you say, and I did see it in him when we first met, he'll recover. What are the police doing to find them?'

'As usual they're hopeless especially that idiot Dickerson and that drunken PC Drew. They said it could be anyone and they wouldn't even question

Ralph without some kind of evidence he was involved. Superintendent Dickerson said the men were probably robbing the place and were disturbed. He thought them most likely not local men but a gang who targeted stately houses.'

'Did they question anyone at all?'

'No and especially not the Morvilles who are almost all in the legal profession and know the police well besides there's no evidence they were involved.'

Sophia fell silent.

Alex paced the room. How could something like this happen in this quiet valley. The homecoming he had so longed for and had thought of for weeks was shattered. There was something about this incident that troubled him that didn't make sense. He could understand the motive of revenge but if these men were also looking for something specific what could it be. His instinct told him they had tried to kill two birds with one stone.

'Sophia, tell me what do you really think all this is about? You must have some idea, or your father and Kevin do.'

Calmer and enlivened by the question Sophia answered as honestly as she could in words that opened her inmost heart and for the first time revealed to herself a long suppressed idea.

'I believe these people were here for the same reason they were here when they attacked and killed my mother. They were looking for something very valuable.'

'And you have no idea what it could be? Has your father ever said anything about it?'

'You have to remember I was only a child. We never discussed mother's death. I know my father thought it would distress all of us if we ever spoke of it.'

Alex breathed deeply, contentedly, the whole idea of it exciting him.

'In that case we'll do our own search.'

For the first time that evening, smiling through her tears, Sophia laughed.

'Of course. That's what we'll do.'

Sophia's cobalt eyes were once again bright and animated with purpose. A decisive hair line crease appeared at the side of her mouth, a characteristic he'd first noticed, that exposed unrelenting determination, when she had argued with her brother Marston.

That night she lay snugly asleep in his arms comforted by his strength and renewed in her resolve.

The next day the media, notified by Superintendent Dickerson trying to make a name for himself, filled the car park at the rear of Henley with vans and cameramen.

Sophia and her brother Marston refused to make any comment except Marston told them all to, 'Bugger off.'

The paparazzi were there all night outside Henley.

The next day news reported the break-in and details of Shenley and Kevin's injuries. There was a photo of Marston felling a cameraman with a blow a bare fist clouter would have been proud of, and a stunning photo of Sophia, leaving from the rear of Henley with Alex beside her, with a caption that read, - Romance at Last for Lady Sophia Allan-.

CHAPTER SIXTEEN

A dappled, hazy light fell softly into their room to wake them from sleep. It was such a beautiful day they chose to walk to Henley Hall.

Alex left Sophia at the Hall steps and turned back towards Barrington.

Perhaps a half mile into his journey he stopped to watch a silent fox, of superb colour, prowling with stiff backed gait towards a clump of trees. His observation was interrupted by a car pulling up beside him.

'Ah! Mr Roedale, thought it was you.'

From the open window of the car the grey spectre of Owen Thomas, the vicar, was staring gauntly in his direction, his sad face shuffling into an enigmatic grimace which in other people would have been a smile but on Owen's face always left one in doubt.

'Hello Vicar.'

'Can I give you a lift somewhere?'

'No, but thanks for the offer. I thought I'd enjoy a stroll, it's such a lovely day.'

Bowing his head in contemplation Owen made no attempt to leave.

'The truth is I need to talk to you. Could you spare me a few minutes?' He said opening the passenger door.

Reluctantly, doing his best not to show it Alex got into the car.

They drove the mile or so towards Barrington without Owen saying much at all.

'What is so important Owen?' Alex asked coldly impatient.

'You see a great deal of Shenley, I believe.'

'Sometimes, but not a great deal, I've been away several months, as you probably know and since my return I haven't been able to speak to him.'

'Have you heard if he is improving at all?'

'I'm told so but it's a slow progress. It would be best to ask the family if that is what you need to know.'

Owen drove through the gates into Barrington pulled up near the entrance and turned towards Alex. He looked every inch a starving aesthetic, but his eyes were kindly Alex thought, recalling how much Sophia admired him.

'Did he ever mention the Green Woman to you?'

'Yes. Why do you ask?'

'Well as many people have done over the centuries he's become obsessed with this ridiculous myth. I have to admit it's a compelling story, a beautiful goddess, an eternal spirit dwelling on Druids Hill.' Owen smiled, 'You know we have hundreds of Americans visiting our church just to look at her image there. Some tell me she's the Earth Mother, a feminine aspect of nature. Then we have a Druidic cult that visits the church to worship her at the solstices. I don't stop them of course because it gives media interest to the church. They are harmless and add to church funds.'

'Are you saying Shenley is part of this cult?'

'Oh no, not that. I meant he has become too obsessed with the story and it isn't good for him. It's all nonsense, I'm sure you'll agree.'

Owen was testing him. 'I do agree but what about all those appearances people mention and the strange phenomenon people report? I've experienced some of that myself, not here but in my travels. In my opinion Shenley is just trying to find out what's causing it all.'

Owen turned to stare at him and Alex thought he was on the brink of some inexplicable anger.

The Green Goddess

'I hope you haven't been sucked into all this?' Owen asked, disdainfully, his eyes narrowing.

'I'm just an observer Owen. I've heard and seen quite a few unexplained things in my life during my travels.'

'Quite.'

It was becoming one of those speculative conversations that could never be resolved or prove anything. Alex opened the car door showing his impatience but before leaving asked, bluntly, 'What is it you want to tell me?'

'I feel my duty, as a minister, to offer some guidance. I have been in this village for twenty five years and know something of these superstitions and I ask you, and warn you, to stay clear of them, for your own sake and the sake of those you care about. Maybe when he recovers you can influence Shenley in that direction.'

Alex stared up at the sky and trees recalling something.

'Once I lived with a Tibetan monk who told me a fellow monk, created by repetitive visualisation a Tulpa, that's a spirit of another monk. It was meant, I believe, to be an exercise in meditation. As you probably know Buddhists believe the mind is eternal and all creative. Well the product of this meditation became reality. Other people began seeing it and began asking who his mysterious visitor was. Eventually, afraid of his creation, he had to destroy it but only after much concentrated effort. I was told he found it easier to create than destroy.'

Owen's mouth had fallen open at Alex's strange anecdote.

'All things we think about and believe in enough become reality good and bad alike. You should know that.' Alex added tersely.

'I only have one faith and belief so can't believe those things but don't say I didn't warn you.' Owen replied, cynically.

'I'll have to leave. I hope you'll excuse me.'

Owen stared ahead quietly, sadly, then asked, 'Could you spare me twenty minutes more?'

Alex looked at his watch. He was curious at Owen's resigned melancholy and he hesitated realising there was something deeply troubling the man.

'It's important?'

'Yes. I'm sure it will help you though I don't know how yet. At least you'll understand my worries better. This must seem very strange to you. You probably think I'm round the bend that I'm just a goody, goody, clergyman trying to save your soul. Maybe I am but I want to show you something very few people have ever seen.'

'Why me?'

The Green Goddess

'I believe with your knowledge of the world you can help in some way. Come with me to the Church, will you please?'

Feeling uncomfortable and wary at Owens's strange behaviour, gloomy anxiety and stricken appearance, he was nevertheless intrigued by what the vicar wanted to show him. Nodding assent Alex answered, 'Alright, let's go.'

The church was dark at that hour of the morning, musty air pervading it's unlit interior, nothing like that lovely sunny morning he'd first seen Sophia there, then it had been light and clean with the scent of flowers.

Owen walked ahead of him along the aisle carpet to the silent altar and communion table.

'Help me with this.'

Taking an end of the heavy communion table, to move it, a candlestick toppled as the altar cloth slipped in his grasp.

With much tugging and pushing they moved the marble topped altar ponderously forward to expose, beneath it, mediaeval mosaic stone tiles coloured in patterns of red and green.

Exhausted Owen paused to catch his breath, 'Wait,' he panted.

He left Alex at the altar table and walked to the rear of the church where he entered a curtained vestry beneath the church tower.

Observing the tiled floor more closely Alex noticed some of the tiles had been loosened and someone had recently scraped their edges clean. The tiles were chipped and heavily scored.

Owen returned with a crow bar and a piece of timber.

'This should do it.'

The frail parson levered the crow bar hard against one of the floor tile edges. Using the piece of wood to give purchase together they forced the tile upwards. It was no ordinary tile. Someone had fixed it securely over a much larger slab of emerald green marble that had an iron ring recessed into its surface.

Removing more tiles they were able to force the crow bar under the iron ring and free it.

'What are we doing vicar?' Alex asked, 'And why?'

'Be patient I beg you. You are going to see something so rare your life will never be the same again.'

Tugging at the enormous ring, inch and a quarter iron and approximately twelve inches in diameter, they dragged the marble slab free.

Below them yawned a four feet square shaft that fell away into blackness. Dragging the slab away from the gaping hole Alex noticed the way it grated and ground noisily. Thinking this somewhat incongruous he saw it was not a single slab of marble but a composite of marble and stone. The slab itself was perhaps twelve inches thick but only the top three inches were of leafy green marble. It occurred to him then how unusual this was. There must have been a reason, he conjectured, the bright green of the surface contrasted so vividly with the other surrounding tiles. Later he realised the distinctive green entrance to the vault was a marker to show, or warn, what lay within the mysterious recesses of the caverns below their feet.

'Ah, that's it.' Owen panted, crumpling forwards, as he wiped perspiration from his forehead with his shirt sleeve.

Alex leaned against the Onyx altar table wondering what all this effort had been about. Other than the sound of Owen's short, quick breath it was depressingly silent in the church. Bending forward he peered into the sloping cavern and, his eyes adjusting to the darkness, he saw there were stone steps leading to a narrow spiral shaft.

'A crypt?' Alex asked.

'I wish, it were'.

Owen's voice was softly subdued with apprehensive fear and his right hand trembled.

'When I arrived here the place had been without an incumbent for years, the previous vicar had absconded, or so everyone thought, without leaving any trace. One of my first tasks was to clean and renovate the place and make it more welcoming. Trying to restore its original splendour wasn't easy and the congregation as you know is quite small. I didn't have any help, except Tamara of course, or sufficient capital to hire someone to do it. When I was a struggling student I had worked part time for a builder friend of my father's so I knew a little of the work involved and Lord Allan kindly donated a huge sum of money to pay for things. One day while I was scouring and scrubbing the floor tiles beneath the altar carpet here I dropped a wire brush and noticed the floor sounded hollow at this spot in front of us. My fear then was that there had been some kind of subsidence and we urgently needed a structural engineer to assess the damage, also it occurred to me there might be a forgotten tomb here. The weight of stone in a Norman Church is quite formidable and since this has Saxon origins I feared the Church might be unsound. Any weakness in a church structure is a threat to the whole edifice so I searched all the church records in the parish chest, the County Record Office and lastly the British Library but I found no mention of a vault or crypt. Then one day I noticed an unusual pattern in the tiles and discovered this slab.'

Owen's face clouded in some awful dread.

'And now I wish I never had.'

Determinedly Owen grasped at an altar candle and taking a box of matches from a window ledge he lit the candle, shielding it until the flame burned brightly.

'Follow me but be careful the steps are narrow and not level.'

Owen with difficulty led the way down.

Alex followed expecting to be shown some oppressive dungeon and manacled skeleton of someone left centuries before without love or light and left to die.

The spiral steps seemed to descend forever.

'What made you become a clergyman Owen?' Alex asked in an attempt dispel some of the apprehension he felt.

'Unhappy childhood drew me to the church, but I am not suited for it, dressing in robes to make one look godly and giving weekly performances. To be a good clergyman you need to be an actor.'

They descended the worn stone steps, brushing sandstone walls that grazed fingers and knees in the restricted winding space, until they reached a depth of some sixty to a hundred feet at which point the steps ended. Here they entered a tunnel approximately six feet wide and about seven in height although this varied at times quite dramatically.

It was a man-made passageway widened out of a sandstone channel, which was obvious from the way the passage turned and varied in width and height.

'Built by the Romans do you think?' Alex asked, 'I read they camped in this region.'

Owen didn't respond. There was no purpose in discussing it, the answer would soon be apparent enough. Shuffling along the restricted passage for what seemed a mile Owen gave frequent assurances over his shoulder that they would soon be there. At the point when Alex was losing patience at the secrecy of the clergyman and about to confront him in the glow of Owen's candle he saw ahead of them a large chamber.

Ahead Owen led into a large cavern that in the light of the altar candle appeared as perfectly chiselled from the rock as any Egyptian tomb. The walls of this remarkable chamber were painted with symbols of eagles, flowers, winged animals and angelic winged creatures and what seemed a primitive script.

'How magnificent,' Alex gasped at the splendidly executed paintings and bright colours of the murals. 'What a remarkable find. If this is what you brought me here to see I can truthfully admit I never saw anything like it.'

Owen made no reply as though afraid even to speak about the things reflected in the dancing

The Green Goddess

light of the candle that he gripped so firmly. Alex had the impression the clergyman was so alarmed he was about to flee the chamber.

Cautiously walking to the far side of the cavern Owen led Alex to another tunnel and commenced walking down this. Reaching the end of it the cleric stopped at the entrance to a second chamber smaller than the one they had passed through.

Extending his arm across the entrance, to prevent Alex going inside, Owen spoke in breathless subdued tones as he pushed the candle to arm's length, to reveal the inner chamber. Thrusting it directly ahead of him he said, 'Look there.'

In truth there was no need for the candle. A soft green translucence, like sunshine through spring foliage, suffused the cell emanating from a most extraordinary sculpture. Perhaps eight feet in height, standing naked on a rock, was the most brilliantly executed sculpture of a woman. Never in all his explorations, or visits to the most famous galleries and museums of the world, had he ever seen anything comparable to it.

The figure stood in upright posture and was far beyond the beauty of any human. The stone she had been carved from was polished as smoothly as glass; every curve of her was perfect in form and more lovely than the wildest imagination. Whoever the sculptor he must have been the greatest of craftsman. It was such an ideal of feminine beauty that both men stood transfixed by its presence and enraptured by the figure in front of them. She seemed alive and watching them with her green eyes penetrating Alex's soul like a scalpel as his gaze followed and lingered on her every curve.

Light from the candlestick, as it trembled in Owen's hand, cast shadows of the figure on the walls and made it seem alive.

Taking his attention away from the sculpture Alex noticed how clean the cave was. The tunnel they had walked along had been free of spider webs and even the air was much fresher than in the church they had left behind. Once more looking at the statue he noticed there was an inscription carved beneath it in letters he couldn't recall ever seeing before.

Thrusting the tremulous Owen aside he entered the chamber. The woman's eyes seemed to follow him as he moved to her side. Then reaching out his hand, to touch the glowing green marble, to his surprise he discovered it was not cold as he had anticipated.

Clambering up onto the rock pedestal he grasped a hand of the Green Statue to pull himself erect and felt a sensation so powerful it numbed his body like an electric shock, sending spasms through his limbs, shaking him from head to foot until losing his senses he fell back heavily onto the hard sandstone floor in a convulsion.

Kneeling beside him Owen stooped over him.

Blaming himself, Owen moaned, 'It's all my fault. Why did you enter? I tried to stop you. I should never have brought you here. Alex.'

Owen's voice sounded far, far away like a very distant rumble, like a voice calling across a mountain waste, and Alex could see the Green Woman, alive, watching him, her gaze gentle, filled with compassion. In his delirium he thought he was looking into the face of God and God was a woman.

Owen lifted Alex head onto his knee.

'Wake up Alex, wake up.'

Alex mumbled, 'What on earth happened?'

'Thank God.'

Coming to his senses Alex remembered they were in the bowels of a cavern. A labyrinth no longer a place of mystery but a cold ominous, dangerous sepulchre.

'Let's leave.' Owen urged as he helped Alex to his unsteady feet.

Picking up the candle Owen led the way back to the spiral steps and stone slab entrance.

Both exhausted from their experience and the long journey back they sealed the entrance leaving it much as they had found it, dragging the altar over it.

'Can you imagine how I feel every Sunday giving communion above this evil place? It is destroying my life and health,' Owen spoke desolately. 'Dear Lord God please show me what to do.'

Unsteady still, Alex was persuaded by Owen to go to the Vicarage.

Tamara opened the door jovially.

'Hello darling. There have been one or two calls. I've written the numbers on your pad. Hello Alex, nice to see you again, you should visit us more often. Can I get you a coffee or tea?'

Alex tried to dismiss from his mind the memory of Tamara in the green grass on the May Day celebration at Druids Hill.

Left by themselves over tea Owen, who had recovered his composure, attempted to explain their experiences in the caverns.

'There's some strange force, as you found out, in the stone itself, that glow must be a result of a form of energy, not electrical, that knocked you to the ground. You know you are probably the only living person who has seen the statue apart from myself. I'm sure you felt the awful power the statue has over people, it is like a living thing, some unknown organism and you can sense a presence a kind of aura that emanates from it. Once I chiselled a fragment from the stone beneath the statue and took it to the British Museum for analysis. Of course I didn't tell them anything other than I had come across it in the church. Well it was some time before they replied and their answer was surprising. They said they'd never come across this kind of stone anywhere before, but that some of its properties indicated it was from a meteorite. They asked if they could keep it for research and I agreed.'

'What about the writing on the stone?' Did you notice it? I don't think I ever saw anything like it before,' Alex asked.

'Yes, very strange I think. Soon after I discovered the place I copied the inscription and tried many years to decipher it but without success. There aren't enough words to compile a comprehensive alphabet so I asked a cryptologist friend at Cambridge to help. As one would expect, it took a long time before I received a reply in fact I had forgotten all about it, when my friend sent me his answer. I didn't tell him where I found the inscription and his letter was full of questions most of which I couldn't answer. I never did tell him where it came from. I didn't want Cambridge people digging up the Church you'll appreciate. Well, his letter said there were sufficient similarities between the script I had given him and a pre-Chaldean or Hittite language.'

'That agrees with Lord Allan's opinion on the sculpture of the woman at the Hall.'

'You mean there is another one of these objects?'

'You didn't know?' Alex realised he had divulged a secret.

'Not at all.'

'Well there are enough similarities to know they represent the same woman.'

'Oh! I didn't know about that.' Owen interjected with surprise and irritability. Opening a draw of his desk he took from it a letter. On it was written the translation sent to him by his Cambridge Don acquaintance.

'From the few letters I wrote down my Cambridge friend suggested the inscription reads,'

'Seek me above all.

The pure of heart shall hear my voice.

In my love is found eternal freedom.'

'What it means is beyond me.' Owen said. 'On the surface it seems innocent enough, a reasonable cult if it makes people feel better but from what I know it hasn't meant that to any of the villagers here nor throughout its history. The Green Woman, if that's what the statue represents, is worshipped as a fertility goddess up there on Druids Hill. I hate to admit it, even to myself, but they believe she is real and a living power more active than the God I revere and worship and teach them about.'

'So you do believe those stories of the goddess after all?'

'Yes. That's why I warned you not to have anything to do with it.'

Owen rested his hand on Alex's forearm.

'You'll endanger your life and those around you. I'm not talking idly. Often we just feel her presence here, and mostly benign, then suddenly without warning she emerges out of wherever it is she exists and all hell breaks loose. Those stories of men disappearing can't be mere coincidence or old wives tales. I believe the previous incumbent at our church, a truly devout man, with rare gifts of intellect, became too involved and as I told you he too disappeared, leaving a lovely wife and daughter and a promising career. He wouldn't have abandoned them like that. It's remained a mystery of what happened to him.' Owen spoke agitatedly. 'My warning is don't fall under her spell. When I first saw her and her overwhelming beauty I couldn't sleep. I'm ashamed of it, of course I am, but I could think of nothing else. It was all I could do not to go there every day to that strange cavern just to be in her company, just to look at her and be near her. Eventually I became ill and feverish for many months, seeing visions of her, hearing her angelic, melodic voice speaking to me and seeing her in the most unexpected places. I longed for her with a passion I would never wish upon the greatest recreant. My work suffered but, strangely,

Tamara was more understanding. If it hadn't been for her support I think I would have been institutionalised. You know a substitute clergyman had to take my place for some time, until I was well again, but after much prayer my recovery was complete and it all passed. A most remarkable thing, when I was at the worst moments in my illness the Green Woman came to me to comfort and reassure. Well I recovered as you can see and she no longer has any power over me.'

The clergyman seemed so exhausted, after recounting his experience, Alex excused himself.

'Thank you for showing me these things Reverend and putting your trust in me. I'll have to go because I have a lot of work to complete.'

Alex stood holding out his hand.

Tamara joined them at the door. With a knowing, secretive glance she touched Alex's arm.

'There's a lot you have to learn about our village, please visit us again Alex.'

CHAPTER SEVENTEEN

In the ensuing days Alex frequently thought of the caverns and the sculpture and was determined to resolve its mystery. What Owen saw and imagined was coloured by his personal prejudices, the result of his religious beliefs. In spite of the clergyman's warnings Alex had been inspired by what he had seen.

It was an exotic find, perhaps one of the great archaeology discoveries and Owen was right they dare not divulge it to anyone, at least until they fully understood it, and it was important not to betray Owen's confidence and trust, besides if anyone else knew of the things they had seen then this lovely, unspoilt village world would, without doubt, be ruined by unwanted visitors, news media and inquisitive researchers and academics and no doubt Druids Hill would disappear beneath bull dozers.

The most he could do for the time being would be to catalogue every detail of the caves and record what he had seen with photographs. This he was determined to do and laid plans to visit, surreptitiously, once again the caves beneath Henley Church.

With this in mind the next time he met up with Sophia he asked, 'Are there any spare keys to the Church?'

'There is a caretaker who retains a set for visitors when they arrive outside of service hours. We get visitors from all over the world coming to look at the monuments and stained glass, sometimes they come in coach loads. For convenience Owen leaves a key with the caretaker. Did you want to visit?'

Looking at Sophia's Alex wanted more than anything to share it with her but his promise to Owen held him aloof.

'I thought I might look more closely at the image of the Green Woman on the pillar and take some photos.' He wasn't lying for he did intend doing this.

'Owen would be more than happy to assist you.'

'I don't feel comfortable asking him.'

'Of course and you would need privacy. If you walk down the lane that leads to the church, next to

The Green Goddess

Harrold's farm, you will see the caretaker's cottage on your right.'

The following day Alex visited the caretaker's, brick and timber cottage.

'You're Mr Roedale aren't you?' A woman smiled at the door.

'Yes.'

'I seen you in the village shop. It's nice havin' a famous writer with us. What can I do for you? Come in an' have a cup of tea in any case, won't you please, if you've the time.'

Alex explained why he had come.

'I want to photograph some of the church interior. It isn't convenient on Sundays when there are so many people there.'

'No, weekdays are best and usually no one's there in the morning.'

'Perfect.'

'Of course, we do get lots of visitors, especially in the summer.' She showed him a heavy key hanging on a hook in the vestibule.

'Don't you ever lose the key? Alex asked.

'I al'ays have several keys.'

'Can I borrow the key for several days? I need to look around and take notes before I decide on the photographs I would require. Then there's the problem of lighting, if I get it wrong then I'll have to try again, so I need a day of bright sunlight. If I had a key I could visit the church at leisure when no one was there.'

The white haired, kindly looking, woman sat silently over her tea for a few moments before answering.

'I'm quite sure it would be alright. We have a few spares and it's not as though this is the busy season. By rights I should ask Reverend Thomas, I suppose, but you're a respectable man an' he'd just say yes anyways. Use it as long as you like. I think though I'll give you the Yale key, if you don't mind, instead of this big thing.' Saying this she picked up the iron key from the table, left the room, and returned with a standard Yale key.

'You'll be able to carry this in your pocket, much better than that old thing. It fits the side door on the right side of the church'

'Have you been looking after the church for very long?'

'I hate to count the years.'

'Did you ever see anything unusual there?'

The old lady smiled, 'Like ghosts an' things like that, you mean? I'm often asked that by visitors.'

'Yes, noises, apparitions, anything strange.'

'No, not me, I'm not that kind of person. God is in a church as far as I'm concerned, that's what I al'ays believe. I don't like to be there alone though

The Green Goddess

I must say. Nothin' I can put my finger on precisely, something not quite right, but I don't think it has anything to do with spirits.'

That evening Alex dined with Sophia at a riverside pub eight miles from Henley.

'Can you help me with some research on Henley Church?' Alex asked half way through their meal.

'The church guide book is very good?' Sophie replied quizzically.

'It's quite general without depth and what I'm looking for is what was there before the church and who built the original church on that site.'

'I can tell you who built it', Sophie answered cheerfully, 'Travelling masons. They travelled all over Europe. To build a church of such proportions was quite an engineering feat so they had to bring in the experts. Does that answer the question?'

'I would like more detail. You know where to look for these things in depth. You read Norman French, and Old English. If I tried I really wouldn't make much progress with it on my own.'

'Of course I'll help you if it means so much.' Sophie smiled searching his face over her glass of wine. 'Why do you need it?'

'To complement the history of the church and Henley with a photographic treatise. It's such a place of mystery. You know that better than I.'

'Oh, many stories. They say a tunnel runs from your house to the church. Did you know that? We could look for it if you wish? Folky, tall stories say another one runs to Henley Hall. It's all village myth. Every stately home and castle has a secret tunnel somewhere but they never find them.'

She sat back in her seat watching him. She loved Alex deeply and knew he wasn't aware of it.

'I suppose.'

'You are beginning to believe in these things aren't you? The Green Woman's got you.' Sophie laughed.

'Not entirely but there is an origin for these stories, something profound or profane even, a secret deeply hidden, long dead perhaps, my intuitive gut tells me. In any case it would make a good story I think.'

'Henley Hall has a superb collection of books on the subject in the library but if its medieval mythology that is not in my field Alex but I can introduce you to someone who studies those things if you like.'

'It would be a start.'

Sophia was smiling, privately, visualising the beautiful professor she had in mind to help him, wondering if she should introduce them.'

'Why are you smiling?'

'Before I help you promise not to fall in love with the professor I introduce you to.'

Alex laughed, delighted. 'So you *are* a jealous woman. I would never have believed it.'

CHAPTER EIGHTEEN

It was a cloudy night, perfect for moving without being seen. An impatient, cool wind shook the sycamores and a resident owl called hauntingly, over Barrington Meadows, as he walked through the fields. Shouldering a bag, in which were a camcorder, camera, a high powered torch, notebook, chalk, and an American hunting knife, Alex was alone. Few people walk the country at night. Crossing the lane he was certain no one would see him entering the church.

The side door of the church opened readily.

Inside, with some difficulty, he managed to move the marble altar, and the covering slab, hiding the entrance to the caves. The spiral steps and passages were easier to traverse this second time round. As an added precaution against losing his way he marked his progress using a red chalk he had stuffed into the pocket of his hunting gilet.

Perhaps only a hundred feet below ground the tunnels seemed a thousand kilometres beyond all that lived and breathed. They had been chosen for secrecy by whoever had helped to carve them. A feeling of vulnerability gave him a keen watchful self-preservation as he negotiated the tunnels. A teenage exhilaration and excitement took control of him like a boy setting out on some new adventure.

In the powerful glare of the torch the tunnel, that led to the central chamber, was this time illuminated in far more detail. What previously he had thought were bare walls he now noticed were painted with figures of men and women holding tapered torches in their hands in a solemn, eternal procession.

The paintings were in vivid hues, crimson, azure blue, greens and yellows and almost all pristine. A few were faded worn away by what he suspected had been shoulders rubbing against them in passing. They were all images from long gone civilisations The processions of figures were moving in the direction he was following as though guiding towards the central chamber. At the head of the figures was a vessel that looked like an ancient sailing ship and in front of it was a brightly painted canopied carriage drawn by four horses, two black and two white.

Reaching the end of the tunnel he stopped to gaze in awe into the cavern of the Green Woman. The statue reflected back the spotlight, he shone onto it, with the full blinding, brightness of a green sun.

Some unknown fear that he couldn't explain possessed him at that moment. The statue gazed at him, like a living soul, alive and watching him, aware of his presence. Her features had been executed in minute, perfect detail and the whites of her eyes accentuated bewitching green irises and the dark dilated pools of her pupils.

Her beautiful face in the torchlight though kindly in its expression was endowed with such power Alex felt a shudder of dread.

Shaking off his apprehension, smiling at allowing himself such ridiculous fears, he rested the torch against a corner, tilting it to illuminate the magnificent sculpture and then climbed on to the base plinth on which it stood.

Examining the figure more closely he was astounded at how perfect it was in every imaginable detail. A woman more beautiful than anything nature could create and beyond all imagining and desire. He put his arms around her, aware of the danger of doing it from his past experience, and touched her lips with his.

An indescribable energy filled and engulfed him transporting him into a world of fire and light and inestimable peace. Lost, unable to prevent it, Alex fell back unconscious to the hard stone floor.

How long he lay there before regaining consciousness he couldn't tell. When he opened his eyes, dazed, he looked up at the strange green marble statue and to his surprise she seemed to have moved and was now standing feet apart, fists on her hips, looking down at him, a smile pouting her full lips and her eyes flashing in what seemed quizzical admiration.

'You also I will set free'. Her voice sounded like blown leaves resonating in a summer breeze. Leaning forwards towards him she laughed, 'In time'.

Alex's head throbbed, his eyes blurred, he couldn't recall where he was. Lifting himself to a sitting position he looked once more at the statue and found her just as he had first observed her on entering the cave.

Rising to his feet he shivered, he was cold, dizzy, disoriented and wanted to vomit.

Supporting himself against the chamber wall, taking deep breaths to revive his half wakened senses, he noticed again how well ventilated the caverns were, without any trace of the stagnancy one would have expected to find in such an enclosed space, so deep below ground.

In spite of his weakness he decided to explore the caves as fully as possible. He had until dawn to accomplish it. Once more taking up his torch he moved to the farthest wall of the chamber where he had noticed a small opening. Stooping to search beyond the entrance he found himself in a long tunnel that curved away to the left. Here there had been no effort to decorate the naturally formed limestone passage, the width and height of which varied so considerably that at times he had to crawl on his hands and knees to make progress.

After a considerable walk the tunnel ended against a fall of rock. About to return his eyes caught sight of another passage on his right. This one was quite definitely man made and cut with precision to approximately seven feet wide. At this point he marked a corner of the junction of the tunnels with crayon before proceeding down this new passage.

Before long the passageway narrowed to shoulder width and became claustrophobic. Still unsteady, from his fall in the larger cave, he toppled very nearly falling down a two stage spiral flight of steps that recurved back in the confined space.

The Green Goddess

Descending he came upon what appeared to be a medieval church crypt sculptured out of the solid rock.

Pausing at the entrance to look inside he was amazed at the structure. Supporting the ceiling were four rows of slender pillars and the interior was brightly coloured with paintings, down each side of the crypt, of life sized figures of knights wearing white mantels. Going over he saw more closely the images painted in vivid hues each one different in body type and facial expression and he guessed painted from life.

Removing his camera from his shoulder bag he photographed the crypt and the individual wall paintings.

At the far end was a simple stone altar and in front of it a bare stone, kneeling rail. On the wall beyond the altar was a painting of the Madonna dressed in a bright blue robe but unlike other images her face was open, direct, smiling.

Walking around the crypt half way along the row of columns Alex noticed another tunnel about two feet six inches square. Impetuously he decided to investigate this believing it would lead to further revelations of caves or perhaps something even more exotic.

Kneeling he crawled inside. The tunnel had been cut out of the limestone and after a few yards turned upwards towards the right in a semicircle and as far as he could judge, towards the direction he had come from. Eventually the tunnel decreasing in height exited into another cave concealed from view by a tall slab of rock, crawling through into this he was at last able to stand upright. Stretching his aching back and rubbing his chafed knees Alex squeezed past the rock and found himself once more in a corner of the cave of the green goddess. He realised at once he had discovered a bolt hole, from the crypt to the cave, created as a means of escape in times of danger.

Returning to the crypt he retraced his steps to the tunnel where he had crayoned marks on the sandstone walls and turned again into another unexplored corridor cut by hand from the rock.

An artist or artists had here also brightly painted the polished walls in bold colours with a procession of men in priestly vestments walking to the chamber of the Green Woman.

Catching his hand brutally against a protruding rock the torch flew out of his grasp to hit the stone floor where it shattered to leave him in total darkness.

Alex knew quite well the predicament he was in. No one knew he was there lost in a maze of passages along which he could stumble and never find a way back to the central chamber of the statue. He blamed himself for not using the string he had brought with him to tie around the statue in the event that something like this might happen. Feeling around the floor he found broken glass and plastic. The torch was useless.

Slowly he edged his way down the passage carefully feeling the rock beneath his feet before taking any step forward. For all he knew some gaping hole might drop him into eternity. The current of cool air, which he had noticed on first entering the caves, seeped in from somewhere and this he would follow as best he could.

Frequently pausing, holding his breath to catch even the slightest movement of air, his path along the passages was excruciatingly slow. Once, when pausing in this fashion, he heard a noise like an echo. It made him sense his desperate situation more acutely.

How or why, he couldn't later explain, an intuitive awareness told him someone else was there. Pausing to listen, in the anthracite darkness, for the sound of breathing or footfall he heard nothing. He was imagining it he thought and moved on then quite suddenly a light appeared ahead of him, no bigger perhaps than a candle flame dancing wildly, playfully, to and fro in the tunnel ahead. Subduing his fear and the sudden panic that strove to engulf him he decided to move towards the light.

Calling out, Alex yelled, 'Who are you? Help me please.'

There was no answer and he was unable to lessen the distance between them. The strange light continued to move ahead as before then abruptly disappeared.

Somewhere from his right was a draught of cool air. Turning in that direction he once more glimpsed the light moving ahead of him. Following it closely it led to yet another limestone tunnel. Air was filling the passage as the dancing light continued ahead.

This tunnel had a level floor and he reasoned it led to an exit.

He must have walked for an hour in that awful darkness. On his left he passed yet another chamber but the light passed by this moving ahead along the man- made passage he was walking.

For the first time he noticed by touching the walls that there were small recesses cut into them at regularly spaced intervals and guessed that these had been cut to hold torches or candles to light the tortuous passages. This discovery renewed his hope of finding a way out of the labyrinth.

Just when he began thinking there was no end to this interminable maze of tunnels the mysterious light that had accompanied him, perhaps guided him, was no longer visible. The tunnel ahead began sloping upwards steeply and he began to perspire and breath heavily in the cold of the caverns. This incline dramatically ended its journey at a flight of steps that he tripped onto. At their apex the worn uneven steps ended abruptly at a level walkway that turned sharply to the left.

Feeling his way along the stone walls he discovered what appeared to be a wooden door of such age it had petrified into an iron like consistency. Moving his hands carefully against the door he searched for a lock or handle. To his delight he found a wood drop latch and lifting this, and tugging, the door creaked open to the scented night, filled with a smell of leaves and fields, welcoming him to the real world.

Searching around, his hands told him he was in some kind of wooden cell, he realised he was standing in what seemed to be the bole of an enormous tree.

A narrow break in the outer shell of the tree allowed sufficient light for him to find a constricted opening and through this he was able to squeeze into the freedom of the darkened woodland.

In almost disbelief Alex to his surprise found he was standing in the natural amphitheatre of Druids Hill and the tree he had emerged from was the trunk of the great, venerable yew in its centre.

Returning to Henley Church he kept wondering about the small light that had guided him to safety. He had read that when the Stone Age fort had been built the surrounding countryside had been a swamp and marshland. Such places were associated with a 'Will of the Wisp' phenomenon, where phosphorescent gases gave off a glow from a distance and moved forward when approached and seemed to follow when one walked away. That must be the answer, he reasoned, yet how had it led him to the exit? Doubt jiggled his thoughts whenever he tried to rationalise the mystery away and he concluded someone else had been present in the caves with him.

The night was already well spent and he hurried to leave everything in the church just as he had found it.

CHAPTER NINETEEN

Several days after the exploration of the caves Alex made a second visit to the church, this time during daylight hours, with the intention of photographing anything that might explain the mystery of the caves.

Being late autumn it was dark inside. The caretaker had left for home. Flowers were displayed in large vases each side of the transept arch. To the left of the transept was the unusual carved pillar, Sophia had shown him, with the image of a snake coiled at its base and the column shaft depicting the bole of a tree. On its capital leaved branches radiated up into the vaulted ceiling. It was unlike any other column in the church. Above the south door was another curious carving, a skull with a timeworn letter 'B' inscribed below it.

On the north side of the church was a lady chapel and to the right of it a tomb and alabaster monument to Thomas Barrington Esq. of Barrington Hall. It had been cut with great skill and so lifelike that Barrington seemed alive in resting posture his head reclining on his right hand. He was portrayed as a handsome young man in the prime of life with serene and kindly face. Below the monument an inscription read,

Thomas Barrington sepulchit 1624.
One brother for good one for evil.
Thom. Barrington was ye sainte among men.
None so fair none so benevolent.
God took him as he did Enoch,
Leaving the world to its wickedness.

There were two other standing sculptures at each side of the tomb. On the left a female figure, draped Roman style, holding an hour glass and on the opposite side another female holding a skull. Alex meticulously photographed everything to study later.

The guidebook explained that the unusual pillar was one of several found in Britain and Europe that celebrated the transition of an apprentice mason to that of Master. The column did not depict the tree of life and Satan as one would suppose but was a secret shorthand of the mason craftsmen. Masons, he knew from discussions with Sophia, travelled all of Europe carrying their secret methods of construction and pre Christian mythologies with them. They were the great preservers of Pagan, Earth Mother worship, leaving testimonies to her by the thousands, in churches throughout western Europe and the Mediterranean. The guide book further explained that the snake coiled round the base of the pillar represented not the power of evil as found in the Bible but the knowledge and cunning of the craftsman. Referring to the skull it was believed it was a memorial to a forgotten Saxon lord whose name had been initialised with the letter 'B' below it. Most likely, the guidebook assured, it was Earl Baldwyn who had fought with Harold at Hastings.

Regarding Thomas Barrington the guide book noted that when his tomb had been opened it was found to be empty. This had been discovered, some decades before, during renovation work on the church. It gave credence, it suggested, to the story that Barrington had disappeared and more likely, though not proven, that his brother had been responsible for his murder. Barrington's body had never been found nor was anyone charged with the crime. The author suggested Barrington had perhaps sailed for the New World.

The history went on to suggest that the rare sculpture of the Green Woman was the work of a highly skilled apprentice who had, because his notable skill, been elevated to that of Master while working on Henley Church and it was he who had been commemorated by the unusual pillar.

Over dinner Alex asked Sophia what she thought of the photos he had taken of the church interior.

'Can you add more than is written in the church handbook?' Alex asked.

'I have some ideas and when I was in my teens did a little research that might be of relevance.' Sophie gave him back one of his photos. 'This one of the skull, do you notice anything unusual about it?'

'The letter "B" of course but I haven't noticed anything else.' He answered intrigued.

'Well, I don't think this skull is of a Saxon lord at all. It isn't the head of a man. It's the head of a woman.'

Looking more closely at the photograph he was perplexed at how Sophie had drawn this conclusion.

'It is very well sculpted, by an excellent craftsman I'd say, and he wanted to be accurate. My belief is he used a real skull as a model. It is carved it in sufficient relief to leave no doubt about it being a woman.'

'How do you know, Sophie?' Alex asked.

'Let's wait until we get home and I can show you on my computer far better than words and you can take a print of what I show you.'

In her study at Henley Hall Sophia sat down at her computer. Alex drew up a chair beside her and watched as she scanned the photograph of the skull in Henley Church. Splitting the computer screen to compare Alex's photo with skulls of male and female from her own computer library she pointed out to him the various points of recognition.

'There are several differences between male and female skulls. This one from the church doesn't have the typical male ridge brow, the suborbital margin. There you see, compare it with this one of a male skull. The other clue is the jaw line, quite delicate. On a typical male here,' Sophia aligned a cursor arrow on the images, 'The male jaw tends to be more square and heavy. But Alex in case there is still some doubt, a point that even most anthropologists miss, is that if you draw a line from the male brow to chin it is almost a straight line but in the female the lower face invariably protrudes much more forward, like an animal really', She laughed at this sudden idea as she turned the images side face, drawing a diagonal line from forehead to chin of each of the skulls.'

'The female is deadlier than the male.' Alex quoted.

'Unquestionably.'

Sophia squinted at him pretending malice but somehow on her it didn't work. On the screen she imposed the photo taken in the church over the male skull for Alex to see the unmistakable differences.

'I would never have noticed it.'

'It's part of my training and research that's all.' She was searching his face trying not to offend him.

'What conclusions do you draw from it?'

'None at the moment. I have no idea what it means except it probably has something to do with the Green Woman.'

'So, let's see, in Henley we have this remarkable sculpture of a Green Woman and a skull. Do you believe they are connected in some way?' Alex asked

'Perhaps, but we can't be sure without more evidence. I think the church itself has a code written into it that only an initiate could understand. I really believe my father thinks so too. He never speaks of it but his reluctance tells me more than words,' Sophia replied thoughtfully.

'Do you mean some kind of secret code?'

'Well, the pillar is a symbol to show that Henley church is very special and different from all others, there is something there of great importance, then we have the image of the Green Woman and the skull with the letter B and we have the tomb of the knight from some holy chivalric order.'

Alex was thinking of the caverns below Henley and all he had seen there but was reluctant to tell Sophia.

'Any other revelations?' Alex inveigled.

'This other picture,' Sophie pushed the photo of the Green Woman at him. 'You've captured it superbly Alex. The emerald translucence of her and magnificent watchful eyes, wonderful photography. It occurred to me however, that no matter how incredibly skilled they were, in their designs and architecture, those early travelling masons were not capable of executing a work like this. It's more the work of a Greek or Roman. Don't you think?'

'I never saw anything so lovely.'

'The work of church masons is quite primitive really but this is equal to or better than Grecian. Recently I was researching Roman Britain. The Romans, to avoid conflict, would often move certain tribes from one location to another to prevent them unifying into some kind of amalgamated fighting force with other kindred local tribes. Another reason, of course, was to utilise skills in regions where they were most needed.'

'You can't mean they moved Greek sculptures into this part of Britain.' Alex said doubtfully.

'No! Not that. Let me finish. There's a lot of evidence from local speech patterns and physiognomy that the Romans moved a tribe from Cornwall, to this region, to mine for iron ore.'

'But that was surely a thousand years before Henley was built.'

'Yes.' Sophie laughed.

'No primitive, ancient Brit, could have sculpted this.' Alex said looking at the photo of the Green Woman.

'The connection, Mr Roedale, if you will please allow me, is not that they were responsible for it but that they were in contact with someone who was.'

'Oh! Who?'

'Phoenicians, they were the great traders of the ancient world.'

'Why would they be in England?' Alex asked perplexed.

'Phoenicians were adventurer merchants, the Greek city of Thebes was founded by them and they are mentioned extensively in Greek mythology.'

Alex wondered if there was a mere possibility Sophie was right. He recalled reading somewhere that Greek writing had been discovered on a carving at Stonehenge.

'The centre of the Phoenician kingdom, as I'm sure you know, was at Tyre. It is said in the Bible Solomon came to them for help in mounting campaigns in the Red Sea. The Temple of Solomon, according to archaeologists, was designed by Phoenicians. Something else, the Phoenicians were so advanced that their alphabet gave rise to the Greek alphabet and eventually ours.

'Well, that's all very interesting but how does it fit in with the Green effigy?'

'The Phoenicians came to Cornwall to trade for minerals. This is well established and known. My guess is it they brought the Green Woman statue with them, and the masons of Henley church knowing of its existence, for whatever reason, copied it into the design of the church'

Alex drank a glass of wine Sophia poured out for him. His head was filled with questions about the paintings and things he'd seen in the caverns below Henley Church.

'Who is she then, this magnificent sculptured woman?' He asked, thinking aloud rather than speaking to Sophia.

'I believe she is Europa or the goddess Athena, maybe Astarte, Venus or Aphrodite, who knows?' Sophie answered, her face lighting up as though in a sudden eureka revelation.

He had lost Sophie's line of reasoning.

Noticing his confusion, before he could ask, she enlightened, 'In Greek mythology, Cadmus, *the Phoenician*, founded Thebes when he was searching for his sister Europa. She was considered the most beautiful woman in the world, so beautiful that Zeus himself fell in love with her. Eventually the King of Crete also fell in love with her. They married and the Royal House of Crete therefore claimed descent from the Phoenicians. Cadmus, the founder of Thebes and Europa's brother was always helped by Athena, the Goddess of Wisdom, and she has always ever since been associated with Europa.'

'And?'

'I believe the Green Woman is Athena, the most powerful female symbol the world as ever known. Before she was born, according to the Greeks, it was prophesied she would be greater than Zeus himself. Athens is named after her and strangely by coincidence Europe derives its name from the goddess Europa. Anyway all those goddesses are the same symbol.

'Sophia, you are brilliant and the most beautiful woman I ever met.' Alex said wrapping his arm around her waist.

'Tell me second only to Athena and I'll be satisfied.'

CHAPTER TWENTY

'Hello, Alex, pleased to meet you at last. Sophia explained to me some of the reason why we should talk.'

The woman addressing him was slender with dark skin and a long angular face that he recognised immediately as Ethiopian. The lean figure, perfect skin texture and large, oval slanted eyes all confirmed it.

'Pleased to meet you Psyche,' Alex greeted delighted by her exotic beauty and now understanding Sophia's jealous remark.

Outside Psyche's study he could see the quadrangle lawns of the university and beyond them a towering university clock.

'I'm grateful you could find time to help me.'

Inviting him to sit down Psyche asked, 'Can I get you coffee or tea?'

They settled into casual small talk of how he had met Sophia and of Psyche's own friendship with her, until eventually Psyche laid out a folder on her desk.

'Well, I've studied the writing you sent to me. I'm almost certain it's a type of Sumerian text but with quite a few differences. I have to tell you I've never seen anything exactly like it. We only know of these Mediterranean cryptic languages from Greek writings and Biblical references, and often we have no way of comparing them. The Sumerian language was quite complex, known as the language of the gods, only priests knew how to write it. Consequently we know very little about it either.' Turning the pages of her folder, Psyche's face brightened, 'As far as the drawings are concerned,' she laid out the sketches he had sent her drawn from his photos, 'They are goddesses from a variety of cultures.' Psyche looked closely at him searching his face. 'I'm sure you already know that. I have to admit though that about a third of them I've never seen before but I 'm sure they are all goddesses of love, fertility and wisdom.'

'Why would they be all together like this?'

'That depends I suppose on where you found them,' Psyche answered quizzically.

'Mostly these goddesses were invoked celebrating the arrival of spring, the goddess giving birth to something new, new life, a new beginning, the old passed away and gone. Some appear to be of the greatest goddess of all, the goddess of Wisdom.'

So Sophie had been correct in her assumption, Alex was thinking, as Psyche explained the meaning of the paintings.

Sitting in front of him, her calm, fatalistic eyes reminded him of the broad open hills and plains of North Africa he'd visited, in his teens, with his parents.

'Some of the images though are rather warlike, I would have thought, with axes and spears,' he commented.

Resting her slender arms and hands on the table Psyche informed, 'Yes, that is true, these goddesses not only gave life but also took it away, to make way for their beloved and the new. They kill and transform and destroy to resurrect life itself.' Folding her hands beneath her chin Psyche asked pointedly. 'Tell me Alex where did you find such a fabulous collection?'

'I have to keep that secret for the time being, Psyche. I'm sure you understand. I'm sorry I can't at this stage divulge more. It might surprise you but not even Sophia has seen these drawings.'

The Green Goddess

'Well you must have a reason and yes I do understand. The moment you expose these to the public gaze there will be all hell let loose, reporters, photographers and academics all over them. I'd say it's probably one of the most spectacular finds I have ever seen. Promise me you will let me be the first to know.'

'Psyche, I want to say yes but I'm not sure the location should ever be disclosed.'

'That would be a true loss to our incomplete knowledge and research. I beg you to reconsider that. I am sorry I haven't been able to decipher the inscription from the statue you mentioned to me. The writing seems very much like early Phoenician, a branch of Sumerian. I will work some more on it and get back to you.'

It was a dull, wet weather, day in appalling traffic, as he drove back from Oxford. Sophia was waiting for him at Barrington.

'Was Psyche able to help?' Sophia asked.

'Yes, she more or less confirmed what you told me so I haven't learned much more.'

'Anything about the Green Woman?' Sophia enthused.

'I didn't mention it, only the inscription beneath.'

Alex couldn't help but notice Sophia was unusually sombre.

'Why are you so unhappy?' he asked, 'Not more bad news?'

Sophie walked away disconsolately. 'Father is ill. The stress of everything that's happened, I suppose. He's never been a truly healthy person you know. I think mother's death has weighed on him all these years and now this near repetition of the same tragedy with Shenley, is just too much for him. I'm very worried about him Alex. The doctor doesn't think he should be left alone for the present and has arranged for a nurse to be with him. He's so distant, doesn't want to speak to anyone.'

'For Henley Hall to be targeted in this way, twice, is more than coincidence. There's something valuable in the Hall people are willing to kill for.'

'I have tried not to believe that Alex but I have to agree you. I've gone over the few memories I have, of when mother died, but I was only a child and I hardly recall anything of it. As for whatever the men were after I have no idea. Daddy never mentioned anything.'

'We'll have to ask him then won't we? He must know something.' Alex advised peevishly, 'Your life may be in danger too for all we know.'

Sophia clung to Alex like a child resting silently beside him on a settee. After dinner they went to Henley Hall.

Friends and neighbours dropped in hoping to see Lord Henry. His nurse, an austere Scot told them, 'The Master is stable but we canna let anyone see him not for the time bein'. It's best to ring if you want information, ye understand.' They were turned away politely but firmly.

Lord Allan sitting in a winged chair, wrapped in a dressing gown, hardly acknowledged their presence. From his huge, silent bedroom he stared into the melancholy twilight descending on the fields of Henley. Sophia kissed his cheek but his only reply was to squeeze her hand.

'How are you feeling?' Sophie asked.

'Much better,' Lord Allan replied perfunctorily in a muffled voice.

Sophia knew he was lying and asked him tersely, 'I want to ask you daddy why were we broken into again? Do you know?'

Lord Allan remained silent. There were no words from anyone, not even his beloved Sophia, that could induce him to answer only a deep sadness pervaded his kindly eyes.

When they were ready to leave Lord Allan surprised them by saying, 'Alex I need to speak to you alone, if I may.'

'Of course, I'll visit tomorrow', Alex promised.

CHAPTER TWENTY ONE

When Alex called at Henley, the next day, Lord Allan was no better. A doctor, about to leave, met him on the way out and advised, 'It will be alright to speak with him but don't let him become agitated.'

In his large bedroom Lord Allan rested back on the pillows of his bed, a coffee tray, cups and a pot beside him on a stand and when he greeted Alex, his voice was weak.

'Alex, I hope you didn't mind coming here but I have something important, perhaps you will think unbelievable, to tell you, but I promise you it is true.'

'Are you any better?'

'No! I 'm not, which is why I have to speak with you. I feel you are the only person I can confide in, and trust with our lives.'

Alex was about to interrupt but Lord Henry gestured silence.

'I belong to a secret society. I don't think any of my family knows that, although they may have guessed it. The order is the most ancient of all such leagues. It has no name since to give it one would have made it easier for people to know us. Individually, also for secrecy, we only know those of our equal rank and our subordinates. Each master alone knows who his subordinates are, that might sound formidable but really there aren't many of us in the world. Over the years we have had to develop this hierarchy, and secrecy, because of constant persecution.'

'How old is the society?' Alex asked intrigued by this revelation.

'Approximately a thousand years but our ideas were handed to us from more ancient sources, from members of similar orders in ancient Egypt, who were advisors to the Pharaohs, and before them others who were active among the followers of Zoroaster. Perhaps it might surprise you but the wise men mentioned in the New Testament were members of one of these orders, like ours, under the authority of the Zoroastrian Parsee. Do you wish me to go on'?

'Yes, of course.' Alex said, fascinated by Lord Henry's story.

'The Temple of Solomon was built by one such fraternity. We were also active in ancient Greece and you can find some of our teachings in Plato and the Neo Platonists. In the Gospel of John there are references to our specific beliefs. The leading exponents of Gnosticism were of our order, the Cathars, Knights Templars, Cabalists, Rosicrucians, Freemasons. All these relied directly upon us in one way or another, adopting our methods and beliefs and accepting our authority over them as a last defence. Our order is above all others, and our members were hidden for safety among their ranks.'

'What is your own involvement in this society?

For a moment the room was silent as Lord Henry in his weariness struggled how he should answer this pointed question.

'I am the Grand Master.'

Alex began to see, before he was told, the answer to the troubled lives of the Allan family. Staring into the face of Lord Allan, testing his sincerity, Alex paused at this new revelation.

'Although our present order is only one thousand years old, in its present form, the disciplines,

The Green Goddess

beliefs and teachings have been continuous since the ancient times I've just referred to.'

'You mentioned persecutions.' Alex was trying to focus on the recent tragedies in the family.

'The Church, our greatest enemy, destroyed the Cathars. Then Kings of Europe, to obtain our wealth tried to destroy the Templars but our order lived on nevertheless, hidden among them, and using our influence we took the remaining Templars to the safety of 'The Order of Christ'. Of that order by the way were the great explorers Christopher Columbus and Vasco da Gama.'

Lord Henry pausing in his weakness lay back exhausted on his pillow.

'Would you like me to come back another time,' Alex suggested realising for the first time how ill Lord Allan was.

'It's important I continue. I'll be strong again in a minute or two. Pour yourself a coffee, I can't drink it at the moment and I ordered it for you.'

Alex looked out over the lawns of Henley, drinking coffee. In the heavy silence of the room the only sound was the laboured breathing of Lord Allan.

'Our enemy at present,' Lord Henry continued, 'is an organisation called P2. They were supposedly disbanded in 1981 when their leader was arrested at his Italian Villa and, for the first time, the organisation came to the attention of the world.'

'I read about that somewhere, Licio Gelli was its Grand Master wasn't he and its members were politicians from all over the West, businessmen, bankers, even the Vatican Bank and some Cardinals?'

'Yes indeed, and more, CIA and NATO officials. One report into their activities mentioned President Nixon. They were responsible for many murders, among them the Italian Chief of Intelligence, and the 1980 Bologna Railway bombing that killed 85 people, the murder of Roberto Calvi, president of the Banco Ambrosiano, partly owned by the Vatican Bank, who was found hanging beneath Black Friars Bridge in 1982, and the murder of the Swedish Prime Minister, Olof Palme.'

'If they were disbanded, why are they your enemies now?' Alex frowned appalled at this revelation.

'They were never disbanded, secret organisations never are. They become more secretive, or change their names'

'What is it then you are so afraid of? What do they want from you?

Alex was beginning to believe that perhaps Lord Henry's illness was affecting his reason.

'Firstly we are their enemies and they want to destroy us, we are just as powerful as they are but with different ideals. More importantly they want the symbol that keeps us together. Many of our treasures, in the past, were stolen from us by monarchs and the Church of Rome, but not the most priceless treasure of all. Through the centuries members of our order have been tortured and killed to obtain it, yet not one of our members ever revealed where it was, or what it was. The Church would do anything to obtain it. They know it is the most sacred object in Christendom. The second reason is its monetary value. The Vatican alone would pay billions to have it in their keeping and any collector rich enough would do the same.'

'I understand, but how does it affect you and your family?' Alex asked troubled not only by the story but also by Lord Allan's condition. He was certainly very ill, his breathing difficult, unfocused, his face perspiring and his speech at times barely audible.

'I am the Grand Master. Every twenty five years the elite of our order meet at a secret location and the object they are after is part of our ancient ceremony. For almost a thousand years our temple has been here in England. There are other sites, of course, one in La Sainte-Baume in Provence, one in Jerusalem. Other of our temples were destroyed, one at Ephesus, one in Tyre, and another lost to us or hidden, but still existing we believe, in Istanbul.'

Alex remained silent while Lord Henry regained enough energy to continue.

Knowing it would take time for this disclosure to sink in Lord Henry deliberated on how much he could tell Alex without exposing the secret fully.

'Perhaps you can understand my dilemma. I am unable to produce the object. This is a disgrace to me and my family and I feel we have lost all honour.'

Lord Henry seemed to visibly fade.

'I still don't understand, why can't you produce this symbol as you call it?'

'You know Sophia's mother was murdered?' Lord Henry said.

'Yes, I heard something of it.' Alex's had a barrage of questions to ask but knew this wasn't the time to ask.

Lord Henry's brows furrowed, his eyes glaring wildly, his face filled with shock and anguish

'Whoever they were, and no one was ever prosecuted, they were looking for the sacred object of our order. I believed they were P2, under the command of Licio Gelli and the Vatican. Somehow Sophia's mother hindered their search. Before they killed her she hid Sophia in the only place they couldn't gain access to and somewhere in the house she also had time to hide the sacred symbol that gives life to our Order. We have never found where she hid it and she left no clues. She didn't have time.'

Lord Allan stopped speaking, deeply affected in his illness and fighting back the tears that struggled to overcome his composure.

'I used to believe P2 had stolen it but when it became clear that they were still torturing and killing, in an attempt to obtain it, I realised Eleanor, my wife, had risked her own safety to secure it.'

'That was a long time ago. Sophie told me she has no memories at all of the event.' Alex enjoined.

Lord Henry sighed, seeming to shrink into his bed.

'That is true, she was only a child and it was an awful experience. There were no other attempts, by the perpetrators, after the murder to find the object here in Henley, though two of our Order were murdered, five years ago, in an attempt to discover its location. During the eighties P2 had their hands too full, avoiding arrests and prosecution in the courts, to make much effort. That is all behind them and once more they are seeking the whereabouts of our sacred object.'

'What is this thing that is so valuable that men die for it?' Alex asked his heart desiring to see it for himself if it was so priceless.

'I can't tell you that. None of our order are permitted, on punishment of death, to disclose its nature or its whereabouts.'

'So what is it you want me to do Lord Henry, you must have a reason for telling me all this?'

Alex was openly exasperated to think that anyone in their right mind would put the life of wife and children at risk for the sake of some antiquated relic. The concealed anger in his voice didn't miss the attention of Lord Allan, who fell back once more on his pillow visibly distressed.

Remembering the doctor's advice not to let him become agitated unnecessarily Alex excused himself. 'Lord Allan, I have to leave, I wish I could stay with you longer but I have some very urgent things to do.'

Grasping Alex's hand, with an urgent desperation in his voice, Lord Allan said, 'It was Sophia they were looking for this time, thank God she was out.'

'Why Sophia?'

'She is the only one capable of telling them where her mother hid it. Before you go, promise me you'll do your best to protect Sophia. Promise me.' Lord Henry demanded.

'I will, of course, gladly, she means more to me than life itself.'

'Be careful of the Morvilles. They have, from the earliest days, when Gelli founded P2, as a breakaway from Freemasonry, and devoted it solely to criminal activity, been involved with that organisation, that and the more crooked side of the

Illuminati.' Clutching Alex's hand Lord Henry insisted, 'Promise.'

Folding his right hand over the hands of Lord Allan Alex replied, 'I promise.'

'None of this conversation is to be mentioned to anyone not even Sophia.' Lord Henry requested.

'No one, '

After Alex had gone Lord Allan lay on his bed thinking of his wife. How he had missed her all those years ago and never been tempted to even look at another woman. The sight of her lying in a patch of blood had never left him. He thought of Shenley, so badly injured, and Kevin, and for the first time wondered whether it was all worth it. In any case without the relic his position of Grand Master would be over. For the first time also he realised he no longer wanted to live, all that was dear to him was gone. If only he was strong enough he could walk into the fields with his gun and end it all right now. He comforted himself that his illness would take care of that, soon.

Alex left Henley with many questions and a growing fear, made more acute by Lord Allan's warnings, for Sophia's life. The valley, he had come to for peace and seclusion, had turned out to be a battleground.

Neither Lord Henry nor he knew that every word of their conversation had been listened to and recorded.

CHAPTER TWENTY TWO

Through Sophia Alex waited for news that Lord Henry's health had improved sufficiently to speak to him about the secret order he belonged to. He was hoping he could obtain enough information to find the relic Lord Henry had spoken about. It seemed to him that much of Lord Henry's illness was psychosomatic, due to the attack on Shenley and the realisation he would have to appear at the sacred temple without the venerable object entrusted to him. As the days passed there was no improvement in Lord Henry.

Sophia had to go to Europe but made daily contact. She was attending a conference on medieval literature in Geneva. While there she was using any spare time to search for references, from European sources, in historic journals, libraries and university research papers, about the Green Woman phenomenon.

Alex wanted to tell her of his conversation with Lord Henry but was prevented by the promise of secrecy.

The next morning Alex received a call from Kevin.

'Well, I'm glad I got hold of yeh at last. I'm afraid to say but Lord Henry has taken a turn for the worse,' Kevin apprised in his distinctive Irish brogue.

'I'll come right away. Has Sophia been told?'

'That she has.'

'How are you also Kevin, surely you should be in bed too?'

'Not at all, I'm in fine fettle and rarin' to go. I ask you though to wait for me there and not to come over here, if you don't mind, because I have things to say that have to be said private.'

'Of course,' Alex answered, alarm ringing through his thoughts like a bell as he waited patiently for Kevin to arrive.

The butler came thirty minutes later, limping and his head bandaged which he had tried to hide with a hat. His left hand was also bandaged and his right badly bruised. He kept them hidden in his top coat pockets. As soon as he had seated himself Alex offered him a shot of his favourite whisky.

'What I'm about to tell ye, I suppose right enough, it'll seem strange to you but it's the truth none the less.'

'After what I've seen and heard lately I doubt if I'll be surprised by anything.'

'The truth is I'm not really what I seem.'

'Yes, I thought as much,' Alex replied, cynically.

'Lord Henry and I met years ago in the military. He asked me, after we both left the service, to be his bodyguard. I was in military intelligence, would you believe it looking at me now. It was a long time ago, of course, just after his wife had died, such a lovely woman she was, like one of God's angels. He felt, and quite right too, that Sophia needed protection. She was just a child then and I took the disguise of butler so no one would fancy why I was there.'

Alex looked more closely at Kevin, there was no doubt he had the bearing of a soldier. He'd recognised, when he first saw him that he had been a soldier of some kind, a man to be relied on he had decided then. Kevin always seemed far more casual than most butlers, giving one an impression he was an equal, not subservient in any way.

'But that's not what I'm here to tell you. I ask you to be careful of what you say at Henley. That's the reason I wanted to speak with you.'

The Green Goddess

'Why do you say so Kevin?' Alex was mildly bewildered.

'The house is bugged.'

'What?'

'Yes, indeed. The day after you visited Henry I was sitting by his bed an rested my hand on the edge of the table beside him. My hand felt a small object there so being curious I looked and found a tiny device.'

'Who on earth?' Alex interrupted.

'After Lord Henry had gone to sleep and the nurse gone downstairs I began lookin' all round the Hall and found five others. There may be more so I'm asking a military associate to search the place more thoroughly.'

'Who would do this?' Alex asked, more of himself than Kevin, and already knowing the answer.

'The same people who attacked me an' Shenley. They're looking for something, just as when Lady Eleanor was killed, an' not finding it, they've bugged the house in the hopes that someone will disclose its whereabouts.'

'Did Lord Allan ever tell you what it was they were after?' Alex asked. If anyone knew surely it would be Kevin, he reasoned.

'That he never did at all an' he must have his reason. I never pressed him about it.'

Finishing his whisky Kevin said, 'We'll have to go quickly but I needed to tell you first. Just remember what I said. At all times when there, even with Lady Sophie, be very careful what you talk about.'

The next time Alex visited Henley he waited in the hall until Lord Henry's doctor came down to speak to him.

'Well, I'm afraid the prospects aren't very good, he's had a stroke and I'm waiting for an ambulance to take him to hospital.'

'Can I see him first?' Alex asked. 'I need to speak with him if possible. It's most urgent and important.'

'You can see him yes, of course, but you won't be able to speak with him. He's lost his voice completely. Not unusual in a stroke case. He is also paralysed down the right side of his body.'

'What are his chances?' Alex asked bluntly.

'I can't say. Sometimes people recover but it often takes years to reach any kind of normality, then again I've seen people recover in an instance. We won't know without more tests. What my concern right now is that he doesn't have another stroke. '

The doorbell ringing loudly interrupted their conversation.

'That must be them now. You will have to excuse me. Go along and see him quickly if you must,' the doctor said in exasperation.

The Green Goddess

Lord Henry lay on his bed not recognising Alex and staring straight ahead he had made a decision to close himself to the world entirely.

'I will do my best,' Alex promised, squeezing Lord Allan's hand, hoping he understood.

Lord Henry's eyes flickered and for a moment there was an acknowledging feeble pressure of his hand.

Several hours later Sophia arrived at the hospital to wait for news with Alex.

'All this has to do with the society he belongs to you know.' Sophia said looking disconsolately at the floor.

'What do you mean?' Alex wasn't going to break confidence with Lord Henry.

'Father has been part of a secret society since before I was born. It's why mother was killed, I'm sure of it, and now Shen and Kevin injured and the house ransacked.'

Lord Henry had said Sophia knew nothing of this. If she knew so much about it he felt no obligation to his promise of secrecy. Alex concluded, after churning the matter over in his mind, he had to tell Sophia. He probed further.

'What kind of society are you talking about?'

'A clandestine organisation. They meet annually, but every twenty five years they indulge in some kind of arcane ceremony. All nonsense really, I can't imagine father being mixed up in such a childish thing. What I feel sure of is that our home has something so valuable hidden there that people will kill and rob to find it. The only reason is it must have something to do with the society that father belongs to.'

'How on earth do you know this if it's secret?'

'Oh! A long time ago, you can't hide anything from children. When I was small I was always exploring the interminable rooms of Henley, hiding behind chairs, listening and peeking. Once father left a wardrobe open that he usually locked and inside I noticed strangely coloured robes. I knew from history books they were similar to those worn by medieval knights and once I saw a book on a table with indecipherable writing in it and engravings of a woman, a copy from an old manuscript I now think. On one was the name Sophia. The same as my own name and I imagined I was named after this beautiful woman.'

'And you think the thieves were after this book?' Alex watched her closely.

'I don't know, maybe.'

'If it isn't the book what do you think then that these thieves are after?' Alex was still reticent of disclosing the conversation with her father.

'I have no idea but my guess is that if we find father's book, with the engravings in it, that I saw as a child, we may find the answer.'

A nurse interrupted them to lead them to a private room.

Lord Henry was there comatose without any recognition of either of them.

Later, that evening, Alex mentioned his conversation with Lord Henry and Kevin's warning.

'Don't even mention the society or anything to do with it,' Alex suggested.

Agreeing, Sophia took his arm and led him to the dining room where they opened a bottle of wine.

Sophia smiled happily, 'We're getting somewhere Alex, I can feel it, we will unravel this mystery you and I, and punish those responsible.'

Ralph Morville was on the phone and at the same time looking around the room. The walls, windows, everything needed attention it occurred to him. This place left to him by the family was draining all his resources. It was then that he decided to get rid of it.

A voice on the other end of the phone broke his thoughts. 'He's in hospital.'

'I'd hoped he might be able to tell us something,' Ralph answered.

'That is now out of the question, he's lost his speech and may not ever recover.'

'Well only Henry Allan and his daughter can tell us where it is, so that leaves his charming daughter.'

'I'll work on it.'

'Don't do anything, not until I tell you,' Ralph snapped back, 'there have been enough mistakes already. For the time being just watch her and that writer boyfriend of hers.'

'Will, do,' the sullen voice replied.

CHAPTER TWENTY THREE

They began in Henley's spacious library but there was nothing Sophia found, among the thousands of volumes her family had collected over the centuries, which was remotely like the book she had seen as a child.

'It's difficult remembering exactly what it looked like after all those years.'

For three hours they searched then had to admit it wasn't there.

Outside, where they could talk privately, sitting in the sunshine, Sophia tried to recall exactly what had happened on the day she had seen it.

'I remember Daddy had been in the room where the Green Woman is. I do remember that, seeing the door left open because he had been called to the phone.'

Sophie's face lightened up and spread into a smile. 'Of course, that's where it must be, in there, and maybe the object he mentioned to you. Let's go.' She jumped to her feet leaving Alex to follow her.

The green marble statue, riveted Alex to the spot the moment he saw it.

'Come on Alex,' Sophia called impatiently.

A marble topped cabinet, resting against one wall, seemed the most likely starting point. The drawers were locked and they had to force them open. Inside the drawers there was nothing to help them. Stepping back Alex glanced more closely at the cabinet realising there was something amiss, a curious design to the cabinet.

'The space in the drawers doesn't agree with the size.'

'How do you mean?' Sophie asked.

'It's much larger than the space available in the drawers. There has to be something behind the rear wooden panelling'

Moving the cabinet, together they slid it back from the wall. Kneeling at the rear panel, placing his ear close to the wood, Alex tapped his knuckles against the pine. It gave a muffled hollow sound. Unsure he tapped the sides of the cabinet.

'Yes, there's space at the back about a foot in depth I would say.'

Alex tried to remove the drawers but found them immoveable beyond their normal length. 'Sophia we'll have to break open the back of this thing, can you find something to help us.'

Locking the room they searched for and found a claw hammer in a stable toolbox, and returning broke through the rear of the cabinet panelling. As Alex had suspected there was a concealed space behind the drawers and inside, on its side to fit neatly into the area they found a carved box. A magnificent artefact it was inlaid with ivory, silver and numerous gemstones.

Sophia took the casket from the cabinet and placed it on the marble table top to look at it carefully. 'Medieval period, carved in the Mediterranean region,' she said softly.

Lifting the box Alex shook it gently. They could hear the sound of something inside but they found no way of opening the casket.

'We will have to break it open, I'm afraid,' Alex concluded.

'No, no, wait,' Sophia pleaded. 'There, look that tiny hole, it's a spring lock, I've seen it before on this type of artefact.'

Using the pin of a brooch Sophia thrust it into the hole and the box top clicked open. There in front of them was a book wrapped in an embroidered cloth. Fastidiously unfolding the linen cloth Sophia froze in wonder as she exposed an antiquarian vellum tome.

'This is it Alex. I know it is.' Sophia said softly, opening the pages.

'Let's take it back with us to Barrington. We can photograph it and inspect it without any interference.' Alex suggested.

In Alex's study at Barrington they once more opened the box and carefully laid the mysterious volume on a desk. Its vellum pages, delicately brittle and yellowing, were filled with magnificent images of medieval art. Opposite on a separate page each illustration was accompanied by a short passage written in a language Sophia couldn't decipher. It was as she had recalled all those years from her childhood, illustrations of women from many different cultures.

On one page was the image Sophia had remembered so clearly, 'The Goddess of Wisdom,' and the name Sophia written in Greek beneath it in brilliantly coloured, medieval scroll, calligraphy.

Reaching the final pages of the book, incongruously, the last two images changed in context to two enigmatic engravings, one of the Holy Shroud of Turin beneath which was written in Norman French the name Gules du Bois; the other was of a woman dressed in Mediterranean attire. Above the engraving was written 'Wisdom' and below, written, in Latin, 'Mary'.

'What are they and why so important to your father?' Alex asked eagerly.

'That I don't know is the simple answer but I do recognise some of these pictures, they are goddesses of fertility, and renewal, and, perhaps for our purpose, more importantly wisdom.' Sophie turned over the pages of the book. 'Athena, Astarte, Tara, Isis, Aphrodite, Venus. The others I am not sure of and here is a mystery the Magdalen.'

'Why would the Magdalen be among them?' Alex asked confused.

'The Medieval Church worshipped the Magdalen more than the Virgin Mary. There were hundreds of churches built in her honour. She was with Christ at some of the most important events, at the raising of Lazarus for instance and he appeared to her before anyone else at the tomb though not all agree about that.'

'But why among a list of goddesses and why wisdom? She was supposed to be a prostitute.'

'The accusation of prostitution was a ploy of the early church to destroy the power of the fertility goddesses, widely worshipped in the ancient world. They were after all mostly images of female promiscuity. My guess is Magdalene was a substitute for a fertility goddess just as the Virgin Mary was substituted for Isis and an Earth Mother goddess. Even the same images were used, in the substitution, to capture the minds of the people. The image of the Virgin and child are simply the ancient image of Isis and Horus. The image of the Magdalene seems to be, though I'm not quite sure, equating the Magdalen with fertility and wisdom.'

Alex was completely out of depth, fields of religion and mythology were subjects he knew nothing of, which had never interested him. He realised then that the puzzle they were trying to unravel would rest entirely, for the time being, on Sophia's ability to interpret the medieval mind that had created this remarkable piece of art.

'I need to copy these pictures so that I can research them further.' Sophie requested.

'I can photograph the whole book right now and print the illustrations off. We can then enhance any image you want this evening or later.' Alex offered.

Fixing his camera onto a tripod, directly over the manuscript, and using a cable shutter trigger to copy every image in the book under different lighting and shutter speeds, Alex obtained multiple images.

The Green Goddess

Satisfied with their painstaking work they closed the book and sealed it in its box.

That night Sophia stayed with Alex at Barrington and the following day they visited Lord Henry. Her father had made no progress and was in truth much worse. Shenley however had recovered remarkably and was back home from hospital and seated in a wheelchair.

'It all has to do with the Green Woman you know.' Shenley said echoing Sophia's own words.

'How?' Sophia wondered if his conclusions were the same as her own.

'These break-ins, mother being killed and now this to me and Kevin.'

'And what do you think they're after?'

'There's something hidden here to do with the Green Woman. That's why they've searched the place and were prepared to kill to get it.'

'What do you think it is then?' Sophia repeated her question.

'No idea, but what I do know is, the Green Woman is not just a myth she's a living power. There's a secret to it these people are after.'

'Or perhaps just its value in money,' Alex interrupted

'That too perhaps,' Shenley replied thoughtfully. 'I often wonder if on the day mother died if

I hadn't been with my aunt maybe I'd be under a stone in the church too.'

'Do you believe you are part of this mystery?' Alex asked, alert now to a new possibility.

'I'm not sure. Father told me when I was a boy that I was part of a great secret that when I was older he would explain to me. He never has though. He may have been just filling me with wonder about the future of course, the way children are told fairy stories and encouraged to believe in Xmas but I've never known him lie about anything.' Shenley stared out of the windows to the green fields. 'Now in his present state there's very little chance I'll ever find out.'

'Father isn't dying, he will get better,' Sophie said, reprovingly, her violet eyes narrowing.

'He doesn't want to get better, dear Sophie,' Shenley replied softly. 'The last words he spoke to me were, 'I've failed.' He's just given up you see.'

'Then we'll have to give him a reason to recover,' Alex said.

Driving her back to Barrington Alex was so silent that Sophia asked him, 'What is troubling you?'

Hesitant, unsure of what he should say Alex didn't answer immediately then flicking a gaze at her said, 'There's something I need to tell you. The images in the book, I've seen wall paintings very much like them.'

'Oh! Where? Sophia asked surprised at this new information.

'In caves beneath Henley Church,' Alex confessed.

Alex uneasy at the questions she fired at him like a salvo explained. 'I didn't mention it to you because I promised Owen not to and I didn't see any connection with the events at Henley or your father's society.'

That night, on Sophia's insistence, they entered Henley Church. She was surprisingly strong and agile, in her excitement and impatience, in helping him move the marble altar and trap door. Their progress to the central chamber of the green statue was achieved expeditiously in Sophia's adrenaline surged enthusiasm.

'Many of these wall paintings are exact copies of the ones in father's book, Astarte, Athena, Isis, Maat, Tiamat, and look, here's the Magdalen. This *has* to be one of the ancient temples he told you of, where father's secret society has met for centuries.'

In the central chamber Sophia stood, as he had done, overcome with surprise and wonder at the statue of the Green Woman.

'It is not only the most beautiful work of art but it exudes such power and dominance.' Sophia exclaimed excitedly.

'Be careful. When I touched the marble I was thrown to the floor.' Alex warned. 'Let's move on Sophia. I think these caves too oppressive.'

Alex led her further into the labyrinth following the tunnels from memory but now he noticed even more passageways that he decided sometime would need further exploration. In one of these, as he paused to pierce the gloom, he saw the same dim light shining in the distance, that he had seen before, as though from a candle or lamp.

Eventually after negotiating the strenuous climb that led to the petrified wooden door they opened it to the fresh smell of woodland in the central glade of Druids Hill. A brilliant moon, sliding behind a torn blanket of cloud, shyly lit up the green hollow.

They woke at Barrington to bright sunlight flooding through edges of the curtains. Sophia rose first, dressed and went downstairs leaving him in a half sleep laziness. He was startled from his lethargy by a cry of alarm followed by the sound of Sophia's feet running up the stairs. Now fully awake, and already out of bed, at her call he ran to the door.

Sophia met him at the top of the stairs and clung to him. 'Alex, someone has broken in. They've stolen father's book.'

Alex photo studio hadn't been destroyed, the thieves, it seemed, had known exactly what they were after. The photographs he had printed of the cave paintings and the Green Woman had all gone. Foolishly, in hindsight, he'd left them on a table spread out for studying and left them for all to see. His small library had been ransacked and the illuminated book was missing.

They waited for the police and drank coffee, both chiding themselves for their unforgivable incompetence and lack of caution.

'All isn't lost, Sophia, I still have the digital card of photos from my camera. It's fortunate we copied them. The book may have gone but not what we needed from it.' He tried to console her.

'I can't possibly tell father.' Sophia moaned. 'It would be the last straw'.

'No need to.' He comforted. 'The best thing we can do is to find that relic of his. There's no time to waste now the thieves know almost as much as we do.'

Sophia agreed tearfully.

Later that morning Miriam, Alex's cleaning lady, greeted them as she entered with her own key.

Alex faced her squarely. 'Miriam, yesterday we left a valuable illuminated book here. Did you see it at all?'

Abashed at his pointed interrogation Miriam cringed in embarrassment. 'I did see it Mr Roedale on your table.'

'Did you tell anyone about it at all?'

For a while Miriam stood silently then said, 'I did mention it to Mr Ralph. He wanted to know if you had been doing research on Druids Hill and if there was anything to do with his family.'

Alex didn't scold but as he walked away he told himself she would have to go.

CHAPTER TWENTY FOUR

Jan Modjeski greeted him, at his mountain home, in the Sierra foothills.
'Glad to see you Alex. I never thought we'd meet again.'

Jan a renowned Polish artist was also professor of mythology and Jungian analysis at Berkley. They had met by chance years before in Vienna. Jan had invited Alex to visit him at his California home and over the years repeated the invitation and now, Alex thought, seemed the appropriate moment. He felt fortunate to know Jan. If anyone could solve the riddle of the cave goddesses and the Green Woman

Jan could. and, hopefully, help unravel the mystery of the ancient society connected with them. Most libraries carried books written by him on the subject of dreams and their relationship to the myths of the world.

They were interrupted by the entrance of a lithe, slender, lanky young woman, smiling graciously at Alex whom Jan introduced as his American girl friend, Dusty.

'While Dusty gets dinner let me show you the property.' Jan offered proudly.

The two hundred acre property in rock strewn low chaparral, of the vast California Sierras was an unspoilt wilderness. Over the brow of a hill a lake shone in the late afternoon filled with fish that thronged the banks when Jan approached the water.

'I bought this whole acreage for forty three thousand dollars then built my home with my own hands. It's worth millions now. We have a few goats running round, Dusty prefers goat milk, an' they keep the brush short. What I liked about the place was the great Sequoia trees further down the valley and the old, Valley Oaks. They're heat resistant you know yet grow larger than their European cousins.'

The land was crowned with pine forests scattered over the hills. Jan pointed out prickly red poppy and spring larkspur already in bloom. In the distance Alex could see an eagle in the pellucid, cloudless sky.

'Turkey vulture,' Jan explained, 'quite common. If you're lucky you might see deer, coyote and mountain lion. They cross here on the way to the Merced River.'

'I look forward to it.'

'You will see them mostly morning and late evening. I've an observation tower at the back of the house and a telescope.'

On the way back to the cabin Jan said, 'When you rang from England you mentioned needing my help.'

'Yes, an unusual problem. I have no idea where to start with it. I thought your studies in mythology and research in the subject could help me.'

'Let's have dinner and we'll talk about it when Dusty's out.' Jan smiled. 'We have three quarter horses and she rides for exercise most evenings. That's probably the best time. You could join us I know you're a great horseman.'

A flaming sunset embraced the mountains like a red blanket as they walked back across the foothills. Sitting at a red wood bench and table, overlooking the blue Sierra hills, Alex spread out the photos taken in the Henley caverns and beside them laid the photocopies from Lord Henry's illuminated book.

'These are what I want to see you about Jan.'

Jan peered at each of the photos in turn, stroked his red short beard and looked away, into the far mountain reaches, before speaking.

'Interesting and you say these are all wisdom goddesses?'

'Mostly, I would say.'

'Well you are right. I have never seen such a lovely collection. You must have travelled far to get them.' Jan was fishing for details.

'All in one place, except these ones copied from the book I told you about. I have no idea why the Magdalene and the Turin shroud are among them though. That's one thing I want to ask you.'

'The wisdom goddesses are easily explained.' Jan stretched his hands behind his head and leaned back. 'Prior to six hundred BC all religion was based on a multiplicity of gods and goddesses, with two supreme deities, one representing the male aspect of creation, the other female. The two supposedly had equal power, however there's a lot of evidence to show the feminine, mother aspect, had the edge since she was the one who gave birth to all things including the male gods. Zoroaster came along introducing a sole, male deity. This has always been, predominantly, a Middle Eastern concept since then. In the fareast

God had no gender. Male and female deities were and are given equal reverence as aspects of the one soul. Judaism took much from Zoroastrian religion, adopting a sole male deity as God. You might like to know I've collected, over the years, much evidence to suggest Jesus was probably a follower of Zoroaster,' Jan added.

'But where does wisdom come in?' Alex didn't want to be side tracked into Jan's pet theories.

'Patience Alex', Jan chided, laughing delightedly. 'First let's have one of our vibrant California wines, straight from the Napa.'

Jan thrust a flagon of red wine and two large glasses on the table, 'One of the benefits of living here, lovely cheap wine, the best in the world.'

They relaxed in the falling sunset while Jan continued at his own leisured pace.

'Judaism and of course the other two religions based on it, Christianity and Islam did their utmost to eradicate all memory of a female deity. Gods and goddesses you know come from a universal unconscious. That's why dreams and myths all over the world are similar in content and story line, even among peoples who have never had any historical connections whatever. The mother of creation is a living reality in the unconscious of the world, and in the soul of man and these religions tried to destroy it.

'Are you saying these gods and goddesses are real?'

'Yes, in a way they are powerful subconscious forces in all of us. Not only I say so but Jung propounded the idea as one of his foremost principles of the unconscious. They link every one of us to the universal soul of all creation. A modern example is the Roman Catholic and Church of England in which the Virgin is a carry- over from Isis and the Great Mother Goddess Minerva. I was born in Poland you know that, to me the greatest Polish composer is Gorecki. In his third symphony the words to the second movement are,

"Mother, do not weep most chaste Queen of Heaven. Support me always. Ave Maria."

These words were also written by a young Jewish girl on the wall of her Gestapo prison. I tell you this to emphasise that the Catholic Church and the Church of England are direct descendants of the Judaic priesthood. It is everywhere obvious, if you care to look, their churches built like the Temple in Jerusalem, the sacrament tent, the Holy of Holies, the manna from heaven, the Eucharist bread, a place for the High Priest, the altar, and a separate one for the people.'

'I don't understand. The Jews, of all people, never believed in a goddess alongside Jehovah.' Alex had lost the trend of the argument.

The Green Goddess

Jan shook his head but before he could reply the conversation was interrupted by a thud of horse hooves on the hard pan chaparral, as Dusty, horse flecked with foam, cantered up, reined in and dismounted beside them. She'd been riding hard, breathlessly she blurted out. 'There are two men, in the valley, coming this way. I didn't like the look of either of them. One is carrying a rifle with telescopic sight. If they're hunting they shouldn't be on our land, should they Jan? But really they don't look like hunters to me.'

'Did they say anything?' Jan questioned.

'No. I didn't give them a chance, one look at their eyes was enough especially the one with the rifle. He looked foreign.'

'Maybe they're just lost,' Jan said unconvincingly.

'Jan, please they are dangerous, I know it. One of them began to raise his rifle when he saw me, that's why I raced up here. I think I am lucky to be alive.'

Jan jumped up from his seat. 'Unleash the dogs Dusty. I'll ring the Sheriff.'

Turning to Alex, frowning, he apologised, 'I'm sorry about this, we do get hikers but never with guns.'

Dusty ran to a rear door. Alex heard the yelping of dogs as they were set free. In the distance the dogs were barking wildly, and then a gun shot, muffled by the trees, shocked the woods into silence.

Alex didn't say anything but in his heart felt apprehensive that perhaps these men had followed him in the hope of finding the mysterious relic.

Jan led to the woods beyond the lake, a shotgun hanging loosely in his right hand. They found one of the dogs dead; blood oozing from its head and side, the other dog could be heard barking some three hundred yards or more in the distance.

'We'd better wait for the police', Alex warned.

'Yes, you're right. Who knows who they are, or capable of.' Jan looked down sadly at the lifeless dog. 'A good old boy', Jan said sadly, 'I'll have to leave him here for the Sheriff. Dusty will be devastated.'

Overhead a police helicopter was flying to and fro across the foothills. Then in the distance the sound of more gun fire echoed across the hills. The helicopter disappeared into the distance.

Five hours later they were answering questions to the Merced County Sheriff.

'They shot one of the Park Rangers we'd called in to track them, they know these mountains and woods better than anyone, and caught up with them at North Fork. One Ranger's dead but before they shot him he managed to wound one of 'em badly. Left a trail of blood. He won't get far you can be sure o' that.'

The Green Goddess

Looking at Alex, suspiciously, the Sheriff asked. 'Do you have any idea who these men are?'

'No idea.' He wasn't going to mention his own conjectures or raise more investigations.

'Strange, you visit here then these men show up. You're foreign aren't you? So are they, from what the lady tells us.'

'A coincidence, America is full of foreigners.' Jan butted in sarcastically.

A mobile phone rang. The Sheriff lifted it from his sleeve. 'At least that's something,' he answered, 'any news of the other one.' There was a long pause. 'I see.'

Ending the call the Sheriff shook his head in disbelief as he addressed Jan. 'They found one of the men dead, the one shot by the ranger, but he looks like he was shot again in the head, mostly likely by the man he was with. He had no ID on him and his partner's missing.'

Two days passed but the police still had no information or clues about the men or their identity. The killer had got away in a stolen car and abandoned it at a private airport.

'Jan I will have to leave,' Alex said over breakfast. 'The police don't need me any longer. It's probably safer for you both if I go.'

Jan looked up from the table surprise registering on his face.

'The men who came here, I believe in spite of what I said to the police, were looking for me.' Alex recounted the recent attacks at Henley.

'You think all this is connected to the photos you showed me? Some kind of mystery?'

'Yes.'

'And you suppose it has to do with this goddess of wisdom.'

'I'm certain of it and the images and statue of the Green Woman in the photos.'

'Intriguing,' Jan puzzled, looking up at the ceiling. 'Last time we spoke of this you said, surely the Jews didn't believe in a goddess. Well, as a matter of fact they did.'

Alex looked at his friend in surprise. 'Another key to the puzzle.'

'If you are determined to leave I want to at least clear up some of your questions. The god of the Bible is a vengeful god, demanding blood sacrifice for sin, a very primitive idea really, a god that punishes severely any breaking of his laws. He is the sole power and there's no escape. The human psyche can't live under this subjugation. To evolve we need freedom to grow our own way. In order to counter the severity of this tyrannical male deity, the Bible introduces the powerful goddess who was there when the world was created, and here's the point, she is no other than the Goddess of Wisdom. A Goddess who brings peace and happiness and prosperity to all who worship her.'

'Admittedly I am not the religious kind but that is the first time I ever heard of such a thing?'

'She's found throughout the bible, especially the Book of Proverbs and the apocryphal book Ecclesiasticus, where we are told she was with God when he created all things. In other words he needed her beside him to accomplish the task. She was obviously considered his equal.'

'And in Christianity?' Alex asked.

'The god of the New Testament is no less bloodthirsty than in Judaism, "Without the shedding of blood there is no remission for sin." As a punishment for sin we are asked to believe Jesus had to be tortured and murdered. Would anyone in their right mind want to believe that? To alleviate this repulsive image, we have the Virgin Mary, the Mother of God, someone kindly and loving whom men can turn to for help. To be pragmatic about it, in the Roman Catholic Church at least, she is the predominant figure of the two.'

'Most people in England are protestant so I doubt if the Roman Church has much to do with these mysteries I've come across.'

'Not if the mystery you speak of is older than five hundred years. Before that all of England was

Catholic. Something the Church tried very much to cover up is the prominence of the female disciples of Jesus yet the bible is full of references to Jesus' female entourage. The gospel of John, it has been proposed, was written by Mary Magdalene. I doubt that. Personally I think it was the Virgin Mary who wrote it because there are stories in that gospel that no one else could have known about. It also contains more passages about love than any other gospel. Definitely a woman author, then the Book of Hebrews, some believe, was written by Prisca, a woman companion of Paul. It's easy to see how a male dominated Church, which forbade women to preach, would hide these facts.'

'The images I saw pre-date Judaism and Christianity.' Alex interrupted.

'Jesus, my research suggests, was a follower of Zoroaster and brought Zoroastrian beliefs into Judaism. When he was born, three Magi from Iran came to see his birth. The Zoroastrians believe in a number of saviours coming into the world, Jesus was one of them and expected at that time. After the slaughter of the innocents by Herod Jesus's parents took him to Egypt. The only city he could have gone to is Alexandria, a meeting place of all the great religions of the world at that time, Judaism, Hinduism, Buddhism, Zoroastrianism, Greek philosophy, and numerous cults, besides being the greatest seat of learning in the known world. At Alexandria was one of the seven wonders, Alexander's Light house. It was called, 'The Light of the World,' by those who had seen it. Jesus called himself 'The Light of the World,' and light was also a major part of the Zoroastrian belief as typifying all good, and god himself.'

'What does all this have to do with goddesses of wisdom?' Alex asked impatiently, doubtful where this discussion was leading.

'Zoroaster received his commission and guidance from a spirit, Vohu-mano, the Goddess of Wisdom. The virgin in the Bible, the Mother of God, is no other than the ancient Goddess of Wisdom in a new form.'

'Let me get this straight. You are saying the goddess of wisdom was the most powerful deity and her worship goes back further than the god of the Jews, that the Jews themselves worshipped her and even in Christianity she is worshipped as the Virgin Mary'

'I believe so,' Jan raised his arms in success, 'and not only that but in Christianity, at least in the RC Church, she is the "Mother of God." Your friend Sophia thought the drawing, at the back of the book you found, was a mediaeval image of the Magdalen because of the name Mary underneath it. I believe she's very close to the truth, but nevertheless wrong. Mary in that drawing might well be the Virgin.'

'Why do you think so?'

'A similar mistake was made by writers and artists for centuries. Take Da Vinci's 'Last Supper'. It's been suggested the figure of John is none other than a woman. We know Da Vinci *was* a homosexual, and many of his male images are feminised, but in my opinion that doesn't completely explain it. Some art historians believe the figure is really Mary Magdalene. I don't believe that either. Let me show you something that contradicts those ideas.'

Going to his bookcase and taking out a volume of Da Vinci's paintings, Jan flicked through the pages, pausing at a photo of The Last Supper. Pointing his finger at the image, in enthusiasm, he turned the book around for Alex to see as he stood beside his chair. 'Look, this is John, now in your mind's eye take out the rest of the picture entirely.' Jan covered the picture with his fingers so that only the head of John was visible. 'What do you have?'

'Well, definitely a woman I think.'

'Yes, quite obviously but it is not the Magdalen.'

'Who then?' Alex asked looking up at Jan quizzically.

'It's a portrait of the Madonna, as painted by many artists before Da Vinci and what's more in a recogniseable pose looking down on the child Jesus.'

Staring more closely at the image Alex asked, 'Why would Da Vinci have put the Virgin in the painting?

'Because she is Jesus' mother. Da Vinci put it there for symbolic reasons.'

When Alex didn't answer Jan asked, 'Still not convinced?'

From a bookcase Jan took down another volume, searched the index, and opened a page for Alex to look at.

'This is a fourteenth century painting from Bohemia of the Virgin holding her child. The head and the angle of the head is exactly the same as the one in Da Vinci's painting and pre dates it. There compare them, apart from the colours of the clothes there is no difference whatever.'

Reaching up for another volume Jan opened it.

'This is a book of paintings by Russian artists. Look at this painting, 'The Appearance of Christ,' and that figure,' Jan pointed at one of the images, 'Is John the Divine. Is that a man or a woman?'

'No doubt about it, it's a woman.'

'This artist was Ivanov, a Russian, but here is an interesting thing he spent the latter part of his life in Rome. These artists were introducing the Mother of God into their paintings so that no one would forget her importance and only the initiated would understand the symbol.'

'Maybe you're right but I'm not competent to say and what about my photos of the Green Goddess? Where do they come in this?'

'Very simply all these paintings in your photos are Earth Mother figures. The great mother creator of all living things is your Green Woman.'

'The Virgin Mary is an Earth Mother figure like the Green Woman?'

'Now you understand.'

'You tell a marvellous story,' Alex laughed still sceptical.

'You asked for my help Alex. The answer you are looking for, I believe, lies in these concepts. You know it's a great pity you won't tell me more.'

'The less you know the safer you are Jan believe me.'

Like a gust of wind portending a storm Dusty bounced in to disturb them.

'Please come back soon Alex,' she said wrapping her arms around him, 'Jan said you were leaving. I'm sorry about all this.' Alex couldn't help detecting through the lack of warmth in her embrace she was happy to see him leave.

His bags stashed in the boot of a car he took one lonely look at the idyllic setting of Jan's home, with its Walden Pond peacefulness, and departed for England.

CHAPTER TWENTY FIVE

Sophia was at the airport. Hugging her, happy to see her, Alex asked, 'Any good news.' Some was definitely due.

'Not much, Shen is improving slowly. Daddy is fairly comatose, doesn't speak to anyone.'

Using side roads on the way back to Barrington he told Sophie what had happened in California.

'We are probably being followed right now,' he thought aloud.

'I think I have been since you left. I can't be certain, just little troubling suspicions, the same car in places it shouldn't be and when I tried to see who the driver was the car always drove away.'

It was late by the time they reached Barrington. Both of them were tired. Perhaps he imagined it but something was wrong, the wild pigeons, which roosted in the trees near the house, should have flapped frantically at the sound of their car on the gravel drive but everything was deathly silent. There was something else, but he couldn't quite put a finger on it, that made him feel uneasy, then it came to him. The security lights hadn't come on, when he approached the drive, and the night light that came on automatically, inside the Hall at sunset, was not shining through the windows. Probably a power surge, all the same after California this was no time to be complacent.

'Stay in the car, I will have to check the fuse box.' Alex said, in a voice Sophia knew was both a warning and tolerated no objections.

Quietly walking around Barrington perimeter remaining below window sill level where necessary Alex moved to the small side windows from which he was sure he could safely observe the rooms. Everything appeared as normal, until he came to the rear of the kitchen. His heart faltered in horror.

The figure of a man, standing motionless, waiting, was distinctly reflected in the glass of a unit cupboard. Alex quickly dropped out of sight.

Using perimeter hedges as a cover he raced back to Sophia. To his consternation she was no longer there. Women he thought. The car door was open but no sign of her anywhere. Alex peered into the dark, searching for her, but could detect no movement anywhere. This discovery threw him into a quandary. He couldn't call out and give the intruder, a warning, yet at the same time the man must have known, by the headlights and the sound of the car on the gravel, they were there. That of course was why he was waiting for them, silently, in the darkened room. He begged fate Sophia would stay away from the house. Where the hell was she?

Somewhere down the lane he heard a vehicle pulling away but paid no attention to it.

Quietly releasing the boot of his car Alex slid a shotgun out of its canvas cover. From a cartridge box he removed half a dozen cartridges, loaded two into the gun barrel and dropped the rest into his coat pocket. Wrapping the gun in a cagoule from the back seat of the car he held it over his left arm as though carrying his coat and shopping to the house.

His entrance had to be one of surprise, from a direction the burglar would not expect. That would give him momentary advantage. At what had once been the Servants Quarters he gently slid the key into the lock and opened the door. Sliding his hand to the light switch, as he had suspected, the power to Barrington had been cut off.

Squatting to his haunches, he clicked the door shut. At least he knew where the intruder was. That was in his favour, and he hoped the man was alone. His fear was Sophia might be in the house, by now. Why on earth hadn't she listened to him?

Barrington unchanged over the centuries retained an ample kitchen with several doors, one once led to the servants quarters, another to a cold cellar and yet another to the dining room. He guessed the interloper, would never expect him to enter through the scullery.

Reaching the kitchen door, waiting, his heart racing and thudding against his rib cage, Alex threw himself into the room, adrenaline heightening his senses, and dropped immediately to the floor.

Taken completely off guard the intruder froze then fired a gun wildly in Alex's direction, and missed, the bullets flying well above Alex's position.

Blinded by the gun flash, Alex took aim and fired both barrels in its direction. There was a cry, the thud of a body against a wall and a heavy fall to the floor.

Rolling aside, and bracing himself on one knee shotgun ready, Alex waited in the deathly silence of the room listening for any movement or any sound but none came not the man's breath or groans, nothing.

After what seemed hours, but was probably less than five minutes, Alex rose, searched the kitchen drawers for a torch and looked at the motionless body. The man's eyes were wide open, a shocked grimace sculptured on his face. Both shots had hit him squarely in the chest. A gaping hole stained the man's clothes with a copious flow of blood.

Alex's immediate concern was not for the deed done, he felt no remorse or regret, but for Sophia. He called her name at the top of his lungs, walking down the corridors, but no answer and he knew she couldn't be anywhere in Barrington Hall.

Going outside he shouted her name again, 'Sophie, Sophie.' No reply.

Searching the car he found no signs indicating a struggle or where she had gone to. Everything in the moonless night was as silent as the man in Barrington kitchen.

He wouldn't, couldn't explain to either Shenley or Lord Allan that Sophie had gone missing, it would most certainly, in Lord Allan's case, have been the last straw. His last words to Lord Allan he remembered was the promise he would protect her.

He had to ring the police immediately.

Detective Inspector Taylor, of the Valley Police, came thirty minutes later with a female detective named Porter who looked for all the world like an all in wrestler. Glancing over the body Taylor rang forensics.

'Did you move the man or search his belongings?' Taylor enquired.

'In no way.'

'You have no idea where Lady Allan is?' Porter interrupted.

'If I did I wouldn't be here, talking to you would I?'

'Why was the man waiting in the house with a gun?' Taylor looked at him suspiciously

'This, I have no idea of either, I suppose he intended robbing the place and heard the car arrive.' He wasn't going to discuss what he knew with anyone.

'Why didn't you ring us when you saw the man inside?'

'And wait for you? So far, with all respect, the police haven't done much to stop these local violent robberies have they?

Ignoring the remark Taylor asked, 'Did you argue with Lady Allan?'

'Not at all.'

'She couldn't just have got out of the car and left you in a huff?'

'No she didn't,' Alex answered exasperatedly, 'nor did she have reason to.'

'There is a possibility someone's kidnapped her for a ransom. Robbers don't usually show up with guns. This man, from what you tell me, sounds like a professional. We'll know more when forensics have done their job. In the meantime do you have anywhere to stay? We have to cordon the house. It will take a few days. By the way don't leave the area until we know what happened here. If anyone rings you asking for money let us handle it.'

'If they want ransom they'll be talking to Henley Hall not me.' Alex pointed out the obvious.

'You have somewhere to stay while we are here?'

'I'll find somewhere. Keep in mind Lord Allan and his son are seriously ill.'

'I'm aware of that. Since you came here we've had nothing but trouble Mr Roedale. If Lady Allan phones you let me know immediately. Detective Porter here will take your statement.'

Alex hardly slept. For three days anxiety tugged his concentration away from all he tried to accomplish. Eventually a call from the police confirmed they had completed their investigation, and he could now return home, but it didn't feel like home after all that had happened.

Meetings with publishers he cancelled indefinitely and for the first time in his life he was depressed.

The morning was bright but cool. A rainy night had left the fields around Barrington smelling of the earth and blossom. Puddles shone alongside the gravel driveway. In his office Alex took out the photos of the cavern paintings and the Green Woman. He couldn't see anything new in them. The will to find any answer had left him. His only thoughts were of Sophia.

He was suddenly disturbed by the Barrington door bell ringing impatiently dragging him away from his morbidity. Opening the door he found Tamara Thomas smiling at him.

'Can I come in?' She held out her hand. Her fingers were long and delicate in his.

'Forgive me. Yes of course, please do. You are always welcome.' He felt relieved to have someone to speak to.

'Drink?' he asked as she sat down on the nearest chair.

'Only coffee this time in the morning, parishioners you know.'

Tamara, folded her long, trouser clad limbs, and rested her fingers on her knees, waiting for him to speak then aware of his sadness she said. 'I know a little of what you must be going through at the moment. It's like a death isn't it? But at least you have hope.'

She got up and walked over to the window. With her back to him she looked towards Druids Hill.

'You saw me that night in May on the hill didn't you? She asked in a soft, resigned voice.

'Yes.'

'Yet you are not judgmental.'

The Green Goddess

'No. Your life is your own. I have no right or inclination to interfere.'

'A civilised viewpoint,' Tamara said. Looking at Druids Hill she remained quiet for a moment then said, 'We believe a goddess lives there. Druids Hill is her shrine. What you saw that day was an age old celebration of her existence. Many of us, I don't say all, worship in the ancient way as the giver of life, the mother of all creation. We enact a drama of the creative power of the universe. Owen doesn't of course believe any of it, well he wouldn't, and he doesn't have a clue about what happens on Druids.'

'If you came to explain to me, I assure you, I will never tell anyone.'

Turning to Alex Tamara stared into his eyes. 'Thank you, but no I didn't come for that purpose, just to see how you are. To be alone without someone to talk to isn't good for you. You can stay with us at the Vicarage if you would like.'

'Its kind but I feel she may ring me here and I have to sort out some problems we were working on together. What do you know of the Green Woman?'

Returning to her seat, Tamara leaned forward and asked eagerly, 'Did she come to you?'

'In a dream the same night we saw you on Druids.'

Tamara clapped her hands in delight.

'Ah! She is calling you. This is the most wonderful thing.' Tamara laughed in pleasure.

'I've had nothing but trouble since.'

'It is good news believe me. You don't understand yet but you will.'

Alex felt as if he was in a Hitchcock movie.

'Tell me more about this cult or religion, or whatever it is you call it.'

'I could talk all day about that. We are so fortunate to have one of her shrines here so close by. You know, we are a world-wide religious group but we never seek proselytes they are always chosen by the goddess herself, that's why I think it's so marvellous she came to you.'

What kind of organisation is it?

'How do you mean?'

'There has to be a hierarchy to give orders, arrange events and so on.'

'Oh! Yes of course. We are just like all religions we have a priesthood and masters at the top. I suppose though people like me and the others, you saw on Druids Hill, are just the ordinary, cannon fodder, followers. I'm sure there's much that happens we never hear about. We aren't told everything.'

'Why not?' Alex probed.

The Green Goddess

'Secrecy, surely you can understand. Can you imagine the furore it would cause if the Church knew anything about us?'

'Yes, I see. Tell me does this cult, you belong to, have anything to do with wisdom goddesses?'

Frowning, puzzled by his question, or suspicious of it, Tamara said, 'I don't know what you mean. Why do you ask?'

Alex knew she was lying.

'What are the attributes of this goddess you worship? I mean why do you worship her?

'She is a reality, a power to those who believe in her, she is all, guides us and helps us.'

Tamara smiling, turning her head to look through the window at Druids Hill, Alex thought her pretty, adolescent, teasing, ultra feminine.

'The order has higher beliefs and interests than the things you saw. It is a journey from our physical nature to a spiritual one to the ultimate union with all of life. She is real you know. She does exist, as I'm certain you believe by now.'

Tamara asked more seriously.

'What are you going to do about Sophia?'

'I'm waiting for the police.'

'Go to the church. Before there was a church at Henley there was a shrine to the goddess on the site, that's why masons incorporated her effigy into the building. Ask her to help you. I have no doubt she will guide you.'

'In a church?' Alex questioned, at the same time thinking that was why the caverns were below Henley Church

'Yes, we believe she was supreme from the beginning. Henley Church was her shrine long before the arrival of Christianity so that's the place to find her.'

CHAPTER TWENTY SIX

Outside Barrington Hall, alone in the dark, Sophia had no awareness of the drama being enacted inside the house. She heard gunfire, muffled and distant. Alarmed by the sound frantically she searched for her mobile phone but before she could ring she was interrupted by a sharp tapping on the car window. Opening the door quickly she cried,

'Alec, I was so worried.'

The face was masked, terrifying in its sudden appearance.

By the time realised her mistake it was too late.

Someone gripped her arm tightly, painfully, forcefully pulling her from the vehicle so roughly her blouse tore and she fell to the hard gravel of the forecourt. A man was bending over her pressing a cloth to her mouth. It smelled strongly of chloroform or some chemical. Sophia noticed it as she dropped into unconsciousness.

The room, she awoke in, looked like a converted cellar. Walls were painted green, in a corner was a washbasin, adjoining it a toilet. A small window, high up was barred and she guessed it was ground level. Lying on a bed, she was still dressed in the clothes of the night before. Looking for a way to escape she noticed the only door to the room was steel and probably securely bolted. Beside the bed were two chairs facing her as though someone had been watching her. No attempt had been made to bind her hands or feet to the bed. They were sure she couldn't escape. On a bedside table there was a tumbler of water and a glass next to it. Sophia's head throbbed and she felt nauseous. Pouring a glass of water she sniffed and tasted it carefully. Satisfied, she drank greedily and it was a mistake, the shock of the fluid on her stomach made her retch. Jumping off the bed she vomited into the basin and continued to heave convulsively. Darkness closed her eyes and she collapsed to the floor. How long she remained there she couldn't tell but when she woke she was no longer on the floor but once again on the bed.

She didn't notice him, he was so still, sitting on a chair near the door. The moment she became aware of him she was filled with terror. An uncontrollable fear made her tremble. Turning away she hid her face in her pillow and sobbed.

'Don't be afraid,' the man said in a calm, almost nonchalant, voice.

Looking back at him, observing him more closely, she saw he was dressed entirely in black, a ski mask covering all but his eyes and mouth. There was something, a tone in his voice and the way he sat, that made her instinctively realise she knew him from somewhere.

'I'm not going to hurt you.' the man said firmly, assuring her.

Recovering herself Sophia asked, 'Then what am I doing here?'

'This you will find out. For now, rest. Is there anything I can get you?'

'I need something to eat and coffee.' Sophia replied hardly knowing what to say in her panic. 'You know who I am?'

'Yes.'

'Then you also know it won't be long before they find me. Are you prepared for the consequences of that?'

The man rose without speaking. He was tall and moved with inbred confidence. Taking a key from his pocket he unfastened the door, locked it behind him and left Sophia alone. She heard a second door being opened and locked. What seemed ten minutes passed then the same repetition of doors unlocked and bolted. Again he came into her cell. He held a tray on which a bowl of soup, fruit and a pot of coffee had been prepared. Placing the tray on her bedside table he stood silently staring into her eyes. She froze at his gaze and instinctively moved further away. The guard let out a laugh and left her alone.

Light from a small window near the ceiling shone at a steep angle and she concluded it was noon, other than that she had no idea of time or where she was. There were no sounds outside. The window was double glazed, perhaps sound proofed in some way. If she screamed her loudest she doubted if anyone would hear. She stood on the chair but still couldn't reach the window. She had to be in a warehouse perhaps or a Georgian building, because of the height of the ceiling.

Returning to the bed she calmed herself and drank coffee. The man, or someone, had put milk in a tiny jug and there was white and brown sugar in a bowl. The tray, was an expensive piece of silverware. This made her suspect she was most likely in the cellar of a house. Near the ceiling she could make out hollows in the wall that indicated an older residence because those recesses, she was sure, had once held oak beams.

She rested, calming herself by letting go, absorbed in a melancholy mood that swung between fear and determination. Her kidnapping would by now have been reported.

What had happened to Alex? She recalled the gunshots and was as fearful for him as herself. She thought of Marston, her wild, unpredictable brother. If he found her they would pay for it dearly. Jumping from the bed she tried frantically to find a way of escape from the room but her few attempts ended always in defeat, she couldn't reach the window and the door seemed impregnable.

Evening came and the light faded from the window. She heard noises beyond the room, the sound of doors being unbolted.

The first guard came in, followed by two men; one dressed in a similar way to the guard but the other man, with greying hair, wore a white gown and surgical mask. In his hand was a briefcase. Panic ceased Sophia. She ran for the door with all the strength of her fear. The guard nearest to the door caught her easily in his arms and held her, looking deeply into her eyes, and she thought he was reluctant to let her go.

'Stop that, put her on the bed and hold her down,' the man in white said to the guards, speaking in an accent that Sophia thought was either Swiss or German.

They took hold of Sophia's arms. She made no attempt to resist knowing it was useless. One man held her ankles the other forced her arms behind her back, the man in white opened his case and removed a hypodermic and needle. At the sight of this she struggled to break free.

The guard said, 'If you struggle you will make it all the more painful. I have told you we don't intend hurting you.'

'You already are,' Sophia replied fierily. 'If you think you will get away with this you are badly mistaken.'

'I think not. Besides we wish you no harm, all we need is the truth.'

'About what?' Sophia angrily demanded.

'Hold her down,' the white coated medic ordered and drove the needle into her right arm.

She had no idea how long she slept but there was no longer any light through the window. She woke and fell asleep constantly. A guard came in, like a shadow in her dreams, and left food. Later the same man, in white, and the infernal needle. She recalled several times crawling to the wash basin and toilet and back to bed then the comforting, painless, forgetfulness of sleep.

Sophia sat on the edge of the bed drifting in and out of awareness. Two men were sitting in front of her, the first guard and the man in his white smock. She felt outside of her body, listening to herself talking freely in brief, lucid moments but there were gaps in the conversations during which she seemed asleep or not alive at all.

'There were noises downstairs. Mother took my hand. We ran as fast as we could from one room to another, then the library I think. She was dragging me through a hall.' Sophia was saying.

'Was she carrying anything?' The guard asked

She seemed to fall asleep again and woke and was speaking without fear or inhibition.

'Try to remember. What did she have in her hands?'

'I'm sure now, she did have something under her arm, very large wrapped in white cloth. Yes I'm sure.'

The two men looked at each other, smiling in triumph.

'I knew it,' the guard said eagerly.

'And what was under the white cloth?' the interrogator in the smock asked.

'I don't know. I am sure she didn't want the people in the house to find it.'

'What was its shape, can you remember that?'

Sophie drifted away as though day dreaming and then once more into a deep sleep. This time when she woke light flooded into the room from the window and someone had kissed her lips. She was lying supine on the bed, the guard sitting on the mattress beside her. Leaning forward he was looking deeply into her eyes, only a foot away. She recognised those eyes from somewhere even with the mask hiding the man's face.

'Where do I know him from?' Sophia asked not certain whether she mouthed the words or spoke them in the silence of a thought.

The guard lifted her to an upright position and gave her coffee to drink.

At times he seemed kindly, at others cruel, his eyes were cunning, capable of all things.

The door bolts rattled again. The man in white walked in.

'She's ready again?' He asked.

'As far as I know, you're the doctor,' the guard answered caustically.

Ignoring the comment, the man in white said, 'Let's try again then.'

He addressed Sophia, 'You were telling us the shape of the object.'

She felt she had no will of her own and was compelled to answer.

'It was hidden by the white cloth.'

'You said it was large.'

'Yes, like a large box. Oblong or square. Mama had difficulty carrying it.'

'So it was heavy?'

'I don't know. I think it must have been.'

'Where did she put it?'

The two men leaned forward frozen, trying to grasp her every word.

Sophia fell silent, trying to remember. 'I just can't remember. The room was cold and mother was afraid. She held me, told me to remain where I was. It was part of a game, that was the last I ever saw her.' Sophia hung her head, tears cutting wavy rivulets tears down her cheeks. She could smell her mother's perfume, hear her soothing voice, feel the folds of her dress in her hands.

Noticing the guard's concern the doctor said, 'It's nothing. Quite usual, the drug frees repressed emotions.'

'What was this room?' The doctor continued his questions.

'I don't know, a hidden room.'

'A cellar, downstairs, upstairs?' the man in white queried.

'I tried to remember but I can't, only the sound of mother, somewhere else, shouting at someone, calling my father's name.'

Sophie blacked out and fell forward. Had it not been for the guard's swift reaction she would have hit the floor. Catching her by the shoulders he gently rested her back on the bed. 'We're getting nowhere.' He angrily admonished the medic. 'You said this would unlock her memory.'

'I didn't say recover memory, only make her speak the truth of what she knew. There's no drug discovered that will make a person recall something repressed. The experience she endured as a child, the sudden loss of the person she loved most, the events surrounding that loss have made her suppress all memory of it to protect her psyche. She may never have known the thing you want from her.'

'So all this was a waste of time?'

'Not a waste of time, we now know her mother was carrying the relic and it must be hidden in the house somewhere. I wish I could help more but I can't. No one can.'

'Would torture free this elusive memory?' The guard asked coldly.

The doctor recoiled, inwardly appalled at the question, his distaste of the man visible in the set of his jaw and mouth, and answered. 'That would simply make it worse. There would be an association with the questions we have asked and the pain caused and just another trauma to add to the first one. It would send her memories even deeper into the unconscious. I am afraid there is nothing we can do.'

'Nothing *you* can do, but I have other ideas.'

CHAPTER TWENTY SEVEN

Returning from the police, a daily routine for the past three days to check if there was any news of Sophia and answer their irrelevant questions, Alex fell into an armchair that gazed out towards Druids Hill.

The primeval eminence towered forcefully over the landscape with the power of a sleeping volcano. After all that had happened to him there it seemed like some ancient temple edifice about to erupt with Shekinah glory.

Could it really be true? A mythological goddess dwelt there? He could almost believe it. Jan had told him the gods of mythology were powerful forces in the collective unconscious of man that were released in moments of crisis when time was ripe. They were living, spiritual beings, the ancient gods of saga and song and dreams. Before he would never have believed it, -but now.

His reverie was broken by the phone ringing persistently.

'Alex Roedale?' It was a distant, disguised, echoing voice.

'Indeed.'

'I have something you want, and you have something I want.' The caller paused then said, 'Listen.'

There was a sound, like a slap, followed by Sophia's sobbing voice.

'Alex,' Sophia called through the receiver.

Alex switched on his phone recorder. Over the years he had found it far more reliable, than trying to recall conversations and the police had suggested he use it if this should occur.

'Now that's what we have.' The muffled voice said.

'What do you want?' Alex struggled to conceal his anger.

He guessed it was only a matter of time before someone rang to tell him what had happened to Sophia but it was still an excruciating and traumatic shock. Relieved she was alive but at the same time filled with an almost overwhelming rage that she was being injured by her kidnappers didn't help the conversation. It took all his self control not to let it loose on the caller.

'What we want is the Allan relic.'

'I have no idea what you are talking about.'

There was a pause then another scream of pain.

'Does that help?' the caller asked in a sneering tone.

'I don't have whatever it is you want,' Alex insisted.

'I accept that but if you want to see your lovely Sophia again, you'll find out where it is.'

There was a click. The conversation had ended.

Alex stood there breathless, trying to regain composure, to collect his frantically, dancing mind. There was no time to waste now and the only person he knew who could help was Sophia father.

Lord Allan didn't turn to look as Alex entered his room. His wheelchair faced open French windows, overlooking the green fields of Henley. He was deep in absent contemplation. All resolve and determination had died within him, grief almost overwhelmed him and his body ached in unison with his soul. Everything he had striven for in his life, all the hard work and commitment to his cause now meant nothing at all. He had failed everyone. It would be so easy to let it all go. He had no more strength to continue and for the first time in his life he thought how peaceful it would be to relinquish everything.

Drawing a chair to sit beside Lord Henry Alex touched his arm.

Lord Henry heard Alex' voice as though in a dream but he had no interest in responding to anyone or anything so deep was his despair.

'I need your help desperately right now, sir. Sophia's in danger. '

There was no response whatever. Lord Henry hadn't recognised him. He seemed not to comprehend anything.

Alex sat in silence bewildered, drained of energy pondering what to do.

Lord Henry had tired noticeably since he came into the room. Alex trying to communicate with him gave up. It was futile. He rang the nurse, who helped Lord Henry into bed and left.

From Barrington he rang Kevin, arranging to meet at the local pub.

'The only chance we have is to find Sophia.' Alex asseverated.

'It can be done, for sure.' Kevin downed his second whisky.

'I've brought this tape of a conversation I had with the kidnappers. Can you have one of your service friends analyse it?'

'Tapes are not easy to work with, at all, but what can be done be sure will be done.' Kevin assured.

Sitting back with a port swirling its bowl in his hand Alex didn't want to admit it but finding Sophia seemed unlikely.

'What's your advice Kevin?'

'Well, let's not have faith in the police that's always a sensible decision. My own belief is we should bring in dogs and a tracker. Do you know a good tracker at all? In your travels you must have met somebody.'

So obvious yet the idea hadn't even occurred to him. Kevin's bold confidence inspired him, renewing his natural optimism.

'I don't but I know someone who will help find one.'

'The weather's been good that's for sure. We could still follow the signs but we need to do it soon.'

.Leaving, as soon as friendship would permit, Alex drove back to Barrington. Several international calls later he'd found an answer in Thor Sorenson, a Canadian Ranger used by the Calgary police.

'I'm sorry I can't come Alex,' Thor said in his distinctive, Swedish, accent, 'However you're in luck old friend because one of our best trackers is in London and far more skilled than I am. I'll make contact for you.' Alex caught a smile in Thor's voice but left it unquestioned.

After a sleepless night, he agreed, through Thor, to meet the tracker at Henley railway station.

The only person to get off the ten sixteen train from London was a woman. It was something Thor, in typical humour, had kept from him. Alex recognised she had to be his tracker by the Canadian Maple leaf logo on her baseball cap.

Corrie Smit was a thirtyish, pretty, healthy looking, red haired Canadian, wearing sneakers, slacks, a white, open topped blouse and shouldering a backpack.

'You're Alex I think,' she greeted smiling, flashing perfect white teeth.

Noting his surprise she said, 'Don't worry, I've been tracking since I was six. One of my ancestors was a Bois Coureur, part French, part Indian, the best trapper in the Northwest Fur Company.'

Alex smiled, 'The Bois Coureur? The notorious, mountain men, trappers, right?'

'Yes, well, done.' Corrie held out her hand in greeting.

Over breakfast, at a Henley village restaurant, they discussed their need for Corrie's skills.

'I've been given more difficult assignments that you just wouldn't believe,' Corrie encouraged.

The Green Goddess

At noon they joined Kevin at Barrington. He wasn't alone. Another Irishman, whose face was an haunted reflection of better days, stood there with three dogs.

'The dogs'll find any scent left by Sophia if there's any to find. 'Kevin said, answering the unspoken question. 'We'll need any clothes she last wore, if you have some here?'

Corrie was silent, a small frown puckering her delicate forehead.

'What's wrong?' Alex asked.

'Dogs, they interfere with any visible track, especially when they lose scent. I'll have to work around that'.

'She had some spare clothes in her car and kept a small wardrobe in the house. I'm sure we'll find something.' Alex answered Kevin.

Placing Sophia's clothes in a basket they watched as item by item the snuffling, tail wagging, dogs dug into them.

'The big un's Norwegian, I've seen him go through a locked door after his prey. The other's a Blood, I'm sure you've recognised, and the other Polish. Each has their advantage.' The dog handler stroked his animals affectionately, 'They're all well trained. I did it me self and they do have innate ability for the job.'

'We'd best follow in the Land Rover.' Kevin suggested as he joined them.

They began outside Barrington walking the driveway and perimeter. The dogs quickly caught a scent and were soon tugging at their leashes. The handler let them go. Running back and forth the dogs led them through an open field adjoining Barrington. To Alex surprise Corrie, whom he had forgotten about, was already there waiting for them to catch up.

'See here? There were two men carrying your friend, I think, but there's no sign of a struggle. The vehicle was a four wheel drive.' Corrie pointed to the soft earth.

The dogs, moving ahead of Corrie, led across fields to a gate then on to a wide track that climbed towards the hills and beyond to quiet country lanes and little used bridleways overgrown with untrimmed hedges and young trees.

'There's no hesitation, not even in the dark. The driver knows this area in the way only a local could,' Corrie told Alex when they stopped to share coffee. 'The dogs agree with my trail. My guess is your friend isn't far away.' She smiled confidently, calmly, without haste in her deliberations. Meticulous, she often lagged a long way behind the dogs, turning over leaves, stooping to run her fingers over any tracks she found, holding the trail between herself and the sun to obliquely distinguish indentations and shadows.

The trail led through a wooded valley, where a wide stream flowed between steep sandy banks heavy with dense shrubs, alder and buckthorn. At this point the dogs lost scent.

On the stream bank the dog handler called, 'There are some tyre tracks here.'

Ignoring his observation Corrie continued along the stream bed pausing frequently to inspect its sandy bottom and gravel.

'That's not it.'

Beckoning to join her she pointed, 'Look, quite devious. They changed vehicles at this point, in mid-stream. The tracks on the other side are the four wheeler OK but the kidnappers followed the centre of the stream in a smaller vehicle, to fool us. They had a vehicle waiting here expecting if anyone followed them they would assume they had crossed the ford further up.'

'Which direction did they go?' Alex quizzed.

'Downstream we'll pick up the trail. Patience my good man.'

Staying close to Corrie Alex was struck by her ability. The dogs following on the stream side had lost all contact but not Corrie. She stopped to inspect branches of overhanging foliage.

'Alex, come look, this buckthorn, the branch is broken, and recently, and here this beech sapling is scuffed. It left a mark on the car roof.'

'Explain.' Alex asked.

'Paint on the branch. I'd say we are lucky. The night before the abduction it rained heavily, the stream swelled and left this soft mud. See where the freshet narrowed, they were forced partly onto the bank.' Corrie squatted to inspect tyre tracks. 'A much lighter vehicle. A trail even an amateur, like you, could pick up.' She quipped smiling.

Alex watched her in admiration, her fingers were slender, hair immaculately brushed and tied back, her face unmarked by extremes of weather. Not what he would have expected.

They followed her, the dog handler saying nothing. Five hundred yards further downstream Corrie stopped at a bank that sloped to the water and grinned triumphantly.

'They were here, definitely.'

Turning to the dog handler she said, 'The dogs won't be able to help from here on, the scent will have disappeared.'

The dogs were scattering to and fro without direction and the handler nodded in agreement

Corrie led them up a slope that formed a snaking path between dense woodland and open fields.

The Green Goddess

Near the apex of the hill the track turned abruptly left, to an open farm gate overgrown with ivy. Going through this the ground fell away sharply to the Morville estates.

Morville Hall was in full view and not far away the lonely church bereft of its village and near bye the Church the isolated, magnificently chimneyed, Tudor vicarage.

Taking her binoculars Corrie viewed the valley below, nothing escaping her watchful eyes, every door, window, chimney and path were examined.

'Someone's there or have been until a few hours ago, that's where the vehicle went, to the house hard by the church.'

'Morville Hall,' Kevin blurted out, as though he had guessed it from the start.

'No not the Hall, the house near the church,' Corrie informed.

'The old vicarage,' Alex corrected.

'Keep the dogs quiet,' Kevin warned the handler, sharply. 'And let's stay out of view will ye all.'

Squeezing into the Land Rover they rolled down the incline, in neutral, hoping the element of surprise would favour them. Using the terrain of trees and hedges they could conceal their approach. Stopping at a small grove of beech trees they parked the vehicle and struggled on foot across a ploughed field to a windowless side of the vicarage. The house appeared deserted. There were no cars in sight,or sounds, from within the building.

'These tracks by this door are certainly from the car we followed. One right front tyre has a smoothed edge. Your friend was brought here, the car stopped and then was driven that way,' Corrie whispered, as she pointed to Morville Hall.

Kevin tried a door to the old vicarage. Finding it tightly closed he impetuously broke the glass of a side window and climbed through. It was but a moment before they were all inside.

A smell of cooking wafted from a kitchen and muddy boot marks led across a large entrance hall to a door to their left. Kevin signalled silence. The Bloodhound, the handler had brought with him, was sniffing the floor, seeking a scent and moved to one of the doors to their left. The dog scratched at it attempting to go beyond.

The door they found was unlocked and led to a flight of stairs and on into a basement. Closing the door behind them following the dog handler they moved silently down the steps. The basement was as large in floor area as the house itself.

'Once the lackey's quarters,' Kevin muttered, 'I should know.'

The hound led them to a door close by a basement kitchen.

There was no one in the basement or house as far as they could tell. The door the dog was sniffing was closed but a large iron key had been left in the lock. Cautiously opening it Alex was faced by a second door made of steel and secured by bolts.

Listening for any sound beyond, they heard nothing that would indicate anyone was in the locked room. Pulling the bolts Alex and Kevin swung open the heavy door. In front of them against a far wall they could see Sophia lying fast asleep on a narrow single bed. Alex, all energy drained away from him, wanted to shout in elation at finding her then immediately his mood changed as he rushed to her side.

Sophia was in a pitiable state. His heart stopped, fearing they had arrived too late. to save her. She lay there motionless, corpse like, there were bruises on her face and arms. She looked emaciated. Looking around, the place looked like a torture chamber. There were ropes at the bed posts and the room was pervaded by such a strange surgical smell it seemed like an operating theatre. He looked down at her his heart breaking.

Kevin rushed over to her, placing his fingers to her jugular.

'Thank god. She's alive, let's get her out of here,' Kevin broke the atmosphere.

Alex wrapped a blanket around her and lifted Sophia in his arms, letting no one else touch her. Kissing her, he murmured softly, 'It's alright my darling you're safe now, safe now.'

There was no response or acknowledgement. Kicking the door open, hoping someone would hear and come running so that he could vent his anger at them, he carried her to the Land Rover Kevin brought across the fields. Climbing inside they bowled along at break neck speed towards the nearest hospital.

In the Land Rover Kevin reached over and lifted Sophia's eyelids. 'She's been drugged, that I'm sure.'

Shaking her Alex achieved a brief, sleepy, response as he touched her lips with coffee from a flask. Sophia drifted into consciousness thinking she had been sleeping a long time, unable to understand where she was. Recognising Alex' touch she opened her eyes momentarily, tears clouding her vision, as she turned her face away from him ashamed that he should see her.

'You can't love me after this,' she mumbled through her swollen lips.

Leaning over, taking her head in his hands he kissed her and whispered gently, 'Love is not love which alters when it alteration finds,' and cradled her in his arms.

The Green Goddess

Sophia smiled quickly and fell away again. She thought she lay in her father's arms again after the death of her mother. He was speaking quietly to her, holding her close, stroking her hair and saying, 'you are safe now my darling.'

Anxiously waiting in the hospital ward, Alex had no desire for conversation. Kevin left him alone while he reported the events of the day to the police.

A doctor came into the waiting room and asked Alex to a private cubicle.

'There's no serious harm done, all she needs is rest. She can do this here or at home, whichever you decide. I'd like to keep her here for a few days, for observation, but the tests show nothing to worry about, no internal bleeding. Has it been reported to the police? We will have to, you understand, by law. Do you have any objections to that?'

'Of course not,' Alex answered sharply.

The police took notes and interviewed the Morville's and after days concluded there was no evidence that Ralph Morville or anyone at Morville Hall had been aware the old vicarage was being used. If it had been it was entirely without their consent. Ralph had been in London on business and had witnesses who could vouch for his presence there.

'Don't believe a word of it,' Kevin told the police, abruptly disdainful.

Corrie Smit stayed on for several days before flying home to Canada.

'I know, for sure, one of the vehicles we followed visited Morville Hall and not once but several times. I followed the tracks, while you were at the hospital, but the police here wouldn't accept my conclusions.' Corrie shrugged her shoulders and smiling said, 'They never use trackers here do they?'

Several weeks passed before Sophia regained any kind of usual buoyant normality. Her bruises healed quickly but the psychological trauma she had gone through took much longer. She recovered, slowly, changing from silent withdrawal to her habitual, customary and youthful, witty confidence.

CHAPTER TWENTY EIGHT

Sophia had acquired a skill, learned from the time her mother had died, of putting painful memories in a kind of sealed room that she locked safely in her unconscious. She didn't speak of her ordeal, it was just as though it had never occurred. Staying at Barrington where Alex could be near her became habitual and she moved into his home more or less permanently.

Shenley had also recovered, except for a temporary limp. Lord Henry however had shown no noticeable recover and the family and friends who visited him didn't, couldn't, tell him of Sophia's kidnap.

'His Lordship has no physical symptoms that I'm aware of. It's a complete psychological withdrawal from the world and life,' the consultant told Marston and Shenley. Occasionally the brothers met when Marston was visiting his father but Marston hardly spoke. When he did his words were full of anger, and certainty, that Ralph Morville had been behind the assault on Shenley and on Sophia's abduction.

'If he thinks I'll let him get away with this he's badly mistaken.' Marston grunted. What he had in mind he didn't tell them but his determination was venomous.

Alex and Sophia had other things on their mind. One way or another they had to discover what the relic of the mysterious, secret society was, find it and bring it to Sophia's father.

'It is the only thing that will restore him to health. We need to know who did this to me of course but, at the moment, my father is more important,' Sophia explained.

There was little time to do it.

Each evening she and Alex explored every line of enquiry they could think of, or imagine, what they already knew and what they needed to know, churning it over and over. Searching the photos, Alex had taken in the Druids Hill caverns, for clues, and studying minutely the copies he had fortuitously taken from the medieval manuscript volume before it had been stolen. Sophia drew up a list of the basic assumptions.

1. The relic belonged to a medieval society similar to the Templars.
2. It was from an ancient civilisation.
3. It had associations with goddesses of wisdom.
4. If the medieval manuscript book could be relied on it involved, in some obscure way, the Shroud of Turin.
5. Likewise in some indefinable way it had an association with one of the Marys of the gospels.
6. There was a clue, if they could understand it, involving a skull and the capital letter 'B'.

Sophia's knowledge of medieval history and manuscripts was an enormous help. Her university term had ended and she was able to focus her time on this subject alone.

One Saturday afternoon, all their notes and scribbles lying on a kitchen table, Sophia stood guiltily looking out of the window towards Druids Hill. A mild wind blew from the south west as the sun sank, over the trees of Barrington, painting a yellow tinge across the darkening clouds of evening. Returning to Alex they both sat in the diffused light from the yellow sky looking over his photos and coloured copies.

'I believe we are misinterpreting the image of Mary.'

'That's just what Jan told me.'

'He is right. It isn't Mary Magdalene at all it's the Madonna.' Sophia gazed intently at the photocopy he had made from the medieval book. 'You recall your friend Jan, in California, said he thought the supposed image of John in the Last Supper was the Madonna. When you think about it what more natural than the Virgin sitting down with the disciples at the table? That's exactly what she does at every Catholic Mass.'

'I have been thinking about this. Jan said that he believed John's Gospel was written by a woman because there were things in that gospel only someone who knew Jesus from the start could have known about, and that rules out all the disciples and Mary Magdalene, leaving only the Virgin herself.'

Sophia looked at him wide eyed, 'Of course. What's more the Catholic Church puts more emphasis on John's Gospel that any other biblical book.' Sophia looked at a photo of Leonardo's, 'Last Supper' that Jan had given Alex.

'Da Vinci speaks in a symbolic language, he may have well been showing the world, something he dare not express verbally, because of the power of the church, that Saint John's Gospel was written by the Virgin and he was showing her to be as important as any of the disciples. To do this, in the place of John in the Last Supper, he puts a portrait that all who contemplate the work will see is the Virgin. In other words what people have believed was Saint John in the painting is the Virgin.'

'Let's assume you are right, what does this have to do with the relic?' Alex probed.

'It means Mary in the manuscript book is the Virgin and she is being equated with Goddesses of Wisdom.'

'That is exactly the conclusion Jan Modjeski drew,' Alex rejoined, 'It's stretching the imagination though.'

'Not really Alex. After all the image of the Virgin and child is similar to Isis the Egyptian goddess with Horus on her knee.'

'Perhaps.'

Sophia left the kitchen. When she returned she had her briefcase and took from it a folder.

'Here's a fourth century writing called 'The Thunder' in which a Jewish female figure called Wisdom is speaking. Some authorities believe the female referred to is Isis. Then in the Biblical wisdom books the Goddess of Wisdom is called the Word. Saint John's gospel begins with,

"In the beginning was the Word and the Word was with God and the Word was God."

'Yes but that refers to Jesus.'

'I don't think so, what it is saying is that Wisdom was with God in the beginning. In John's gospel Mary is mentioned more times than in the other three gospels. Mary was also officially called 'The Mother of God' by the Church. That is quite profound because it says she was there before God.'

'Before Jesus.' Alex corrected.

'Yes, but Jesus was God, according to the scriptures.'

'You mean to say the gospels are telling us, without being specific, that the source of all things is a feminine power. It's a secret gospel understood only by the initiated?'

'Maybe, in any case it does have something to do with father's secret society. I believe they are initiated into an esoteric knowledge. It isn't so far-fetched when you consider it. Almost all the ancient world believed in a Great Mother goddess. Look, here is another of your photos showing Cybele,'

Sophia lifted the photograph off the table for Alex to look at.

'Cybele was known as the Earth Mother supreme. She was life and death and rebirth, a goddess of all life, and this is important, was associated with caverns and mountains. In fact she was called the Mountain Mother. I found in the Book of Proverbs, in the Bible, the same sort of thing where it says,

"Listen, Wisdom is calling out, She is making herself heard on the hilltops."

Saint John after calling her 'The Word',i.e. the Goddess of Wisdom, says,

"Through the Word, God made all things. The Word was the source of life."

It's quite obvious 'The Word' means wisdom without which God couldn't create anything. Wisdom *is* the Great Mother.'

'So you're saying we would expect to find her in the hills and caverns as we did under Druids Hill? The Green Woman is Cybele, is that what you mean?'

'Cybele, Saraswati, Isis, and a hundred others, what she is, is the Great Mother goddess and that Alex is why she is green. She is the creative force of the Earth.'

Sophia sat back in sophisticated satisfaction smiling. 'The Virgin Mary is part of this mystery.'

The following day found Alex in a library working on a task Sophia had set, to find details of men who had disappeared without trace. It was intriguing to say the least. Sophia had ordered him to exclude any suspected murders. He narrowed his search to only include disappearances of people who had, reputedly, enigmatically vanished.

In one County History tome he discovered a reference to a disappearance at Barrington Hall in the eighteenth century.

"Lord Hungerford, the owner of Barrington Hall, who was thought to have been involved in occultism, disappeared one night near Druids Hill, an ancient iron age fortress, near his home."

Other remarkable disappearances Alex came across were;

A church minister in America, seen by his wife and friend, walking across a field towards them, waving a greeting, quite inexplicably vanished from their view. Thinking the man had fallen the minister's spouse and friend searched the area but he was never seen again. Alex discarded this tale immediately as a pair of lovers getting rid of the embarrassment of an unwanted husband, in a puritanical society.

There was a man named James Worson who in 1873, while taking part in a race, suddenly gave out a loud cry and then disappeared into thin air. Many people attested to this strange phenomenon.

There was Ambrose Bierce, an American journalist and renowned traveller, known for his interest in esoteric mysteries, and also, like Lord Hungerford, suspected of belonging to a secret society, who disappeared from the City of Chihuahua while reporting on the Mexican revolution. It had been the most famous disappearance recorded in American history and had never been explained.

At home that evening, after visiting Shenley and Lord Henry, Sophia snuggled beside Alex, their backs resting on double cushions on the bed, while they went over his notes and the details he had photocopied from reference libraries, that day, regarding Ambrose Bierce. In one photocopy was a nineteenth century photograph of Bierce shown standing next to a skull on which he had laid his right hand.

'This is significant perhaps.' Sophia murmured thoughtfully. 'It's the first connection we have with a disappearance and a skull.'

'Yes, that's what I thought, much like the skull in Henley Church, with that letter 'B', Alex agreed.

'Yes, but the 'B' in the church couldn't mean Bierce, that's just a coincidence. The skull carving in Henley Church is at least nine hundred years old.'

'Yes, I know. Anyway you told me the skull in the church was probably another wisdom goddess.'

Ignoring his comment Sophia remarked, speaking her thoughts aloud, 'We have to find it.'

'Find what?' Alex began to laugh.

'What the skull means of course.'

The following day was mild, with broken sunlight sprinkling through grey clouds that threatened a rain that never came. Fields around Barrington were in full bloom and the lanes jammed with farm vehicles.

On waking Alex's mind was clearer after sleeping so soundly. There was something obvious they were missing. It was there at the back of his mind struggling to be recognised. Dropping the thought he turned to Sophia, kissed her and went to the kitchen to make coffee and it was then he remembered. When he first came to Barrington and heard those wild stories of Druids Hill and read of the disappearances of Lord Hungerford and Thomas Barrington there had been an article describing a religious order of knights that had chosen a Temple site near Druids Hill. When he first met Sophia, in Henley Church, she had shown him the tomb of one of those knights. That is what they had overlooked.

Sophia was still deep in slumber when he made up his mind, dressed, and wrote her a note saying he would be away for several days and would ring her that evening. He kissed her cheek and left for Oxford.

After two days of ineffectual searching, through piles of articles and books, and when just at the point of abandoning the project he came across a reference, in a Victorian Gentleman's Magazine, that mentioned an abstruse order of knights who had built one of their temples near Henley. The article referred to an older paper written a century earlier. After an hour or so this document was located by the history librarian. The manuscript, hand written, yellowing and fragile, had been written in a consistent, precise script that he had little difficulty reading. Using gloves to protect the manuscript's delicate pages he eagerly read through it.

"This mysterious order of knights came of ancient origins with a descent traced through the history of many persecuted religious sects. The Order, comprised of men from the noblest of families, were invited by the Albigenses, or as they are sometimes known the Cathars, to protect them from the Pope and Catholic nobles of France and England. The Order of knights agreed. They journeyed with their most hallowed relic, without which they believed their Order could not exist.

Pope Innocent 111, dismayed by the success of the Albigenses in attracting converts, and their growing threat to the Papal hold over the crowns of the Empire, raised a bloody crusade against them. The Sacred order of knights who had agreed to assist the Albigenses fought so valiantly that the war lasted almost forty years. Finally, under the rigours of a long siege at the Montsegur mountain fortress, the Albigenses capitulated. However, before the opposing army entered the citadel four of the knights of the Sacred Order were lowered down the sheer face of the mountain by ropes and thus made their escape carrying their treasured relics with them. This was to ensure their continuance."

Leaning back in his seat, contemplating the content of the document, he realised here was the first piece of real evidence he had come across that mentioned the sacred object. Although it was a valuable find it still gave no clue as to what the relic or treasures were.

Sitting opposite, in an adjoining carrel, unobserved by Alex, a man in blue tinted glasses had been watching him closely. When Alex left his desk the man had walked over and noted the documents requested and followed him to the reference catalogues where surreptitiously he gazed over any books or papers laid out or requested there.

When the search had been completed and he was back at Barrington Alex confided in Sophia and laid out his notes for her observations.

'I discovered a mention of an order of knights among the Albigenses so I researched the beliefs of the Albigenses. A point I thought significant was they believed in a feminine side of creation. Their hierarchy included male and female of equal position and status. Basically they taught that one's religion must be based on an inner experience emanating from the Divine Spirit within and, here is the point, that inner guidance was Wisdom.'

'What does all that mean?' Sophia asked.

'Obviously they believed Wisdom was *the* supreme power and just as significantly, I believe, they studied Arabic and Hebrew and were on friendly terms with a large Jewish community living with them.'

Sophia inspected closely the photocopies and rapidly written notes Alex had brought with him.

'This is interesting but what about the Templars you were supposed to be researching.'

Alex smiled at her impatience.

'The Albigenses asked an order of knights, who sympathised with their beliefs, to protect them from the Pope and, the crucial bit is, these knights carried a sacred relic and treasure with them. I also came across this,' Alex took a photocopy from the pile in front of them. 'It refers to the Knights of Druids Hill.'

Sophia read in silence.

'A hierarchical, secretive branch of the Templars existed whose task had been to defend the Templars from the powerful influence of monarchs and church and retain their own most sacred teachings. At the shameful, bloody dissolution of the Temple Order this body of holy knights, it was believed, also perished. However by some means they still functioned secretively among the most powerful families in Europe and built hidden temples in isolated regions of England, France and the Holy Roman Empire.'

Sophia looked up from the papers in front of her.

'Yes I see. Henley Church was under construction just about the time the Templars were destroyed and this other order moved into the area. They could have been responsible for deliberately having the church built over the caverns.'

'What about the disappearances that are part of the myth of Druids Hill?' Alex questioned.

'I believe not all the disappearances you looked up are genuine. Probably Lord Hungerford's is but Thomas Barrington I feel sure ran away and that man Worson is a figment of journalistic imagination. That only leaves Lord Hungerford and Bierce.'

While she was talking Alex suddenly recalled the Shroud of Christ painting in the medieval book they had taken from Henley Hall.

'Why do you think there is a painting of the Turin Shroud in the book?' Alex asked Sophia. 'It certainly isn't of a goddess of wisdom. It seems out of place.'

'Christ disappeared and that was the image he left behind. There may be a clue here. The Shroud only appeared on the historical scene at the disbanding of the Templars and, by inference, this order of knights on Druids Hill.'

Alex got up stretched erect and said, 'Sophia let's go a walk. I feel exhausted by this. We have all this information but we aren't getting anywhere.'

Sophia sighed in acquiescence, of course he was right.

In the exhilaration of the countryside and spring air, freed of the clutter of notes and speculation, Alex brightened. Putting his arm around Sophia's waist he plucked a wild rose from the hedge and pushed it into her hair. Her lips red and sparkling parted and he pulled her to him and kissed her passionately.

They broke apart and continued through the fields towards Henley Hall.

'Cheer up, we have made some progress,' Sophia soothed, breaking the silence.

'Not enough. One night I sat up looking at the copy I'd made of the Shroud and I don't think the person on the Shroud is Jesus at all.'

Staring at him quizzically, Sophia asked, 'Then *who* do you think it is?'

'The head is long, the beard typical of a crusading knight. You can see a hundred effigies on tombs throughout England and Europe that have a similar face. The man is North European without doubt, that's my opinion, and my guess is he was a Templar or perhaps one of the Druids Hill knights.'

She knew she had never loved anyone as much as Alex, except her father. Sophia turned to look at him, his firm jaw and kind, humorous eyes. She loved his, calm courage, the perpetual quiet sadness, like a man who had gone through hell and come out the other side. It was a part of him she couldn't touch and at times felt like a barrier of ice. She loved him so intensely her heart ached.

Sophia kissed his cheek. 'That's it, of course, that's why the Shroud is in the book. We need to know who the king of France tortured to death, at the Templar dissolution, please if you could look that up. While you do that I'll search connections between Mary Magdalene and the Madonna.'

Two days later, in a Walmley village café, they met to compare notes.

Sophia dropped her leather case on the seat beside her.

Alex watched her, as she tugged her seat beside him, admiring her elegant beauty. With her landed title Sophia's photograph was often in the weekend newspapers and gossip columns. So far she had kept his name out of them. Her fan mail, he learned from a Henley housekeeper, was large and she answered every letter.

'This is what I found out,' Sophia began, looking closely at him, her eyes sparkling, twinkling, and laughing as though reading his very thoughts.

Unnoticed by them a man had entered the cafe, the same that had followed Alex to Oxford. He sat at a distant table drinking coffee, scribbling in a pocket sized notebook, hardly ever glancing their way, an earpiece giving him access to every word of their conversation.

'Don't you think it strange that, at the resurrection, Jesus' mother wasn't present? He was her son but she wasn't at his tomb. This, the woman the Church calls the Mother of God. The gospels are not in agreement yet they all say Mary Magdalene was there, some say with her were Joanna and Mary the mother of James. St John says only Mary Magdalene, and that Jesus appeared to her alone at the tomb. Logically I would have thought it was Mary the mother of Jesus. This led me to the idea the Gospel writers, who wrote many years after Jesus's death, confused the two Mary's, either that or the church fathers didn't want to give Jesus' mother the prominence she deserved, because of the Earth Mother, Queen of Heaven, similarities in the ancient world. They were trying to displace that ancient image. In the Catholic mass, Mary Magdalene is never mentioned but the Virgin Mary is in every mass.'

Sophia had become animated her lovely eyes dancing with enthusiasm.

'Your friend Jan was correct the image in Da Vinci's 'Last Supper' is not, as it has been suggested, the Magdalene but the Madonna. Common sense tells us the woman the church call the Mother of God would be at the Last Supper and at the tomb. What else would you expect from a loving mother but to be there at the last communal meal and at his grave. Some group within the early church prelature tried to take the Virgin Mary out of the picture because they realised she would take a predominant place over the disciples and revive worship of the Great Mother of all creation. Four hundred years later, when it was safe to do it, in the fifth century, the Third Ecumenical Council corrected this view by agreeing the Virgin Mary was, 'The Mother of God', and stated the early disciples had always held this to be true. At last, after all the centuries of denial, the Virgin was given her rightful place as the Great Mother.'

'What you say may be true but there definitely was a strong following of Mary Magdalene in the Church, wasn't there?' Alex interrupted. 'Look at the number of churches dedicated to her.'

'At one time there was a cult of the worship of Mary Magdalene, yes. She was supposed to have travelled to Ephesus with the Virgin. Later, it was believed she went to live in Marseille where she converted the whole of Provence to Christianity. After her death her bones were transferred to the Abbey of Vezelay, in Burgundy, an Abbey founded by Gerard, the Duke of Burgundy. That seems unlikely, why preserve her bones when those of the disciples aren't preserved? Anyway from there they were moved in twelve seven nine A.D. to a sepulchre in the oratory of Saint Maximin at Aix-en–Provence, one of the loveliest and finest Gothic Churches ever built.' Sophia enthused.

'In Sixteen Hundred, Pope Clement the Eighth had the body of the Magdalen placed in a specially designed sarcophagus, but the head for some reason was moved to a separate reliquary. These relics were taken during the French Revolution but the skull of Mary was later rediscovered and is now back in the church of la Sainte-Baume.'

'And?' Alex questioned.

'That means, the Skull of the Magdalen, can't have anything to do with the one we are looking for. There has to be another skull connection somewhere.'

Alex leaned back in his chair and inhaled deeply. 'And we also know the Templars were active in Provence.'

'Seems most likely,' Sophia was pleased with herself. 'We are looking for the skull of a woman but it can't be the skull of Mary Magdalene.'

'Who then?'

'In the earliest copies of John's Gospel the woman at the tomb is stated quite clearly as the Virgin

Mary, later copyists changed it to Mary Magdalene. I feel certain of this. The Gospel could have been written by the Virgin Mary, as your friend Jan said, but the church altered its content.'

'Forgive me if I'm slow in following you but what has that to do with Mary Magdalene in Provence and her skull in the cathedral?'

'I don't believe the skull in the cathedral of La Sainte-Baume was that of the Magdalen at all and I believe it was a fake in any case. The idea for this lucrative forgery was because they knew the knightly order in Provence carried an ancient skull with them and worshipped it. The Church was doing what they did with all relics cash in on elaborate forgeries and cleverly concocted stories. The real skull, not the Magdalena's, is hidden somewhere at Henley Hall.'

Sophia herself was surprised at the conclusion. 'I admit I am confused still about it all and we may be on the wrong track.'

'The reason?' Alex enquired.

'Mary Magdalene, in church mythology travelled to Ephesus with the Virgin Mary. Then it appears the Virgin moved back to Jerusalem and was buried in the Valley of Kidron.

Sophia was meticulous in everything she did, bordering on compulsion, so Alex listened patiently to her conclusions making a mental note of only the salient points of her argument.

Noticing his hesitation Sophia leaned over and grasped his hand gently in hers.

'I have had to go over this Alex to eliminate all possibilities. The skull in Henley Church is that of a female. The only female skull relic recorded, that I know of, is that of the Magdalene so I had to prove it couldn't be what we are looking for.'

Alex drank his coffee in silence taking in Sophia's conclusions. He loved the smell of coffee especially in the morning. Opening a brown foolscap envelope, stained by raindrops, he took out a scatter of A4 paper notes and laid them on the table.

'My own search revealed our knights of Druids Hill, had a hill fortress near Jerusalem close to Gethsemane. There is a church there, and a sepulchre of the body of the Virgin. The early church fathers agreed Mary was translated into heaven but her body was left behind. In Jerusalem it seems likely they were guarding the Madonna's remains and it suggests to me the reason for them having a fortress there. The knights did show up in Provence as you say and it seems feasible they came not with the Magdalene's but with a holy relic of the Virgin.'

Sophia beamed enthusiastically.

'The relic is the skull of the Virgin Mary, stolen from her tomb by the knights that settled on Druids Hill.'

'If we are correct what a find? I can hardly believe it, even I want to hold it in my hands, to gaze on it, to feel its weight in my palm, The Mother of Christ.'

Alex held up his hands as though holding the skull, gazing at it in his imagination.

'Who wouldn't want this sacred object or desire to bow to it. It explains the willingness of these knights to die to preserve it. For them it had the greatest symbolism, the reason for their existence. They had vowed to protect the remains of Mary with their lives. And that's what they have done all these centuries.'

'Father told me he needed to present the relic on the 15th August. That is the date of the Assumption of Mary into Heaven. I never thought of that before. Its another clue and it confirms we are right. It has to be the skull of the Madonna.'

They sat in silence contemplating the significance of their conclusion.

'It would explain, more precisely, why men through the centuries have killed to lay their hands on it, why they killed my mother and injured Shenley,' Sophia brooded, bitterly.

'Yes that's the sad part. Imagine its value to the Church, or on the open market, the most treasured religious object the world has ever known.'

Sitting inconspicuously, at the far side of the café, a man who had been listening avidly to their conversation lowered his pencil to the table and with solemn, disquiet removed his ear piece, stuffed it and his notepad into his jacket, and left.

CHAPTER TWENTY NINE

A chauffeur met Ralph Morville carrying a card, with Ralph's name on it, held above his head at Milan airport.

Driving north into the lonely mountains, on which summer leaves bloomed in wide pallets of green, the Italian driver hardly spoke except to mention the rising cost of life in Italy and the rocketing prices of homes.

'Too many foreigners coma to liva here for sun and life styla. My Poppa he say country nota same as when he grew up. He wana to leava thisa place. Soon everybody liva somaplace else,' the chauffeur added in his accented version of English.

Under his breath Ralph wished the driver lived someplace else.

Licio, the Italian Minister, had ordered Ralph to an urgent meeting.

'You will meet a representative of the Vatican Bank and a senior cardinal to discuss these things.' He had said curtly.

'You have to be there Mr Morville or the deal is off, that's what they say and with what you know the consequences for you could be serious.' The voice was threatening.

Ralph didn't like to be threatened but held his anger back knowing a time would come for revenge.

The journey was tortuous, even the wild beauty of the gothic mountain scenery couldn't change that. The driver spun precariously close to cliff hanging roads that promised a long swift flight into eternity at the least careless lapse of concentration.

They reached the heights of a mountain range that expanded into spectacular views and the road levelled to a plateau that spread out into verdant pasture. On the horizon a castle dominated the landscape. Perched on the very edge of a vertiginous cliff face it looked like a medieval fortress, or some forgotten monastery, in its cold, grand isolation. The palace had originally been built as a hidden retreat for a highly regarded Austrian prince.

Ralph was met and accompanied, at the base of the fortress, through steel doors opening on to a wide medieval hall displaying wolf and bear skins, antlers, shields and swords and then to a lift that stopped at a third floor where he was shown into a magnificent suite, with views of the mountains on three sides, and left alone

Dropping his small valise on the floor Ralph stood surveying the panoramic grandeur from the windows of the modernly decored room. A phone, in the room, rang startling him, reminding him why he was there. His heart missed a beat.

'Mr Morville,' Licio greeted in a subdued, charming voice. Hope you had an enjoyable journey.'

'Yes.'

'I've arranged dinner for you. Afterwards we will meet on the promenade. It has some lovely views, an ideal spot for our meeting.'

A tall, slim, blonde woman, speaking perfect English, though her bone structure told him she was undoubtedly Slavic, met Ralph at his apartment door and led him to a banqueting room. Five men, silent as monks, sat at nearby tables. They all turned to look inquisitively at him and turned away. No one spoke to greet him. He guessed they were, as he was, complete strangers to each other.

Ralph, sitting alone at a separate table, was joined over dinner by the blonde woman escort.

She was a gesture from Licio to make his stay more comfortable. Helping him with the Italian menu she ordered dinner for them both. When they were finished she led him to an upper floor and onto a wide stone promenade that circled the fortress like the deck of a ship.

It was a mild evening, close with little or no wind. Venus had already opened her bright eye and a ghostly moon was beginning to silver the mountain tops.

Smiling charmingly the woman left him alone to his thoughts as he waited for Licio to appear.

'Mr Morville,' Licio said joining him. 'How is your distinguished family? Your uncle came here several times before his unfortunate death. Life is very short sometimes and tragic. We never know what lies around the corner.' Licio was smiling but there was no mistaking the threat in his voice.

Ralph knew Licio as head of the Illuminati, and as one of the men suspected of killing his uncle, a rare virus, had been stabbed into his body on a London Street. There was no proof, of course, only rumours and suspicions. In any case it had been his uncle's own fault trying to defraud powerful Swiss banks controlled by the secretive financial hierarchy of Illuminati. Still whether it was his fault or not he resented having to meet this Italian, political slime ball. Ralph had been surprised when Licio had even been so temerous as to contact him for help.

Licio walked beside him along the terrace till they came to a broad patio on which were chairs and tables, and two men, one of whom rose to greet Ralph. The other, ignoring him, sat there coldly gazing over the mountains.

'This is Angelo, the head of the Vatican Bank,' Licio introduced. 'And our other guest, seated,' Licio remarked admonishingly,' is Cardinal Alfredo.'

After mild pleasantries, during which the blonde brought several bottles of wine for the table, Licio opened to the reasons for the invitation.

'We are not satisfied with the progress you are making,' Licio informed Ralph firmly, but apologetically.

'Not an easy task you assigned me. You can hardly blame me, for nine hundred years people have sought to uncover this secret and you don't appear to know what it is we are looking for.' Ralph spoke arrogantly, wondering, if he could get away with tossing the suave politician over the precipice.

'The cardinals, whom his eminence Alfredo here represents,' Angelo motioned to his silent companion, 'Are concerned that you had a member of the British aristocracy kidnapped and injured.'

Before Ralph could reply Cardinal Alfredo added, without looking at Morville, 'His Holiness, from the beginning, said no violence of any kind or the contract would be nullified. We haven't informed him of this particular matter, of course, since the young woman was not seriously injured, but her brother has been. You should know it is a serious matter to disobey a direction of our Supreme Pontiff. If there are any more mistakes you will pay dearly.'

Ralph stared at the Cardinal. He didn't like the man, his head was large, his body over indulged, his shoes shabby and his trousers not pressed.

'Are you threatening me, your Eminence?' Ralph asked icily and with noticeable sarcasm in his voice.

'We do not threaten only advise from two millennia of wisdom. Inevitably you will pay. No one, no matter who he is, can escape the judgement of God.'

'No doubt it applies to you also, your Eminence.'

Licio joined the conversation trying diplomatically to assuage the growing enmity between the two men.

'What we want is results, nothing more. Tell us what progress have you made?' Licio asked mildly.

'A great deal, though I don't wish to discuss details at present. You will definitely have the object, of that be sure, and when I have it you will put the three million in my account as arranged and restore me to my uncle's position in the Illuminati.'

Angelo turned to look questioningly at Licio but said nothing.

'Of course, it has all been arranged. We never go back on our word. I will have to discuss the matter of the Illuminati further with my superiors but I am sure of their acceptance.' Licio assured, without looking at his companions.

The cardinal nodded his agreement.

'I hope so,' Ralph answered sharply, 'or no relic.'

'Nothing is to be documented, no phone calls and only personal meetings to advise of progress.' Angelo reminded them.

'I prefer to do things my way, without conversation.' Ralph rasped.

'Why was this woman kidnapped?' The banker asked.

'She's the only one who knows where the object is.'

'And you found out where?' The cardinal butted in.

'No.'

'Then what was achieved?' the Cardinal asked acerbically.

'She has no conscious idea where it is?' Looking towards Licio, accusingly, Ralph said, 'The trauma caused by the murder of her mother left her mind blank. I'm sure you know of that episode.'

'It wasn't our attention her mother should die. That was accidental.' Licio cringed under the gaze of the cardinal.

'Whatever,' Ralph re-joined.

'Now what is your plan of action?' Licio asked, trying to hide his resentment.

'They will have to recover the object by the fifteenth of August, because on that date the sacred order meets and it has to be with them for their ceremony to continue.'

'The date of the Assumption of the Mother of God,' the cardinal breathed, crossing himself.

'How will you know if they find it?' Angelo queried.

'We have the people involved under close surveillance. They are making progress and will lead us to it I'm certain.'

'Let us drink to it.' Licio raised his glass.

The stars were clear in the mountain sky, clearer than Ralph had ever seen them before. Portentous? He wondered.

Before retiring for the night, the tall blonde was waiting near his door.

Leaving the Austrian border in their wake and driving on through the Dolomites, Ralph sat in the back of the chauffeur driven car thinking of the three men he had left behind 'The good, the bad and the indifferent,' he grinned to himself. Did they really think he was such a pushover, if so they had a lot to learn, these holy mafia pussies?

Disturbing his thoughts Ralph's mobile vibrated against his chest. Answering it he listened in disbelief.

'It's what?' Ralph gave a short, explosive laugh and paused long enough for the person on the other end to say, 'Hello, hello, are you still there?'

'Yes, I'm here, so that's why they are so anxious to lay their hands it.' He listened carefully to the man's voice at the other end then switched off his phone. Ralph had no intention of letting Licio obtain such a valuable object or give such a paltry sum after the effort put into finding it. On the clandestine, antique market he could get a damn sight more than they had offered and he intended to.

After Ralph had left, the three men, Licio, Alfredo and Angelo sat around a dinner table in the castle banqueting room.

'He is a dangerous man.' Cardinal Alfredo said.

'He could become so, just as his uncle did a liability to our cause and the Church.' Licio nodded.

'Can we remove him after the relic is in our hands?' Angelo, the banker wondered.

'It will have to be done somehow.'

'But the Church.' The cardinal was fearful of disobeying his superiors.

'They need never know.'

'I also gave my word to the Holy Father.' Angelo moaned for the ears of the cardinal.

'Do you want the Pontiff to be involved in this matter then?' Licio asked.

Angelo, embarrassed, made no answer.

'Then leave it in my hands.' Licio clasped his hands together closing the matter.

The Cardinal looked askance at them both. 'I don't trust this Englander. What happens to him will be God's will and not ours. We need the holy relic above all. Everything is acceptable to preserve our holy faith.'

'I will have him followed. Nothing he does will go unobserved, you can be sure of it.' Licio chuckled, 'The arrogance of the man. The Illuminati would never accept him or any member of his family, not ever again, into our ranks.'

'Of course,' Alfredo assented, drinking his wine.

In England, whilst Ralph was absent, trotting along a path he followed every day, summer and winter, a powerfully built rider halted on a wooded elevation overlooking the Morville Estates. With him another rider reined in to look at the scene before them.

Marston Allan, Sophia's brother grinned to himself. From his mount he gazed over the lush valley below. A cloud of smoke and an uncontrollable conflagration shot brilliant sparks and flames into the sky from the building in the middle of the valley.

Sitting astride the horse beside Marston was Kevin, his father's butler.

'It makes a lovely sight on such a salubrious morning.' Kevin said in delight.

'Thought he could torture my sister and get away with it, the bloody fool.' Marston rasped through clenched jaw.

The old vicarage, where Sophia had been held, was in riotous flame, fire engines raced across the fields to the inferno. The firemen must have known they could do nothing to stop it.

'Like a drop of whisky?' Kevin held out his flask to Marston.

'It's a celebration, why not. Thank you for your help Kev. I will see you right.'

'It's kind of ye, and appreciated, I did it for Miss Sophie an' it needs no reward for sure but I'll accept the offer.'

The two men drank the flask empty as they watched smoke drifting in a wave of black and white flags across the valley. Snorting, the horses hoofed the ground as smoke clouded the sky above the valley and the scent reached them.

A loud explosion reverberated over the hills, startling the horses, which paced back shaking their heads affrighted and one neighing and rearing in alarm. This time it was Morville Hall that rocketed into flame. One of the fire engines stopped mid field to retrace its path back to the new inferno.

'You are sure they were all away?' Marston asked, clearly astonished at the noise of the explosion and the rapidity with which the old hall was being convulsed by flames.

'No one there, I'm sure,' Kevin answered calmly.

'Any way the device can be traced?'

'Not a glimmer of a hope.'

Marston leaned over and shook Kevin's hand. 'Well done.'

'It was for sure, an' it's time enough, Morvilles have been here too long. This'll be the beginning o' their end.'

'We'd better lie low, for a few weeks, Kevin old boy.'

'Best go about your duties as though nothin' happened at all, that way you're completely innocent.'

Both men laughed in exhilaration and camaraderie.

'Serves the buggers right,' Marston spat.

Several days passed before an interrogation by the police.

'The belief is someone, out of revenge set fire to Morville Hall.' Detective Inspector Taylor apprised.

'The Morvilles have enemies, everybody knows that,' Marston shrugged, reminding the inspector.

'Yes, and you especially, if your assumptions were correct that Ralph Morville was behind the kidnap of Lady Sophia.'

'A man in my position can't be involved in personal vendettas, you know that inspector. Besides, if you can't be certain who kidnapped my sister how can you imagine we took revenge on someone who might not have been involved.'

'Maybe not you, but Mr Roedale might have.'

'In that case ask him. I don't think he could have. Very unlikely I'd say, not the sort really.'

'I intend to. There was that attack on Shenley and your butler, then robbery at Barrington Hall, the kidnap of Lady Sophia, an intruder killed and this fire at Morville Hall, and none of you know any reason why,' the inspector stated impatiently.

CHAPTER THIRTY

So absorbed were Alex and Sophia with their analysis of countless documents, and the urgency of their task they were oblivious to the constant, voracious surveillance of all they were doing, or of the people who were stalking them as coolly and precisely as a wild beast follows its prey. Even Barrington had been bugged, in their absence, in spite of Kevin's efforts and assurances.

After dining at The Talbot in Mawley one afternoon they came home to find that Barrington had been ransacked again. All their research notes, so foolishly, absent mindedly and confidently, left on the tables for anyone to see had gone.

'They're professional, probably ex foreign service.' Kevin told them. 'The device they planted, this time, I've never seen the likes of.' He held up a tiny monitor in the shape of a wood screw.

'It was screwed beneath the table in the study. There's most likely more in every room. We'll have to de-bug again but short of tearing the place asunder I can't be sure we'll have everything. My advice is conduct your business somewhere else. Change the location every time. Keep your peepers open, anything suspicious, you understand, avoid. Your cars are not safe they may well be, and probably are, monitored too or followed, very easy these days of satellite.'

From that moment they spoke, privately, outdoors, or in bars and cafes beyond Henley.

'What we should do is go back to the caves 'neath Henley Church.' Sophia proposed after Kevin had returned to the Hall.

'Will we find the relic there?' Alex asked sceptically.

'We have to try everything. There might be something we've missed and I have a feeling we should do that. Call it feminine intuition if you like. If you won't come I will go alone.'

'We would have to meet separately, not go together. Be especially careful and we'll go at night. Agree?'

'Agreed,' Sophia assented.

How could he refuse her even if it was a wild goose chase, he thought, looking at her worn and distant expression.

The following night was auspicious for their purpose, cloudy, without moon or stars, and gave them ideal conditions to enter the Henley Church unseen.

Dressed in an old coat Sophia left Henley Hall by rear staff access and walked the path from there to the Church. Alex set off from Barrington at first by car and later by foot over tumbling, overgrown public footpaths, with only a pencil torch guiding his steps through the ink black night. The evening air was close, and the church forlorn, in its dark and ancient loneliness.

Entering the caverns, now they knew so much of their history, they seemed the holiest place on earth. There was a silence, and a presence of some great spiritual power, that overwhelmed Sophia's reason, sucking her into another dimension.

'Could the relic be hidden here?' Alex wondered.

'I don't think so. I'm sure when mother died she was carrying something, so valuable, she gave her life to protect it. It isn't here but maybe there is a clue to help us.'

Taking her hand, Alex quickly, easily located the large central cave in which the statue of the Green Goddess shone gloriously with her strange luminescent glow.

Alex was, he admitted silently to himself, afraid to go anywhere near it but Sophia rushed impulsively forwards, like a moth to a flame, drawn by an incomprehensible, forceful desire she couldn't resist.

'No Sophia, don't.' His cry came too late.

Sophia touched her palms to the beautiful, serene figure of the goddess then froze falling back as though an electric shock convulsed her whole body. Her eyes were wide, staring blankly, as she fell backwards, her head hitting the sandstone floor with a dull and sickening thud.

Dashing to her, Alex saw her eyes were still, open and yet unmoving, cold as marble. Very slowly her eyelids closed. In that awful moment he thought she was dead.

The cave was silent but he knew it, could feel it, someone was watching his every move.

'Sophia! Sophia!' he cried out, his words echoing back from the caverns in some sarcastic mimicry

Touching her jugular, the pulse was normal but there was hardly any breath in the rise and fall of Sophia's bosom. Opening her eyes, he saw they were rolled back in unconsciousness. Removing his coat Alex folded it carefully beneath her head turning her body to its side. She needed medical help immediately. Unless he could bring her round he had no choice but to fetch someone to her and then as a consequence reveal the thing they had been doing their best to keep secret. The only other choice would be to carry her himself out of the caverns to the church but carrying her along passageways and up the narrow steps to the church altar wouldn't be easy. She might not survive such a journey. Not knowing what he should do, he recalled seeing, somewhere in one of the caverns tunnels, a pool of water in a naturally formed sandstone font.

Leaving Sophia with her torch beside her he took his own from his shoulder bag and set off through the passageways. Passing through the cave of the Green Woman to the other side of the statue, he searched for marks that would identify his path on that first visit of exploration alone in the caverns, until he found the bowl shaped declivity in the rock, worn naturally by the constant drip of water from the sandstone rocks above. Removing his riding boot Alex filled it with water and returned to Sophia.

She lay, where he had left her, still as death. He determined to get her out of the caverns by himself resolving not to leave her there alone.

Looking at the green statue Alex shouted angrily ait it. 'You did this.'

Kneeling beside Sophia, he carefully dripped water to her forehead and neck and leaning over kissed her.

'Wake up my lovely, please.'

The shock of the icily, cold water startled her into arousal. Murmuring, her eyes flickered momentarily open. Staring wildly around, at the cave and the statue, Sophia struggled to rise.

Lifting her in his arms to sitting position Alex opened her lips brushing his fingers across them, moistening them.

Reviving, gazing at him, unable to remember where she was, Sophia wrapped her arms around his neck.

'My precious Sophia, I thought I'd lost you, forever.'

'Not that easy.' She purred, tired as though waking from a deep sleep.

'Let's get out of here into the fresh air.' Alex urged. 'Can you stand?'

'I believe so. But I feel so sick Alex, I'm sorry.'

Clutching her waist as she struggled on with wobbling, faltering steps, they staggered through the passages until they reached the safety of the church.

Letting Alex restore the altar over the cavern entrance, Sophia slumped on a pew, sucking air in deep inhalations struggling to bring life back to her dull limbs and lethargic senses.

Outside, in the fields, she turned to Alex and said, 'Something very strange happened to me in there. I seemed to leave my body and was enveloped in a blinding white light then the green statue came alive and bent over me smiling. I was taken back to Henley Hall, to my mother on the night of her death. It was so unreal, like watching a film. My mother was running with me again to the room with the marble statue. She pulled me inside and I saw her secure the door.'

Sophia rested her head on Alex' chest, clinging tightly to him, and stared into his face intensely, 'I now know where mother hid the relic.'

'We'll talk about it later. You need a doctor. I'm taking you to a hospital the moment we get home,' he said, brushing her imaginings aside.

'It wasn't hallucination, my memory really has come back, all the details are there, the noise of the men, what my mother was wearing, even the smell of her perfume, all of it.'

'If the doctors give you a clean bill of health, we will see if you are right but it may just be a dream or false memory caused by the fall, you really did hit that floor hard. I'm surprised you're alive.'

Alex gently placed a cushion beneath Sophia's head, covered her with his car blanket and drove to a private hospital in the pre-dawn, early hours.

The consultant, who knew Sophia and all her family, after numerous tests was satisfied she was suffering mild concussion.

'There is a large bruise on her head but that will go away. She will need to rest for at least three days.

I will see her again after that. It would be a good idea if she stayed here at the hospital for us to keep an eye on her.'

'Not at all,' Sophia interjected. 'I will be perfectly well soon.'

Sophia wanted to search the marble room at Henley Hall, immediately, but Alex refused, insisting she rested. Her health was more important to him than some archaic relic, no matter who it belonged to or how valuable and he told her so, more firmly than he had ever spoken to her before, and to his surprise she submitted. The days passed impatiently, Sophia doing her best to be indolent, something she was not good at, and trying at the same time to prove she was well again, but Alex never relented.

Eventually the time came. They went to Henley Hall, and entered the marble room.

The beautiful statue on its plinth, alive in its perfection, he could have sworn was watching their every move.

Unhesitatingly Sophia rushed directly to the statue and kneeling down beside it, pushing hard, against a corner of the plinth, a side of the marble pedestal moved almost noiselessly to reveal an oblong shaped cavity beneath the statue. Reaching inside Sophia pulled out a most beautiful, jewelled box. Laying it on the floor at Alex' feet, he could see it was entirely of silver and tooled exquisitely with intricate design. The lid of the box was covered with inlaid gemstones, of superb cut and brilliance, diamonds, rubies, sapphires and many others he didn't know the names of. Squatting next to Sophia, they tried to open it but could find no join at any of its edges. Eventually they gave up.

'We have to tell father we've found it. He's probably the only person who knows the secret of how to open it'

Returning the casket securely to the receptacle beneath the statue they closed the wall of the plinth, locked the marble room and entered Lord Allan's rooms.

'How are you papa?' Sophia asked, kissing his cheek.

No response came from Lord Allan's lips. He sat in his bed, propped against his pillows, obliviously staring through the open windows.

Alex walked over to the windows and closed them then taking a notepad, from the table beside Lord Allan's bed, he wrote:

'We have found your missing relic.'

Thrusting the note in Lord Allan's hands, he held it up, prompting him to look at it. Lord Allan showed no inclination to do so until Sophia leaned across and whispered in his ear. Looking down

Lord Allan's eyes opened wide and, for the first time since he had fallen ill, he spoke

'Is it true Sophie?' His voice was the hollow murmur of someone in deep pain.

Laying a finger to her lips, impressing silence, Sophia nodded.

Like a corpse rising from the dead Lord Allan's face filled with colour. A small tear appeared in the corner of his eye. Taking Sophia's and Alex's hand he shook them warmly.

Within days Lord Allan's health had improved, he was almost his old self invigorated by the news. He was able to walk once more in the gardens of the great house.

Walking with him one morning Sophia asked bluntly. 'Daddy is the relic a skull?

Henry Allan looked at his daughter in wide eyed astonishment.

'What makes you think that?'

'You should know you can't hide anything from a woman especially me.' Sophie smiled.

'You were always gifted Sophia. I named you after the goddess of wisdom and you have never failed to live up to your name.'

'Well, am I right?'

'Then you almost seem to know it all. Members of our order will soon come from all over the world, some of the most influential and powerful men.

No one, except the initiated, can know anything of our society, not even you. You've already suffered enough just as did your poor mother.'

'Is it a skull?' Sophia persisted.

'I can't tell you what it is. After the ceremony it will be hidden again and you will never know. '

Sophia explained where she had found the jewelled case omitting the caverns from her explanation.

'But we couldn't open it.'

'Lucky for you,' Lord Allan said, relieved.

'The relic is inside isn't it?' Sophia stood in front of her father confronting him directly.

'It has great power in it. I myself wouldn't dare gaze inside without absolution, penance and fasting.'

'What is it Daddy?' Sophia begged.

'That much I can't tell you, at inception and acceptance we are sworn, on our lives, to secrecy. You already know far too much Sophia.' Taking her shoulders and looking kindly into her eyes, Lord Allan spoke regretfully. 'If I could, I would tell you.'

Sophia realising it was a useless quest walked beside her father leisurely back to the house.

Stopping before they reached the Hall Lord Henry said, 'Close to a thousand years ago the Holy Knights were in the Valley of the Kidron, near Jerusalem, when they were attacked by the

Arab Caliphate. They were formidable warriors the Arabs, gentlemanly, scholarly and skilled horse fighters. The Holy Order would never retreat, by rule, unless outnumbered eight to one. In this case the enemy were three thousand against sixty knights. Fearlessly our Order fought until they knew they would all die unless they retreated. They fell back losing half of their men in the attempt, to the pool of Siloam where there was fresh water. Close by was the Church of the Holy Sepulchre. This had been a place of holy pilgrimage for centuries. Their enemies, the Arabs, were encircling them within it. Fearing loss of the relics held in the sepulchre, realising they couldn't save the church and all it contained two knights took what they could of the relics and among them the most revered object of all.'

'The skull,' Sophia said excitedly.

Lord Allan scowled at his daughter.

'I have warned you, Sophia, never speak of this idea of yours.'

'So that's it,' Sophia muttered to herself.

'I will tell you this. It is the most powerful, sacred symbol in the world.'

Taking his daughter by the shoulders Lord Henry warned, 'Things could become very, *very* dangerous around here, soon. Please Sophia don't interfere anymore.'

The Green Goddess

Hugging his daughter, fearful for her, Lord Henry was thinking of how his wife, the fairest of women who walked the earth, had died so cruelly, unnecessarily and tragically, all those empty years ago.

CHAPTER THIRTY ONE

A splendid sunny morning woke Alex early. In his office at Barrington he gazed over the fields to the mysterious Druids Hill. It looked an image of Arcadian peacefulness. He knew that to be far from the truth.

The phone rang. It annoyed him this morning, an intrusion on his time, callers rang about his books, photos, lectures and then went on to discuss personal problems and life in general. Almost he didn't answer the persistent ring. He lifted the receiver.

'Mr Roedale?'

Alex recognised, and welcomed, the distinctive sultry voice of Psyche immediately.

'Yes, good morning Psyche.'

'I have some news for you, the photos you showed me of that green goddess with the inscription beneath.'

Alex held his breath trying not to miss a word.

'Well, I still haven't transcribed it completely but I'm sure it's a Phoenician-Hebraic text. The important thing is, I've deciphered something quite exciting and incredible. You have somehow uncovered one of the greatest archaeological finds ever. Part of the inscription reads,

'Hiram of Tyre, made this at the request of Solomon the Great.'

'You mean King Solomon of the Bible? Alex asked in astonishment.'

'The same and it means we can date the statue at almost three thousand years. The most important thing however is the name 'Hiram of Tyre,' that explains to me the Phoenician-Hebraic.'

'You have heard of this person?'

'Yes, indeed. Hiram had a Phoenician father and a Jewish mother. What's more he is mentioned in the Bible as being sent to Solomon as the most skilled craftsman in all Phoenicia.'

'That's wonderful Psyche. Can we tie it to the group of wisdom goddesses?'

On the other end of the phone Alex could hear Psyche laughing in the way women everywhere do when excited.

'My dear Alex, Solomon of all people was known for his great wisdom. He believed it was a gift to him from God. He was also renowned for worshipping multiple gods and wrote of the Jewish Goddess of Wisdom, whom it seems, from his writings, he worshipped.'

Alex silently tried to understand this new twist to the enigma.

'Mr Roedale?' Psyche called on the phone puzzled by his silence.

'I'm trying to take it in. You mean we have found Solomon's Goddess of Wisdom?' Alex answered coming out of his reverie.

'I would say so. There is more to the inscription but I wasn't able to decipher that yet.'

'How on earth could it have disappeared from Palestine and arrived in England?'

'I wouldn't know but one explanation could be that when Phoenicians raided the Temple and took away, according to the Bible, all its silver, gold and treasures that was one of the objects. You already know Phoenicians were the ancient tin and silver traders of Cornwall and maybe it came via that route.'

'If I were there I would hug you.'

'You can do it anytime Alex,' Psyche laughed.

Alex put the phone down and went over everything Psyche had told him. The Green Woman was sculptured for Solomon some three thousand years ago and could have arrived in England with Phoenician traders. Where did that fit into the puzzle? He had no idea, just more information that led nowhere.

Alex's father had been, until his early demise, a successful entrepreneur. He had hoped Alex would follow him in the business empire he had worked so hard to create. Disappointed at his son's reluctance he had let him go, but in parting gave him a hard earned piece of business knowledge.

'To succeed in anything one needs enthusiasm, determination and the best advice. Ask experts in their field, get more than one opinion, then trust your own judgment.'

That morning Alex after recalling his father's words rang various Synagogues and set off to meet a Rabbi renowned for his knowledge of Jewish history.

Sheepcote Street a tired looking piece of Victoriana, lay in the centre of Birmingham, surrounded by the noise of reckless traffic, adjoining one of the most notorious nightclub areas in Europe. An unlikely place to find a city Synagogue, but in the days when it was built Birmingham had then been known as the Puritan capital of England.

Rabbi Jacobi, a kindly looking man with bright, intelligent eyes, led Alex to a spacious library office. Alex had expected, from the exterior of the building, to find a Dickensian study with poor light and dusty books and papers everywhere. What he found was a meticulously arranged bright modern office, spotless, newly painted, with computer and cordless phone. Any businessman would have felt at ease there.

'Sit down Mr Roedale. Can I get you a tea with lemon?' The Rabbi asked cheerfully. 'I don't get a lot of visitors and hardly any non-Jews.'

Alex waited silently while the rabbi made tea.

'I asked to see you because I was told you are the leading scholar in Jewish history and mythology,' Alex explained.

'People exaggerate but I do the best I can. You said on the phone you needed to know about King Solomon's wisdom and his beliefs?'

'Yes, and more specifically is it true he worshipped more than one god?'

'Sadly, but you didn't need me to tell you that because in the Book of Kings in your own Bible it makes it quite clear he worshipped Ashtoreth.'

'Who is that precisely?'

'Precisely, that I can't do because we don't know all we would like to about these Mesopotamian gods and in this case goddess. Ashtoreth is Hebrew for the goddess Astarte sometimes known as Ishtar. The Greeks called her Aphrodite, the Romans Juno the wife of Jupiter. She was associated with Venus. Representations of her, you perhaps know, were mostly nude depictions. In Egypt she was quite often exhibited as an Isis figure with a child on her knee. One of her symbols was the dove the Christian Church adopted as a symbol of the Holy Spirit.' The Rabbi looked up at the ceiling thoughtfully. 'You know in Russia they still set doves free at weddings. The power of enduring folk memory,' the Rabbi observed. 'As a goddess she represented love and fertility. She also was a goddess of war. Well, marriage is a battle and all is fair in love and war.'

The Rabbi's face crinkled with infectious humour as he drank his tea. 'Is that what you want to know?'

'I honestly can't say, but tell me could Ashtoreth also be a goddess of wisdom?'

The Rabbi contemplated this query for a moment.

'It's a difficult question but in my own opinion, Solomon I believe, saw her as that. Let me show you a passage from your own Bible, found in the book named, The Wisdom of Solomon.'

Pushing half-lens, pinz-nez glasses on his nose the Rabbi reached behind his chair, picked up a

Bible, shuffled the pages and opened to the passage he had referred to.

'Here it is, Chapter Seven.'

"The spirit of Wisdom is intelligent and holy. Wisdom moves more easily than motion itself; she is so pure that she penetrates everything. She is a breath of God's power a pure and radiant stream of glory from the Almighty. She is a reflection of eternal light. Even though wisdom acts alone, she can do anything. She makes everything new, although she herself never changes. From generation to generation she enters the souls of holy people, and makes them God's friends and prophets. Wisdom is more beautiful than the sun and all the constellations. Her great power reaches into every part of the world. Wisdom has been my *love*."

Rabbi Jacobi looked up to see if Alex had caught the significance of the words, before continuing.

"I courted her when I was young and wanted to make her my bride. I fell in love with her beauty. She glorifies her noble origin by living with God, the Lord of all, who loves her. So I decided to take Wisdom home to live with me."

All the while the Rabbi had been reading Alex was thinking of the green marble statue that men fell in love with.

The Rabbi looked up over the top of his glasses. 'I believe this answers your question. Solomon worshipped Ashtoreth the goddess of wisdom. He even built a temple to her near Jerusalem.'

Alex took the photo of the Green Woman from the pocket of his jacket and dropped it in front of the Rabbi. 'Could this be Ashtoreth?'

The Rabbi looked at Alex's photo with startled concentration.

'This is remarkable. Where did you see this?'

Opening his desk draw the Rabbi pulled out a magnifying glass to view the photograph minutely. 'What wonderful craftsmanship,' he admired.

'Is it Ashtoreth?'

'I can't of course tell you that without knowing more of its history. There is nothing I ever heard of like it from that period.'

'What if I tell you it was made for Solomon by Hiram of Tyre?'

Rabbi Jacobi, rubbing his eyes, sat quietly for a moment his hand nervously touching his mouth. 'What makes you think this? He asked.

'An inscription found with it.'

'If what you say is true, it would certainly be one of the greatest of archaeological discoveries. If this was made by the man you mention, an acclaimed craftsman that worked on Solomon's Temple, then this,' the Rabbi tapped the photo in front of him, 'Is Ashtoreth. What a work of art, unsurpassed, and what beauty.'

Taking the photo back Alex said, 'Thank you, you have been of great help to me. Before I leave, something else I would ask, what is the earliest date for the Jews in England?'

'You are full of surprises, sir. Why would you ask such a question?'

'This sculpture arrived here somehow.'

'In England?' The rabbi asked in astonishment.

'Yes.'

Leaning back and folding his arms the Rabbi said, 'No one can say exactly when Jews arrived in England. You do have the tale of Joseph of Arimathea, the supposed uncle of Jesus. It is possible some came with Phoenician traders. We know there were Jews in Tarshish, often mentioned in the Tanakh, the Hebrew Bible, and some scholars believe Tarshish was Britain. In Spain a Jewish signet ring was found dated at eight hundred BCE. Now I want to ask you a question. Was this object found beneath an oak tree?'

This time it was Alex who fell into surprised silence. It occurred to him the Rabbi knew more of the sculpture than he was admitting.

'Yes, but how do you know that?

'Abraham our ancestor came to the sacred tree of Moreh at Shechem and God appeared to him there and promised the land of Palestine to him. Abraham settled there. Jacob the founder of Israel also came to the trees at Shechem and hid the idols of his tribe under the mighty Oak of Shechem. Until the destruction of Shechem, and the sacred oak and grove there, the place had become, for the children of Israel, a meeting place. I would like to say if this beautiful object, you have shown me in this photo, was found beneath an oak in a grove of trees, then they were Jews who placed it there. Can you tell more about it and would it be possible for me to see it with my own eyes?

'I wish Rabbi Jacobi that I could take you there, but I can't. I don't own this object. I'm not sure the place should ever be disclosed to anyone.'

'Ah! Yes, you are probably correct. The destruction, the jealousies, the professional infighting, this I understand.'

Rabbi Jacobi stood to signal the meeting was over and held out his hand.

'One other question,' Alex said taking the Rabbi's hand. 'Do you know of any connections between the goddess of wisdom and a skull?'

'The name of the sacred tree of Moreh meant wisdom or oracle. The skull I can't help you with. I never heard of such a thing. Wait though there was a story of a talking skull. Yes, now I remember. We have a legendary story of a famous Rabbi of Moravia, in what is now the Czech Republic, named Rabbi Loew. He was a mystical man with great powers. One day a young Jewish man was lured to a supposed wedding, in an Arab land, but when he arrived there he was put in a library to study wisdom all his life. In the library he found a talking head that couldn't lie. The head told him of the dangers of the place where he was a prisoner and how to escape. The head belonged to another Jew.'

'Where would such a tale come from?

'Many of our folk tales are very, very old. The context of an Arab land and wisdom and the talking head perhaps has a meaning for you?'

'I'm not sure yet,' Alex answered.

'May I keep the photo you showed to me?'

Taking the photo from his pocket Alex gave it to the Rabbi. 'It is the least I can do.'

Rabbi Jacobi took the photo in his hand, staring at it affectionately.

Driving out of the city, avoiding the heavy traffic of motorways, Alex took a country road to Oxford, through market towns and orchards teeming with blossom among black timbered villages. At Oxford he stayed with friends. Leaving his car with them, the following morning he caught a train to London where from the Holborn tube, in a sudden downpour of squalling rain, he walked to Great Queen Street to a grey building that looked like a confused amalgam of art deco and Hindu stupa.

A tall, neatly dressed, middle aged man welcomed him inside.

'The person you wanted to speak to asked me to apologise, he couldn't meet you personally as he had hoped. He is away on urgent official duty. I'm his secretary by the way and he asked that I give you full assistance. Let's hope I have the answers you are looking for.'

They sat in a roomy lounge of wing chairs facing each other.

'It was kind of you to agree to help me.' Alex said sitting down. 'I needn't take much of your time.'

'We are always happy to help.' The secretary smiled.

'Is it true that Masons are another name for Templars?'

'Strictly speaking? No, because our structure and purposes are different. However, they were our antecedents and we carry on many of their traditions.'

'And esoteric knowledge?'

The secretary looked directly at Alex trying to measure why he had asked this and how he should answer it.

'Yes, according to many authorities.'

'Would you have any idea what a skull with a letter 'B' beneath it could mean?'

The secretary frowned, puzzled by the question.

'I am not sure about that. You are perhaps referring to the skull of the Templars? There was a medieval rumour, used as an indictment against them before they were disbanded, that they worshipped a talking skull. I think that is all anyone can say about it. It was just propaganda against the Templars, concocted to destroy them, so historians assert.'

'What could the letter 'B' stand for?'

'I have no idea unless it means Baphomet.'

There was a sudden shift in the secretary's face and voice and a less than friendly glance that indicated Alex should pursue the question.

'Who is Baphomet?'

The secretary sighed. 'There is much debate about that. The Templars seem to have worshipped an idol, some say a relic, of some kind by that name. It was so long ago no one knows for sure. They were, after all, a brotherhood with many secrets. The name itself is obscure. It has been conjectured it refers to the Prophet Mohammad or some Islamic Sufi saint.'

Alex aware of the secretary's reluctance to voice an opinion or discuss the matter, pressed further. 'What do you think?'

'I am not an expert on these things.'

'You have an opinion, I'm sure,' Alex persisted.

'An accusation against the Templars was that their source of great wealth and strength came from

The Green Goddess

the idol Baphomet. The name, in my less than knowledgeable belief is that it means, 'The seat or source of understanding.' That view comes from Dr Hugh Sconfield, a scholar who worked extensively on the Dead Sea Scrolls. He said the word Baphomet, means Wisdom and was a Jewish codename. To be honest about it Jewish authorities disagree with that explanation and it really is sensationalist nonsense.'

At last, Alex thought, he was getting somewhere. He wanted to leave and return to Barrington immediately. Instead he sat there doing his best to be polite.

The secretary continued, 'Another explanation, which is most certainly nearer the truth, is that the name Baphomet comes from the Greek words, 'Baphe' and 'Metis' which together mean 'Baptism of Wisdom.' Personally my view of this matter is, if the Templars had such a relic, it was used in some kind of Baptism ritual, or ceremony, merely to serve the purpose of reminding them of the brevity of life.'

'This agrees with my own conclusion,' Alex said affably. 'Tell me though what is the story behind 'Apprentice Pillars' that are found in churches associated with the Templars?'

Smiling broadly, crossing his legs and placing his hands on the arms of his chair, the secretary was pleased the conversation had turned within his own knowledge of the history of the movement. He nodded his head.

'It is true that they are often found in churches with Templar connections, but not always, and they have nothing whatever to do with apprentice masons.'

'What then?'

The secretary laughed quietly. 'Can you imagine a wealthy aristocrat allowing some trainee mason to indulge himself, at his expense, in an edifice that was built as a mausoleum to his family and to last for a thousand years? These rich lords built out of their devotion to the church, and to have a lasting monument to their largesse, for their own honour and peaceful repose and I suppose earthly immortality'

'What is the meaning of these pillars then?' Alex enquired.

'They reveal that the benefactor, the lord who paid for the structure, had reached the highest level of esoteric knowledge. It was perhaps a hidden signal of his status in the Temple hierarchy. What they really depict is the 'Tree of Knowledge,' mentioned in the Bible.'

'Intriguing,' Alex replied standing and shaking the secretary's hand.

'May I inform his Highness we were able to help your research?'

'Absolutely and more than I'd hoped for.'

Sophie held Alex hand as they unbolted the wooden door of Henley Church. She loved the feel of his strong masculine fingers in hers. It was cold inside the church and the air pervaded by a musty lingering smell. The afternoon sun, suffusing light through the stained glass of the windows, fell delicately on the pews and altar, accentuating the silence and serenity.

'I believe you are right Sophia. It's here right in front of us if we could recognise the clues.'

Sophie turned her head towards him nodding agreement.

Alex watched the exquisite beauty of her face in the half light. There was no one like her, as beautiful, in his eyes, as the Green Goddess herself.

'Yes, I know I am. I knew, by some kind of feminine intuition, the answers we are looking for have been built into this wonderful church.'

Sophia remembered the times she had worshipped with her family, in the church, from her earliest childhood without even contemplating the secrets it held. She felt a certainty in her heart that within the church lay the answer to their quest, infallible and sublime. The church had been built with clues hidden in its fabric that only the initiate of the Order would recognise, the tombs, the caves of the goddess, the pillar of knowledge, the effigy of the unnamed knight, the woman's skull with the letter 'B' as the baptism of wisdom, the sculpture of the Green Woman that had disturbed Alex, by its powerful presence, when he had first attended Sunday worship there with her.

Impulsively Sophia let go of Alex's hand to walk into the Lady Chapel. Behind and above the votive candles was a statue of the Madonna. It was a powerful image but more like a Greek goddess than the delicately demure Virgin. Why hadn't she noticed before she wondered? It had the same compassion and love in the eyes, and perfect childlike face, but there was also a power in it she hadn't noticed in other similar sculptures. Sophia realised for the first time, in a eureka moment, that this was the Green Woman in the disguise of the Madonna.

CHAPTER THIRTY TWO

Ralph swinging himself out of the car took a hip flask from his pocket and drank from it several times. Returning the flask, he lit a cigarette and blew a ring of smoke into the still air of the afternoon then, in an afterthought, grinning, he twirled his forefinger around the smoky circle and pushed his finger through the centre.

He was looking at the shell of the once stately, historic Morville Hall. A melancholy scene of devastating loneliness.

Strange how much of a building could be destroyed by fire, the roof had gone, all the floors, and at ground level lay the sad rubble of eight hundred years of history. Just a windy pretence. Ralph didn't show any sadness in his decadent, finely chiselled face, nor did he feel any. Running his fingers through his tousled blonde hair he once more drank from his flask, raised it in a final salute and smirked. Looking into the distance, at the hills and woods, he remembered days when the Hall had been a happy place, when each summer the villagers and farm children had been entertained with their parents on the green lawns. He sighed, all that ended when his father, flying their private aeroplane home from France, had plunged into the channel. He thought of his mother how he had seen her sitting for hours staring sadly over the gardens. She died of grief, he was sure of it and now he was old enough to see it and understand. At fifteen he had been left to the care of a brutal governess.

He was, he reminded himself, happy to see the last of the place, nothing but a drain in the pocket. The land was still his, much could be done with that, then there would be the twenty eight million in insurance on the property coming to him and Jane, perfect. It would be sufficient compensation for the house and its valuable art collection all the best of which had been moved, many moons ago, to his Gloucestershire mansion. The insurers didn't know that. He laughed silently at his astuteness and foresight and unexpected good fortune.

Tossing his cigarette to the drive, he crushed it flat with his shoe, got back into his car and drove slowly away.

The journey to his Gloucester home took, at his furious pace, one and a half hours down the tree lined M5. His home was a lordly manor house built of Cotswold stone during the fifteenth century.

Ralph poured a glass of wine and reclined in an easy chair. Jane, his wife, was at their Spanish villa so here he could relax with his mistress, sitting in pink panties, across his knees. Squeezing her, he pulled her closer and kissing her passionately, trickled wine across her nipples and sucked it away to her delighted squeals of pleasure.

'So you will be even more rich?' she said, peering into his eyes, seeking the truth.

'When the insurance comes, yes.' He knew the fever, wealth roused in her avaricious heart. As he ran his hand along her thigh to her crotch he wondered if she knew the pain wealth dragged forever in its wake.

'Twenty eight million! Oh, my god'

Caroline threw her arms in the air lifting her incomparable breasts into soft, intoxicating, fluid spheres.

'Tell me more about this relic, you've been talking about.'

Running his hand over her breast Ralph folded his arm around her waist.

'There isn't anything to tell.' He parried her question.

'What is it?'

'At a wild guess, I'd say, probably a skull of great antiquity and spiritual value.'

'That's why the Pope wants it?'

Ralph had met her when she was fifteen. They had been together for seven years and he had watched her develop into a lithe cat like grace that turned men's heads. Every moment they were together he felt a fire that was unquenchable in his loins.

He should never have told her any of this, but his resolutions faded whenever he looked at her. She could extract anything from him and he was helpless before her beauty.

Caroline sighed and looked away in disbelief.

'Sometimes your stories are so incredible no one can believe them.' Folding her arms around his neck she stared deeply into his eyes. 'Is it really true?'

'I believe so.'

'How much will you make if you find it?'

Ralph loved feeding her unquenchable avarice. 'At least a billion, maybe more.'

'Aah! She rose from his knees to jump from one foot to the other, her arms flailing around as she spun in circles.

'I don't believe it, I don't believe it.' She laughed, and screamed, her face turned to the ceiling.

Grasping her, rolling her to the carpet, he lay on top of her pushing her legs apart with his.

'Then believe this you hungry bitch.'

Caroline rose early, quietly taking her clothes off a chair and tip toed into the bathroom. Stretching her naked body she rubbed her skin vigorously with the palms of her hands. Looking at her reflection in the mirror, she combed her curling, strawberry blonde hair, tying it back with a blue clasp. She peered more closely at herself, her eyes were puffed, and with horror she saw tiny hair line rays at the corners of her eyes. Yesterday she had noticed a single grey hair above her left ear and in panic had plucked it out.

'He did this to me.' she thought angrily.

Dressing quickly she silently entered the bedroom. Ralph was still fast asleep. She glared at him maliciously. There was no love in her icy gaze. Piqued, she felt an inner anger clutch her heart, she could never forgive him for marrying that plain socialite instead of her. Turning away from him, she crept downstairs in her bare feet and left the house, closing the door softly behind her, before putting on her shoes. She would make him suffer for it.

A mile or so down the lane Caroline stopped her car, looked at her watch and rang a number on a slim illuminated phone.

A month previously, arriving home in the early hours at her country cottage, she had put the key to the door when she was startled by a man standing beside her, confronting her, preventing her entrance to the cottage. Caroline drew in her breath deeply, in fear, too afraid even to scream.

'Please don't be afraid,' He said in a European accent.

Recovering she asked angrily, 'What do you want?'

'I have a business proposition that could bring you a great deal of money.' The man thrust a piece of paper in her hand with a phone number. 'We need information. We think you could help us. Think about it. If you are interested please ring this number.'

'What kind of information? Caroline had asked her interest aroused.

'Even I don't know that. I was just asked to speak to you.' The man left and was gone into the darkness of the country lane before she could question him further.

The Green Goddess

After several days Caroline rang the number. An Italian voice answered and passed instructions to her. She had been elated at the money they offered her for such a small thing and agreed.

Now holding her mobile, waiting for the other end it was pay up time. A voice answered gruffly, sleepily, in Italian.

'Salve.'

'Mr Pollino?' Caroline asked.

'Si. Chi e?'

'Mi chiamo Carolina, you asked me to ring if I had any news.' She was deliberately evasive, they had warned, severely, about mentioning anything specific over the phone, to anyone unless it was Pollino.

Pollino, wide awake now, raised his corpulent frame upright in bed. He recognised the voice of the woman, 'Si, si.'

'The object you are searching for is a skull,' she said, clearly and precisely, like a child in a verbal examination.

This meant nothing to Antonio Pollino. He was just a courier contact. His instructions had been to repeat verbally all he was told by this young woman.

'I will pass this on right away,' Pollino said.

'And the money?'

'Whatever you were promised, our word will be kept. In one week, I have been instructed to tell you, the money will be in your account. Also I was instructed to thank you for your help, it is appreciated and we won't forget.'

The phone went dead. Caroline smiled and breathed deeply. Now she could leave that immoral pig for good.

From his Italian villa Antonio Pollino rang the Sardinian number of Licio's palace.

Licio, known for his early rising and minimal hours of sleep, paced up and down his room. Outside, the sprinklers had already begun the greening of the lawns and flower beds of the gardens. Looking down at his thin legs he tugged his boxer shorts higher up his waist and laughed quietly, Shakespeare was right, age, fat bellies and thin thighs. Taking a Cuban cigar, from a marble case on a coffee table, he snipped the end and did a jig around the room, as though his feet were on fire, before lighting up and drawing peacefully the thick taste into his mind and heart.

So they are looking for a skull? Why would such an object be so desirable to the Vatican. His mind raced over the possibilities. Whose skull? That was the question. When he knew the answer to that the amount they had offered him would have to be negotiable.

The Green Goddess

Staring over the lawns to a fountain he noticed a lone bird sitting on the edge of its dripping fountain bowl. He couldn't say why but the sighting of this solitary creature, amid the splendour of his estate, surreally prevented his momentary exhilaration, inexplicably changing his mood to one of fear. Wrapping his initialled robe around his body he grabbed a phone from its cradle and dialled.

'Roberto!'

'Si'

'The moment he has the object, eliminate him.'

Licio listened, impatiently, to the man at the other end of the line. 'What? No the details are not important. It must be done without trace Roberto.'

CHAPTER THIRTY THREE

Helicopters disturbed the tranquillity of fir and beech woods as they came in low over Henley estate, flattening leaves and grass, bending ornamental bushes and flower beds and sending waves of tremor across the fields. Flocks of startled birds flew across the sky. Horses in an adjoining paddock stamped and snorted, raised their heads, shook their manes, and took flight at the whoosh and rhythmic thud of the helicopter blades. Dust phantoms blew across the courtyard and lawns of Henley Hall.

Ten guests arrived that morning in six flights. Lord Henry met each on the steps of Henley Hall greeting each man by name and accompanied them inside where everyone was shown to his own private room.

They were old friends, the hierarchy of the ancient order, descendants all of the original founders of the brotherhood. It was their custom to meet annually and every time he noticed the physical changes since they last met. The spirit in a man never changes only his outer shell he ruminated but it was time for new blood to be added. Shenley should and would be joining the order on this most special of occasions.

Lord Henry enquired about their families with intimate interest. The history of each he knew as well as his own and he was bound by honour to share all with them.

As he shook their hands there was an unspoken renewal of loyalty, faithfulness and duty to each other. Some things are temporal, some fashionable, some eternal such as trust, courage and endurance. Every member knew they relied on each other, leaving no room for animosities or shuffling for rank. Their lives depended on their closely knit camaraderie.

Behind the scenes, of this brotherly union, Kevin had set up heightened security. Though ostensibly fulfilling his duties as butler he was unobtrusively watching each guest as they engaged in their daily activities. Around the perimeter of Henley, and inside the house, hidden cameras observed every movement. A monitoring room had been planned many months before and was set up in private quarters of an isolated wing of the Hall, sealed to everyone except Kevin and three military officer comrades.

'We need to cover the area twenty four hours. I am asking for a three shift system but you have freedom to work within that, whatever personal arrangements you have, so long as we do it, an' of course I'll be here as a backup if I'm needed.'

'Food?' An officer asked.

'Malt?' Another quipped. The men tumbled in laughter.

'Well now, the whisky'll come but only if you do a good job, and the refreshments, you can be sure, won't be army rations and they'll be brought here by meself.'

It would be long and exacting work, cameras and monitors operating, every minute of the seven days they would be there.

The guest list was impressive; a president of one of the largest metal companies in the world, an oil magnate, three European aristocrats, two prominent European politicians, an American General, a renowned surgeon and an Anglican Bishop.

Lord Henry, as Master of the order, more than anyone was acutely aware of the dangers they would be exposed to. In five days time the relic would, if all went well, be taken to the caverns as part of the

Order's ritual. Between now and that moment anything could happen.

By evening Henley's dining hall was brightly lit with candles, as the sole source of illumination. Lord Henry had spent lavishly on the affair. A grand table was spread sumptuously, with fruit, game and steaming vegetables, on large oval platters in medieval style. When all was ready the guests entered attired in mantels of white, embossed with a blue Maltese cross, the insignia of the order, over their dinner jackets.

At the head of the table, standing, smiling at every man and nodding a welcome, Lord Henry stared along the length of the banqueting room towards the distinguished company. Watching them as they took their seats he was afraid for them. The men ceased their chatter and humour to turn their heads expectantly toward him. He raised a golden goblet embossed with a skull, 'To the Queen and Our Lady.'`

The men stood in unison with gold goblets and responded, 'The Queen and Our Lady.' All drank deeply until the goblets were empty.

Putting his cup on the table Lord Henry raised both hands expansively and gazed around at his companions.

'It is wonderful to see you again. Lords and Gentlemen please be seated.'

Clasping his hands behind his back he was hoping none of them sensed the tremors and uncertainty he felt inside.

'We are good friends, comrades all, joined in a single purpose as our ancestors were for a thousand years. Just as in the past our lives are in danger at this time. You are all aware of this I know. We always depend on each other for our safety, secrecy is our shield, loyalty our defence, courage the barrier around us none can penetrate. Once it was the military prowess of our Order and the power of the sword, that humbled the abuses of monarchs. Now the pen, persuasion and influence are our weapons. Once our enemies came on horseback, and in armour, now in expensive cars and tailored suits. Their motives are the same, a lust for power at the expense of others. Once they sought the subjugation of peoples with their armies, now they exploit with global business and political manoeuvring. Our motives also remain the same, to staunch the flow of blood, to defend the defenceless, to support the weak and encourage resistance. We are still the same warriors though in a different garb. Without our Order the world would be a far worse place, more unjust, less equal, more tyrannical. Our enemies now are just as real, tangible and deadly as the ones our ancestors fought through the centuries of our existence. The treasure we revere is the same, our dedication and purity the same, our enemies may have changed but their desire is unchanged and to that desire they have added a new lust to steal our sacred relic for gain.'

Lord Allan paused, carefully choosing his words, the room remaining silent waiting for him to continue. When he spoke again his voice was filled with repressed emotion.

'If anything happens to any of you the pain and heartbreak it would cause to all of us here cannot be expressed, so we will be determined, alert for ourselves and each other.'

Lord Allan wiped his forehead in a gesture of comic, mock distress dissipating the tension in the room.

The Hall burst into blusterous laughter.

'Now gentlemen all let's enjoy ourselves. Every one of you has his own favourite wine or drink in his goblet and more still in the pitchers directly in front.'

Lord Allan raised his cup and waited while chairs were kicked back and all stood to join him. Steadying his voice he shouted, 'A toast to Our Lady, the Goddess of all, and to our endurance and success.'

The golden goblets flashed in the light of the candles as the men lifted them at arm's length shouting in one unified voice, 'To Our Lady.'

A loud metallic ring echoed in the hall as the goblets clashed.

Like students in a college hall, the men let out an approving roar, stood, removed their white tunics, flinging them to the floor behind them, and sat down to their banquet and camaraderie.

This would be their only indulgence until the final day of their ceremony. Each made the best of it, until sated one by one they retired to their rooms.

The routine over the next few days was accepted by the guests at Henley. There would be a day of relaxation on the estate, under the watchful, ubiquitous eye of Kevin, for the more energetic or a leisurely day in a club room atmosphere inside Henley for the older members. On the third day a three day fast would be declared during which period everyone was expected to examine their conscience and confess. During this time of devotion and purification the chapel inside Henley, that had been built for secret worship during centuries of religious persecution, was open day and night.

Each morning, at ten thirty, Bishop Tom Langham held a service with helpers chosen at random from among the small group of worshippers. The men came in attired in the white mantels of the Order to kneel facing the altar. General Brett Sanders knelt awkwardly, quickly and then sat, relieving the pain that gnawed at his knee wound.

Langham, waiting for their silence, addressed them, his white mantel over his clerical vestments confirming he was no more than one of them an equal, though a priest and Bishop.

The service differed little from established church liturgy. All knelt at the communion rail and Langham prayed over them.

'O Lord our God, who art of purer eyes than to behold iniquity: Have mercy upon us, we beseech thee, for our sins accuse us, and we are troubled by them and put to shame.

Father, Eternal Mother, guide us with your light. Help us to recognise you in this worship.'

After the group responded with 'Amen' Langham crossed himself. 'Please be seated.'

'Gentlemen, brothers, I know for some of you these services are irrelevant and boring, but I would remind you if there is any need for it we have always, from the earliest of times worshipped in this way. It is our tradition, a good one and a valuable one. None of us dare look upon our sacred relic without a pure soul and intention. During the almost thousand years of our existence some tried and all paid the price. That is why we are here fasting and cleansing our consciences.'

An untidy, involuntary noise rose from the group as they shuffled uneasily in their seats. They all knew of the fearful anecdotes that, whether true or false, shouldn't be ignored.

Langham continued, 'Each of us must be clean of heart, pure in motive before we enter Her presence. In the moments of contemplation, of your life, renew your vows of total surrender. Ask if you have put the welfare of others foremost, have you injured anyone except to preserve good, have you betrayed the honesty, right speech and action our Order demands of you, have you promoted justice, equality and peace in the world?

Seek God's forgiveness for your failings. Together we have accumulated great wealth and prominence so recall also the good things you have achieved and ask for the will and strength to achieve more. Above all thank let us thank God and our Eternal Mother that we have been able to better this world, this vale of tears, we were chosen to serve. Finally, fasting isn't easy, as you know, use it to lose self and to seek union with God.' Making the sign of the cross the Bishop concluded, 'In the name of the Father, the Son, and our Eternal Mother.'

All stood until the Bishop left then most followed, talking idly, but General Sanders, Rudolph Seidel and Baron Clos, remained seated in silent prayer.

It was a difficult three days, the men hardly speaking. When they did they were curt, irritable, fighting their hunger, longing for the ordeal to end. It galled them to endure the imposition of the fast.

One of the least affected was Sanders. Used to privations as a veteran of many conflicts, Vietnam, the Gulf, South America, Iraq he carried on without complaint.

'Three days without food,' he laughed at the discomfort of the others.

The most affected by the deprivations were the aristo's and politicians, Seidel the steel man and Keefe the oil had spent years building fortunes on sixteen hour days, sandwiches and coffee. Sanders grinned. There was little difference after all between war and business. Discipline and austerity was an essential part of both.

Leaving the chapel, Sanders walked through the Hall into the sunshine of a clear, bright morning. This is what he liked about England, the smell and lush verdure of the fields.

On the patio Seidel and Clos sat together drinking mineral water.

Through the windows of Henley, Seidel caught a glimpse of Sophia and drew in a long easy breath. 'You know fasting increases libido?' He said to his friend Clos.

'An ancient remedy in Europe for over indulgence,' Baron Clos reminded.

Both men laughed.

'That daughter of Henry's is the most beautiful woman I've seen.'

'A pity we are not younger,' Clos replied.

Sanders passed the two men without speaking and sat alone at a table in a secluded corner of the wide patio that overlooked the garden fountain and the hills beyond. Straightening his leg he rubbed his old knee wound. Hearing footsteps he turned sharply to see Kevin approaching, tray in hand with a steaming pot.

'Hi, Kevin, good to see you,' Sanders greeted.

'Lovely day General, I thought you'd like coffee.' Kevin dumped the tray, with coffee pot, brown and white sugar and several cups and saucers, each painted with the distinctive Henley coat of arms, on the patio table.

'Well, thank you. That's a thoughtful gesture. I don't suppose you have a Jack Daniels to go with it?'

'I'd like to oblige. At the moment it isn't advisable sir,' Kevin grinned, 'Sure but I knew you were a man after me own heart.'

Sanders chuckled, 'Indeed I am and in more ways than one.' Turning to face Kevin, Sanders asked, 'You're a military man Kevin?''

'An' what would give you such an idea?' Kevin answered taken aback at the unexpected exposure.

Sanders waited for Kevin to pour the coffee and cream before answering.

'Sugar sir?' Kevin offered.

'No thank you. To answer your question, you can drop the pretence, I've been a professional soldier for longer than I care to acknowledge, as I'm sure you know. Do you really think I don't know a fellow officer when I see one? It's that carefree humour, born on the battlefield, the live now resolve in all you do, the quiet individuality that soldiers develop even within the restrictions of discipline, the way you stand, walk, observe. Shall I go on?'

'Well you could be right. I was in the military once.' Kevin smiled stiffly. Changing the subject a little too quickly he said, 'England's lovely in the summer, but not quite as green as Ireland. What do you think sir?'

Sanders' features spread into a good humoured smile. 'You can stand at ease, Henry spoke of you and your exploits, thought I would need your help. Sit down colonel, I know all about you.'

Kevin remained passive for a moment unwilling to be exposed, then relaxing sat down and poured himself a coffee. 'Not all I hope, an' am glad to say it. I'm sorry it's not whisky.'

'Well Kevin what do you think? Are we in danger?' Sanders probed.

'There's no doubt. Someone is watching us from those hills day and night.' Kevin nodded towards the tree clad heights.

Not turning to look, Sanders poured coffee for them both and gazed pensively at the upper windows and roofs of Henley. 'Any there weak links, that might be got at, among us?'

'I have no idea. My guess is not at all.'

'What are the plans to protect everyone?' Sanders enquired.

'At the moment all we have is surveillance.' Kevin knew this was not sufficient to ensure safety.

'Do you have night vision glasses or scopes?' Sanders asked.

'All we have is two powerful spotter scopes, no weapons of course apart from shotguns. They'll have more sophisticated equipment I'm sure, an' they won't have spared expense.'

'Alright,' Sanders answered, reminding himself this wasn't America. 'I want the two scopes put in a private room, up there,' he glanced up to the top of Henley Hall, 'With good all round views if that's possible, and a map of the estate.'

'There's a better place I know of than up there an' less likely to have been bugged. Meet me in the stables in say thirty minutes an' I'll show you.' Kevin rose and collected the tray.

At one time the extensive stables had held over fifty horses in the days of carriages and county hunts. Lord Henry now maintained just a mere half dozen. In the shade, out of the August heat, the stables smelled of fresh hay and ordure. Sanders caught the scent. It reminded him of his West Point days as cadet and the smells of his Oregon ranch. Somehow that moment gave him renewed confidence. He ambled over to the horses, still in their stalls, and stroked their muzzles affectionately. A sound disturbed him and he turned to find Kevin approaching, folder in hand.

'Military timing,' Sanders jested looking at his watch.

Handing the map to the general Kevin led to a space between two stalls where he moved an old, round runged, ladder from the wall. Raising it to a ceiling trap door he rested its securing hooks into a recess below the trap and climbed up. At the top he unbolted the door and swung it up and outwards. 'Follow me General,' he called down.

They had entered a turret where Sanders noticed a six foot long refractor telescope pointing towards a sloping window light. A large metal toothed wheel as large as a yacht steering connected to a similarly toothed rail running around the centre of the octagonal turret. On one side of the room was a single bunk bed, next to it a table and a chair and a bookcase filled with volumes on astronomy. Windows gave views on all sides. There was a wash basin, heater and electric wall plug.

'Lord Henry's father had it built to study astronomy, then Henry used it as a boy and still does, when he has time, an' Master Shenley. The turret as you can see revolves to give a three hundred and sixty view. It's an ideal observation hide. The mechanism is easy enough, you just turn the wheel an' the tower revolves. It's likely though you won't be needing to move it at all. Three parts of the estate can be seen from here easily.'

Kevin stood back hoping it would meet with the approval of Sanders experienced eye.

'Let's look at the map?' Sanders suggested, opening the folder Kevin had given him, spreading the map on the table. 'The estate is irregular in shape and that's to our advantage.' He jabbed his finger at two places. 'See here Kevin they can only watch the house from these three points and that narrows the field.' Sanders straightened and looked out of the windows. 'Perfect! With just a little adjustment of your wheel there we'll cover all those points. Hands on hips he stared across the peaceful, green landscape. 'What we need to do is locate anyone out there.'

'I'll ask the keepers to be on their guard,' Kevin added, 'We don't want any innocent folk caught up in this.'

'Yes. If we do find anyone up there we'll attack first.'

The two men looked quickly at each other and laughed.

'We'll have 'em for sure,' Kevin enthused, experiencing once more a resurging exhilaration of combat, with its adrenaline spurt, springing life and enthusiasm into the moment.

Sanders would get a US helicopter and pilot to survey the area. They both agreed it would be the best option. Sanders knew of several bases in England that wouldn't refuse his request but they didn't have much time to accomplish their goal, in four days the ceremonies would take place.

'It is enough.' He assured himself.

'Leave me alone now Kevin. I promise we'll meet soon.'

'I will bring coffee, sugar, milk and a kettle for your comfort, when I have a moment, you're going to need them.' Kevin's years of experience left him with no illusions about how difficult a long vigil was, how it sapped ones concentration, and that could mean the difference between success and failure.

As soon as Kevin left Sanders pulled a wood, table chair over to the window and positioned the spotter scope in front of it. In turn he stared out of the windows across the incomparable, English landscape.

Sanders had joined the military as soon as his young age permitted and had through his father's influence gained a scholarship entrance to West Point. It was what he had desired more than anything. He had felt it a man's duty to defend the things he loved, his family, his country and his beliefs. Perhaps naively, in hindsight, he had become a soldier to fight injustice. 'Injustice?' He'd seen a lot of that in the world and here the situation oozed it. Those men in the hills, he had no doubt, were there waiting, were willing to kill for monetary gain. They needed to be taught a lesson. He had come to the right place, at the right time, again.

The woods and fields opposite were peaceful at the moment. Sitting, Sanders shuffled the chair to a more comfortable position in which to manipulate the scope. Satisfied any movement in the terrain could be observed he settled back. The very stillness in the trees, the way the sheep in the lower fields stopped feeding to stare at the woods told him someone was in the hills. Focusing the scope he ranged the woods minutely but could see nothing to give a location of any intruders. To the right of where he was looking was a dense patch of woodland fir. He made a mental note to focus on that particular spot later.

Getting up he moved the chair to another window where he carefully positioned the second telescope. The landscape was different on this side, the ground concealing hollows, undulations and wild undergrowth, 'Ideal terrain,' he mused. Sweeping the landscape he saw a flock of pigeons fly upwards, startled, and in the distance heard the raucous moan of a magpie. Leaning over to the table, grabbing his map, he found the place and marked it with a cross.

A noise below the tower, disturbing him, told him Kevin was back. The trap door was pushed open, and Kevin's head appeared for a moment only to disappear and reappear. Kevin held a tray of steaming coffee, and a kettle, handed it to him and disappeared again to return with a loaded hamper of food. This time climbing inside and closing the trap Kevin panted, 'I think I'm out of shape,' and laughed. Flinging open the lid of the wicker hamper he pulled out a bottle of Jack Daniels. 'I know, I know, it's breakin' the rule but after all we're old soldiers. A lapse is due, I'm thinking'.

They drank their coffee laced with whisky and Sanders explained what he'd observed.

'Once I've found them, and I will, we'll go up there, after dark, and disable them and any equipment or firepower they have.' Sanders commented. 'We'll leave it until the day before the ceremony, that way they'll have no chance to regroup or re-equip.'

'I agree General, but I've been thinking we need a decoy on the day you move the relic. I can get *my* men to lure them to a false trail. The least it can accomplish is get rid of a few of them. We have no idea how many of them are waiting.'

'It's unlikely there's more than a half dozen. It would be too conspicuous and unreliable. That's my opinion. We have to *assume* they have military training but they may just be a bunch of amateur assholes,' Sanders corrected, 'But that Kevin is a good idea of yours.'

Sanders paused then asked.'Is there anyone, not from here, who could go and look at these places?' Sanders leaned over his map and showed the places marked with a cross. 'Someone with his wits about him who could look at these as though he was out walking?'

'Ah! Well, there is come to think of it. There's Alex Roedale over at Barrington Hall a friend of Sophia Allan, an explorer, travelled even more than we have, in the most inhospitable, dangerous places on earth. We can count him a close friend for sure, reliable and determined.'

'OK. Enrol him colonel. Get him up here ASAP.'

Alex was going over all he and Sophia had accomplished and endured in finding the relic. There was a pang of disquiet over Sophia's safety. It would be better if she left this place, until the Order's ceremony was over and done with, then he could sleep at night. His thoughts were broken by the sound of a phone ringing.

'Hello, Roedale here.'

'Mr Roedale, this is Kevin. We need your help right away, just a little job to help us an' nothing to worry about. Are you free?'

'I am.'

'Come over to the stable block at Henley as soon as you can please. I'll be inside with the General. He'll show you what we want.'

Apprehensive at the call Alex drove to Henley, parked, and walked to the stables. Inside Sanders met him, map folded neatly, and shook his hand.

'Nice to meet you Alex, Kevin has told me a great deal about your adventures.'

Alex, staring out of the corners of his eyes at Kevin said, 'I hope it was all true.'

'This is General Tom Sanders,' Kevin introduced.

'Glad to meet you General. What can I do for you?'

Spreading the map over a stall Sanders pointed out the three places he had marked. 'We need you to inspect these spots. It's important no one suspects you are doing it. That's why we've asked you here. Can you do it?'

Alex didn't reply, but nodded his assent, still not quite sure what they wanted.

Sanders folded the map. 'Come with us.' Going to the ladder he led the way up into the tower.

Alex was puzzled at what he saw inside the turret and by the spotter scopes directed across the estate.

'Look here,' Sanders said, going to the window, opening the map and holding it in front of them. 'See that group of firs? We think someone is hiding up there and watching our every move.' Leading Alex to the other window Sanders pointed to the uneven ground, 'I feel sure someone is there also. I might be wrong and they may be just hiking or going about normal duties, whatever you do here in England, but we need to know for sure. Then see over there?' Sanders, narrowing his eyes, pointed at an oblique angle to the right of the window, 'My guess is, that's one of the best places from which to observe the Hall. It would be my choice anyway and, no doubt then, theirs also.'

Straightening up, Alex said, 'I'll need a pair of binoculars, a shotgun, double barrelled and ammunition, just in case. I'll go over there on horseback, better than on foot.'

'Excellent. I'll be watching you from here.' Sanders agreed. 'If by any chance you meet trouble fire the gun twice, if possible, then every hour a single shot. Here take this,' Sanders opened his coat, to expose a leather tooled belt holding a sheath and hunting knife. Unbuttoning the belt he gave it to Alex. 'Don't hesitate to use it if the need arises that way you'll live.'

The Green Goddess

Alex stroked Gazalla's nose as he tightened the saddle girth. She lowered her magnificent head, nuzzled his cheek, and snorted.

Returning, carrying a canvas bag Kevin unzipped it on the stable floor, took out a shotgun and binoculars and presented them to Alex.

Leading the horse out of the stable Alex turned to Sanders, 'I know the paths and bridleways intimately.'

Sanders smiled approval and shook Alex hand. The robust physique and quiet deliberation of the younger man was all the assurance he needed, a man to rely on, who wouldn't let go.

It was a lovely bright day of slow, cumulus cloud and who on such a morning would imagine that danger lurked in this quiet backwater of England. Mounting the mare he cantered towards the trees that skirted the hills of the Henley estate.

Crossing a narrow, hawthorn hedged, lane he rode at a gentle trot along the paths that entered the woodland and fields to the rear of the area Sanders had indicated on the map.

Alex knew of a hill from which he could survey the woodlands and so he set the mare in that direction. It was a strenuous climb but the mare took it easily and soon they were on an eminence above the woods that presented an oblique view across the whole expanse of the estate.

Dismounting Alex hooked Gazalla's bridle over a low hanging tree branch as he stood beside her scouring the landscape with binoculars, concentrating on places Sanders had suggested. There was nothing that gave indication of movement anywhere. Mounting again he rode directly towards the first point on Sander's map, looking closely at the soft, sandy tracks that led through a beech grove and into dense, fir woodland. The mare struggled up a steep incline, which led to a grassy sward.

Gazalla, a shy mare, who at the first sign of danger would stop and raise her magnificent chestnut head to snort a warning, Alex knew he could rely on for her heightened sensitivity.

The ground they were riding along showed signs of recent activity. It was dotted with fresh boot marks. Alex's heart began to beat faster, someone was definitely close by. Quite suddenly the mare halted, raised her head, her ears twitching and turned to face a path to their right.

A man stepped out of the trees, walking towards them.

'Morning,' Alex greeted. 'A lovely day for a walk.'

The man said nothing until quite close then asked, 'What are you doing here?' A beard stubble darkened the jowls of the man's tired looking face. His eyes were puffy from drink or lack of sleep.

'I might ask you the same question,' Alex turned the mare to face the man, keeping him at a distance, in an unmistakable warning. 'You know this is private property.' Alex rested his hand on the stock of the shotgun.

'I'm just bird watching.'

He was lying. The speaker carried nothing to indicate he watched birds.

'Well, this is a good place for it but much better where the fields skirt the woods. Are you alone, in case I meet more of your friends?' Alex asked coldly.

The man's eyes peered beyond Alex, into the trees, just as Gazalla turned her head, her eyes wide, staring in alarm.

Turning the mare sharply in the direction of her gaze they were confronted by two men, one of whom held a hand gun pointed in their direction.

'Get down,' the man rasped pointing the firearm at arm's length.

Alex momentarily froze then in a spurt of adrenaline nudged Gazalla with his heels and rode her full gallop towards the men.

Taken by surprise the intruders attempted to avoid the charge. The mare at full throttle caught the gunman with her shoulder spinning him off his feet, knocking him heavily to the ground. The other opponent jumped free of the mare but, catching his foot in a tree root, tripped headlong to the earth.

Pulling in the horse Alex turned her to face his assailants once more and pulled the shotgun from its saddle pouch.

The fallen gunman had hastily risen to his feet and retrieved the weapon that had been knocked out of his hand. In an instinctive split second Alex raised the shotgun and fired at the man's legs. A report from the man's gun, muffled by the trees as it went off, sent a bullet towards Alex that missed by inches and harmlessly gouged a groove in a nearby tree, sending splinters into the air as the man once more fell to the earth. Screaming his pain into the soundless trees, the man's right trouser leg was in tatters and blood running from a wound that had torn away flesh to the bone.

Raising the shotgun, pointing it at the man who had first met him out of the fir trees Alex waited for him to help his companion to his feet and for them to run back to the safety of the trees.

Riding over to the man, lying doubled over, holding his wounded leg in both hands, Alex dismounted and stood over him.

'You'll regret this,' the man growled, through clenched teeth, staring viciously with angry, half closed, eyes.

'Not half as much as you.' Alex retorted. 'Take off your shirt.'

The man unbuttoned his shirt, staining it with blood from his hands, tugging it free of his trousers and shoulders.

'Now bind your leg tightly above the wound,' Alex commanded, at the same time watching the trees confirming they were still alone in the airless, silence of the woods. Breaking the muzzle of his gun Alex pushed in a fresh cartridge and snapped the barrel into place. Holding the gun to the man's other leg he rasped, 'Who sent you here?'

Staring at the weapon then into Alex's cold, blue eyes the man grunted quietly,

'We were contacted in London to watch the big house down there.' He nodded in the direction of Henley Hall, 'And to report on all activity, day and night.'

Alex noticed the man spoke in a southern English accent.

'Who?' Alex interrogated.

'I have no idea. We just do what we are asked to do, and no questions asked.'

'How many of you are here? Alex pushed the shotgun barrel cruelly into the man's good knee resting his hand threateningly on the trigger.

'Six others, besides me,' the hasty reply was a groan in pain.

Lowering the gun Alex pushed it into the saddle sheath, mounted Gazalla, but before leaving watched the man stumble to his feet, the shirt binding his leg trailing blood stains, along the earth.

'With any luck someone might come before you bleed to death,' Alex taunted and rode away.

CHAPTER THIRTY FOUR

Henry Allan, restored to health, paced his study, hands folded behind him, his head bowed thinking of the coming conversation with his son. He stopped his pacing for a moment to look at his watch then at the door, listened, and walked over and opened it. 'Come in Shenley. Take a seat' he invited softly.

'Morning father.' Shenley came in breezily, still limping slightly from his injury, and took a seat near the empty marble fireplace.

'Are you enjoying the commotion,' Lord Henry asked smiling.

'Interesting to say the least.'

'You know in a few days you will be part of it. You'll be one of us.'

'It's a pity Sophia isn't part of it, she would be a far better candidate.' Shenley considered with reserve.

Lord Henry sat down beside his son and thought of his daughter.

'Not at all. Sophia *would* be admirable of course, but women are excluded you know that. In point of fact you have all the qualities, Shenley, and more, that could be expected of anyone. Since you were a child you've been the most promising of candidates. The Order doesn't accept everyone only those most suitable.'

'So I've been spied on and monitored since childhood' Shenley said reproachfully.

'Not quite like that Shenley. A report on your progress was submitted, by me, to the Order annually, about your education, physical prowess, emotional stability, integrity, your social concerns for the welfare of the people working for us at Henley and in the village. These and other aspects of your character were recorded each year. No more than a school master would do.'

Moving forward in his seat to place his hands between his knees and stare at the floor, he couldn't hide his mixed feelings about being part of any secret organisation, especially one that placed family second in importance. Yet Shenley didn't wish to disappoint a father he loved so much.

'And if I don't want to be part of this society of yours?' Shenley remarked defiantly, staring at Lord Henry. 'I don't know anything about the Order at all. I knew of course, from childhood, you were involved in some kind of secret society but I never imagined I would be a part of it. It's caused our family nothing but grief.'

Shenley walked to the windows to look at the fields of Henley and their peaceful setting. Turning to his father he asked, 'How can you expect me to be part of such a society, my mother murdered, Sophia, myself and Kevin injured. It almost destroyed you with grief. What has it done for us? What have been the benefits from belonging to this secret organisation you have sacrificed us all to?'

Lord Henry, reddening, faltered for a moment.

'I can't deny what you say, but the world is an evil place. We all have a choice either to let the world remain as it is or try to change it.' He spoke gently, understanding the conflict inside his son. 'The majority of people do nothing to change the world for the better except at the polling booth. Some don't even have that choice. As a group of influential men our Order has greater power than that, and more so because no one knows we are there, behind world events. It is through our secrecy we sway the opinions of governments, stop wars, generate funds for poor nations. We hold a vision of the future of our planet. We are a shining sword for change, not just nationally but internationally. It may not come in our lifetime but be sure there will be the world government we are striving for, one day, with equal rights and a sharing of the wealth of all nations for the good of all. That is our goal Shenley. That is our dream. What better ambition could there ever be? Whatever you choose for your life there will be problems, no one can escape that.'

Lord Henry rose from his seat to face his son. 'Will you be a part of us, you are the finest candidate we have had in a lifetime. If you refuse there won't be another opportunity.'

Deliberating, unable to answer, knowing initiation would begin within a few days, Shenley feeling anger and reluctance was finally overcome by the sense of duty and family tradition instilled in him from childhood. He would do as his father wished. His mother's death wouldn't and couldn't have been in vain, whoever did it he would make them pay for every drop of her blood, no forgiveness only justice. He would dedicate himself, all his energies and all he possessed to avenge her and promote his father's ideals.

'I will be a part of it.' Shenley assented.

It was as though some mechanism had instantly changed his life and stamped it forever into a mould from which he could never escape and unexpectedly with it came peace within himself.

Lord Henry going over to his son held out his hand. Shenley shook it firmly to seal his commitment.

'One day you will have enormous power and influence, kings and presidents will shake your hand, just as you have mine, seeking your advice. This house and estate one day will be yours.' Lord Henry waved his arm across the expanse of windows.

Surely it is Marston's by right.'

'Marston will receive the Scottish estate, it suits his character better. Sophia will take over all my business interests. I have been proud of you Shenley ever since you were a child. The Green Goddess, the goddess of Wisdom herself chose you ever before we did. Your obsession with her, the dreams and visions you had of her when you were just a boy were from her.'

'Who and what is she?' Shenley asked recalling the way the Green Goddess had enchanted and bewitched his life.

'The spirit of God in all of us, the creative energy behind life, the Shekinah glory, the divine stream that inhabits the universe,' Lord Henry explained.

As he spoke Lord Henry could feel her strength, the fire she gave to all who knew her, enlivening, reviving his energy and aspirations.

'I understand it now. At times I thought I was going mad she filled my thoughts day and night, like an obsessive nightmare.'

Lord Henry laughed, 'Indeed and Sophia actually believes you still are.'

'She had reason. I can see my behaviour wasn't always rational to say the least.'

Lord Henry rang a staff bell.

A smiling young woman in a blue and white uniform entered the study. 'Sir?' she addressed Lord Allan and cast a shy glance at Shenley.

'Fiona, can you get a coffee for us.' Lord Henry ordered.

Leaning his elbows on the study desk Lord Henry, though looking at his son was staring past him to a distant memory as he gathered his words to meet the occasion.

'What I am about to tell you will surprise you.' Leaning back in his seat his arms folded over his chest he turned his gaze over to Druids Hill. 'Up there, more than two thousand years ago, a group of Jews of the Diaspora built a temple beneath Druids Hill. They brought with them two marble statues representing the Holy Spirit, in the image of a Mesopotamian Goddess. One of them is here at Henley, as you know, the one you fell in love with when you were a boy,' Lord Henry smiled quietly at the memory of his son's frequent visits to the marble room and its green statue. 'The other and a far superior sculpture is hidden in a series of tunnels below Druids. The first Lord Allan found the caves below the hill and brought one statue to this house and though our Hall has altered beyond recognition, over the centuries, she has remained.'

Frowning in disbelief Shenley interrupted, 'I find it an interesting story but you can't believe such a dubious tale surely. Jews here, in this quiet corner of England, and *their* statues? I thought the commandments forbade worship of idols?'

'Yes that's true but Solomon's Temple did have effigies of angels and Seraphim and they weren't idols. The statues found below Druids represented the Holy Spirit, the spirit of wisdom, the first of all things created.'

Aware of the scepticism and doubt in his son's eyes Lord Henry opened his desk drawer and took out an Apocrypha.

'Here read this, written by Sirach about one hundred and eighty BC. These passages are quoted at times in the most frequently used prayer in Judaism, the 'Amidah.' Read the verses I've marked and, if you doubt me, note verse sixteen. It has special relevance to what I'm telling you.'

Lord Henry opened the yellowing pages for Shenley to read.

Feeling a pang of guilt, he had never known his father make any assertion without giving deep thought to its validity, Shenley glanced at the book and read,

"Listen to Wisdom! She proudly sings her own praises among the Israelites. I am the word spoken by the Most High. I made my home in the highest heaven. I ruled over all the earth and the ocean waves. He created me in eternity before time began and I will exist for all eternity to come. I grew tall, like the cedars in Lebanon, like the cypresses on Mount Hermon. My breath was the spicy smell of cinnamon of sweet perfume."

Lord Henry had highlighted a passage in blue to make it stand out from the rest of the page.

"Come tell me, all you that want me, and eat your fill of my fruit, you will remember me as sweeter than honey."

Looking up at his father Shenley waited for an explanation.

Patiently, yet animated in tone, Lord Henry persuaded his son, pointing to the book on the desk.

'You can see from this the Jews recognised Wisdom as a female deity created before any other thing. Ancient peoples understood this concept and worshipped her as the one from whom all things were created. The Catholic Church adopted her as the Queen of Heaven. Now see here.' Lord Henry turned the Apocrypha round and read,

"Like an oak I spread out my branches, magnificent and graceful."

'When the Jewish exiles came here to this secluded place they found the caves and at the entrance to them planted an oak over it, to conceal it, and a yew tree beside it to hold it there and give it longevity.'

Shenley's blue eyes flashed excitedly. 'That's why I've seen those strange phenomena and have been so drawn to the old oak and yew. You say an entrance is hidden there?'

'Indeed, and so concealed it's remained undiscovered outside of our society.'

Turning once more to the book on the desk Shenley asked, puzzled, 'What does it mean?' "Come to me, all you that want me, and eat your fill of my fruit."

'Her fruit is the wisdom and guidance she gives to anyone she has chosen. She comes only to worthy men and women with high moral purpose and intellect. Some she appears to in visions as she did you, others hear her voice and some feel her presence. If you listen she will guide you in all your ambitions.' Lord Henry explained.

Not wishing to say more Lord Henry took the shoulders of his son. 'You'll be told more of these things after your initiation, before that however I have arranged for Bishop Langham to instruct you and discuss the things you need to know. Put your thinking cap on because everything must be committed to memory. We refuse to have any written documentation of our proceedings or beliefs.'

Looking quizzically at his father Shenley asked pointedly, 'What is this strange relic people want so much?'

'You'll be shown it when you're confirmed in the Order, not before. It's the most sacred, the most valuable object in the world.'

Noticing his son's agitation and dissatisfaction Lord Henry changed the subject. 'I want you to fast with the others then tomorrow Bishop Langham will meet you in the chapel. There you will confess your doubts and remain in prayer until you feel peace. He will lay his hands on you in blessing. It's possible you might at that point feel your body on fire or experience a sensation like an electric current flowing through you. It will last for a few seconds only, don't be alarmed by it. From then on you must surrender the whole of your life to God and our Order.' Lord Henry's voice rose in excitement at the prospect of his son's ordination as he devotedly recalled his own. 'At that moment, believe me, your life will be transformed, the world will not be the same, you will find a new purpose, new direction and will be walking with destiny.'

CHAPTER THIRTY FIVE

Brett Sanders wiped perspiration from his forehead. He was as fit as any man could be at his age but it was a hot, cloudless day and he never had acclimatised to the humidity of English summers. Walking into the gardens of Henley he took a mobile from his shirt pocket and dialled a number at Lakenheath, the US operated base of the Royal Air Force near Cambridge.

'Give me Rowan Peters.' He grunted at the operator.

'Who shall I say is calling sir.'

'General Brett Sanders.'

'I'm putting you through sir.'

In a moment an American voice answered. 'Is it really you Brett? I thought I'd never hear from you again after that spat with the Senate.'

'As always I'm back and the Senate as usual had no idea what they were talking about. I couldn't agree to the war, destabilising the Middle East for political reasons and business interests, so I openly opposed the President.'

'I can't always agree with you Brett but no one can deny you have integrity and courage.'

'It's all behind now. Senator Duane Rees pulled me out of that scrape with lobby support. By the way he's here with me in good old England.'

The formalities over Sanders bluntly got down to business. 'I need your help Rowan. Is it possible you could do a one off surveillance for me over the Welsh borders?

'I am not sure. I'd need permission from the British Defence Ministry for that.'

'There isn't time, could you put it down as training exercise or something after all they don't own us. All it will be is a simple reconnaissance. Apart from yours truly and Senator Rees I have to protect some prominent European politicians and aristocrats. If anything happens to them it will be an international incident,' Sanders persuaded.

The voice at the other end fell silent for a moment. 'Hell yes. Why not? I don't see why these RAF guys should tell us what to do. What's the situation?'

'Myself and a few European dignitaries here are being spied on by some private organisation. I want to disable the enemy as quickly as possible. All I need is for you to tell me where they are. After a day or two we'll all be out of danger. Could you let me have a Sixty G Pave Hawk with two personnel for a night mission reconnaissance.'

'How soon?'

'Tomorrow night.' Sanders requested.

'Give me an hour to arrange it and I'll call you on this number at fourteen hundred.'

'I owe you.'

Outside in the shade of an aging cedar Sanders waited for the expected call from Lakenheath. When it came he found the reference, he had jotted into a pocket notebook, and read the co-ordinates taken from Kevin's maps, out to Commander Rowan Peters.

'They'll fly over there at around two hundred hours. The data will be relayed to you immediately they find anything. It will be a good exercise and a piece of cake.' Peters said confidently.

Sanders smiled, he knew he could always count on Peters. He closed his mobile feeling a new exhilaration. This wasn't going to be another boring get together after all.

At two am precisely he heard a distant, steady, muffled pop, pop sound across the distant hills alerting him the Pace Hawk had arrived. He and Kevin had sat up waiting for its distinctive rumble since midnight.

Designed for military search and rescue and emergency evacuation on day or night missions, the Pave Hawk was fitted with automatic flight control, night vision and an infrared system. Using a satellite, secure voice communication it was the perfect craft to ferret out any intruders lurking in the hills and terrain around Henley Estate.

The Pave Hawk circled and hovered, over the woods and fields of Henley, sweeping the landscape with an infrared monitor. A co-pilot read off the bearings and plotted them onto a terrain profiler. In the dark hills they could see the blurred images of make shift shelters and men huddled within and close by. Satisfied the pilot swung the helicopter slowly in the direction of Henley.

In the room, above Henley stables, Sanders and Kevin, dressed in light weight combat attire, were drinking coffee, as they waited. Near the trap door, two small rucksacks had already been prepared and beside them lay double barrelled shotguns and serrated combat knives. Without sleep for twenty hours the vital eagerness they felt to begin their attack on the men in the hills imbued them with fearless, adolescent energy.

A short wave radio burst into life.

'PH calling GS,' the pilot's voice signalled, 'Three targets. Seven personnel. Grid bearings...'

Sanders was leaning forward over a table, marking the coordinates given on the map in front of him. 'Well done, PH,' he congratulated.

'Acknowledged, over and out.' The radio became silent.

Staring closely at the map Sanders took a pen and joined the bearings, given by the pilot, into a triangle and sighed, 'I was beginning to think I'd die of boredom in this place.'

'A feeling I'm most acquainted with General.' Kevin shot back.

Fingering the map Sanders explained, 'They have almost the whole of Henley covered from these points. This wooded coppice would be our best approach but even then there's a hundred and fifty yard gap from here to there.'

'I'd like to suggest General that we have Alex drive over from Barrington Hall with Miss Sophia accompanying him. Whoever is watching will think he's dropping her off. He could park in the garage. We could then lie hidden in the back and he could drive back towards Barrington They know his car by now and it will seem innocent enough and they shouldn't suspect anything.' Kevin offered.

Glancing at the map, finding Barrington, Sanders agreed. 'A good suggestion. Let's do it. Ask him to drop us off here.' He jabbed a finger at a narrow road at the edge of dense woodland. We could make our way to this hide of theirs from that location.'

'I'd like to make another suggestion.'

Sanders narrowed his eyes and looked aslant at his companion, a warning without serious conviction that he was in charge, but it was merely theatrical and they both knew it. 'Well?'

'I believe it would be useful to have Alex Roedale with us. He's an excellent shot, as reliable as any man I know and knows the paths in the woods better than me. An' besides he has a stake in protecting the family.'

'Lady Sophia.' Sanders conceded

The General would have preferred a purely military exercise but conceded Kevin had a point, someone who knew Henley would save time and he grudgingly agreed.

Thirty minutes later they heard Alex's vehicle on the road and the gear changing pause as it negotiated the distant entrance gates. They were already prepared and waiting for him inside the garages adjoining the stables.

Alex swung out of the four by four to open the door for Sophia. Grasping her waist he lifted her down. It was the first time Sanders had met Sophia and even in the dark he thought her the most beautiful woman he had ever seen and that was saying a lot. In her high heels she was almost his height. She flashed him a welcoming nod then turning graciously to Kevin gave a smile of unmistakable affection.

Sanders glancing from Sophia to Alex made a quick assessment of the man and satisfied greeted him. 'Alex.' Shaking his hand he said, 'Kevin and I have a proposition to make. We would like you to guide us through the hills.'

Alex answered cheerfully. 'I was hoping you would ask.'

'Walk Lady Sophia up to the house Alex, behave naturally and then join us in here.'

At Henley door Sophia kissed Alex warmly, her face flushed in anxiety for him and hugging him whispered, 'Be careful darling.'

'No one, or anything, will keep me from you.'

Strolling to the garage he changed into boots and corduroys. Taking his shotgun from the back of the vehicle he broke the barrel and pushed cartridges into it.

Sanders was staring at the map again, on the bonnet of the four by four, with the aid of a penlight.

Joining him Alex thrust a finger to the map. 'There's a fir wood here and, from the places you've marked, they wouldn't be able to see us.' Pointing at the map he commented, 'Here, there's a single dirt road that will take us to that limestone edge. I know it well so we will only need dimmed lights if any. My suggestion General is use that path. We could drop down the side of this escarpment and from there it's a downhill track to the first of these places.'

Looking up, Sanders appraising Alex agreed then he and Kevin stashed themselves inconspicuously in the back of the vehicle and Alex drove away in the direction of Barrington.

There had been no rain for days. It was a dry night of scattered cloud filtering a brilliant full moon. Skirting a hill Alex entered on to the narrow dirt track that led upwards to the escarpment. Before reaching the ridge he stopped the vehicle. They all clambered out. In the intermittent light of the moon they followed the sandy footpath Alex led them to. Within twenty minutes they were close to the first of the hides marked on Sanders' map. Following the General's hand signals they fanned out each side of the path.

On a slope of the escarpment, looking directly onto Henley Hall, the lights of which were clearly visible in the distance, a man stood, with arms resting in the fork of a tree, steadying binoculars to his eyes.

The man heard the sound behind too late. Kevin had him by the throat, slowly cutting off the blood to his brain. Without a sound he fell backwards, unconscious, into Kevin's arms. Within seconds Alex joined Kevin while Sanders hid in the darkness securing them from surprise. Removing his own shoulder bag Alex, taking out tape and rope, swiftly sealed the man's mouth and tied his arms securely behind him. They carried him deeper into the fir wood where they secured him to a tree. Seizing the man's binoculars and emptying his pockets, they tossed his mobile into the trees, removed his shoes and a .38 pistol from his belt and leaving him there they set off into the dark woods, Alex leading the way.

Fifteen or so minutes into their walk Sanders signalled silence and pointed along the slope of the ridge. Ahead of them a small light was moving with swaying, rocking motion towards them. The three men moved off the track and into the trees. As they did so, a bird, startled by the movement, screeched a warning and shot noisily into the sky. The light ahead of them stopped and was extinguished.

On hearing the wild cry of the bird the man stopped, waiting, and alarmed and turned off his torch. Reaching to a side leg pocket he drew a knife and flicked the handle. A double edged blade, gleaming in the moonlight jerked from his hand. Stepping off the path and dropping to his haunches, making himself less conspicuous, he waited in the silence of the woods.

Kevin, Alex and Sanders were walking each side and off the path in the direction they had first seen the light.

To the left of the path almost stumbling over him in the darkness Kevin saw the man too late. A stinging sharp pain, seared through his side. He couldn't see his assailant in the total blackness of shock as he grasped the wound below his rib cage. The man rose and lunged again from his half bent position. It all happened within a second. Both men began their combat to the death acting on instinct alone.

Hearing the struggle Alex and Sanders rapidly came upon the man and Kevin rolling on the ground seeking advantage in their desperate battle.

Drawing his combat knife Sanders grabbed Kevin's attacker by the hair and with the butt of the knife handle struck the man sharply below the right ear. The man fell unconscious to the ground. Dragging him into the trees, unaware Kevin had been severely wounded, they bound the still unconscious intruder, tying him to a tree well away from the bridle path. It was only after this was done that Alex noticed Kevin's heavy breathing and saw blood on Kevin's hands. Looking more closely at his friend he saw his combat shirt was wet with blood.

Signalling silence Sanders laid Kevin on the sward. Opening Kevin's shirt he saw the wound bleeding steadily from a two inch wound in his right side and saw Kevin was on the point of collapse from the unrelenting flow.

Unfastening Kevin's combat suit to the waist, Alex took tape from his pack, closed the wound and patched it tightly before binding it with more tape around Kevin's chest and waist.

Sanders, accustomed to the sight of wounded men, signalled Kevin towards the Hall. Realising the futility of protest Kevin nodded his assent.

Wiping away pine needles that lay on the earth at their feet, Alex drew, with a twig, a route on the sand that would take Kevin quickly back to Henley Hall.

Leaning double in pain, holding his side, Kevin smiled faintly and set off alone into the trees.

'We have to hurry General. I think that wound is serious enough to be fatal.' Alex whispered the urgency unmistakable in his voice.

'Let's get the other men then we'll attend to him.' Sanders rasped back through his teeth. He knew Kevin had been trained for such occurrences and all his training had taught Sanders wounded men were a secondary matter in war.

After leaving Sanders and Alex, Kevin made a slow and dizzy progress towards Henley. Though the track was well trodden and easy to follow he stumbled often due to an inexorable creeping weakness and nausea. At times his eyes wouldn't focus on the track ahead and he paused, hand against a tree trunk, breathing heavily, pushing oxygen into his failing limbs. Blood was still seeping from the wound and was soaking through the edges of the tape Alex had applied and fixed there. He could feel the warm trickle of it down his leg and into his boot. Feeling his trousers, they were wet through to the skin. Experience and common sense warned him to sit down and wait, that was always the order given, when wounded in combat and out of the field of fire, but his Irish truculence pushed him on. He was determined to reach base alone. In his weakened state, delirious, he was no longer in the woods of Henley but fighting for his life in a jungle of unseen enemies. He stumbled and fell, losing his torch. Looking around quickly to observe if he had been seen or heard, he knew he had to leave the beaten path. Reaching into his blood drenched pocket he took out his compass tried to focus on its shaking dial and set off eastwards into the trees.

Taking his cell phone, from a breast pocket, Sanders texted a number at the control room at Henley.

'Get two men up to Brereton Hill. Kevin badly wounded, coming down alone.'

He clicked the mobile shut. Signalling Alex forward they set off along the path that would lead them to the second hide.

From the Pave Hawk pilot's report Sanders expected two men at this second location and three more at the third. Twenty more minutes of strenuous uphill climbing, nearing the spot they once more spread out into the trees, stealthily approaching the co-ordinates given by the pilot.

In the overwhelming darkness of the firs they nearly passed the hide. A sudden sneeze from the branches of a tree stopped them in their tracks. Sanders and Alex, unable to see each other, both heard the sound and stopped. Alex the first there, saw, as the clouds drifted past the moon, silhouetted in its light, the shape of two men with night vision glasses capped around their heads staring intently in the direction of Henley. A double tap on his shoulder made Alex aware Sanders was by his side. Gesturing up into the tree Alex indicated the presence of the men.

A glint of humour filled Sander's face and to the complete surprise and consternation of Alex Sanders called loudly, 'Pisht,' upwards to the men.

A cough came back then a voice, 'That you Bernard?'

Shining the full glare of the torch into the eyes of the men, the intensity of the light temporarily blinding them, Sanders ordered, 'Get down,' and swung the torch in Alex's direction so the men could see the shotgun pointed at them.

Without hesitation the men sulkily climbed down. Both in their twenties they had no stomach for a fight. They hadn't been paid for that.

The one who opened his mouth to speak was struck in the chest by the butt of Alex's shotgun and within minutes both were dragged into the trees and bound.

Sanders, stretched backwards, hands on hips, satisfied with the night's work so far. 'A bunch of amateurs,' he commented, shaking Alex's hand. 'Go back and see to Kevin. There's only three left and I'll be OK from here on.'

It was not the time to argue. In any case Alex was deeply worried about Kevin. The wound had gone deep, the blood flow indicating serious internal injury. Kneeling, in the light of his torch he drew a line of paths for Sanders to follow. The two men shook hands then parted. Alex set off in the direction he believed Kevin had taken.

It was thirty minutes of rapid walking before he came across signs of Kevin's faltering progress.

He had stopped to remove and adjust the tape bandages. In the light of the torch the sandy path was flecked, unmistakably, even in the sandy soil, with large drops of blood.

In the valley below Alex could hear darks barking. Kevin's army friends from Henley were climbing up towards them. Within five minutes he came across the body, crumpled face down, well off the bridle path, where Kevin had stopped beside a tree to support himself and had obviously fallen, leaving a trail of blood down the bole. Touching the jugular there was barely a heartbeat. Carefully he rolled Kevin on to his side, making sure his air passage was free, before stripping off his own vest and fastening it tightly over Kevin's wound.

That done Alex climbed a tree, flashed his torch six times, and repeated the signal in the direction of the search party below them, until he saw their three returning flashes. From his mobile Alex rang Henley police insisting they send air ambulance immediately.

'We only have one air ambulance in the county. It is out on call at the moment. The earliest we can get someone there would be two hours.'

Alex switched off his phone in disgust and sat down heavily at Kevin's side resigned to waiting until the rescue team from Henley appeared. It seemed an interminable stretch of time. Light was beginning to glaze the eastern sky before two men with a folded stretcher came for Kevin and carried him to a waiting Land Rover further down the slope.

An ambulance was waiting at Henley when they arrived. Sophia was standing beside it when the search party returned. Running over to Kevin she placed her warm palm onto his cheek. 'You will be safe now,' she whispered, brushing the sand and leaves from his hair.

Alex beside her, she kissed him, clutching him tightly in her embrace, letting her anxieties drain away.

'I was so afraid for you my darling.' She held his face in her hands, looking into his eyes. Breaking away she went to the ambulance. Kevin was still unconscious. The ambulance medics were fastening a drip into his arm and a respirator to his face. Climbing in beside him she leaned over him and took his hand. There was dried blood on his clothes, his eyebrows and face powdered with dust. Removing tissues from her shoulder bag Sophia wiped his face clean. She had known him since she had been a child. He had been like a second father to her when Lord Henry had been away in London and abroad.

'Fight my dear, wonderful Kevin the way you always have for Me.' she said tearfully.

Sophia felt his hand respond and couldn't hold back the tear that trickled silently down her cheek. Turning to Alex she said, 'I will go with him to the hospital. I know I am in the way here with all this madness going on but I have to be near him if anything goes wrong.'

Alex nodded agreement, he knew of her attachment and love for her wounded bodyguard and friend.

CHAPTER THIRTY SIX

They were tired, it had been a long night of vigil and now they sat in the crypt chapel of Henley. Bishop Langham faced the small congregation that for the first time included Shenley Allan.

'Let me first of all welcome our guest Shenley Allan who has been proposed for membership of the Order.' The Bishop folded his hands and smiled his welcome. 'We are honoured to have you with us.' Turning to the congregation he said in his clear, forceful tone. 'In the name of the Father, the Son and Holy Mother,'

'Amen,' the unified masculine response returned, rolling, like a peal of thunder, in the ancient chapel.

'If any of you wish to use confession I will be in my booth for one hour this morning. This evening as you are aware our ceremony begins. Each one of us must show vigilance as protectors of the Order. That said this is a joyful occasion, and a precious moment, to once more gaze on our sacred relic, to renew our vows, and draw strength from her presence. She will be with us, as she always has been, in these moments of crisis, guiding and invigorating. It is this sacred ceremony that draws us together into our most holy calling.'

Gazing down at the Bible opened on the lectern in front of him Langham read,

"No one has ever found where Wisdom lives or has entered her treasure house, and those who have tried have vanished, the rulers of the nations, those who accumulated vast fortunes of silver and gold, which everyone trusts and will do anything to get, and those who worried and schemed to make money but who left no trace of their work behind. No one has ever gone up into heaven to get Wisdom and bring her down out of the clouds or bought her with precious gold. No one knows how to get to her or how to discover the path that leads to her. All who hold on to her will live. Turn to Wisdom and take hold of her. Make your way to the splendour of her light. Do not surrender our glorious privileges to any other people. How happy we are, knowing what is pleasing to God."

Langham closed the book and raised his head to gaze at the men of the Order listening so intently to his words. 'Tonight, we will meet Wisdom in all her glory, beauty and holiness and touch the sacred object that reminds us of her presence among us.'

Miles away from Henley, Ralph Morville drawing on a filtered cigarette, strolled between the camellias and Japanese maples that lined the narrow walk on a driveway to the extensive gardens of his private mansion. 'In the name of heaven how could seven men be caught while watching Henley? Shit, oh, absolute shit.' Morville thought. He wanted to roar his scream of frustration and invective into the blue sky. 'I should never rely on other people,' he told himself.

Walking back to the house the excruciating pang of disappointment almost overwhelmed him. Climbing into his car and opening the top to allow the breeze of the morning raise his flagging spirit he raced up the lane to see Caroline.

Skidding onto the grass verge next to her cottage he got out and walked, through the blooming, scent filled, flowerbeds to her door. He knew little of flowers or gardening but enough to note how carefully she had laid the beds and blended their exquisite colours. For the first time he noticed how much she loved her cottage garden and the care she took with it. For the first also he knew how much he needed her.

Using his own key he opened the door and immediately noticed the coldness of the place. Running up the narrow staircase he called her, 'Caroline, Caroline,' he sang the words in his enthusiastic excitement at seeing her again as an erection struggled against his clothes.

At her bedroom door Ralph stopped abruptly. The room was empty, vacant in some way. Opening her wardrobe door confirmed it all of her clothes had gone. Swivelling to look for her he stared in panic, an icy numbness creeping into his heart. A letter was propped conspicuously on her bedside table with his name on it in her childlike scrawl. Hastily he reached for it, tearing it open impatiently, already guessing its contents and hoping to heaven he was mistaken. Reading its contents his heart wavered in that lonely, anxious moment.

Darling,

I am praying you will understand.

Thank you so much for all you have done for me, over the years, for all our happy times together. I know I will miss you terribly. You will always be in my heart, for ever and ever and I am truly sorry to have to say goodbye. After your marriage I just felt guilty every day as though our relationship was bereft of all decency. It is necessary for me to find my own life as you have yours. I know you will understand. At least you have a wife to go to whereas I have no one.

Take Care.

Caroline. x.

Anger flushed Ralph's face crimson as he screwed up the letter into a tight ball, in his fist, and tossed it to the floor.

'I know you will understand. I know you will understand,' he repeated aloud. 'You won't get away with this you cunning bitch.'

As he said it he knew the words were futile empty threats and there was nothing he could do. She hadn't left an address or phone number. God damn the evil bitch. In any case there wasn't time to chase her not with the more pressing problems of Henley. How stupid he'd been to trust her, to divulge any of his private affairs.

Driving back to his home, that too seemed more empty now she was gone than the shell of Morville Hall, he threw a few clothes hastily into a capacious valise, checked the Beretta he took from a bedroom draw, lifted a shotgun from its rack and dropped a box of cartridges into the bag.

Jogging to the stables he growled at one of the men cleaning the stalls. 'Morgan, get that bloody hunter into the horse box as fast as possible with my favourite saddle and blanket.'

Ralph left the stable and drove away towards Henley recovering some of his fire in the exhilaration of the fresh morning air. He smiled broadly, knowingly. Caroline was already disappearing from his consciousness as the adrenaline surged in him at the prospect of getting the priceless relic in his hands.

Pulling over in a shelter of trees off the side of the lane he rang the two friends he knew he could trust with his life.

'Randy, meet me in the lane on the south side of Henley Hall, can you do that? I'll make it worth your while. Bring Duffy.'

General Sanders completely unaware of Ralph's proximity concluded all serious threats to the Order were over. Of course caution would be necessary, just in case, but they could feel less anxious about the ceremony taking place that evening. There was no longer any need for the decoy Kevin had suggested besides without the colonel to arrange it there was insufficient manpower to do it anyway. The enemy whoever they were couldn't possibly re-form in the time left before the ceremony.

With one hour to go before sunset all the men were assembled in the foyer of Henley Hall. Looking at the group Lord Henry grinned at their appearance. From their three day fast some had noticeably lost weight, their faces looking haggard from the experience, but for all that they were keen eyed and vigorous. Others, already slim and athletic before their penance showed no physical change whatever. Several had let a beard stubble grow as a part of the ancient ordeal.

Each knight was dressed in a cowled, white mantle emblazoned with a Maltese cross. From each man's waist trailed a sling and heavy sword.

In a discreet canvas bag slung across his broad shoulders Lord Henry carried their precious relic of the Order. Ideally it would have been carried before him but security considerations dictated this expediency. Unlike Sanders he was not convinced it was safe for them to journey the distance they would walk to Druids Hill. He refused to entrust the relic to anyone else not only for its protection but also for theirs. If they were attacked then he would be the target and he placed this burden on himself. He and Sanders were the only ones armed, packing a gun secured in a holster beneath their mantles.

Driving behind Morville Hall stables, Ralph skidded his Lotus in a tail spin before driving into the garages.

The stable block, a good distance from the Hall, had escaped the ravages of the recent conflagration. Saddling his hunter gelding, Ralph calmed the horse by stroking its neck and murmuring softly to it. Checking the girth straps before mounting, he secured a shotgun in a sheath at the side saddle and tucked the Beretta into his trouser belt before galloping off across the expanse of his estates and into the hills and woods that led towards Henley.

'Come on my beauty, let's get them before it's too late,' Ralph prompted his mount as he rode full gallop recklessly into the trees.

By late afternoon he was ensconced in thickets and dense woodland no more than three hundred yards from the entrance to Henley, his two friends beside him. They sat in shade on the fern strewn hillside and waited.

Thirteen men set out from Henley Hall in silent procession, looking like a group of comic revellers off to some fancy dress party.

Ralph laughed at the spectacle. 'What a bunch of fools. Duffy pass that brandy flask.'

At the head of the procession Lord Henry was accompanied on each side by Tom Sanders and Shenley. The rest of the cortege followed in pairs behind them.

Ralph resting on his elbows watched with humour the slow procession leave Henley estate while Randy and Duffy in the meantime passed the flask of brandy between them.

Even in the deepening twilight Ralph could easily recognise Lord Allan at the van guard of the

Order. Narrowing his eyes into aggressive slits he grinned. From the direction of their movement it appeared they were heading for Druids Hill but he was at a loss to understand why on that ancient mound they would be holding their ceremony in the open for anyone to see. It was going to be far easier than he had imagined. Lifting his shotgun, checking the Beretta in his belt, Ralph set off in pursuit followed closely by his two companions.

The men from Henley were easily visible and not hard to follow in the evening light however after they had ascended Druids Hill, and had climbed to the stone age plateau at the top, Ralph lost sight of them in the yews that crowned the fortress. The column of men were making for the mysterious centre of Druids Hill with its ancient yew and green enclosure, of that he felt certain, where else could they gather on that bleak edifice.

Darkness had descended by the time Ralph and his friends reached the top of the mound. Their horses were panting after the steep climb across the fortification and dried out moat. Dismounting they paused listening for the revealing sounds of human presence, footfalls or broken noise, but all was silent as a sepulchre on that eerie hill, there was only a breeze and an absence of light that was almost palpable in its intensity among the avenue of yews. A cold foreboding gripped Ralph. He had never liked the place from his childhood when his nanny had filled his head with tales of goblins and demonic creatures hiding in the archaic depths of the hill fort.

They made stealthy progress towards the central arena of the hill. Randy and Duffy gazed in fearful awe at the giant oak and yew tree locked in their eternal embrace. There was no one there but themselves, nor any trace of the twelve men or indication of where they had disappeared to.

Retracing their steps, avoiding well-trodden paths, they walked the whole circumference of the fortification until disappointment sapping their confidence they finally all sat down on a fallen tree. Ralph was frustrated and angry and in utter disbelief and despair. Regaining composure he reasoned the men they had followed were on Druids Hill somewhere, of that there was no doubt, and he was determined to find them.

Returning to the edge of the climb into the fort, where he had last seen them, he took a torch from his jacket pocket to search for signs of their direction of travel. Thirteen men walking in the same direction couldn't hide their progress no matter how they tried. Thirty minutes more of searching revealed he had been right, the trail led conclusively to the centre of the fortification and the ancient yew. But where were they?

The Green Goddess

Ralph stood in the grim silence of the amphitheatre staring at the yew and oak. Perplexed, he began wondering if the stories of people disappearing on Druids were true after all. His father had often told him to stay away from the hill fort, insisting it was a place of evil, and had forbidden him ever going there to play.

'Absolute nonsense,' Ralph thought. 'The men of Henley were there, somewhere.'

Watching from the windows of Sophia's apartments Alex and Sophia closely observed the procession of men after their departure.

Sophia knew her father would never flinch in the presence of danger. A momentary tear moistened the corners of her eyes at the bravery of these idiotic men and their dedication to an impossible ideal. It was like a tale from Cervantes. Looking at them one knew they could never change the world in any way. Yet life was so strange, appearances were often wrong, the most unlikely events changed history all her studies had taught her that. Those caves under Druids Hill reminded her of the tomb of Saint Peter. The Romans must have thought him an insignificant old man but now the eternal Empire had gone and in its place the most magnificent church in the world and a city glorifying itself over Peter's bones. Silently to herself she breathed a wish willing them on, 'Let them have safety and strength.' She was encouraged that Shenley was beside her father at the head of the column. He was the true image of the saintly knight among them like a victor from the pages of Mallory. If there were need he would fight to the last and undoubtedly win.

'What are you thinking?' Alex asked, disturbing her romantic, morbid flow of thought.

'Just their bravery and apparent insignificance.'

Using a spotter scope, she had often used since childhood, Sophia was able to follow the direction of the men, their white mantles visible even among the trees. 'They are going up to Druids, just as we thought,' she told Alex.

Alex stood behind her, pulling her close to him, as they watched the procession disappear into the gloom of the twilit sky.

'Let's go Sophia, its time. We'll have to be quick to get there before they do.'

CHAPTER THIRTY SEVEN

Darkness had fallen by the time Alex and Sophia entered Henley Church and the moment they entered they realised someone had preceded them. The altar table had been moved and the pitch black opening in the floor told them someone had beaten them to it. Alex's heart fell, fearful of what lay ahead and for the safety of the men of Henley.

Signalling silence he approached the bolt hole entrance to the caves. Kneeling, listening, he could hear no sounds breaking the ominous silence but a smell of burning wax rose on the air in a draught from the entrance to the caverns.

Reluctant to switch on their torch and give their own position away Alex and Sophia began the steep descent down the stairs into the catacombs of the Green Woman.

The origin of the scent was soon apparent to them. The length of the narrow corridors were lit brightly by candles placed inside draught proof holders and set into the recesses of the cave walls, Alex had noticed on his first visit there. The candles lit the way towards the central cavern and the great womb like cave that held the statue of the Green Goddess.

In the dancing candle light the wall paintings inside the caverns, shining in all their brilliance of colour and craftsmanship and appearing alive in the flickering light as though imbued with life, urged them on in their procession of adoration. Sophia gazed at them in awe, so enthralled that several times she forgot the reason why they were there. She wanted to exclaim to Alex their exquisite beauty but drowned the words in her mouth for the silence she knew they must maintain.

Alex leading Sophia by the hand through the narrow passages abruptly stopped, causing Sophia to stumble into him. Ahead of them, where the passage turned, and formed a junction with an unlit corridor, a light was moving towards them. Grabbing Sophia's arm he pulled her against him into an unlit passageway barely in time to avoid being seen.

A tall woman, in a long white robe, that trailed in a ghostly train to the floor behind entered the corridor they had just vacated and passed in front of them. In her left hand she held her white dress from the floor in front of her feet and in her right held a candle the light revealing her features grotesquely but not enough to prevent Alex and Sophia recognising the face of the willowy, libidinous Tamara Thomas.

Sophia clasped her hand to her mouth in shock and surprise.

Waiting for Tamara to be out of range, Alex whispered, 'She's lighting the caves.'

'Who would have guessed?' Sophia replied quietly in disbelief.

'I was certain she knew more about the Green Woman than she told me. She must be in your father's confidence. They are obviously entering the caves by way of Druids Hill and will leave from this direction after the ceremony, to prevent attack in case they were followed, that's the reason Tamara is lighting the tunnels towards the church,' Alex suggested.

Continuing onwards to the great cave of the goddess they could see bright lights ahead of them from the luminescent glow that began to fill the tunnels ahead. Cautiously they hugged the walls closer and crept slowly forward.

Twenty or so yards from the central cavern Alex motioned to Sophia to wait while he went on alone.

To his surprise the cave was empty. Waving to Sophia he waited until she was beside him.

The cave of the Green Goddess had been lit brightly with candles placed high on the walls. Their glow, from every side, shone back in a blinding, reflected green radiance from the statue. The Green Woman, her beauty in its perfection arresting time, seemed to be watching them with her enormous eyes, angrily warning them.

'Where are they Alex?' Sophia brought him back to reality.

Taking her by the waist, pulling her close, Alex spoke in a whisper. 'I know exactly where they are.'

They would hold the ceremony in the crypt not here in the cave of the Green Woman. Some other ceremony must take place here later.

'Follow me Sophia and be careful.'

Going to the slab of rock in the far recesses of the cave Alex squeezed passed and into the bolt hole he had discovered on his first visit alone to the caverns.

Their journey on all fours seemed to last beyond Sophia's endurance, he constantly waited for her, tired, distressed by cobwebs and the dark. Eventually in the distance ahead they heard a low murmur of voices and saw a faint glow of light guiding them to the ancient temple.

The lights inside the crypt shielded the darkness inside the bolt hole entrance that Alex and Sophia now peered from. Lying silently side by side they were able to watch undetected the ceremony being conducted before them.

Sophia pressed herself warmly against Alex, laying her arms across his back and kissing his cheek. It was like being a child again watching, from a secret corner, her father and his guests and forbidden things.

The scene in front of them was like some animated pre-Raphaelite painting. The knights in their white mantles with a blue, Maltese cross emblazoned on them were standing reverently, swords and daggers by their sides, gazing towards the altar, their faces lit only by candles the light of which flowed and danced with shadows in a warm yellow glow. Surrounding them, the wall paintings of the medieval knights seemed to be standing guard over this sacred moment.

Facing the roughly hewn stone altar, upon which stood the engraved casket the men were waiting for Bishop Tom Langham to speak. Beside him and to the left stood Lord Henry Allan his face glowing with pride and unabashed relief that thus far they had arrived safely.

Tom Langham lifted his hands and made the sign of the cross. 'The Lord be with you.'

'And also with you,' resounded and hollowly echoed the unified response.

Sophia recognised the men she had seen with her father. At the rear Rudolph Seidel, the steel manufacturer; the American Senator Duane Rees, next to them Baron Herman Clos and Count Phillipe Lanais; in front of them was the oil billionaire William Keefe whom she had grown to like for his positive good humour and determination, and near him was Prince Gottlieb. In the front row were General Sanders, Karol Lindberg the politician and his friend Andre Malinn. Standing in front of the group there was a man without the knightly mantle of the Order. She couldn't make him out, his face was hidden from the view she had from the floor. While wondering who this could be General Brett Sanders moved, easing the strain on his wounded leg, and she saw quite distinctly the face of her brother Shenley. She gasped in surprise putting her hand to her mouth to cut off the sound. She touched Alex's shoulder, to gain his attention, nodding in Shenley's direction, but Alex had already seen and grasped the situation before she had. Glancing sternly at her he cautioned her into silence.

Langham continued addressing the knights.

'We have with us for the first time an acolyte, Shenley Allan, who will join our order this Holy

Day. Come forward Shenley Allan and kneel on the stool before you.'

Shenley walked to the Altar facing Bishop Langham and his father and kneeled on the stone stool at the front of the assembly and bowed his head.

'Do you affirm the precepts of our Holy Order?' Langham asked.

'I affirm.'

'Then repeat dutiful knight of our Holy Order those precepts that will from this day bind you to our brotherhood.'

Shenley addressing them and speaking clearly, determinedly and unwaveringly, that all might hear, all doubt had left his mind. He was sure this is what his life had been destined for.

'I affirm that from this day forth I will act with courage, show mercy, be brave in opposition, that I will defend the fatherless, the widow, the defenceless, the poor, the outcast and the needy and all disadvantaged wherever they may be. I will champion good against evil, be generous with my worldly goods and with all my Godly endowed abilities and possessions and bring justice to the world. I will assist my brothers at all times. I will be gentle and gracious to all women, be respectful of age, be a brother to my brothers and a father to the young. I affirm that from this day forth I will abide by the rules of our Order and will be obedient to my superiors in all matters, in the full knowledge that they act justly and with integrity. I will defend our sacred Order and our brotherhood unto death. I will never disclose our secrets or our treasure.'

Shenley recited without faltering, he had taped the monologue, listened to the words over and over, repeating them until he knew every phrase and pause and nuance under his father's watchful and critical tuition.

'Well-spoken brother,' came the reply.

The Bishop lifted a gold tray from the altar on which rested the neatly folded white robe of the Order. 'Take this and wear it with pride.'

Shenley rose took the mantle and raising his arms above his head let the mantle fall around him the hood falling loosely on his shoulders.

'Kneel, Master Shenley.'

Shenley knelt once more on the stone footstool. His father Lord Allan took a sword that had been resting in its scabbard on the altar behind the sacred casket and drew the blade. Going over to his son he touched both of Shenley's shoulders with the point and spoke, quenching the emotion in his words, in a stentorian voice that all could hear.

'Rise brother to a new life. Let all the things of the past be as nothing to you. Reach forward to the goal set before you, run your race to win and carry with honour the memory of those who went before you. You may now rise.'

Shenley rose to stand before his father and Bishop Langham. Tears welled in the eyes of Sophia as she watched her incomparably, handsome brother stand erect, confidently, looking every inch a knight of romance and the dreams of women.

A sword was buckled over the mantle around his Shenley's waist and he stepped back.

Raising his arms Lord Allan addressed the assembly. 'Let us welcome Shenley into our sacred Order.'

As one the brothers drew their swords and struck the ground at their feet shouting with a roar whose sound grew in intensity and crescendo so that it reverberated deafeningly through the chamber until terminated with a cheer of, 'Aye.'

Shenley bowed to the brothers and turned again to face Bishop Langham.

Holding his arms aloft in benediction the Bishop ordered,once again, 'Kneel Master Shenley.'

Shenley dropped to one knee facing the altar.

'From this day the Lord God will bless your work and everything you do.'

Resounding cries of, 'Aye,' came from the assembled brothers as they struck their swords to the floor.

'The Lord God will make you the leader, not a follower.' 'Aye,' came back the reply from the brothers.

'You will always prosper and never fail.'

The assembly roared their chorus.

'Your enemies will approach you in one direction and flee in seven. Do not be afraid for God himself gives you the victory.'

The waiting brothers repeatedly beating their swords against the stone floor, until the ground shook beneath them, hailed in their crescendo, 'Aye,' before dropping to their knees as one to face the altar.

Blessing them Langham said, 'In the name of the Father, the Son and our Goddess, the Holy Mother.'

A unified response from the men reverberated within the cavern, 'Amen.'

'You may stand.'

Bishop Langham stepped to the right of the altar while Lord Henry took his position behind the jewelled casket and its precious relic.

CHAPTER THIRTY EIGHT

On Druids Hill darkness was total except for an occasional glimpse of stars that broke the canopy above. Ralph was puzzled, unable to understand where the cortege had disappeared to. He and his two friends gazed round the site of the yew and oak but could find nothing to explain how such a large company could have vanished into thin air.

Ralph shone his torch onto the great Yew tree and walked over to it. Yews are always hollow inside and the thought of this one having a hidden chamber began to form out of the confusion of his thoughts. He searched the rugged red bole and the oak that had grown into its embrace but could find nothing to suggest an entrance into the trunk. Then quite unexpectedly he heard a sound like a loud reverberating hum emanating from the tree itself.

'Randy, Duffy, come here. What do you make of this?' The sound had gone but the three men listened nevertheless with their ears pressed against the bole of the tree.

'Nothing that I can hear,' Randy said, stepping back.

'Maybe a squirrel', Duffy suggested.

Before Ralph could answer the ground beneath them vibrated, barely perceptibly but sufficient for them to notice. A reverberating thud like a minor tremor shook the spiny leaves of the yew branches and once more the sound like a distant drum.

'In there,' Ralph gesticulated towards the yew. That's where they went. There has to be a way in.'

'How could a dozen men get inside there?' Duffy asked.

Ralph laughed, 'For God's sake Duffy. Help me find the way in.'

The three men began tearing at the bark of the tree wherever it was split or broken.

'Here,' Randy grunted squeezing past a mat of vines to expose an overgrown opening that led into the tree trunk and to the ancient, heavy door.

Forcing his way through the tangle of vines and looking around the huge hollow inside the trunk of the yew Ralph calculated twelve men could easily stand together within it capacious girth. Going to the door he tried to open and then force the rusting ring handle of the lock but the door remained obstinately secure. Going outside, leaving the trunk to his companions he searched the amphitheatre for a lever of some kind, anything to use as a tool to batter away the door and rusting lock. Duffy came to help but search as they might nothing useful or strong enough came to hand.

In exasperation, for a moment, with his friends watching him, Ralph felt defeated.

'Get bundles of sticks, grass, moss anything and do it quickly,' he ordered, chagrined.

In a short time the old oak door was alight, flames taking hold and licking away at its parched dry wood. The three men watched as the yew and oak were engulfed in smoke billowing from the aperture in the trunk. The fire had not yet turned into a conflagration but the ancient trees moaned as though crying out in their despair and anger.

'Let's hope you are right. This is likely to burn down the whole woodland and us with it,' Randy hissed disparagingly.

'The clearing should give enough fire break to protect us if it does as long as the wind keeps off,'

Ralph answered looking around at the trees. 'In any case we'll be under Druids not on top of it.'

Holding his coat over his face Ralph pushed his way through the smoke and into the hollow trunk of the yew and kicked hard at the door, burning slowly like black charcoal. The oak door splintered around the lock and its centre fell away into the cavern on the other side.

'Come'. Ralph waved to his friends. In moments they were moving down the candle lit arteries of the caverns.

While absorbed watching the ceremony Sophia shuddered beside Alex and he felt a cold chill come over him and goose bumps prickling his arms and legs. Instinctively he knew something had changed somewhere deep in the maze of tunnels but he gave it no credence so engrossed were he and Sophia with the ritual enacted in the chapel.

Bishop Tom Langham opened a book on the altar and read.

'Wisdom cannot be bought with silver or gold. The finest jewels cannot equal her value. The value of Wisdom is more than crystal or rubies, the finest topaz and the purest gold cannot compare with her. Where can she be found even death and destruction have only heard rumours of her? God alone knows the way to where she is found and he reveals her only to the pure of heart. Her light shines like the Father's light, she the eternal power, is the image of the perfect and invisible virgin spirit, the perfect glory among the realms of light.'

Langham closed the book and faced the congregation of knights. They responded in unison with, 'Eternal Father, Holy Mother, of you, we ask forgiveness.'

Sophia observed the ceremony with emotion and awe and the faces of the men lit by the candles that lined the walls of the crypt.

The Bishop continued in accord with the voices of the men before him.

'I confess to you Almighty God, and to you my brothers, that I have sinned through my own fault, in my words and in my thoughts, in the things I have done and the things I have failed to do, and I ask you compassionate Father and Eternal Mother to forgive me for all my sins. Amen.'

The gathered knights knelt on one knee their heads bowed.

Langham prayed, his arms raised to heaven. 'We come to you asking you to bless our work, to keep us faithful in your ways and commands until the day of our death. All we have is yours, comes from you and we give it back in gratitude that you have entrusted us with our authority, abilities and talents.'

The knights rose to their feet. Lord Henry took his place at the altar table, in front of him the shining, jewelled casket that in the light of the tall, altar candle, took on flashing brilliancy and luminosity.

Reaching to the casket, Lord Henry pressed several emerald jewels at the top. Two silver rods moved outwards several centimetres from the casket lid. Pulling these outwards he lifted upwards and the lid of the casket came away.

For a brief moment Lord Henry gazed in reverential awe at the relic inside the jewelled box. Slowly, cautiously he put his hands inside the casket. Everyone held their breath.

Sophia longed to move from the constriction of her position, her buttocks were cold, her legs numb and her feet tingling, but from the cramped space they were in she dared not.

Lord Allan lifted the object above his head for all to see. Sophia glanced at it transfixed, longing to touch it, hold it to her breast and stare into its empty cold face.

She had been right after all, it was a skull.

'Brothers, behold the head of the Holy Mother, the Virgin spouse of God, the Goddess of Wisdom and the Mother of our Lord.'

The temple was unnaturally silent, no one moved and the words fell like a thunderbolt on Sophie's ears. She turned to Alex, her eyes wide, soft, excited, exulting. He was not a believer of such things but even he experienced for a fleeting second the sacredness of the object. It was something tangible that gave plausibility to the biblical life of Christ. Merely by being in its presence one left the realm of myth and was transported back to those miraculous times.

Lowering the skull, returning it carefully into its receptacle, Lord Henry preceded by Bishop Langham, holding the altar candle before him, walked to the exit followed in sombre single file by the men of the Order.

Waiting until they had all left the chamber Alex and Sophia at last stretched their aching bones and stood alone in the crypt.

'We will have to hurry, and,' he looked sympathetically at her, 'Return the way we came.'

'How do you know where they've gone?'

Sophia wanted to follow the procession as the most sensible of choices. The very thought of crawling again through that confined bolt hole dismayed her beyond words. Briefly she wanted to defy him and gazed into his eyes, pleading, shaking her blonde hair aside.

'I know where they are going, to the cave of the Green Woman.'

'Oh! Alex.' Sophia groaned, rubbing her knees strenuously, warming them against the ordeal ahead. Stretching, setting her resolve, she wrapped her arms around his neck and kissed his cheek and in a plaintive mew said, 'Ok, let's go.'

The journey back seemed longer, dustier, the temperature had inexplicably dropped. Sophia shivered from the penetrating change in the air.

Nearing the cave of the Green Woman filled Alex with a foreboding he couldn't explain, an anxious surge pumped his heart driving his breath in short, fast bursts. He focused ahead, all his senses keenly alerted, in preparation for visible danger.

When Alex and Sophia reached the end of the bolt hole, they had so painfully struggled through; they crawled out to stand behind the slab of sandstone that hid the entrance to it from the chamber of the Green Woman.

Through a crack between the slab of rock and the wall face they were presented with a full view of the great cave and the astounding statue in its centre.

The procession of men had begun to enter. Walking single file they took their places, forming a circle around the goddess and knelt in prayer.

Langham stood before the statue, his head bowed, holding the casket aloft, and warned, 'Do not forsake her and she will preserve you. Love her and she will keep you. Wisdom is the principal thing.'

The Green Goddess

Langham lowered the casket to the floor in front of the goddess and the men stood again in respectful silence.

From a silver tray, carried by Lord Henry, on which was a goblet of wine Langham walked among the knights and presented it to each in turn.

Joining his father Shenley stood before the Green Woman. She seemed alive in her shining, emerald beauty and stern gaze. Lord Henry bowed his head, afraid even to look into the large green eyes that stared at them both, but Shenley, hypnotised by her seductive allurement was unable to look away.

'I present to you Holy Queen, our new son and brother and ask you to watch over him to further your purpose here among men.'

Once he had spoken Lord Henry stepped to the rear leaving his son alone before the peerless sculpture. Everyone, unmoving, held their breath.

Faintly at first but growing into a brilliance that almost blinded their eyes the statue began to glow with a pellucid green halo. A ray of fire shot from her, like a flash of sunlight, to strike Shenley and smite him to the stone floor.

Sophia, watching from the shadows, instinctively moved forward as though to go to Shenley's help. Alex took hold of her firmly, placing his hand over her mouth, choking off the cry that rose in her throat. She was trembling in his arms.

In the centre of the cave, at the foot of the statue, Shenley lay unconscious on the floor. Not one man moved, they all remained in their places heads bowed in prayer. Langham stood over Shenley, arms raised to heaven. Unmoved, Lord Henry watched his son on the floor and waited.

Unaware of his surroundings Shenley thought himself in a night sky filled with stars. He could see them without time or distance as though floating among them. They were filled with colour and enchanting beauty. He felt a profound sense of peace and wonder. In the midst of all she appeared, a living creature, filling the whole of the heavens. Smiling, taking his hand, her faultless splendour dazzled in its magnificence and power and overwhelmed him.

'Who are you?' Shenley asked, his voice unnatural and distant, as though speaking in a cave or resounding an echo through eternal, mountain valleys. He longed to be near her forever.

She replied in a voice singing with feminine metre like tinkling bells or a wind shaking the leaves of the forest.

'I will be with you, guiding you, protecting you, within you. Close your eyes and I will be there.'

Leaning forwards she kissed his lips and faded away into the timeless mystery of the skies.

Shenley found himself back in the cave of the Green Woman. The statue lifeless as the day it was carved from the marble thousands of years before. He understood now why she had obsessed his thoughts so indelibly since childhood.

Langham pulled Shenley to his feet.

'You have been accepted. Welcome brother.'

The knights drew their swords and struck the stone floor as they cried aloud in their humming, pulsating, 'Aye.'

Tugging black masks over their faces Randy and Duffy followed closely as Ralph pushed ahead. Reaching the cave of the Green Woman, unseen or heard due to the vociferous clamour of the men congratulating Shenley, they watched the ceremony, their backs against the limestone wall of the corridor entrance. Ralph narrowed his eyes focusing on finding the relic. Seeing the casket, bejewelled, glistening in the light of the candles in Bishop Langham's hands, he burst into the cavern with shotgun loaded held at torso level towards the gathered men. Randy and Duffy remained guarding the exit their weapons ready for firing.

'Stay where you are, everyone, if you want to leave here alive.'

Morville spoke calmly and resolutely walking behind each knight. 'Drop your weapons, useless as they are, to the floor. I won't hesitate, nor will my men, to shoot anyone who dares to show resistance.'

The body of knights taken completely by surprise were grounded to the spot in disbelief.

Rudolph Seidel was the first to move, turning he swung his sword at Morville but as he turned was struck to the floor by the butt of Morvilles shotgun against his left ear.

None of the men gathered there, apart from Sanders and Lord Henry, had been trained for combat. At the sight of Seidel lying unconscious on the floor, blood trickling from a gash to the side of his head, all resistance froze in them.

Ralph's shotgun pointed in his direction Bishop Langham faced Morville fearlessly.

'You have no idea what you are dealing with here. To enter this holy place with violence and murder in your heart will bring such a retribution you couldn't imagine.'

Laughing at the Bishop, Morville grinned, 'Well priest it seems to me you are the only one with any mettle and isn't shitting himself. Keep your threats of retribution for the gullible.' Raising the gun to his shoulder Ralph pointed it towards Langham's head. 'Now hand over the box and the relic.'

The Green Goddess

Lord Henry lunging out from the group of men, unable to get at the gun beneath his mantle, drew and threw the ceremonial dirk, he carried as master of the Order, at Morville and then dropped to the floor out of line of fire.

Flying as straight as an arrow at its target the knife struck Ralph just above the heart. Losing his grip on the gun barrel, a reflex in his right hand jerked the trigger.

Bishop Langham fell hard to the floor a wound through his side. Still clutching the casket he turned his eyes to Lord Henry silently pleading for help.

Alex watched the drama taking place, in front of him, with trepidation then instinctively moving from the shelter of the rock he appeared at the side of the altar and called to Lord Henry. 'Throw it here.'

Tugging the casket from Langham's hands Lord Henry attempted to hurl it towards Alex, but Randy seeing Ralph's predicament as he collapsed against the wall ran into the cave towards the casket and at the same time fired his shotgun. Lord Henry fell wounded to the floor on top of the jewelled box.

Shaken from their frozen immobility some of the knights grabbed Randy as he attempted to dart passed them.

Ignoring the commotion around him Alex pulled Lord Henry off the casket, lifted it beneath one arm and fled to Sophia and the safety of the bolt hole.

'Take this and go as fast as you can, as you've never run before.' Seeing her hesitation he shouted angrily at her, 'Go!'

Sanders, seeing his chance in the mayhem around him, picked up his sword and with it struck Randy's arm with all the force he could command behind the heavy sword. The gun fell from Randy's hand to the floor and his arm, crushed above the elbow by the blow, hung limp, bone protruding through his hunting jacket and blood flowing freely in a rivulet to the floor.

Realising all chance of recovering the casket had gone and unable, in his condition to follow Sophia, Ralph turned and ran to the exit that led to Druids Hill.

Duffy who had, until this moment, stood his ground near the entrance to the Cave raised his shotgun and fired in an effort to protect Randy and Ralph as they made their escape.

Count Phillip Lanais and the French minister Andre Malinn groaning and doubling in pain fell to the floor of the cave wounded.

Shenley so far unscathed drew the sword his father had presented to him and ran in the wake of Ralph Morville who had by this time reached the exit tunnel. His way blocked by Duffy, reloading his shotgun Shenley swung the sword brutally but missing Duffy's head he struck his shoulder and Duffy fell to his knees in a paroxysm of pain. Leaving him there Shenley was about to continue his pursuit of Ralph when a hand grasped his shoulder, halting him abruptly. Sanders stood beside him.

'Let him go. Your life is worth far more than his. We can get him later. Here take this.' He handed Alex the handgun carried beneath his mantle. 'Run after Sophia, make sure she and Alex get through safely. We have no idea if there are others waiting for us. We'll meet up with you later.'

Looking around at the destruction and chaos in the cave, five men seriously, perhaps fatally, wounded, the floor of the cave wet and spattered with their blood, Shenley nodded agreement and followed after Sophia and Alex into the bolt hole. Before leaving he turned to the Green Statue. Her eyes burned with an un-assuaging, implacable anger and a lurid, emerald glow emanating from her sent a shiver through him.

Sanders, and the others who had escaped unharmed, bound the wounds of the brothers as best they could by tearing strips from their white mantles. The worst injured, Bishop Langham, needed medical attention immediately. The men under Sander's direction made a stretcher out of their mantles and they all set off for Henley Church.

Phillip Lanais and Andre Malinn though badly wounded could at least walk without much assistance. Lord Henry's wound though slowly seeping blood was however minor and he was able to help the stretcher bearers negotiate the confined corridors by leading them through the confined spaces of the caverns. Maintaining silence they extinguished all the candles as they passed so that no one could follow their passage to Henley Church.

In the general confusion Duffy had seen his chance to escape. Throwing his arm round Randy he helped him to his feet and out of the great cave. Together they left, unopposed, following Ralph's stumbling progress through the constricted alleys of the caves towards the only exit they knew on Druids Hill.

Alex and Sophia struggled through the bolt hole rapidly. Sophia knowing all depended on her successful escape from the caves, to the security of Henley, moved swiftly ahead no longer conscious of the pain in her knees. When she and Alex exited to the candle lit passages they were well in front of the slowly moving column of knights. Alex joining her attempted to take the casket from her to relieve the strain on her arms but still in shock of seeing so many men injured in the cave of the Green Woman she refused to let it go feeling its safety lay with her

The Green Goddess

and no one else. She hardly recognised Alex in the fixation that had grasped her mind like a vice.

Holding her close, whispering, Alex assured her, 'Everything will be all right now. They can't follow us and we'll be out of here soon.'

Calmed, her breath easing, her heart slowing its beat, Sophia looking into his eyes wildly, gave him the casket, and let go, sobbing, clinging to him like a child.

'We'll be in Henley Church very soon. I'm sure the others are coming this way, they can't go back towards Druids Hill that's for certain.'

Ralph had fled without any compunction at leaving his comrades behind. He heard them calling his name in the dull echo of the chambers but gave no heed, 'One lives alone and dies alone,' he said pushing ahead as fast as he could. In the caverns he could smell the wood smoke from the door they had set on fire and knew he was near the yew and oak. Hurrying on he intended not to get away but to meet up with Lord Henry and his friends. In his exigent flight he had almost forgotten the wound in his chest but now suddenly he weakened, felt dizzy and stopped, clutching at the walls of the corridor for support, and vomited. His legs were weak, trembling, and his lungs hurting at each breath. Feeling beneath his sports vest he touched blood, tackily wet, soaking his clothes and trickling down his ribs.

Taking off his hunting vest he drew his knife and cut a sleeve from his shirt then placed it against the gash in his chest. Struggling back into his vest he fastened his shirt to the topmost button in an endeavour to keep the makeshift dressing in place. Breathing heavily he made for the exit as quickly as his failing strength would permit.

Randy further back in the caverns was struggling to continue, the pain from his arm so excruciating he felt he just couldn't go on. Blood, from his shattered arm left a trail behind them, which sank into the stone floor of the tunnel turning it a dark ochre hue. He leaned against a wall exhausted.

'Go on without me,' he urged.

'We're nearly there, come on.'

'I don't have the energy anymore to go on. That shit Ralph just left us here. If I live I will by God get even with him.' Delirious, not aware of the words spoken he drifted far away then staring gauntly at Duffy said, 'Promise me you will make him pay for this.'

'We'll both make him pay for it.' Duffy said propping his companion securely against the wall. Taking off his belt he tied a tourniquet above the broken and severed bone, ignoring Randy's scream of pain, then removing his shirt he tied Randy's arm against his chest. 'Take deep breaths, and let's go.' He said firmly, 'Or I'll bloody well drag you.'

Randy began to laugh, uncontrollably, insanely, at their unforeseen predicament, and blindly struck off along the tunnel encouraged by Duffy who had taken his friend's uninjured arm over his shoulder.

Henley Church was cold and unwelcoming in the early hours when Sophia emerged from the trap door that led from the caverns. Alex passed the jewelled casket up to Sophia and climbed out. They sat in silence, exhausted, gaining their strength. Eventually breaking the silence Sophia interrupted with, 'I think we should just go immediately to Henley. If the others are coming this way as you say then they'll follow us. First of all we need to secure the casket safely somewhere. I understand why mother was willing to die for it now I know what the relic is and its importance.'

'I agree Sophia but the two of us stand little chance if there are more men waiting outside to get their hands on it. Let's wait just a little longer please. The others can't be far behind. The more of us there are when we leave here the better.'

Alex' words were timely. At that very moment they heard the sounds of the men on the stone steps beneath the altar. Rising to meet them Alex assisted to bring out the makeshift stretcher and wounded cleric to the altar floor.

Finally all were through, Shenley exiting last of all. He and Sanders sealed the entrance to the caverns behind them and tugged the marble altar over the top.

Waiting for an ambulance to arrive, Lord Henry stood in front of the altar and raised his arms towards his cortege of men feeling himself to blame for their injuries and unfortunate encounter with the thieves.

'Let's thank God and our eternal Mother who has not let our enemies destroy us. We have escaped like a bird from a hunter's trap, the trap is broken and we are free.'

The men of the Order bowed solemnly in prayer while Alex and Sophia watched for the ambulance through the windows of the church entrance.

Within twenty minutes an ambulance arrived to take the wounded men to a private hospital. Daylight was spreading embracing rays across the horizon and clouds were swaddling a yellowing dawn with a blanket of grey by the time the rest of the men reached Henley Hall.

Alex was the first to notice the smell of burning on the wind as they reached the entrance to Henley. 'There's smoke coming from Druids Hill,' he pointed out to Sophia.

Swinging open the door for him Sophia stared at the distant trees and rolling landscape, 'Farmers burning off the chaff,' she said.

CHAPTER THIRTY NINE

Grappling against an awful weakness, cold and fear that gripped him Ralph reached the burning yew and found the exit from the caves. The door they had set alight had burned through rapidly under the convection currents of air in the caves and fanned the embers into an avenging, pernicious fire that consumed the ancient yew and oak.

Lifting his gilet around his head and shoulders Ralph ran through the smouldering gap, of such intense heat that it singed and set on fire his hunting jacket, into the exhilarating air of Druids Hill.

The woods were brightly lit by the conflagration as the fire licked its way up the boles of the woodland to dance along the branches of the trees.

Ralph was overwhelmingly tired and so weak he could hardly stand. Leaning forward, gasping, filling his lungs with the smoke filled air he stopped, and attempted to regain some of his flagging energy. Lifting up and pulling his shoulders straight he was astounded to see that the glade in which he stood, the natural amphitheatre, was filled with a lurid green glow, bearing down on him like a fog, squeezing the very life from his limbs. Leaning forward he rubbed his eyes and looked up at the burning yew and companion oak.

A report like a distant explosion shook the trees as a great bough of the oak, weakened by the blaze broke loose. Ralph watched it as in slow motion, unable to move, his legs numb and the will to flee gone, as the great bough fell and a torn branch knocking him to the earth penetrated his upper abdomen.

Flames danced along the heavy branch that skewered him to the ground. With a last thrust of energy he struggled to free himself from the branch and awful scene.

As life ebbed from his body he saw the Green Woman standing in the flames that consumed the trees. In a voice like waves crashing along a cavernous shore, her words accused him, shrivelling all his remaining hope.

'Did you think you could escape my wrath?'

The earth around the ancient yew trembled with the sudden force of falling timber and a rumbling like late summer thunder filled the glade. The two great trees, groaned in their death throes as their timbers broke apart and the ground beneath them fell into the depths of the caverns where they burned with the ferocity of a volcano.

After the long traumatic night of the events in the caves it was late afternoon by the time Shenley woke. He could have slept all day he was so tired. From the breakfast room of Henley Hall he could see Druids Hill. It caught his attention immediately. There was a rising column of smoke spreading like a cloud over the yew grove. 'Vandals or campers probably,' he told himself. There was too much dry timber up there and dry undergrowth at this time of year.

Unless they acted soon the whole forest would be ablaze. Grabbing his phone he rang the County Fire Department. Within minutes a helicopter was flying over Druids Hill and Shenley's phone rang. He could hear the popping, whining hum of the helicopter engine and its rotors over the line.

'There is a potentially serious fire up here sir. Some of the trees in the centre are on fire. There's a real threat of it spreading if the wind picks up. I'll ask forest fire team from the county to drop retardant over the area and put it out. That should do it but we'll have to monitor it for several days. I'll have some men go up and clear the area in case there are intruders.'

'Thank you,' Shenley replied, putting down the phone wondering if the events of the previous night had in some way been responsible.

Late that evening while Shenley, Alex and Sophia were dining, they saw a red fire service vehicle enter Henley drive followed by a police car.

'What now?' Sophia folded her head in her hands, tired and irritable, her whole body and mind stressed from a long sleepless night.

'Stay here I'll go.' Shenley offered, leaving the dining room.

Ushering the men into the hall then to the study, Shenley enquired, 'Any News?'

The cynical, plain clothes, police officer answered first. 'We found two bodies up there sir.'

'What! Who? Sophia joined in.

'We don't know yet. Both unrecognisable at the moment and we found a third man there named Charles Duffy who is alive but not able to say much. It seems the fire started sometime last night. One of the dead was burned to a cinder, we aren't sure yet if it was man or a woman, the other was killed by a fall of rock probably when the earth collapsed under the trees.'

'That said, the good news is we've contained the fire.' The fireman explained.

'We might have to ask you all to come down to the station for questioning when we know more,' the police officer said. 'Maybe this man Duffy can throw some light on what happened.'

'Of course, anything I can do to help.' Shenley answered, dubiously, as both men left.

A week later, in the absence of his father, Shenley was visited once more by a police detective.

'This is just a routine matter sir. I hope you understand.' The Inspector switched on his phone recorder apologetically. 'It appears from DNA that the burned corpse was Ralph Morville of Morville Hall. I believe he was known to you. Our files show that over the years you have had several disputes with him. He had in fact reported your family as being responsible for burning down his ancestral home but he had no proof of that to charge you or anyone else. Now it appears he himself probably set fire to the trees on Druids Hill, in way of reprisal perhaps, and by accident died there.'

'Poetic justice,' Shenley murmured.

Looking at his notes Inspector Porter said, 'The other man was Sean Randolph, he was with Morville and Charles Duffy. They were all close friends. He died when the ground collapsed as far as we can tell. Duffy is alive but mostly incoherent.

You'll be happy to know the only persons to blame for these terrible accidents are the men themselves. The coroner concluded the cause of death was accidental with no evidence of foul play.'

'This is a sad affair Inspector. It's true of course we never did like the Morvilles but we wouldn't have wished this on any of them. What exactly did the man Duffy say?'

'Oh, he blabbered about some green statue and secret caverns, all nonsense. He did however confess to starting the fire and we will charge him with that.'

After a month the anguish of the events fell away in the pressing cares of life and slowly became less shocking.

Langham was well on the way to recovery at his West Country home. The other wounded men had recuperated and flown home.

One evening over dinner and wine Alex asked Lord Allan, 'What is the connection with the Order and the Holy Shroud in the medieval manuscript book?'

'Firstly I would say it is indeed a holy shroud, but not because of the image of Christ but because the power of the Holy Spirit, Sophia, our Green Goddess entered the body of Sir Gules du Bois, one of our Order during the twelfth century. After his execution by the King of France his body lay secretly in one of our temples prior to internment. The night after he was carried there a white light filled the temple and his corpse. Those present recorded seeing his soul leave his body. The shroud that covered him was burnished by the brilliant light and that shroud became the Holy Shroud of Turin. Over the years the shroud became a relic and for propaganda reasons our Order were never mentioned.'

Lord Allan picked up his wine glass and shrugged, 'Who knows the truth Alex, I certainly don't, but that's the story passed down in our Sacred Order through the ages, and a good one it is. By the way the knight in Henley Church was one of our Order as Sophia surmised, you can't hide anything from her, and like Sir Thomas Barrington is buried in the temple under Druids Hill.'

'What about the stories of Barrington and other people disappearing, is there any truth in those?' Alex enquired.

'Like all folk tales there is some truth in the stories. Due to the secrecy of our Order Barrington's death and burial couldn't be divulged to anyone. Thomas Barrington was killed by his brother over a love affair that's true but it was not for a mortal but for the Green Woman. He refused to reveal the secret of the caves or the Order to his brother and died for it. Similarly with other mysterious disappearances they were members of the Order and were buried secretly.'

'Tell me, how is Tamara Thomas involved in all this?'

'You saw her?' Lord Allan asked in surprise.

'Only in passing. When she was in the caverns we saw her lighting candles in the tunnels. Why was she there? I don't understand, I thought you were an all-male society.'

A glint of humour flitted over Lord Allan's face.

'We are, but Tamara somehow found out about the caverns, did research of her own, she has a keen intelligence, and came to me. Her enthusiasm is harmless enough and she is devoted to us and tends to the temple and caves.' Lord Henry laughingly added, 'She worships the Green Goddess in her own free spirited way.'

'One other question that intrigues me is how did the Morvilles become involved in all this?' Alex asked.

'That's a long story, going back nine hundred years. Sophia with her knowledge of history could tell you more than I can. Like all our great families the Morvilles were Norman in origin. Sir Hugh de Morville founded the family with a castle at Seagate and their banner was a lion on one side and on the other the Virgin Mary seated on her throne as the

Queen of Heaven with the baby Jesus in her arms. Their feast day was fifteenth of August the same as the Feast day of Mary's assumption and coincidentally the date of our ceremonies also. Sir Hugh made an attempt to join our Holy Order but was not accepted. It was thought he lacked chivalric qualities and was too mercenary. Sir Hugh had gained knowledge, from somewhere, of our relic being sacred and set out to obtain it as of value to the Roman Church and to gain favour with the Pope. Of course he had no idea what the relic was. His descendants throughout the centuries have tried periodically to snatch it from us.'

When Kevin had fully recovered from his wounds Lord Allan asked him privately into his study and poured out a whisky for him.

'Tell me Kevin, how are you now?'

'Scarred but none the worse, Lord Henry,' Kevin replied.

'Glad to hear it.' Lord Allan clinked his glass with his bodyguard butler.

'How would you like to lay down your arms at last and retire to the place you always dreamed of?'

'A man can dream,' Kevin answered refilling his glass from the whisky decanter. 'This holy water cures all ills.'

'Holy fire I think you mean.' Lord Henry lifted his glass. 'Kevin, I have written you a cheque for five hundred thousand pounds. Go and fulfil that dream. You have been the best friend a man could wish for and not only to me but my whole family. You didn't hesitate to lay down your life if needed for us and how can something like that be paid for? It's just a small token of gratitude.'

Lord Allan opened his desk drawer and gave Kevin a white embossed envelope.

With slight hesitation, silently thoughtful, Kevin took the envelope then said, 'Thank you. I suppose all things end. I'll buy the hotel in Ireland I've often thought about near the Wicklow and the Hollywood crowd.'

Holding out his hand Lord Henry said, 'Good Luck Kevin.'

CHAPTER FORTY

Pietro Licio hadn't slept. He kept going over the details, repeating them like a song dinning through his thoughts. All his efforts to get the sacred relic had failed and ended in futility. He should have known better than to trust the competence of a Morville in the first place.

Ralph's death was timely. He would have had to take care of him anyway. What bothered Licio most was how he could save face with the Vatican who had helped to secure his political appointments and business successes by funding him whenever he needed their finance and influence. He rose from his bed, tired, feeling his years. He always felt the pain of failure more than anyone.

Looking from his window he gazed with sadness over the green lawns of his Sardinian mansion.

'All great men come to their point of failure and begin again to reach even greater pinnacles,' he pondered, positively, but the thought didn't help this time. He was becoming old. Time was running out for greatness. He made the sign of the cross, acutely aware of all the times he had failed so many people.

Licio's meanderings were halted by the sound of helicopters overhead. He looked at his watch. It was five thirty am. No guests were expected today. The drone grew louder, two helicopters lowered over his home to come down and finally rest on the lawns.

Licio went to stare out from his bedroom window.

Armed Sardinian Police, in bullet proof vests, jumped from the helicopters while the blades were still beating their steady, pulsing, phut, phut rhythm. Licios' heart paused, a pang of anxiety engulfing him. Involuntarily he slumped down a premonition telling him what was coming.

Without ceremony the armed men burst into the mansion, guns ready to fire.

Running up the stairs an officer approached Licio without deference to his political status in the Italian government.

'Pietro Licio?' The officer asked, knowing full well who he was speaking to, everyone knew Licio.

'Of course! What do you mean by entering my home uninvited and armed like this?'

'You are under arrest for murder and an attempted murder in California, for a murder in the United Kingdom and attempted robberies. Put your hands behind your back Senor Licio.'

Obeying calmly Licio protested. 'I refuse to say anything to your preposterous charge and demand to speak to my lawyers.'

'You may call them from Police Headquarters.' The officer agreed as he handcuffed the perspiring politician.

Licio's wife appeared at the door, scampering tip toe in her bare feet. Running over to Licio she asked, 'What happened my darling? What happened?'

Gaining his composure, Licio reassuring her, spoke tenderly, 'Nothing for you to feel alarmed about Alessandra. Just some misunderstanding. Ring our lawyers, tell them what happened. I'll be back soon my treasure.' Licio leaned forward and kissed her cheek.

Alessandra angrily confronted the police. 'You will all be reported to the Ministry and your superiors for this conduct. How dare you force your way into our home like this? Every one of you, leave your names and rank before you go. If you have a job by the end of the month I'll be surprised.' Turning back to Licio she said, 'Everything will be alright Pietro, I have some influence of my own, they won't get away with it.'

Her words were to be prophetic. One year later Licio was still a free man, meeting heads of governments, as though nothing had happened, enjoying the solace of their friendship and sympathies, many of them thinking it could easily have been one of them.

A year later also saw dramatic changes in the Allan family.

Marston had moved north to oversee his father's Scottish border estates. Sophia was absent much of the time travelling between Paris, Munich and London involved in a directorship of Allan companies. It was often months before she and Alex met together. They were still deeply in love and like all true lovers would be for ever. Alex was busy writing a travel documentary, of the South Pacific Islands, for an American television series and this also kept them apart and prevented him joining her in Paris.

One lovely spring day Alex, who had returned to Barrington for a brief respite from work, walked over to Druids Hill, his mood sadly pensive. Here he had lain beside Sophia, enjoyed the frolics of the May festival, rode with Shenley, caught Tamara in the shadows, seen a vision of the Green Woman and had almost died there. It was the first time he had visited the hill since the incidents of the previous year.

Bluebells were once more blooming in the open woodland and among new green saplings. A clean, fresh aroma of spring filled the air.

The trees on Druids Hill had for the most part escaped the fire that had destroyed the old yew and oak. Walking through the avenue of yews to the central enclosure Alex could still feel the enigmatic, timeless presence of the woodland grove, watching him, closing around him. When he arrived at the open sward, charged stumps and debris of the great trees filled the amphitheatre. Passing through it he stopped to look at the remains of the once great yew tree. To his surprise he saw that out of its centre another shoot had grown and beside it an oak was beginning to sprout once more.

© Edward Dyas 2014
Hereby asserts and gives notice of his right under s.77 of the Copyright, Designs & Patents Act 1988 to be identified as the author of this work.

U.S.A. Copyright registered.

Made in the USA
Charleston, SC
17 January 2016